THE JANUS AFFAIR
A MINISTRY OF
PECULIAR
OCCURRENCES
NOVEL

PIP BALLANTINE &
TEE MORRIS

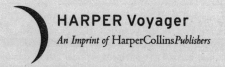

HARPER Voyager
An Imprint of HarperCollinsPublishers

This is a work of fiction. Names, characters, places, and incidents are products of the author's imagination or are used fictitiously and are not to be construed as real. Any resemblance to actual events, locales, organizations, or persons, living or dead, is entirely coincidental.

HARPER Voyager
An Imprint of HarperCollins*Publishers*
10 East 53rd Street
New York, New York 10022-5299

Copyright © 2012 by Pip Ballantine and Tee Morris
Cover art by Dominick Finelle
ISBN 978-0-06-204978-0
www.harpervoyagerbooks.com

First Harper Voyager mass market printing: June 2012

Harper Voyager and) is a trademark of HCP LLC.

Printed in the U.S.A.

10 9 8 7 6 5 4 3 2 1

Wherein Our Heroine Makes a Startling Discovery About Our Hero . . .

"Eliza!"

Both of them jumped when Wellington's hand clamped down on her wrist. "What are you doing here?"

She shrugged. "Forgive me—but when a house shakes like that and smoke starts coming from every orifice I think you might need a helping hand."

"Oh tosh. It was a little experiment I left brewing. No need for alarm."

"I am so glad you don't 'brew' experiments in the Archives."

The smile he shot her was both wicked and rather enjoyable. "As far as you know." He turned back and flicked off a row of levers.

"This is quite impressive, Welly. And by the by, I thought you disliked guns! Have you been withholding information from me?" She pointed accusingly to the dismantled Gatling on his workbench.

"I dislike *using* them. That doesn't mean I don't like the engineering challenge of working with them."

"A Gatling gun on a velo-motor? Remind me not to cross your path when out on the town."

By Pip Ballantine & Tee Morris

Ministry of Peculiar Occurrences
PHOENIX RISING
THE JANUS AFFAIR

To our parents, Roger & Pamela and Wayne & Nancy,
who never expected their kids to travel back
in time by airship and save the Empire
but understand that sometimes it is required.

ACKNOWLEDGEMENTS

There is always that daunting task after you write a book, people want more. Sure, it's always good when people want more. It means they like you. (They really, really like you!) So you get started on the sequel . . . and that's when it sinks in—you've got to clear the bar you've set for yourself.

The good news about a sequel: You're not in this alone. There are so many people out there pulling for you, and it is that drive that keeps us going.

To our friends and fans on Twitter, Facebook, and social networks far and wide, thank you for your unending support in letting people know about Agents Books and Braun, and The Ministry of Peculiar Occurrences. We owe a lot of our success in part to you. To Laurie McLean, our full-time agent, part-time cheerleader, and eternal friend—thank you for keeping us on the right track. To the writers (past, present, and future) of *Tales from the Archives*, thank you for opening up our world to the steampunk curious and encapsulating the global scope of this Neo-Victorian era. To the steampunk community for their accolades in the 2011 Airship Awards and the 2011 Goodreads Choice Awards. Your praise and admiration mean we must be getting something right.

A book can't happen without an editorial staff behind it, and we are so fortunate to have the talents of Diana Gill, Will Hinton, and Eileen DeWald at HarperVoyager. This is the team who helped us get the Ministry in order. And a special thank you to Stephanie Kim and Pam Jaffee for opening doors and opportunities for us in our first year of the Ministry and making us feel like steampunk rock stars. We look forward to what you have in store for us and *The Janus Affair*.

THE JANUS AFFAIR

Wherein the Perils of Train Travel Are Made Plain

It was the smell—the smell of metal baking under a summer sun—that alerted Lena to the terrible fact that her getaway had been a failure.

The sharp, hot odour burned her nostrils, reawakening the blind panic she had pushed back earlier in the evening. Now it wrapped invisible, chilling tendrils around her throat again. Unconsciously, she touched her face with one gloved hand, wincing as her skin flared under even this lightest of contact. Still, if a light sunburn was the worst she'd got away with, then she would not complain—not with what she had witnessed.

Lena had nearly been lulled to sleep with the repetitive rattling of the train, being wedged between its window and a rather rotund woman with a hatbox perched on her lap. Even after what she had seen back in Edinburgh, she dared to take some reassurance once the hypersteam had reached full speed. Her next stop would be London. She would rush home to Adelaide, hold her close, and then together they would pack up Lily and head out from the city. Having a plan, even as threadbare as hers, added to her sense of security, like that of a babe in a mother's arms.

That was before the scent tickled Lena's nose, sending her blood into a heady rush. Every primitive sense screamed at her, *Run. Run now!*

Ignoring propriety and decorum, she shoved her way past the damnable woman—not even bothering to excuse her lack of manners as the lady's ridiculous hatbox tumbled to the floor. Outraged complaints of her fellow passengers packed tight in this third-class car were reduced to distant clatter as she took long strides down its length. Manners and decorum held no consequence to her now. Had they known what she knew—witnessed for themselves what had happened to Maude Wilkinson—they would have understood. Undoubtedly, they would have joined her in a terrified flight.

She rested one hand on her stomach while her other clutched at her skirts, lifting them slightly. Her stride grew longer, then faster. Against the momentum of the train she felt that sinking illusion that she was only running in place. Beneath her corset, her heart raced as fast as the random thoughts flashing in her mind. Why didn't she wear trousers this morning? They would have been so much more efficient when running for one's life.

What of Adelaide, waiting at home? What would her love think if she didn't come back? Would she believe Lena had abandoned her and their sweet Lily?

What if—heaven forbid—the abomination caught her?

The desire to live, to escape, choked her throat, so huge that it seemed impossible. Yet Lena had seen so many impossible things today. So many. Too many.

She stumbled to the third-class door, and the rush of winter's chill cleared her mind as well as stirred the passengers unfortunate enough to be in the seats closest to the junction between cars. The bitter cold lingered against her exposed skin when she slipped into second-class. Another two carriages remained ahead, and then came the private compartments of first-class. One more car, after this one.

She concentrated on that as she strode forward. She dared not look back. If she did, she knew the abomination would be there, on her heels. The last thing she would see. The other end of her present car grew closer but on catching a whiff of hot brass in her nostrils, her mind flashed again and again on what horror she had witnessed in Scotland.

Much as in third, the second-class passengers closest to the door grumbled and barked at Lena as she continued into the junction. Now in the tiny gangway between cars, the wind biting at her skin, an idea came to mind. To her *educated* mind.

Madness. Nothing, other than madness.

"Madness," she heard herself whisper even as she slipped out of her overskirt and tossed it into the darkness, even as her fingers released the catch on the iron gate, even when her hand gripped the metal rung of the ladder. There was no reason to say it again as her heels locked into the rungs under her, nor when she began to pull herself upwards. Then Lena cleared the top rung and any civilised thought she might have entertained disappeared as the wind struck her hard and relentlessly. At their present speed of seventy miles per hour across Her Majesty's countryside, the January chill ripped though her clothes, through her chemise; and against her skin Lena felt invisible needles tear into her.

She needed to disappear, if only for a moment. Yes, this was madness, but also her only chance.

Lena was thankful, still. At least it wasn't snowing.

The phenomenal speed of the hypersteam train was tearing at her eyes, yet she dare not spare a hand to wipe them clean. Her gloves, satin creations that were far too respectable for her current exploits, grasped the roof's edge, her fingers searching for any purchase. Lena suddenly felt warmth, only to feel the cold for fleeting moments, then warmth once again. Is this what that peculiar extension running along the rooftops of passenger cars was all about? She tried to imagine the train car before her. What else would be up here for her to grab on to? A small chimney? Yes. Somewhere along her progress, somewhere in the near-darkness, she would see it. Would she catch its scent first?

A scream drowned out the locomotive's rhythmic *chuff-chuff-chuff* and caused her grip to tighten. Something was happening to the air around her, and in moments each breath caused her to gag and retch. A stale, earthy taste continued to fill her mouth. What was happening?

My God, we are in a tunnel!

Her jacket could not filter out all of the foul soot from the engine's main stack; but using its sleeve as a mask, she could at least take small, shallow breaths. Those breaths, though, threatened to choke her. How long was this tunnel? Could she manage to make it to its end? What of the abomination? Was it also following her, or had she evaded it with this daring, if not foolhardy, escape? Hardly a victory if she were to suffocate due to the soot and ash—

Another terrifying scream and then the deafening howl returned to her ears. She drew in the hard, cold air, and found a peculiar solace in its chill, its taste, and its freshness.

Lena also took comfort in not catching any trace of the sharp, deadly odour that had driven her to this precipice. Maybe she had outwitted her assailant, unlike poor, slow Maude.

The world opened up around her, and Lena felt her heart leap into her throat. A hunter's moon now emerged from behind a curtain of dark clouds, its ivory light reflecting in the water far below. One slip and she would either meet a quick death on the bridge or fall into the abyss of the gorge they now crossed. In this brief second, the train hurtling relentlessly on, humming underneath her like a beast, Lena considered jumping into the night, into the great expanse around her, but that *educated* mind—the same one that told her to escape via the carriage's rooftop—conjured images of Adelaide and Lily.

No, she insisted. *I have to live. For them.*

Then Lena saw in the moonlight a tiny smoke pipe, demarcating the end of the car. With her right hand daring to crack the edge of the vent she held, her left reached out. Through the ruined gloves, she brushed the ladder's top rung. She looked up, and the gracious lunar companion that had restored her hope was now disappearing into darkness again. Lena fixed her eyes on the ladder. So close. She threw both hands towards it, and watched the fixed iron disappear into the night as the cloud bank high above her devoured the moon. Her world tilted, slow and languid, and then a stillness wrapped around her like a blanket.

Lena pressed her temple and cheek against the ladder; and with a grunt, she pulled herself off the second-class car's roof. The stinging in her skin, the cold, and the exhaustion all abated. The train rocked Lena back and forth as she descended, as if trying to shake her free of it, but still she managed to drop safely onto the gangway.

Lena looked through the finely decorated glass of the car. No sign of the abomination. Now what? Back the way she came? Forward, gambling that it had continued that way to the engine?

She kicked open the door of the car behind her, her eyes raking over its passengers who had no clue that mere moments ago she was above them, lost in a Bedlam outside their comfortable, cosy, shared compartment. Lena knew she must have looked terrifying: soot-stained, wearing finery torn by the elements and rooftop décor. Amidst the looks of revulsion, she saw a face looking at her with something different—recognition.

"Lena?" the woman mouthed silently.

It was the colonial. The sister that she'd been introduced to more than a year ago. She'd taken tea with her only the day before—even though it felt an age past. Lena smiled, relief flooding through her whole body. Finally, Fate had dealt her a decent hand in the form of an unexpected ally. She would tell this sister from the South about Maude and then everything would be all right.

Lena took a step, her mouth opening to call out her name, and then the warmth wrapped around her. She only had time

CHAPTER ONE

In Which Miss Braun Protests
Her Innocence and No One Is Fooled

Wellington had excelled in debate and the oratory arts during his time at university. His previous experiences in discussing imperative issues and pressing matters of Queen, Country, and Empire had never involved an opponent quite like the one standing over him. The fact that they were holding this debate on the *very public* platform of the York train station where they had been forced to make an emergency stop seemed to make little difference to his opponent, employing an unknown but hardly unsurprising strategy in keeping the upper hand with him: passionate contradiction.

"No." He tried to murmur as covertly as possible.

"Yes." Her retort was nowhere near as subtle.

"No."

"Yes."

"No."

"Yes."

"Miss Braun—"

"Oh, come on, Welly—"

On hearing that nickname—the nickname that worked

like Paris' arrow to Achilles' vulnerable heel—he dared to look up. Those sapphire eyes of hers could easily bend his will as would reeds in a strong winter wind. This time, however, he had steeled himself.

"Miss Braun, I can say it for you in the Telegu dialect of India—*Kaddu*. I can say it for you in Nepalese—*Ahaa*. The Nandi dialect of Kenya? *Achicha*. A Mandarin variation? *Bu dai*. Or would you prefer your homeland's Maori dialect? *Kao*. Pick a language that you tend to grasp better than the Queen's English because I think I am clear as crystal when I say *No*!"

"But Welly—"

"Yes, I know, we were right there." He pinched the bridge of his nose, screwing his eyes shut . . . and he instantly regretted the now habitual gesture. The fresh sunburn on his face brought an extra sting. Exactly what had happened on the train, and how it had caused such damage to both himself and his colleague, was a matter he planned to investigate, once he had calmed Eliza down.

He stood, and suddenly the need to pace overcame him. Perhaps he also needed to calm his own nerves. No matter how hard he squeezed his eyes shut, that woman bursting into the carriage car still remained etched in his memory. The scarlet in the stranger's skin revealed to him she had been exposed to the elements, either for a prolonged period or in a brief intense burst at high speeds. He had caught the recognition in her eyes along with Eliza's reaction just before all went dark in their car, followed seconds later by the crackle of electricity. Thin bolts of blue, white, and violet danced around her figure, caressing her body's curves and crevices. Then came the flash, followed by the wild panic of passengers. When the car's lights flickered back to life, the stranger was gone.

A stranger to him, perhaps, but not to his Ministry compatriot.

Those closest to the lost woman were left not only horrified, but also slightly burned. Most assuredly, this affair would fall under the Ministry's jurisdiction. Or, more to the point, it would fall under a London field agent's jurisdiction.

And here was Eliza's point of contention, as it always had been since her demotion. She was, officially, no longer a London field agent.

Wellington stepped aside as a man working the levers of his Portoporter steamed towards the door. "Eliza, now you know it was sleight of hand and quick thinking that managed to keep our hides as well as our jobs with Doctor Sound last time."

"You forgot cleverness. The tale we spun was quite clever," Eliza stated proudly, pushing her dark russet hair back into a braid that had come loose.

"Be that as it may, we were—and no doubt, still are—held under scrutiny, with that whole Phoenix Society brouhaha. It is imperative we remain on our best behaviour, a feat that you did not exactly manage effortlessly with your shenanigans in Edinburgh."

Eliza huffed. "Tosh, Wellington. Had I shown up for the meeting, I think that would have caught Doctor Sound's attention." She snickered. "Now if I had shown up early, that would most assuredly make him wonder what the game was."

"And there we are, missing the point. Once. Again." Wellington clicked his tongue as a thought—a new strategy—came to mind. "Consider then how compromised this occurrence would be if the Director deemed it proper for you to investigate."

Eliza's brow furrowed. "Come again, Books?"

"Much like our previous little adventure outside of the Archives, you are the last person who should investigate this case due to your attachments to it!" He returned to the bench and considered her for a moment. "She knew you!"

"She knew me a little. There is a difference." She rubbed tentatively at her own rosy skin. "I think we will need to get some of that wonderful Ministry cream they issue in the tropics. I fear I may tan." She winked at him, when any real lady would have been horrified at the prospect.

"Don't change the subject," he warned, his eyebrow crooking slightly. "That woman who disappeared in a ball of lightning right in front of our eyes knew your name—and I want to know how."

She finally took a seat by Wellington on the bench, her hands smoothing long azure blue skirts. He secretly wished she would wear dresses more often. The look did suit her quite well. "All right, I confess, I had met the girl previously. We had a few pints at the pub with the Edinburgh Suffrage Chapter, talked a bit about the forward progress of women in our society, and she was making overtures towards me—"

"Well, there's a shock," Wellington snipped.

"Not like that! She was making overtures to me about speaking at her Women's Society back in London. Her name was Lena Munroe."

"Eliza, must I remind you, you are no longer a field agent. You are my partner and protégé within the Archives. Our responsibilities and priorities remain there."

As if on cue, movement in the corner of his eye caught his attention. He recognised the form instantly.

"Welly?" Eliza leaned forward. "Welly, you've gone ashen. What is it? Do you have the vapours?"

With the scent of oil, metal, and steam filling his nostrils, Wellington took in a deep breath and brought himself back to his feet. Eliza was still talking to him, but he really didn't take in the words. They made no difference now. Eventually, her head turned to see whom had grabbed his attention.

"Agent Books." Doctor Sound beamed. "And our beloved Agent Braun! Archivist and junior archivist."

Eliza quickly rose, and Wellington noted her smile seemed eerily relaxed and charming—even though she loathed the use of her new official title. "Sir, what brings you—"

"Oh do not think me a simpleton. An incident occurs on

the White Star's prototype hypertrain, the same hypertrain that you and your mentor here happen to be riding on, and you believe that it wouldn't warrant my attention?"

"Well, it is late, Doctor Sound," Eliza said. "We didn't anticipate you being awake."

"Oh, normally at this hour, I am enjoying a deep sleep after a delightful hot toddy. Strangely enough, I have been having a right bother of a time falling asleep ever since you left London." Sound turned his attention to Wellington as his expression darkened. "Happens with every trip the two of you undertake, I've noticed."

Wellington watched Eliza loose a wink, as her back was now to Sound.

Doctor Sound checked his pocket watch, nodded, and then said, "Well, I hope you can regale me with the astounding events that occurred on your train ride home."

"But of course," Wellington began, about to return to the bench, "After we—"

The Director cut him off. "Perhaps we could walk as you give me your unofficial report."

"If you don't mind, sir," Eliza added, "It's lovely to be stationary after the long—"

"I insist." Doctor Sound's brows furrowed.

Wellington and Eliza shared a look; and then with the tiniest of shrugs, the two followed the Doctor down their platform.

He shot them an appraising look. "If I didn't know better I would think both of you had gone to the Indies, not Scotland."

Wellington managed not to raise his hand to his face. "Sir, it appears whatever happened had some unusual side effects."

"I hope we don't keel over before luncheon," Eliza replied brightly. "My friend Marie in Paris is working on some—"

"I also hear," the Ministry Director cut her off curtly, "that you were engaging in some social time with suffragists while you were in Scotland?"

"Yes, sir, but strictly on my time. Not the Ministry's," she reassured him.

Wellington added, "I saw to that, Doctor."

"I'm sure you did. And this is where you met—"

Eliza cleared her throat. "Lena Munroe, sir. A suffragist from London. There was a ladies' group from the City giving support to an Edinburgh chapter. Strength in numbers and all that. I only met the girl a couple of times, but she was quite outspoken."

"Perhaps one reason you two got along so well, Miss Braun," Wellington muttered from beside her.

Her elbow never failed in finding a pressure point that could steal his breath. Blinking back tears, Wellington remained quiet as a church mouse while Eliza continued. "We met for breakfast along with many of the other ladies from both the London and Edinburgh groups."

"And was this breakfast why you missed the meeting at Deputy Director Wynham's office?"

He saw the muscle twitch in Eliza's jaw. She dare not tell him what she'd been actually up to, and that the previous day had in fact been when she met with Lena. This, Wellington surmised, was his cue; and unsettling as he found it, it was proving easier and easier to lie for Eliza. "Yes, sir. I was already there—"

"So he told me in a wireless."

"Ah," Wellington gestured to Eliza and said, "then he told you that Agent Braun really didn't need to be there. It was really only a courtesy, since we already had what we needed from their archives."

"The wireless was hardly that detailed." Doctor Sound then turned back to Eliza, stopping hardly by chance at their train car. "So, Agent Braun, you and Agent Books here collect your case files from the Scottish branch, you board the train, and then—"

"And then we settled in for the ride home. I had no idea Miss Munroe was also sharing the hypersteam with us." Eliza motioned to where she had seen the suffragist appear.

"She burst into our car, saw me, and looked as if she would break down and cry."

"More out of relief than out of despair, Doctor Sound," Wellington offered. "I do not mean to sound cheeky saying that, but it was true. This woman recognised Agent Braun here, and looked awash with relief."

Doctor Sound furrowed his brow. "Relief?"

"Yes, sir. It appeared as if she wanted to tell us something"—Wellington took a deep breath and then motioned along the car—"but then—"

"But then, all hell broke loose," Eliza chimed in.

"Really now?" His eyebrows were up again. "And the Gates of Beelzebub just happened to open in the car that two agents of the Ministry of Peculiar Occurrences occupied?" Doctor Sound pursed his lips. "Fancy. That."

Wellington gave a light shudder.

Eliza lifted her chin slightly. After spending months with her, Wellington had observed this usually happened a moment before she did something dangerous. "Sir, I know how this may look—but I can assure you this is completely coincidental."

"Agent Braun, you are, indeed, a force of nature. You do not command the arctic winds to plunge Old Blighty into a harsh winter nor do you call upon the sands of the Sahara to blind the ancient home of the pharaohs. Nay, you attract mayhem, chaos, and anarchy wherever your delicate feet tread. Around you there is no such thing as coincidence."

"Why do you think it is always me, Director?" Eliza protested. "It could be Books. My father always told me to beware the quiet ones!"

"Yes," Wellington grumbled. "In my spare time outside of the Archives, I tend to get into the occasional pub brawl or even the odd boxing match, to work out the tensions."

Eliza blinked. "You? Boxing?"

He turned to look at her. "The tension just so happened to arise last summer when I was assigned a charge in my Archives. Do you think that is coincidence?"

"A tiny one."

"That will do, the *both* of you," Doctor Sound said, his voice remaining calm, though effectively cutting through the clamour of the train platform. The Scarborough Dasher chugged past them into the station, bathing the area for a few moments in steam. The Director seemed to revel in the atmosphere. He drew in a great breath before continuing. "Whether you meant to or not, you attracted a great deal of attention to yourselves in this fateful moment. From what I have managed to gather from eyewitnesses is that the woman was quite a sight, her eyes fixed upon you, and that was when the screaming started. The screaming, and the *lumières fantastique.*"

"Doctor Sound," Eliza began, and Wellington's stomach felt as if it were gripped by a metal fist. "As Agent Books and I were present during this obvious peculiar occurrence, perhaps you could allow us to be lead investigators on this case?"

Directly, and to the point. How utterly colonial of her.

Doctor Sound tucked his hands into his pockets. "I believe even a junior archivist would agree that, as the peculiar occurrence directly involved you, your judgement and impartiality have both been compromised."

Wellington leaned towards her ear and muttered, "I told you so."

She heard him, but chose not to listen. "Hardly, Director. As I mentioned, I hardly knew the girl; but for the brief moment that I saw her, she asked me for my help. Asked *me*. I believe that it is my duty when one of the Queen's subjects asks of me—"

"Stop—right—there." Doctor Sound raised a finger as Eliza went to protest. "No, Agent Braun, I will not hear another utterance from you on this matter. Once you have offered your account of events, you and Agent Books will return to the Archives, where you will resume your duties unless the primary investigator calls upon you again."

Eliza crossed her arms. "Who would that be?"

Doctor Sound motioned behind him, and Wellington felt

a tightness form in his throat as he made out the man striding towards them through the parting steam.

"You cannot be serious, sir," Eliza grumbled.

"G'day, Eliza," Bruce said, flashing her what he apparently believed to be his best smile. "I have a few questions for you." His eyes flicked over in Wellington's direction. "Books. Be with you in a moment."

This was going to be the longest interview of Wellington's career at the Ministry.

Eliza, once again, displayed her monumental lack of tact. "You cannot expect Campbell here to have the wherewithal to handle this case?"

"Oh, I know that Agent Campbell is more known for action in the field rather than investigation; but when I received word on this matter, I was pleased to see him step forward and agree to take on the assignment. Considering his current caseload, I am glad to see such initiative." The Director turned and actually beamed at the Australian.

"How fortunate for the Ministry." She scowled.

The crash made Wellington, Eliza, and Campbell jump. The three turned to see a cart of large, heavy cargo—at first glance, the corner of an armored safe was visible—now covering the bench that Wellington and Eliza had earlier occupied. Two workers were yelling at each other over the scattered remains of the Portoporter. The bench meanwhile had been reduced to a pile of splintered wood and bent iron.

"Good Lord," Wellington finally uttered, "Had we still been there—"

"Yes." Doctor Sound agreed, glancing back at the site of the accident, and then looking back to Wellington. "Most fortunate we stretched our legs, eh Books?"

He paused in his reply, tilted his head to one side, and then slowly nodded. "Most."

Why was Doctor Sound smiling at him?

"With the strange happenings on your train and the superstitious nature of the working class," Sound said, motioning to the scattered luggage and twisted bench, "this platform is only going to fall deeper into disarray. Therefore, Campbell will need to collect statements straightaway—starting with yours." He considered the two of them for a moment. "Can you do that?"

"Yes, sir." They replied—though Eliza's was considerably less enthusiastic than it should have been.

Wellington's eyes followed Doctor Sound to the incident. It appeared as if the Director was studying the random accident up close, for some strange reason. His attention was immediately yanked back to the broad-shouldered Ministry agent flipping open a small pad and touching the tip of his pencil with his tongue.

"Right then," Campbell began, his tone so civil it was offensive. "May I have your name for the record, Miss . . . ?"

"Eliza Braun," Eliza sneered. "Here, I'll spell it for you—B-U-G-G-E-R-O-F-F."

Bruce nodded. "That is a beautiful name, miss." He looked up from his notepad. "Very exotic."

"Eliza, please," Wellington said, "Agent Campbell here has others to interview before the night's over. Just cooperate."

"Oi, mate," Bruce snapped, stepping closer to Wellington, "I think I can handle her myself. I don't need some *limey* offering assistance."

Just as charming as Wellington remembered him.

Bruce suddenly spat on the pavement—dangerously close to Wellington's shoes—before giving him one more warning glare, and turning back to Eliza. She herself appeared ready to explode, perhaps in a grander fashion than her favourite incendiary.

Campbell cleared his throat, and resumed his interview. "Now then, Miss Braun—that is right, Eliza Braun, yes? Why don't you tell me what happened, in your own words."

Wellington checked his watch and looked around them, noting the tired passengers and skittish hypertrain personnel. A long night's journey home had suddenly become much, much longer, and his bed seemed a very long way off.

CHAPTER TWO

Wherein Our Dashing Archivist Receives an Earful at Speakers' Corner, and Our Colonial Pepperpot Finally Comes to Grips with Her Past Transgressions

Two hours had passed by the time Agent Campbell finished with Eliza; two long, tedious, and excruciating hours. Wellington knew from his training that questioning a witness—even if one was considered to be the prime suspect—should never take longer than thirty minutes. Brevity was not only the soul of wit, but it was key in keeping an investigation moving. Some of the questions for Eliza were purely trivial, and Wellington could not help but let the odd "*Oh for God's sake . . .*" and "*Agent Campbell, please . . .*" slip.

When it came Wellington's turn, however, Campbell was anything but civil. Simply put, he was nothing less than rude. He cut off Wellington in the middle of answers and yawned outright during crucial testimony. Still, Campbell's contempt meant Wellington's interview took a fraction of the time compared to Eliza's.

At the very moment that Campbell's notebook flipped shut, Doctor Sound re-appeared. He looked well rested, so he had most likely taken a moment to relax at the Royal Station Hotel. Wellington found himself thinking rather bitterly that he had probably found time for tea—something that Campbell had deliberately denied them.

"It seems that Campbell and I will both be joining you as our airship had to return to London," Doctor Sound shouted over the building hiss of the hypersteam engine. "No need to come in tomorrow. You both have endured a rather extraordinary evening. Now, off with you both."

While Wellington and Eliza returned to second-class, the Archivist watched with a pang of longing as Sound hopped into his *first*-class car. The budgetary concerns were apparently not an issue—for the right people. Campbell, Wellington noted, was disappearing into the crowd.

The hypersteam train, the centre jewel of technology's crown, finally pulled into King's Cross at three in the morning. An hour *after* the standard steam train arrived to its platform.

Wellington barely remembered getting home, he'd been so exhausted. The next morning he was able to take inventory of his complaints: aching eyes, sunburned face, and a sore backside from so long on the train. What a ghastly affair the whole thing had been.

However, he couldn't afford to coddle himself—not when he'd promised Eliza a repast at the establishment of her choosing. Wellington knew it was the least he could do for surprising her with the hypersteam train tickets; had he simply bought them passage on a standard steam train, they would have enjoyed true luxury—blissful sleep all the way to London.

With Doctor Sound's admonishment to have a day off, Wellington concluded his partner would take full advantage and arrive for work tomorrow, sometime after lunch most likely.

The huge pile of cataloguing waiting for them in the

office was not a job to tackle on his own, and so with a slight pang of guilt, Wellington decided not to go into the office until tomorrow either. Instead he walked down in the fresh late-morning air to the main street and hailed a cab outside the *Old Bull and Bush*. Luckily, the cockneys who often journeyed to the pub on their off days were nowhere to be seen. They often caused a bit of a scene in the area.

Grateful of the lack of drama—at least thus far in his journey—Wellington travelled on to his partner's residence. With a generous gratuity added to the fare, Wellington thanked the driver and then proceeded up the stairs to Eliza's rooms.

The sound of his feet scuffing against the stone steps made Wellington Thornhill Books return to memories he would much rather have left in the past.

A gentleman walks with confidence, boy, his father would say as Wellington rubbed the back of his hand. Arthur H. Books was quite adept at using a ruler as a device of discipline. *Scraping your soles like that tells the world you do not walk upon this earth so much as you lumber. You, Wellington, will not be an embarrassment to me.*

Wellington splayed his fingers and then slowly balled them into a fist. He had tried so hard as a youth to please his father, but eventually he had worked out how little the elder Books' regard was worth.

All these unpleasant childhood memories were haunting him now for one very good reason: he was exhausted. He'd just realised that, when the door above him swung open, and Eliza appeared before him, looking rather smart. If she had been a gentleman.

"Oh come along, Miss Braun," Wellington began.

"Not a word about my trousers," she barked. "You booked us passage on the new McTighe contraption—"

"The hypersteam engine is a Barrington invention, not a McTighe. The Edinburgh Express is the first train to be fitted with it, and White Star is usually known for their comfortable travel—"

"For the *first-class* passengers, yes." She gave him a stern look and a slight shake of her head. "Awfully considerate of the Old Man to invite us to ride along with him."

"But he didn't."

"I know, Welly. I was being sarcastic." Her eyes narrowed on him, her tongue running inside her cheek as she pulled her coat in tighter. "Your brilliant plan to get us back to London in 'half the time of the usual express' was a bit of a bust, Welly, so you owe me this morning. Therefore, my attire is not open to your criticism, understood?"

Wellington cleared his throat, went to reply, thought better of it, and instead took in a deep breath.

"If I am a bit grumpy," she continued, slipping on her decidedly masculine jacket and shutting the door behind her, "it is because I did not get enough proper sleep."

"Lack of sleep makes for an irritable Eliza." He nodded. "Right then. I shall keep that in my memory lock'd, and I myself shall keep the key of it."

She glared at him but did not reply.

They walked in silence then, Wellington doing just as he'd promised himself he would do—following her lead. As expected, Eliza's fashion was attracting many a disapproving look from passersby.

"Wellington." Eliza finally spoke, her eyes still fixed on the pavement as they walked. "I know a little café with a lovely view of Hyde Park. Thought that might be a pleasant way to enjoy luncheon. So much more enjoyable than last night."

"Quite."

Their rapid pace managed to keep Wellington warm against the chill. They were most fortunate that it had not been a characteristically windy sort of January day; but whatever this café promised, Wellington was looking forward to a good, hot cup of tea and a scone fresh from the oven. However, Eliza's stride began to shorten the closer they drew to Speakers' Corner, and Wellington's curiosity was piqued.

The crowd gathered here consisted mainly of women, with

a few gentlemen patiently and politely paying attention—perhaps because they were escorting their female relations. In front of the group, but obscured from Eliza and Wellington's point of view, a woman could be heard addressing the crowd. Near the back was a small group of men, continuing—rather rudely—with their own conversations. This would have not been so much of a bother had the men not been carrying on so close to the woman speaking. The din from the men was enough to make a few of the ladies turn their heads and shoot them angry looks.

From the sound of their guffaws, they really did not care.

Eliza shook her head and barged her way through to them, not even bothering to mutter a "*Beg your pardon*" or "*Excuse me*" as she joined the other women.

Wellington easily walked around the men and clearly heard their opinions.

"Bloody suffragettes," the portly one remarked, loud enough to make certain he was heard. "Caterwaul all they like, they're not likely to get the vote in this country. Not even Queen Vic likes 'em."

"I don't mind if the hens get the vote," another man stated, quickly silencing his compatriots, "so long as dinner is waiting on the table."

"I wouldn't mind if that dish—" another said, his eyes taking in Eliza's curves, "—served herself on my table."

Wellington paused. He swallowed back a reply, and tried catching up with Eliza. They mustn't draw attention to themselves—especially after their recent misadventure with the Phoenix Society. He was certain that Doctor Sound suspected their involvement in the downfall of that hedonistic society. He could only hope the Director was not keeping them under surveillance.

He brushed by the crass gentlemen, thinking how lovely it would have been to rap the varlet with a walking stick, at the point of vulnerability between the tibia and fibula. Sadly, today such actions would have to remain only in Wellington's imagination.

When the Archivist stepped clear of the small "Gentle-men's Club," the woman's voice suddenly came to him clear and resonant. And resolute. In fact, overflowing with resolve.

The women standing there, decked in half-cloaks and the large sleeves and muffs to stave off the late January chill, looked to all intents and purposes like they had just stepped out for a brisk winter's stroll through the park. Their outward expressions however, uniform in their intensity and sombre look, were contrary to their dress. They remained stock-still, paying rapt attention to the woman at the podium.

"A question. A question is not a harmful thing. Our children ask us questions every day. And it is our responsibility to answer them truthfully, honestly. It is the answer to questions that build character, integrity, and morality. The very foundations of Her Majesty's Empire. And yet, when my daughter asks me why her questions are not answered by her teacher, when she is told, 'That is not your concern,' what am I to tell her? All we want is an answer to a question, a moment to ask our leaders 'Why?' when their decisions are, most assuredly, our concern. For it is the decisions of men that send our sons off to war, turn our daughters into widows. We want our voice to be counted, and our questions answered."

The women's applause managed to drown out the dissention from the cads behind them. Wellington cast a glance to his partner, her once hard, sour expression now radiating with optimism and hope.

"Really?" Wellington asked her, his own hands also offering up a polite applause. "This is my penance? To be your arm decoration at a suffragette rally?"

"Suffra-*gist*, Welly," Eliza politely corrected as the applause settled. She leaned in closer to his ear as the woman resumed her speech. "You should endeavour to know the proper address of such dissonant voices within the Empire?"

"Dissonant?" Wellington objected. "What do you take me for, Miss Braun?"

Eliza crooked an eyebrow on that. "Do you want an honest answer to that?"

He shook his head and turned his attention to the speaker. "I do not know this woman's name, but I respect her words and her voice. She is quite right. A woman's opinion should be heard."

"Why, Wellington Thornhill Books, Esquire," Eliza began, "aren't we the forward-thinking gent?"

"I mean, who raises our children, cooks our meals, and assures that house and home remains tidy and in order?" he went on. "It is, most certainly, not a man's job, now is it?"

"If our voices do not count," came the suffragist's words, her voice now stained with real ire, "why should we be so supportive of decisions that, society tells us, are not our concern?"

Wellington nodded, offering his wordless support for the woman's plight. He happened to glance over at Eliza and felt a sinking feeling on meeting her gaze. Eliza was just staring at him. He noted shock in her eyes, a touch of anger roiling just underneath her gaze.

"What?" he asked, completely unaware what he might have done to earn such temper.

The speaker paused for a moment, leaned down so that a nearby woman could whisper into her ear, nodded, and then stood tall with a smile. "Perhaps there are some of you that may think this is a fool's errand we are embarking upon—"

"Finally!" barked one of the gents from the back. "The voice of reason!"

Only the men gathered there found the comment amusing. The men alongside their ladies would chuckle but covered their approval in a cough.

"Perhaps, a word from one of the Empire's children would give you a touch of reassurance."

From behind a group of ladies—a group of ladies which, Wellington noted, were all armed with small clubs seen usually in the hands of police officers—a figure emerged that caused Eliza's breath to audibly catch. This newcomer carried herself with confidence, her modifications, while striking, seeming only to add to that bearing. The morning sunlight caught the gleam off the brass fixture of her jaw while the light where an eye would have been flared with an emerald glow. She was still able to smile warmly, even as half her face was covered in metal and clockwork. A few of the women closer to the podium stepped back, but she did not take offence to it. Even the men behind Wellington and Eliza went deathly silent.

"Good morning, my sisters," this new speaker began, "for while I do look quite extraordinary, do not think for a moment that we are not sisters. We are. Under the flag of our beloved Queen Victoria, we are one, part of the great British Empire."

Eliza, recovering from whatever her shock was, whispered, "Kate?"

"I am Kate Sheppard, a citizen of New Zealand and a servant of the Empire. I also have a voice, a voice that came with a cost," she said, motioning to her face. "A cost that, I believe, was well worth paying."

There was a smattering of applause. Wellington looked over at Eliza. Her eyes were welling with tears.

"You know this woman?" he murmured.

The nod was imperceptible.

"Back home in my beloved land of New Zealand, I have a voice. Perhaps it is a quiet one, at present, but it is still a voice. A voice that, rest assured, will no longer remain ignored."

"You overestimate yourself, tinkertot!" shouted a heckler from the group of men. He waved his cigar as he added, "I can easily shut out your shrieking. How about a ding-dong? *All things bright and beautiful . . .*"

Then the rest of the men joined in. *"All creatures great and small, all things wise and wonderful, The Lord God made them all . . ."*

Wellington looked back to Kate who raised a single finger to the wall of women originally shielding her from the audience. His eyes jumped to Eliza. The emotional display he had seen earlier was all but gone now. He was expecting her to be staring down the hecklers. Instead, Eliza was watching Kate, a grin across her face. She was clearly expecting a rebuttal from her New Zealand cousin.

Kate waited until the men reached *"God made them high and lowly, And ordered their estate . . ."* verse and burst into laughter. She turned to an attendant and motioned to a small box behind her. With a nod, the attendant hefted the box up into her arms.

"Gentlemen, your song is quite apt as God did make us all. As the child's hymn proclaims—none are better or worse. And yet, gentlemen such as yourselves are content with having us stay silent, still, and making your dinner."

The hecklers watched as Kate's attendant set the box at their feet, and turned the lock on its lid. The box fell away to reveal a skinned goose, frozen solid.

"You gents want dinner?" Kate asked the men, reaching underneath the podium. What came into view next caused the women up front to scream in horror and the crowd to part as if they were the Red Sea and Eliza's New Zealand cousin was Moses. The staff this Moses brandished in Speakers' Corner took aim on the goose in front of the retreating gentlemen. Kate pulled back the bolt on this monstrosity of a rifle, bringing the beakers on either side of its chamber to a wild, furious bubble. The air around the rifle's barrel-bell distorted and wavered until brilliant pearlescent rings of heat and power burst from it, striking the frozen bird over and over. Wellington, who had been the only one remaining where he stood, watched with fascination as the goose went from a sick pale colour to yellow. The smell tickled his nostrils when the fowl turned to a golden brown, and his mouth instantly began to water.

Kate released the trigger and hoisted the rifle upwards, her green eye flaring brighter than ever. "Gentlemen, your goose is now well and truly cooked."

The crowd, even some of the men keeping company with their wives and sweethearts, erupted into applause. The hecklers, however, were slowly regaining their composure while in front of them a large goose sizzled. Wellington gave her a healthy ovation as the crowd gathered back around him.

Over the thunder of appreciation, Eliza called to him. "Welly, time to go."

"Did you see?" Wellington exclaimed, the crowd still cheering on Kate Sheppard. "That's a Matford-Randleson Ætheralternator rifle your friend has there."

"And she knows how to use it. Now let's go."

He motioned to Kate who was now passing the rifle to her attendant. "But don't you want to—"

"When Kate gets this way, the bluebottles are not far behind, now com—"

Her word caught in her throat as an odd scent in the air made them both pause. Stray hairs that had escaped Eliza's braid waved back and forth a fraction. The expression on her face said this was—for once—not her doing. Wellington looked up to the podium, and saw the young attendant reach for the Ætheralternator—only to recoil as if shocked.

Now, overpowering the cooked goose, there was another odd scent in the air. Like copper baking in the sun, or . . .

"Ye Gods, Kate!" Eliza said before shoving her way through those around them.

A mix of men and women were now being thrown into Wellington's arms as Eliza fought her way through the crush of bodies. The crowd had not seemed that large to him when they first arrived at the rally, but now there appeared to be more people between them and the stage than he'd estimated. His nose burned with the building scent of electricity, but he pushed aside both men and women in order to keep Eliza in view.

Then he was through. Instead of a thick press of fabric and flesh, he only saw Eliza, running undeterred. As she was unhindered by skirts or cloaks, Eliza bound for the podium and leapt for Kate. He heard their bodies impact with each other, and that was when he turned to face the crowd.

"Get back!" Wellington shouted, stretching his arms

wide and running back towards the mass of people. "Get! Back!"

The concussion threw him forward, pushing him into the curious that were trying to watch the excitement on the stage. He knocked at least five over when he went flying; like he was a ball and they were the skittles. Wellington gingerly pulled himself free of the startled ladies, some of them trying to gather their wits, while a few looked at him and blushed.

Pulling himself up to his feet with apologies flowing left and right, Wellington gave a tug on his lapels and ran back to the smouldering podium.

"Miss Sheppard," Wellington called, "are you well?"

Kate Sheppard, the voice of the women's suffrage movement in New Zealand, was still trying to get her bearings. She must have landed hard against the ground when Eliza tackled her. Her head lolled from side to side, but came to an abrupt halt when she locked here eyes, both real and substitute, with her saviour.

"*Kia ora*, Kate," Eliza said, flashing her a friendly smile. "Been a while, hasn't it?"

"Eliza?" Kate asked, her breath short.

Wellington looked around them. "Eliza, who was—"

The scream cut through the lingering silence.

Kate's glass eye swiveled around, and she jerked upright. "Melinda? My goodness, where is Melinda?"

Eliza shot a look back to Kate. "We'll have to catch up another time. Good to see you." She grabbed Wellington's forearm and used it to pull herself up to her feet. "Sounds like near Grosvenor Gate, Books!"

Again they were pushing their way through the stunned crowd, though it was easier going since many of their fellow audience members were streaming away from the podium. Once beyond the initial impact zone, they reached pedestrians who had no idea what had happened and were instead enjoying the remains of the morning. At least until they processed that terrified screaming was coming from somewhere up ahead. Wellington remained only a few steps behind Eliza until they came within sight of Upper Grosvenor Street. By then, the screaming had stopped, but the crowd of onlookers had started to gather.

Eliza and Wellington forcefully managed their way through the gawkers to the source of the cries.

The young girl was trying to speak, but found she couldn't as the thick iron bars comprising the large gates surrounding the apartments were now running through her throat. And her chest. And her skull. She was no longer holding the Matford-Randleson Ætheralternator, but it never fell to the ground as it had also been fused into the gate. The body, being part of the ironworks, twitched as much as it could; and Wellington gave silent thanks that he and Eliza had not taken in a tea or an early lunch. He swallowed back the queasiness and, with Eliza at his side, approached the poor girl who was gasping out her final moments.

"It was the rifle," Wellington whispered. "She had taken it from Kate just before you got her out of the way. The rifle must have attracted the electricity to her."

"What does this?"

"I don't—"

The woman gave a tiny whimper, and Wellington felt completely impotent. The victim was looking at them both, though, and her brow was creasing. Then her eyes looked out and then down. Out, and then down. Again. And again.

"Wellington," Eliza said, causing him to jump. "Her hand."

The woman was trying to make a fist of her right hand, all except for her index and middle finger. She had wanted them to see this gesture.

"Two?" Eliza asked her.

The hand relaxed, and the woman looked at Eliza and smiled. Or at least, tried to.

Then her eyes stopped looking at them, and now looked through them to some place they could not see.

In the distance, a police whistle sounded out.

"Eliza," Wellington muttered to her. "We need to go. Now."

So much for that low profile that he'd hope to maintain. As they disappeared into the bustle of London, Wellington considered exactly what he would tell the Director tomorrow.

Where Many Things Go Bump in the Night

The clouds above the greatest city in the Empire were grey and thick, and just before midnight they finally let loose their promise of retribution.

Most of London was hiding inside from the downpour, but Sophia del Morte loved the rain and thunder. It was not just that her nefarious comings and goings were less likely to be noticed—she also enjoyed the way nature's opera rattled her bones. Unfortunately, it also made her feet, braced as they were into the window frame of London's Natural History Museum, slightly slippery. She was wearing the latest fashion in rubberised footwear, but even that was having difficulty in these conditions.

When her foot slipped Sophia sneered, shaking her head in disgust. Breaking and entering? This was an utter waste of her abilities. True, being an assassin meant she was well versed in stealth and infiltration—but she was not a common cracksman. She had served aristocracy, minor nobility, and on the rare occasion high ranking members of government. It was most likely her mention of procuring the plans for Lord Fontaine's time actuator that led the Maestro to believe this sort of thing was part of her repertoire.

She'd managed to suppress her disdain for this charge

when in front of her master, but now she was free of such restraints. While she knew nothing could keep her from gaining access to what she wanted, it appeared citizens of a most law-abiding nature were attempting to slow her night's progress. It only contributed to her wrathful mood.

One such device that had put a proverbial stick in Sophia's spokes this evening showed all the hallmarks of the McTighe-Fitzroy Laboratories. It was bad enough to have Julia McTighe taking up the family business, but since she had teamed up with the young Verity Fitzroy, their combined inventions had become far more complicated. Sophia contemplated sending them the bill for her ruined chemise and time wasted when she could have been dining at the Savoy with a delightful Argentinian trader.

When she'd first arrived at the museum, it was immediately apparent that the doors, main and side, were locked with a cypher that would take her until morning to crack. She simply didn't have the time—or indeed the inclination for such things. Luckily, that arrogant little strumpet Fitzroy was not the only woman with devices on hand. The ascent claws strapped to her palms and her knees had got her this far up the side of the towering stone building in rather quick order.

As they approached a new century, the British had begun to build temples to science and art. None of them was as beautiful as Rome's, but they were certainly harder to break into. This building was impressive with its multistory stone façade, rows of stained-glass windows, and square towers at each end. *A cathedral to the natural world*, she mused while rain poured down her cheeks, *but at least one thing it contains is most unnatural.*

The thunder was getting louder and closer. She ducked her head instinctively but kept moving higher. Her master was not one to be put off—not even for a day. So, she climbed on, muttering under her breath things she most certainly would not have repeated in his presence.

Just as Sophia reached the roof, the sky lit up, as if announcing her arrival. It was nice when Mother Nature was in agreement with her own mood.

Wiping water out of her eyes, Sophia ran over the slate roof tiles of the façade towards the roofline of the Central Hall. All the museum's windows were protected with McTighe's annoying etheric sensors, but to the well-informed there were ways around such inconveniences.

Reaching the great barrel roof of the Hall, Sophia smiled, wiped the water out of her eyes, jerked her satchel around in front, and removed from it another of her master's devices. Her informants had passed on the news that work was being done on the leaks in the Central Hall windows, and the sensors were disengaged for a few days.

Perfect for her purposes. As was her Maestro's device. It was a narrow rope that looked strangely as though it were made of metal, but woven in ways she'd never seen metal worked before. Sophia liked how it felt in her hand: smooth, slick, and strong. One end she wrapped around herself, cinching it tight around her waist, while the other she snapped onto the ridge of the roof. It locked tighter than a crocodile on a person's limb. The rope itself was very fragile looking, but she trusted her Maestro and his devices implicitly. He was more than the equal of any McTighe or Fitzroy, she thought with reflected pride.

One more thing was needed. Sophia fished out strap on soles for her boots. Sooner or later even the fools at Scotland Yard might stumble on her activities, so it was better to put another of London's numerous felons in the frame.

Then she leaned hard into the rope, and turned on the little box that held the ropes tight about her. When she flicked the lever, the gears began to turn, the rope loosened out, took her weight, and then she simple walked down off the slate roof tiles to the windows that comprised the sides of the barrel vault.

She came to rest with her boots against the glass, as if out for a morning vertical stroll evening as thunder crashed and rain fell. In the interests of not being obvious, she crouched down and pressed another of the Maestro's gifts to the surface of the glass. A diamond edged knife cut a small enough hole in the window that she was able to wriggle her way through.

She released the catch on her line, and dropped down into the Central Hall, leaving the wet bootmarks of Fast Nate Lowell behind. He was going to have some explaining to do.

Then she withdrew the slightly bulky goggles she had not dared to wear outside in the rain. As Sophia slid them over her eyes and adjusted the oculars on each side, a soft scarlet glow bathed her field of vision. Something about the curious illumination always made her uncomfortable, but it gave her the night vision of a cat, which was beyond useful in these circumstances.

Sophia didn't pause at where she had landed for long. Instead she scampered up the central stairs as quickly as possible.

The lightning lit up the great vaulted ceiling through the museum's many windows, and for a minute she saw nothing while the oculars were overwhelmed by nature's own fireworks.

Sophia chewed her bottom lip while waiting for the Maestro's device to compensate—which they did eventually. Now below, she could see the shapes of the watchmen's lanterns, which in the oculars looked a deep blood red. They were triangular glows in the vastness of the room below, and there were only two of them.

These telltale lights were moving slowly enough to tell her that—like most guards—they were bored with their lot. Certainly there was not much in the Natural History museum that was worth stealing; mostly old bones and preserved skins from distant parts of the Empire. At least that was what most people thought. Sophia knew better than that.

She watched the guards negotiate around the displays for a moment. They were among the fantastic exhibits of fearsome animals from the wilds of Africa, the menagerie of beasts all frozen in time in various states of alertness, curiosity, or combat. During the day, their mechanical skeletons would resurrect them and show visitors how they lived and, considering the lions' poses, how they hunted. It was something her master could have enjoyed or at least appreciated.

A soft rumble thrummed in her ears and flashes of white light illuminated the side of the gazelle's snout.

Sophia smiled. The prey. She understood prey.

To the accompaniment of thunder, she turned and entered the geological gallery. Lightning illuminated all the treasures surrendered by the earth. Most were pretty hunks of rock or crystal but worthless.

However, the museum had recently acquired the Carrington Collection, a collection made by the kind of people England specialised in—the eccentric. The Carringtons had apparently cleared out the attic, and felt philanthropic enough to donate what they found to the museum. One of the items in particular had caught the eye of one of the Maestro's collaborators. She'd seen it and known what it was immediately, but apparently lacked the courage to take it herself. Typical of many of the clankertons Sophia was forced to deal with, he'd sent her to do what they could not.

Looking down into the display case through the oculars at her prize, she was almost blinded. The square crystal looked like a pulsing heart through them, with blazing lines of lights darting deep within. Her master, not usually given to sharing information, had told her that the ancient civilisation now lost beneath the waves had once powered its cities with such stones. It was just the thing his little protégé could make use of.

Though it irked her to be an errand boy, her fear of his wrath overrode any sense of pride. She'd seen what he'd done to those who displeased him—and had tended to the mess afterward.

Lightning flashed once more, followed only a heartbeat later by the rumble of thunder. The storm was right over the museum now; and Sophia glanced instinctively up, the instinct blinding her as the nocturnal lenses compensated. Clamping her hands over her eyes to give the device time to recover plunged her into darkness, and that was when Sophia heard movement. Behind her.

Somehow one of the guards, blundering about like a drunk elephant, had by sheer chance managed to catch her unawares. Sophia spun about with a soft curse and jerked off the oculars.

The guard, a huge oafish-looking man, was staring at her—something that she was quite used to. Not for the first time her beauty saved her. While he was still gawking, his mouth hanging open fish-like, she reached into the tiny pouch hanging off her belt, grabbed one of the tiny missiles, and flung it at the man.

The British liked to play at darts in their public houses and probably thought themselves masters of the art. They had not however ventured up the Amazon to study with the Huian tribe as she had in her youth. Her aim was perfect.

The guard reached for the sudden sting in his throat, but already his knees had given up on him. Sophia heard the thump his body made as it hit the hard marble floor, but she did not see it. She was already picking the lock on the case, and removing the stone her master had sent her for. The unlucky guard was already forgotten.

The rock was warm and heavy in her hand, but without the lightning and the oculars it really did not seem that remarkable. After wrapping it in a handkerchief, Sophia pressed it under her corset and between her breasts.

She scooped up the oculars, stepped over the guard who was twitching and convulsing the last moments of his life away, and slipped from shadow to shadow until she found her exit. Outside the rain was still coming down hard, and so she had to be cautious on the slick roof, crouching low until she reached the parapet. Then she affixed her rope to one of the stone griffons looking out over storm-tossed London, and slid down it to the ground.

The knot she flicked loose, reclaiming her equipment with smooth efficiency. As for the repelling equipment she had used to gain entry, it disappeared in a flash once she pressed the detonator's trigger. The curators would know someone had been in the museum tonight on account of damage to a window, a dead guard, a few puddles of water, and Fast Nate's footprints. It was a matter of professional pride, though, that she would leave nothing of hers behind.

The streets of Kensington were still quiet but definitely wetter than when she had gone in. She raced across the road and around the corner to Thurloe Street where the reinforced carriage awaited.

Sophia del Morte took a moment to smooth her hair and adjust her clothing before entering. The interior was dimly lit, and her master sat in shadow.

"I take it you were successful?" His voice came out accompanied by a series of steam hisses; she had come to think of it as his own little orchestra.

Withdrawing the stone from its intimate hiding place, she held it out to him on a trembling palm. It was terrifying how dull and ordinary it looked inside the carriage. She held her breath. Her heart was racing, her body near to aching with stress.

For the longest moment she hung suspended between pleasure and terror, until he finally released her. "Indeed, it appears you were."

One brass gauntlet appeared out of the shadows to take the stone from her. Her master leaned forward and examined the stone through the brass helmet that obscured most of his features and expressions. Sophia suspected the articulated suit he always wore was fitted with the same ocular devices as he had given her, because he nodded. "A nice piece that will do the trick for my little investment."

He dropped it back into Sophia's still outstretched palm. She blinked at it for a moment worried that he would ask her to return it from where she had stolen it; he could be capricious like that sometimes.

"Take it to her," he snapped, his voice distant through the grate of his helmet.

Sophia tightened her hand on the stone and nodded. "Yes, Maestro."

And then, just like that she found herself standing on the street, in the rain watching the carriage disappear into the night.

No acknowledgement of her abilities. Not even a word of thanks. It was so hard to know what he thought of her, and she so desperately wanted to know.

Her body was trembling, but it was not with fear anymore—it was from accomplishment. What had begun as a relationship based on terror had begun to shift to something else entirely—but just as primal.

Sophia del Morte wondered if the Maestro had noticed that too.

CHAPTER THREE

Wherein Our Intrepid Heroes Return Home, Our Dashing Archivist Settles into His Routines, and—Sadly—So Does Our Beloved Colonial Pepperpot

The analytical engine sounded off with a single chime, and Wellington's morning tea tickled his nose. He took it into his hands and gave a few soft blows before enjoying its mid-morning bite. He was hoping it would clear his head of the previous morning, but all he could see were the confused, terrified eyes of that young girl trapped within the bars of the gate. He glanced at his newssheet for what could have been the fifth time, reassuring himself that indeed he and Eliza had eluded any mention. The girl was no longer nameless to him—Melinda Carnes. She had come from a family of wealth and privilege, like many in the suffragist movement. She had been part of the Ladies Auxiliary of London for three years, and her assignment to assist Kate Sheppard throughout her speaking tour had been regarded as a real honour, according to the papers. The voices of her parents and fiancé spoke in Melinda's memory, and along with pride there was in their words a powerful sense of loss.

All the better, Wellington thought, *that you did not witness her final moments as I did*.

Perhaps it had not been in vain, however. She had managed to communicate the cryptic "two," just before the light in her eyes dimmed and then disappeared altogether.

Eliza had not voiced any interest to return to Speakers' Corner, which came as a surprise to Wellington. He believed his partner would have leapt at an opportunity to speak with a fellow antipodean, but even she appeared to want to keep a low profile. They'd escaped from the scene before a crowd could really gather and long before Scotland Yard appeared.

The Archivist blinked, and that was when he noticed the cup of tea in his hands had gone from hot to tepid. He had been sitting still, engrossed for some time.

By their desk, a small coal furnace glowed cheerfully. Wellington stoked the remaining embers within it, and then added two additional scoops. A few minutes later, he felt the coils built into the underside of the shared desk surge with a delightful warmth. He examined the Archives' long lines of shelves, and pondered how he could somehow contrive a similar heating system throughout its cavernous interior; but coming up with such a contraption would take longer than his analytical engine.

Besides, he had *plenty* on his worktable back home—and even more sitting before him.

Staring back at him were his own two sheets' worth of notes that were in reference to the archives transfered from the Scotland office. The clock residing at the meeting point of the shared desks read just shy of eleven o'clock. He looked back at the closed hatch of the Archives. Locked, as it had been when he arrived. Wellington concluded his partner would arrive sometime after lunch, as was her fashion. That suited him very well. With this recent acquisition from Scotland, there was plenty to do.

Suddenly, his stomach growled, and that was when Wellington remembered he had forgotten to eat breakfast.

"Dash it all," he whispered.

His eyes darted up to the pillars of crates around their desk. He slipped on fingerless gloves and sighed as he looked at the top box, labeled 1891. Perhaps with Eliza alongside him, this process would take half the time; but alone as he was, 1891 appeared as the easiest place for him to begin. Stepping away from the comfort of the heated desk and into the chill of the Archives, Wellington wrapped his scarf about his neck and extended the keypad to him.

He typed:

ARCHIVE RETRIEVAL
1891

The machine clicked and whirred and then . . .

"Now just a moment," Wellington muttered. No one about, so no need to display his "inability" to type. He double-checked the display. It was the right command.

He pressed the "Enter" key again. Again, the analytical engine clicked and whirred . . .

This time, the engine's display responded:

FULFILMENT FAILURE.
SYSTEM CURRENTLY ENGAGED.

He looked back into the Archives, then back to the engine's amber display. This can't be right. *Such a failure would mean Eliza is already—*

Wellington took long strides as he went deeper into the Archives, looking down each year's aisle, but seeing only darkness—that was until he reached 1892.

At the far end of the shelves was a single, familiar figure sitting at the reading table, poring over a case.

He could hardly believe his eyes. "Eliza?"

"Morning, Welly," she answered cheerily, gathering up the open files before her.

"Good—" Wellington started and blinked. Eliza had been here? All this time? *Before him?* "—morning?"

"What's wrong, Welly? Would you care for a spot of tea, or perhaps something stronger?"

"I—I already have a cup."

"Well, I certainly could use one myself," Eliza said, walking past him and returning to the Archive's analytical engine. She punched in a code, and within minutes the sharp smell of gunpowder tea filled Wellington's nostrils.

The scent seemed to provide the jolt the drink would have eventually given him. "I never programmed—"

"Oh, come along, Welly," Eliza chided him, "did you really think with all the adjustments you have made to this creation of yours, I wouldn't follow suit?"

"But how did you—"

"I opened up your tea sequence, cracked the computations, and then adjusted it for *my* preferred brew. Did you not know that cryptography was a new passion of mine? You're partially to blame for it you know, considering that trick you pulled in Antarctica."

He felt a blush rush to his cheeks. She still remembered, and now she was interested in the art of cracking codes herself? It was almost charming.

Wellington, he snapped silently at himself, *focus! She was here, in the Archives, before you!*

As he returned to their desk, his colleague slid towards him a large jar of ointment across the desk. An aroma of mint, medicinal salve, and lavender tickled his nose. "I popped up to the clankertons' lair and stole this wonderful ointment for our unexpected sunburn from the past two days." She smiled brightly. "It really does do the job." Wellington peered closer, and yes indeed, it did appear Eliza's skin glowed a little less red than it had.

Before he could make a move for the jar, she had darted

around to his side of the desk, sat herself down on the edge, and put one hand under his chin against his neatly trimmed beard. The Archivist was quite unsure what to do with the fact that his partner had him in such an intimate grasp. It was . . . most improper, yet he found himself allowing her to tip his head this way and that. She leaned forward and examined his injuries with an intensity that would have done Miss Nightingale herself proud.

Wellington avoided looking into her eyes.

"Yes," Eliza finally declared. "You seem to have caught a little more of it than I did. My hat provided some shelter on that train, and then yesterday we—Kate and I, that is—were low to the ground, out of the blast radius." She dipped her finger into the jar and began to apply it to his cheeks.

He could have done it himself, however he found at present he didn't want to. Despite himself Wellington let out a little sigh of relief. The ointment was delightfully cool and immediately eased the discomfort of the burns. Eliza's fingers were gentle in their ministrations, and for a couple of minutes they sat in silence while she worked her magic.

Wellington finally met her gaze. "Thank you, Eliza."

Her grip on his chin softened slightly and an uncertain smile hovered at the corners of her lips. "Quite all right, Wellington. I know how you men do fuss." She turned him in his seat and clicked her tongue. "Oh, but did you get a delightful burn on the back of your neck. Hold still."

The back of her fingers slowly worked the ointment into the nape of his neck, and the Archivist felt the heat return to his cheeks—hotter than ever.

Thankfully, Eliza slipped down off the desk and re-treated back to her side of it. Her next comment took him completely off guard.

"You know, we really should name your mechanical monster here. Between us, it is developing quite the personality. I've always liked the name Lisa."

Wellington was relieved to be back on ground he knew all too well—Eliza's magpie-inclined mind. It did so like to hop about. It still didn't answer the overwhelming question in his head. "All right, Eliza, out with it—you've been playing with the æthergates again, haven't you?"

"Are you mad, Wellington? Or need I remind you of the last time I used them and appeared in the Sultan's harem wearing only my pounamu pistols?"

Wellington gave a start. "I don't remember that from your case report!"

Now it was Eliza's turn to blink. "Oh, wait—I left that bit out. Saving it for my memoirs." She relaxed in her chair and released a sigh that coalesced into a mist in front of her. "Yes. That *was fun.*"

"*Miss Braun,* what are you doing here? *Before me?*"

Her mouth twisted into a smirk as she shook her head at him. "Really, Welly, you think you are the only one who will walk that extra mile once a bee is in their bonnet? I, my dear colleague, am engaging in a bit of background research," she said, motioning to the case files before her. "We have a few cases—I have found ten, so far—of missing ladies disappearing under the strangest of circumstances."

"Missing ladies?" Wellington groaned. She was at it again. "Now just a moment—"

Her eyes flicked up to the ceiling as she held up a single finger. "Is this the 'You promised not to do this following the Phoenix Society' talk?"

He choked back his words and adjusted his spectacles. "Well, that seems most appropriate. You did promise to—"

Eliza raised one hand, "Actually I did no such thing, Wellington Thornhill Books. What I recall saying is that I would refrain from getting involved unless something *took my fancy.* Something about two women disappearing in a ball of light has done just that."

They glared at each other for a long minute before Wellington glanced down at what she had on her desk. "Dare I ask, while I know I will regret what you will tell me, what you have found?"

"These ten cases I've discovered between 1892 and pres-

ent day all report eyewitness accounts of women disappearing into a fantastic display of light. More to the point, these
women were all connected, either financially or idealisti-
cally, to the building suffragist movement. Have a look," she
said, handing Wellington an open case file.

"Do I really want to?"

"You know you do," cooed Eliza.

Wellington took the case file and immediately his eyes
fell on the disappearance of Mildred Cady, treasurer of the
Women's Franchise League. "There was a strange crackling
in our ears, and the smell of metal baking in a summer sun
surrounded us. There was a flash of light, and she was gone.
Those close to Mildred were covered in burns as one would
find after an Egyptian holiday." He glanced at the date of
the report, then looked up across the desk. "This is from
December 1895?"

"One of ten," Eliza said.

His eye returned to the report and, with further perusal,
he recognised the handwriting. More of the same was visible
in other case files before Eliza. "You seem to be referencing
open cases that have been passed along to us by their primary investigator—"

"Oh, I have some very strong thoughts concerning that,"
Eliza said, nodding.

"I am sure you do, but I hope you recall another of the
discussions we had."

"The 'Doctor Sound was clear as fine crystal that we are
not to interfere' talk?"

"The very one," he blurted.

"Oh now, go on, Welly. Did we *really* interfere that much
in Dominick's case a few months ago? He was stuck on that
business coming in from Cape Colony, and the Archives
was politely providing additional research."

"Yes, and let's talk about that 'additional research,' shall
we? Unsolved Case 18510421UKSL, where you picked up
the trail of the Sword of the Lost Legion."

"Happenstance!" Eliza implored. "Dominick confessed over drinks he was a bit stonewalled on how the Spear of Yemaya was constantly eluding his associates back in the Dark Continent. I recalled an unsolved case where the Sword of the Lost Legion was also eluding agents back when."

"And so you took it upon yourself to undertake the trail of the Lost Legion, did you?"

"Begin where Hadrian's Wall once stood and work your way back to where the Celts made things nasty for our Roman Legionnaires, eh what?" Eliza leaned back in her chair, quite proud of herself. "And while my predecessor in Case 18510421UKSL indeed had close encounters with this sword, it simply wasn't in the cards." She gave a light laugh. "Or should I say, stars?"

"Eliza—" he warned, rising to his feet.

"And when I closed that case—"

"Thanks to some clever tale spinning from your partner."

"*And when I closed that case,*" Eliza repeated, arching an eyebrow at him, "I left it on his desk."

"In sight of everyone, including Doctor Sound who—if you failed to notice—doubled the frequency of his surprise visits to the Archives."

"What you call interference, I call a fellow agent aiding another. After all," she said, as her grin widened ever so slightly, "isn't that our job?"

"And are you telling me, Miss Braun," Wellington countered, "that this is your intention with Agent Bruce Campbell and his current fieldwork?"

The choked laugh that left Eliza caused him to start. "Hardly! I intend to take some investigative work of my own and present it to Doctor Sound straightaway."

Wellington took a moment. He felt a chill slip under his skin, and he gripped the arms of his chair as he sat back down.

"I—" and he paused as he went to take a sip of his now cold tea. The cup rattled against its saucer as he considered

Eliza's strategy and his next words. "I beg your pardon, but I want to fully understand your intentions: Are you in fact questioning Campbell's competency in the field?"

She opened several cases in front of her and motioned to them as she answered, "Yes. And the proof is here in all these unsolved cases of the Archives.

"1894. Key officers in the National Society for Women's Suffrage started disappearing. Chapter presidents, secretaries, and influential members—*disappearing.* Not all at once, mind you, but their cases—pardon me, these ladies' *existences*—have all ended here. In the Archives. All of them unsolved."

Wellington looked at the collected cases. All of them bearing Campbell's handwriting. "I fail to see what you are concluding from all this."

"Don't lie to me, Books. You can't, for starters."

Wellington straightened slightly on that. She only called him "Books" when her temper was beginning to slip. He found her calm unsettling as she placed three more case files in front of him. She knew he was not expected to read them. She was out to prove her point.

"After I caught a few winks, I came here straightaway and started from the end of the year, working back. These are ten files that I've found so far."

"All in the Unsolved Cases archives?"

"All of them with Bruce's signature. Five just in the past few months. He barely spent a week on them."

"And the reason you were in the 1892 stacks?"

"Now here's where you will be so proud of me, Welly—"

"Overwhelm me with wonder, Miss Braun," he interjected.

"When I came across this pattern, I cross-referenced them with solved cases in or around the same time period. I even stepped back to Campbell's first year, just to see what kind of an agent he was when recruited. Regardless of what a git he is, Campbell is a cracking good investigator. Or was."

Wellington shook his head, slumping back in his chair.

His heart was already racing. "This is a most dangerous course you are plotting. You are challenging Bruce Campbell, an agent of the Ministry with an outstanding record—"

"Provided you are not taking into account his luck with Missing Person cases."

"Eliza!" Wellington snapped. Dammit, she was not seeing what he saw, what he *knew*. "Perhaps you would rather not care to recognise the severity of your actions."

"The facts speak for themselves!"

"They may very well do so, but what they mean could be lost in translation." Wellington began closing the numerous files in front of him. "People disappear in the Empire all the time, never to be seen again. Some leave deliberately, some go abroad, and some simply move house and leave no forwarding address."

Eliza looked betrayed. The opposite of his intentions, really; but he could read in her cold, hard gaze that she didn't see that. Not at all.

"Books . . ."

"Eliza, please . . ."

"These women are not statistics to be simply cast aside." Wellington wanted Eliza to be screaming at him, wanted her voice to be filling the spacious Archives with her fury. Her control terrified him. "That is exactly what Bruce did here; and for two years, ten ladies *that we know of* have remained nothing more than a bunch of hysterical women gone missing in the streets of London. These women were something far more important than notes in our files." Eliza spread out the files. "Annette Pritchard. Glenda Rooney. Mildred Cady. Clara Gleeson. They were lives. Wives. Mothers. Sisters. Friends."

"You have to look at this objectively—"

"How dare you!"

"*Oh for God's sake, woman, would you listen to me for once?*"

The drone of the Ministry generators filled his ears, alongside the pounding of his own heartbeat. She was the one who was supposed to be losing her composure, not him; and there he was, on his feet, his fists trembling tight at his sides.

Well done, son, the voice whispered in his mind. *The colonial needed a reminder.*

His father's ghost was not helping. Not one jot.

"This is not personal, Miss Braun." But it was. Wellington did not wish her to fall any further; and while she did not see it, Eliza D. Braun's feet were now close to the precipice. "You know I would never challenge your deductions. I trust your detective skills implicitly."

Eliza gathered up the case files from Wellington's side of the desk. "And yet?"

"You are about to accuse an active field agent of negligence. You are intending to march into Sound's office with your own findings and question Campbell's competency."

"That is the idea."

"Tell me, Eliza . . ." His heartbeat quickened as the words left him. "When was the last time Agent Campbell was reprimanded—let alone *demoted*—for his actions in the field?"

The cold stare he had earlier received was replaced by one of anger.

"And what would you know of Ministry protocol and politics?" she spat. "You have spent your career here, alone, in this bloody hole."

A valiant effort. Wellington pressed on.

"I was an officer in the Queen's Army. I watched many a peer and subordinate openly question another officer's judgment based on patterns they thought they saw. Those Queen's soldiers would find themselves reassigned to the front of the charge. They either died a hero's death, or returned home to their sweetheart with the ability to embrace them with only one arm, if they were fortunate."

"What happens upstairs is hardly akin to campaigns in Afghanistan or Burma."

"Very well then. The direct approach. I am your superior,

appointed by Doctor Sound himself, and you will heed my order: stand down, and let this matter go."

She took a step back on that. He was surprised his own stance had not faltered.

"You are too close to this," he continued, "and your judgement—the objective eye and opinion that is essential in crime investigation—has been compromised. And I will not have you jeopardising yourself or your fellow agents in the field. Therefore, you will cease all exploration into these missing persons. That is a direct order."

Eliza gave a slight tug at her jacket. She was staring at the files as she asked, "Is that all?"

As if his stomach were responding to her voice, a low growl rumbled from him.

"No, in light of yesterday's events and my own lack of sleep because of it, I forgot all about breakfast. Would you mind?" Wellington reached into his vest pocket and pulled out a few shillings. "A ham sandwich, please. Light on the mustard."

The sharp rap of her heels against the stone floor caused his head to flick up. Eliza held her salute until Wellington made eye contact with her. Her arm lowered and then she gathered her coat and made her way to the hatch with no further word.

Naturally Eliza was angry. Ye gods, she must be furious with him right now. She was failing to see, though, what Wellington knew down to his soul was how close she was sailing to a guaranteed expulsion from the Ministry ranks. The Archives had been a reprimand, a demotion from the glamorous life of a field agent to a far more quiet one of logistics. When she had first arrived, Wellington did his own share of research on her. She achieved results. No one would question her abilities there; but after Agent Thorne's demise, Eliza's risks made her a growing liability. Then there was his daring rescue from the House of Usher's Antarctic hideout. A single act that brought her here.

Wellington had initially thought it some sort of pun-

ishment on him for being captured. Now, less than a year
later, the Archivist did not want her to leave. Perhaps he had
grown accustomed to having a partner, or perhaps it was
Eliza herself. She was hardly the kind of woman he asso-
ciated himself with; but a part of him looked forward to
Eliza's company.

Or maybe after seven years of singular service to Her
Majesty in the Archives, it took the colonial's daily presence
to show him how lonely he was.

Eliza mattered a great deal to him, even if she presently
couldn't see that. A demoted agent questioning the ethics of
a commended Ministry operative—an agent that even Wellington could tell, from his isolated seat in the Archives, was
as thick as clotted cream—would be her final act. The Ministry Director was hardly of the same mettle as his cavalry
superiors, but he would have to maintain order amongst the
ranks. There was also the possibility of the field agents' fra-
ternity turning on her.

Wellington pushed aside the archive inventory sheets and
cast his spectacles on top of them. His eyes fixed instead
on the empty space across from him. Was he truly looking
after her best interests, or was he being selfish? For all those
traits and quirks that Wellington weathered, he didn't want
to lose her.

The sudden *fump* from the catch-all underneath the
chute caused him to start. Replacing his glasses, Wellington crossed over to the still-swaying basket that held this
new folio from upstairs. He released its cover and pulled out
from it a relatively thin case file.

He opened the folder and held his breath as he read what
was written there. Wellington looked up at where the agents'
offices would be.

"You cocksure bastard," he whispered aloud.

How Wellington hated it when she was right.

CHAPTER FOUR

Wherein Miss Braun Takes
Some Air and Meets Someone Unexpected

How Eliza hated it when he was right.

The man was insufferable, but the rational part of her mind only echoed what Wellington Books had told her: this was a dangerous game she was thinking of playing.

She recalled a frank discussion Harry and she had shared regarding one agent, Timothy Cuthbert, head of the Jamaican office. The "whelp," as Harry had referred to him, came from a family of wealth and influence, and that was how he'd landed a director's job in what many considered paradise. The cases coming out of Jamaica, though, were usually dismissive and poorly handled, resulting in the unnecessary deaths of two agents. Agents that were friends of Harry. He had to remain silent, though, as questioning Cuthbert's judgement would have opened a political maelstrom between offices and government officials.

Cuthbert, however, managed to bring about his own downfall when Doctor Sound made an unexpected visit to the outpost—and discovered Cuthbert managing a rum-running business between Jamaica and the Americas.

After Cuthbert's ousting, Harry had told her, "*Take care,*

Lizzie. Even when you have the facts in your favour, you may not be able to openly question another agent's competency. It's a silent code we all must adhere to. Eventually, secrets herald one's downfall."

When Eliza emerged into the front shop of the Ministry, most of the paper shufflers in their rows of desks ignored her as they did any agent who entered their domain. Those who had dared to peek up from their work immediately ducked their heads lower and looked even more studious than ever as she passed between them. No one wanted to get in the way of Eliza's dark glare.

Out on the street it was chilly but beautiful. *Damn it,* she thought bitterly, *I am taking the sodding long way. Let his stomach tie itself into knots for all I care.*

"Eliza!"

The woman's voice broke through her anger and stopped her in her tracks. Turning, she felt her tension abate, if not disappear completely, on seeing Agent Ihita Pujari running to catch up with her. The young Indian woman had only arrived in London the previous month, but already the New Zealand agent had grown very fond of her. They had a somewhat similar sense of humour—though Ihita's was hidden beneath a layer of gentility. Her sleek black hair was tied in an elaborate braid, but, much as Eliza did, she wore men's clothing—and wore it well. The effect was even more striking with Ihita's dark skin and sparkling brown eyes. It was like putting a sleek jungle cat in tweed. It threw her beauty into stark contrast.

"Good morning!" Eliza did her best to conceal her annoyance. It was after all not the other woman's fault. "Off for a spot of lunch?"

"Yes, Brandon is quite buried in paperwork," she paused, tucking her hands into her pockets. Her eyes looked aside as her dark skin grew slightly ruddier. "And I know he won't have a chance to get out."

Eliza raised one eyebrow. Ihita would not be the first woman to fall under Agent Brandon Hill's curious charm. If she was lucky he might even notice her.

"You're fetching something for Agent Books?" It was a neat way of changing the subject, but Eliza was only too ready to let off some steam.

"It serves as an excellent excuse to free myself temporarily from the Archives," she muttered as she kicked a stone across the street, "lest I break his arm."

Her companion chuckled, but then, on catching Eliza's gaze, stopped short. "Oh, I see."

Their stroll following the curve of the Thames was not what could be called "a scenic walk" such as you might find further up the river, but that was what Eliza needed. The smells of river life, unpleasant but familiar, distracted her from the pit of anger in her chest. The catcalls of the port workers and drivers were only to be expected, but Lord have mercy on any man who thought to lay hands on Eliza D. Braun this afternoon.

"It must be quite different where you come from," the New Zealander offered. "I mean, I find it strange enough, but London must be even more of a shock."

Ihita shrugged. "There are just as many people in Delhi, and men are the same the world over."

"Unfortunately, that is very much the truth."

Eliza's tone made her friend jerk her head around. "I thought you and Books had come to a satisfactory arrangement?"

"Me too, but today we hit a little bump in the rails. In fact I think we are near to careening off them."

Ihita slipped her arm into the crook of Eliza's and gave her a gentle squeeze. "If you don't mind me saying so, I think you are a little hard on our studious Agent Books. He is a good man, and he is only looking out for you and your position in the Ministry."

It wasn't what Eliza wanted to hear, but it made her curious. "How do you know what Books is like?"

She gave a little shrug and stated, "We've enjoyed one another's company over lunch a couple of times."

"Really?" Eliza gave a light chuckle. "I remember my

first social night with him. I do hope you had more success in conversations with him than I did."

"Oh, he was quite delightful." Ihita thought for a moment and nodded. "A bit shy, at first. Later on, though, it can be hard to get a word in, depending on the subject at hand." She considered Eliza for a moment, her smile turning sly, and then added, "You'd never guess it but he has a bit of a taste for saag. In return for my own recipe, he loaned me a novel of his. *The Time Machine*. It's quite wonderful."

She looked at Eliza with such innocence that the New Zealander could not possibly snap at her, so for a long moment she said nothing at all.

Ihita tilted her head at this oddity, wondering no doubt what was wrong with the other woman. "He takes his job very seriously," she said softly as a goad.

Eliza cleared her throat. "That's as may be—but he should also remember we have sworn an oath to protect the citizens of the Empire. That is more important than any silly bureaucracy. Far more important than any political nonsense."

"Political?" Ihita asked. "Whatever do you mean?"

She opened her mouth, wanting to confide in her Indian friend about Wellington's objection to her claims against Agent Campbell. Her instincts though, gave her pause. Sharing her revelations of what Campbell was doing could place Ihita in an awkward position within the Ministry's ranks.

"Another time, Ihita," she finally replied, "perhaps over a dinner at my apartments."

Eliza quietly cursed her sudden moment of reason. This was Wellington's influence, and she didn't care for it—not one jot.

Their silence lingered as they turned left, the ports changing to shops that supplied services to the workers who could be found there. Many a gambling den, disorderly house, or pub was located here—but also the best sandwich shop this side of the Thames. Eliza was grateful that Albert Southward's business was so close to the Ministry, and sometimes she wondered if that was not altogether by chance.

They had to pass the eel-jelly stand to get there—but that still did not put the women off. Watching Londoners slurp down with real relish something that looked like it had been sneezed out of their noses was another oddness that Eliza had not quite gotten used to. The smell alone convinced her that everyone in line was completely mad.

"And they call what we eat in my country strange," Ihita whispered behind her hand.

They were both still chuckling by the time they reached Albert's sandwich establishment. The crowd at the shop was miraculously short—so they had picked the right moment.

"So much better than jellied eel." Eliza smiled.

"Oh, much!"

Eliza could feel her mood lift a bit, so much so that she felt herself capable of prying—just a little. "You know it suddenly occurs to me: there is nothing at all you can eat as a Hindu at Albert's. It's all very . . . well . . . beefy."

"Oh, no," her fellow agent responded quickly. "I'm here for Brandon's sandwich."

Eliza's eyebrow shot up. "Fetching lunch for *Agent Hill*, Ihita? Isn't that a bit forward of you?"

"It's just lunch!" her friend protested, but she would not meet Eliza's eyes.

"Well, if you ever want it to be more than that, you will have to tell him directly. Brandon is a handsome man, but truth be told he's as thick as a brick about women fancying him." Eliza tapped her fingers on her purse. "It will never ever cross his mind that you like him at all. Lunch will merely make him think you are mates."

They moved a few more steps in the line while Ihita thought about that. "I couldn't possibly tell him." Her whisper was barely able to be heard above the hubbub of the street, so Eliza had to lean in to make it out. "What if he doesn't feel the same?"

"Then you move on."

Her friend vehemently shook her head. "I'm not like you, Eliza. I've been able to get past some of the traditions I was raised with—but I don't know how to tell a man that I like him." Her eyes gleamed with frustration.

Eliza's first instinct was to offer to tell Brandon herself, but the look on Ihita's face said that would be a very bad idea. "I promise I won't say a word," she said reassuringly, "but I can't promise I won't interfere. I am always so much better with other people's problems than my own."

Ihita blinked. "Agent Books, you mean?" She gave a small huff. "Perhaps if you stopped thinking about Agent Books as a problem . . ." she hazarded, but Eliza was already deep in contemplation.

The two men in front of them were taken care of and then Albert smiled broadly as they stepped up to the counter. "Miss Braun, Miss Pujari, what can I do for you lovely ladies?"

It was his usual greeting, but Eliza still smiled. "Nothing while your missus is looking on, Albert," she responded tartly. Maybe a bit of harmless flirting was what she needed this morning to get the taste of Wellington's betrayal out of her system. Ihita merely blushed.

Maggie waved from the corner where she was making quick work of the bread slicing. "Sure you won't take him off my hands? He snores loud enough to wake the dead."

"'fraid not," she replied, casting an eye over the steaming pile of beef before Albert. "Though I do like the look of his meat."

Wellington would have suffered a conniption hearing her banter in such a common manner with these two—and somehow that knowledge took the edge off her anger. Eliza's companion couldn't help stifling a giggle.

Albert's laugh was deep and genuine. "Then what can I get you?"

"One roast beef, and one ham . . ." She paused and smiled wickedly. "And make sure there is *plenty* of mustard on the last one if you please." Albert's knife moved with consummate skill, slathering butter on the bread, slapping on the meat, and giving it a good lathering of yellow mustard on the ham.

"And you, lovely Miss, the jewel in the crown of the Empire, what can I get you?" Albert leaned on the counter and smiled sweetly at Eliza's companion.

"The usual for Mr. Hill, if you please."

"Oh, I see—buying lunch for that smart co-worker of yours *again*?"

Her smile was bright, seeming even brighter as her skin darkened a bit when she blushed. "I am surrounded by matchmakers!"

While Albert took care of Brandon's ham order, his daughter Ida took the sandwiches and wrapped them separately in brown paper. Eliza waited on her friend, and then together they went out onto the street.

"Not much in the vegetarian line in there," Eliza wiped a line of mustard off from top of the packaging and licked it off the tip of her finger. "I take it you bring your own food to the Ministry."

Ihita shrugged. "Actually, though I do not consume anything that came from a cow, we do eat lamb dishes. Unfortunately, Mr. Southward does not often have it for his sandwiches." She tucked her hand under Eliza's elbow. "If you like, tomorrow I shall bring extra of my *rogan josh*. It's my mother's recipe."

The combination of Albert's sandwiches and talking about Indian delights was making Eliza quite hungry. The bundle in her hand began to smell more and more tempting.

"You know Albert's secret," she said, trying to stave off hunger pangs. "He always has the best beef and ham—mostly because his brother is a well-to-do butcher in the West End. Quality ingredients, even done simply, always make for the best meals. My mum taught me that while working in our pub's kitchen."

"Isn't it the way of the world? The way to a man's heart is through his stomach, and we are lucky to have mothers

that love us and look out for us." Ihita nodded appreciatively.
"I'll make sure I bring home a new recipe when I visit my
mum next month."

Eliza swallowed hard. She'd gotten a letter from back
home last week, but it didn't ease the tight feeling in her
chest. A worry that she might never see them again. It
seemed like an age since she'd felt her mother's arms around
her, and despite outward appearances she needed that now
and again. For some reason Wellington's turncoat attitude
had struck her deeply, and made her yearn for someone
who was on her side. Someone who understood that things
needed to be set right.

"I miss my mother too, Eliza."

She blinked at the comment. Ihita was smiling warmly,
and Eliza considered herself quite fortunate to have a com-
rade in her. "It is a long way back to Delhi and seeing my
home once every two months . . ."

"But that is what makes us different, Ihita. You *can* go
back home."

"All we have to make up for that is the work we do."

Such bitter, melancholy thoughts were occupying her
mind as they turned the corner, reluctantly making their
way back towards the Ministry, and the men who awaited
them. That was why she didn't see the gent whose path in-
tersected with theirs, and why, for an instant, her reflexes
failed her and both sandwiches began to topple to the muddy
earth underfoot.

The man she had collided with stepped deftly off the
pavement, pivoted on one foot, caught the first sandwich,
then, twisting about, ducked down to catch the second on
top of the first only a breath above the muddy road. Eliza felt
the apology on her tongue, and even tried to summon up a
soft smile, but that was before she looked into his eyes. All
words and thoughts failed her.

For the second time in two days, she had run straight into
her past, into the world—or at least a part of it—she thought
was far and away from England.

He looked exactly the same as when she had last seen him—tall, handsome, and dressed impeccably—but with the rakish smile that had always been able to melt her.

Once he had smiled at her. Once those dark eyes had sparkled with love. Once those lips . . .

Eliza D. Braun, who had faced death and disaster time and time again, who always had a witty reply or a pistol at the ready, found herself completely and utterly speechless.

"Good afternoon, Eliza." The gentleman tipped his hat, flashing a brilliant smile. "What a delightful happenstance."

"Douglas?" Eliza finally managed. A heat surged beneath her cheeks. The history between them could not have been more complicated. "A bit far from Lambton Quay, isn't it?"

"Quite." He cleared his throat and held up the sandwiches balanced on his fingertips. "Your lunch?"

Perhaps it was the smell of the sandwiches, the comforting warmth they still had, or feeling her fingertips brushing his; but suddenly Eliza's wits returned—with a vengeance. "A delightful happenstance? Really, Douglas?" She fixed him with a sharp look, and eventually even he succumbed to it.

"I misspoke," he conceded, standing a little taller, "since you are correct. I came here hoping to find you. One of the local suffragists recognised you from your rather daring exploits the other day."

"Daring? Tosh." Eliza stared down at Wellington's slightly crumpled lunch for a moment, and then her eyes flicked up to his. "You know very well my line of work, Douglas."

"And I know you, and how you tend to tempt Fate." His smile darkened slightly before he added, "Thank you, Eliza. It could have been my mother in that grate instead of poor Melinda."

Eliza felt heat rise in her again—but this time not only in her cheeks. Catching her breath, she noted Ihita looked between them, one of her eyebrows crooking. In her confusion, she had almost forgotten her colleague was with her. "Ihita Pujari, may I present Douglas Sheppard."

Douglas tipped his hat to the Indian. "Charmed."

Eliza had never seen Ihita's eyes grow so large. "Douglas *Sheppard*?" she asked. "As in *Crossing the Void: My Adventures Across the Serengeti*? As in *Touching Heaven: On Scaling Mount Everest*?"

"Oh, you've read my journals?" Douglas blushed slightly, earning a silent eye-roll from Eliza. "Thank you so much for taking the time."

"Eliza, you never told me you were friends with the adventurer and explorer Douglas Sheppard!"

Now it was Eliza's turn to blush. "Ihita . . ."

"Just friends?" Douglas smiled ever so slightly. "Well, I shouldn't be surprised. I should have tried harder, I suppose."

Ihita looked back and forth between the two New Zealanders, and then understanding washed over her face. "Oh. Oh, I see. Well then . . ." Her imagination had to be running at a pace rivalling the White Star hypersteam. "I have no doubt the two of you have a lot to catch up on, so I'll be off. Good day."

Then she was gone, clutching Brandon's sandwich with both hands.

Eliza knew there would be *many* questions to answer over luncheon tomorrow. She turned to her new companion. "I am glad to see you, Douglas."

"And that's why you stopped to chat up Mother after saving her life? Find out if I had come along, how I was managing?"

"Douglas—"

"Perhaps the Good Lord gave you a sign the other morning? You are not some villain in our eyes. You've saved Mum's life. Twice now."

"The first time the cost was too high," she stated.

"Are you still carrying that burden? It was Premier Seddon, not Mother, who sent you away. We miss you." He dared to gently lift her chin up to him. "I miss you."

They stood there for a moment, their eyes locked in a

stalemate of wills, until he relented by offering her the crook of his elbow. She took it easily. Despite it being years since she had seen him, some habits and relationships remained etched in the memory. His cologne also had not changed—clean and crisp, it reminded her of the Pacific.

"So tell me," Eliza began, breaking the momentary awkwardness, "what would truly possess Douglas Sheppard, gentleman, adventurer, and New Zealand man-about-town, to go just a bit out of his way—"

"Oh, come now, would passage across two airships, one transcontinental train, and the Manchester express really put me out?"

"Douglas, please don't." She kept her voice light, though being this near to him was reminding her how they had once promenaded around Auckland in such a manner, but with her head resting against his shoulder. "Why are you here? Talking to me?"

"Do you think you really could just give my Mother a quick *kia ora* and then disappear without so much as a word on how you've been?" He cleared his throat. "I came here with her on this tour, more for moral than physical support. She's got that bloody honour guard, the Protectors, courtesy of the local chapter after all. This was the first time she actually had something for me to do." Douglas looked at her, crooking his eyebrow. "She sent me to find you."

"Oh." Eliza hadn't meant the sound to give such an impression of melancholy, but now that it was out there, she went on. "Forgive me if I seem surprised that she did so."

They turned the corner and once again, there was the Thames. The boats of all shapes and sizes disgorging the spoils of the Empire, and ferrying people up and down the river, provided a moment's diversion where former sweethearts did not have to talk to each other. *With the right company,* Eliza thought to herself, *it is almost scenic here.*

"Eliza, you need to stop this. Now. She's mended well enough—some have even suggested she is better than before. The only reason I have not heard her speak your name aloud since the incident was on account of your departure." Douglas adjusted his ascot, a gesture she remembered well. "That brought on more pain than her surgeries, I can attest," he said, a touch of spite in his words.

It was hard not to let that revelation hurt—but then she couldn't blame Kate. The circumstances surrounding the vital petition granting women the right to vote, had been . . . incendiary. No one had felt that more keenly than the redoubtable Mrs. Sheppard.

"Despite the nature of your departure," Douglas began after a time, "you did your country—and my mother—a great service." The statement was said so quietly that she might have missed it.

Now she shoved him away, her outrage quite overwhelming the propriety she was trying to maintain in front of him. "That was most certainly not what you said when it happened!"

"Eliza!" he snapped, and then looked over his shoulder to see if anyone had noticed. "Eliza," he continued in a more moderate tone, "I was nursing my mother back from the brink—by Jove I thought she was dying! I am sorry I did not have enough time or inclination to spend on your feelings. When I had a moment to gather my wits . . ."

"King Dick passed his sentence on me, making certain that I could never return. I had barely enough time to utter the word 'goodbye' to my mother and father, so please, refrain from adding 'guilt' to my burden." She closed her eyes. "And please don't stand on ceremony and commend me for my love of country, because I am no longer welcome there."

"That's not true."

"Douglas," she said, "I am banished, assured imprisonment if I ever set foot back on God's Own." She bit her lip and took a long, deep breath. "I miss it, Douglas. *I miss home.*"

"Stuff Richard Seddon," he swore. "We would have fought for you."

Eliza looked out over the river, trying to calm herself.

The painful emotions of that event were something she thought she'd gotten under control—but apparently it only took Douglas Sheppard's handsome face to undo all that good work. "Kate had done enough fighting for a lifetime. She needed to enjoy that victory."

Douglas laid one of his gloved hands on hers where it rested atop the wall. She wanted to jerk her hand back, but memory and a stirring of old emotion held her in place. His posture was so straight, and he was so quiet that Eliza for a moment didn't quite know what to say. Both of them remained fixed to the spot in a tangle of strange emotions.

"My mother never stopped trusting you," he said, his hand tightening over hers. "The first thing she communicated to us in the hospital was that the whole incident was not your fault. Naturally it was scribbled on a blackboard, since she . . . well, she had inhaled some of the smoke and fire."

The agent closed her eyes for a moment, seeing the destruction, and hearing her friend's call but being unable to answer it.

"And after yesterday's heroics," Douglas removed his hand from hers, and straightened his lapels. "I know she wouldn't mind me finding you like this—asking for your help."

"Then let's be having it," Eliza said in a light tone, as if they were strangers just meeting at a dance, rather than a pair of old lovers on foreign shores with a dark past lying between them. "Tell me why you've gone to such pains to track me down."

"You know I have seen many things between the North and South Islands, and across the Pacific. However, my instincts tell me they pale in comparison to what you have seen." A tiny muscle in Douglas' jaw twitched. "But there is a thread of panic running through the movement that is growing hard to miss."

She involuntarily tightened her grip on the railing. "Has there been any thinning of the ranks at the meetings? Perhaps a few less people attending than usual?"

"I have no doubt Mother has more details than I do, but from what the men have told me, incidents like yesterday are . . ." His voice trailed off. It would seem that Douglas had arrived at the scene of Melinda Carnes shortly after they left. "I'm concerned.

"The London Auxilliary shipped us both over to give the English suffragists a kick in the pants—or skirts—and she's been doing quite the job of it." Eliza caught a glimpse of the smile she recalled so very fondly, but the moment was fleeting as he added, "but in this month alone, what we were told were 'isolated incidents' and 'misguided sisters' are appearing less and less random. I am sure that you will be able to find out more than what the Auxiliary is willing to tell me. You were always good at such confidence gathering." He offered her a card. "Mother has asked you to join us here for morning tea. Say you will attend?"

Taking the card between two fingers, she gave a brief nod. "I will."

"Until then. Good day, Eliza."

Douglas tipped his hat to her, spun on his heel and walked away, quickly swallowed by the crowd on the street. Eliza turned back to the Ministry. Now there remained only one thing left to do—recruiting Wellington Books to her cause.

As soon as she explained to him the ruination of his sandwich.

INTERLUDE

In Which the Frailties and Fears
of Mortal Men Are Considered

Agent Bruce Campbell's bed was very large and very comfortable. Still, Peter Lawson, Duke of Sussex, would not have expected anything else. The man, after all, apparently spent half his life in it, though hardly alone.

Sitting in the dark of the apartment, awaiting the return of the colonial, he kept his hand tucked in his pocket. The pistol he felt there served as a reassurance of his sensibility. He had been pushing the agent hard in the last few months. It would not have been reckless to dare the lion in his den without proper precautions—but dare him he must.

It would have been naïve to believe someone would want to play Judas within an organisation they had served happily. This apprehension had blossomed to a full feeling of suspicion. It was time to teach this boy who was the master.

A growing clamour from the other side of the door alerted Sussex to prepare himself. Laughter. A man and a woman, their giggling an indication they appeared to have taken more than their fair share of liquor. *Even better*, he thought to himself, straightening his back.

The lock proved difficult by the sounds of a key scraping on metal to the accompaniment of more snickers. That a member of Her Majesty's service should behave in such a manner really was beyond the pale. Sussex certainly would have no qualms about putting him in his place.

The door popped open and the tall, broad form of Agent Bruce Campbell staggered in. His face was illuminated by the light out in the corridor, but the apartment was only lit by the moon through the open curtains. Sussex sat very still, not alerting the Australian to his presence immediately. This could play out even better than he had hoped.

The woman who stumbled in after and threw herself into Campbell's arms was very well dressed and quite a beauty. Her blonde hair gleamed in an elaborate style that had already come adrift in some places. She appeared well-bred, though her conduct resembled that of a slattern.

"Oh Bruce," she giggled. "Do you think anyone saw us? I felt so light-headed at the gaming table that I'm not quite sure what I said."

"You were a real lady." Campbell bent and kissed her so passionately that Sussex was sure indeed she was not. "Those folks weren't your usual crowd—so no one knew who you were on any account."

He lifted her off her feet and twirled her about closer to the window—probably to see what he was about to do better. The Duke let them proceed, watching with narrowed eyes and pursed lips. He was not at all surprised with Campbell—but disappointed in the lady.

As they kissed, Bruce's fingers began to pull at her buttons. It was time.

"For propriety's sake, Campbell," and in the darkness of the apartment, Sussex found his voice did indeed sound rather terrifying. "I suggest you stop right there."

The women shrieked and clutched at the Australian while he pushed her behind him and pointed a pistol in his direction. The man might be a bit of a dolt, but Campbell was unquestionably quick and deadly. Ingenious as well, as Sussex noted the gun appeared to be attached to some apparatus either in his coat sleeve or fixed around his forearm. As for himself, the Duke concluded the best course of action was to keep his own weapon concealed.

Sussex inclined his head forward, clicking his tongue lightly as he turned up the lantern burning next to him. "That would make a mess not to mention quite a scandal shooting a member of the Queen's Privy Council in your apartments. People would ask questions I dare say—especially of the lady."

"Bloody hell!" Campbell strode over and lit the gaslight above the fireplace. His frown was thunderous, and his lip was pulled back in a snarl that would not have looked out of place on a Bengal tiger. "What in the blazes are you doing here?"

Sussex smoothed his moustache and rose from the bed. "Waiting for you of course. We need to talk." He tilted his head and looked at the horrified woman.

Campbell's face settled in stern lines. "You better have my man see you home, Nancy. This is business."

The blonde readjusted her clothing as best she could and scuttled for the door. Just as she was about to make her un-dignified exit, Sussex smiled. "Do convey my regards to your husband, Lady Waynethrop. I believe I will be seeing him at the club on Friday."

Her blue eyes widened, and he took some small satis-faction that he had cracked the renowned icy demeanour of Nancy Waynethrop. Next time she chose to ignore him at the dinner table he would take pleasure in reminding her of this moment.

Once the door closed behind his guest, Campbell strode around the room, lighting as many fixtures as he could—as if illumination would somehow banish Sussex. Then he turned to face the Duke. He did not point his revolver at his guest, but neither did he let go of it. "You better have a damn good reason for coming here like this." The venom in his voice was quite impressive.

Sussex smiled at the posturing. It was trite, but quaint.

"Coming here at this hour, yes, I have a very good reason, my crass colonial." He took a step closer, so that there would be no mistaking his own anger. "Unlike the married ladies of the English aristocracy, I am not content with small favours. You have been stringing me along about getting into the so-called Restricted Area at the Ministry."

"Your Grace," Bruce started, retracting the gun back into his sleeve. "I hope you understand that drawing on you is out of habit, not manners."

"You are such the gentleman, particularly while in the company of married companions." Sussex gave a snort as he crossed over to the table of spirits. "Most gallant, your protecting Lady Waynethrop. I hope your courage is double that in the presence of your own wife."

He eyed the crystal bottles of various heights and shapes. Quite the lifestyle these Ministry agents led.

Then he considered Campbell's concealed weapon.

"Any particularly good spirits in these decanters?"

Bruce remained silent, until Sussex looked over his shoulder at him. "The square one." Sussex lifted a single eyebrow. "And the bulbous one with the square stopper."

His hand went to another bulbous decanter with a long neck, a teardrop stopper decorating its mouth. Sussex took a sniff, and nodded. "I would have never guessed you appreciative of a good cognac."

"If I may be so bold, Your Grace," Bruce replied, "you tend to underestimate me in a lot of things."

He paused, his mouth twisting into a grin as he poured himself—and the colonial—a drink. "Oh, I do like it when you bite back." He handed him a glass. "Join me. I hate to drink another man's spirits alone."

Bruce cast a glance at his glass. Sussex waited.

"You don't trust me, Your Grace?" Bruce asked.

Sussex gave a light shrug. "I'm not underestimating you, my dear colonial."

"Cheers then," Bruce said, raising the glass to his unexpected guest. He took a deep draught of the liquor and smiled. "A man can have his beer and his hard whiskey, but cognac is a gentlemen's drink."

"That it is," Sussex said, before setting his glass down. "And best partaken amongst them rather than here. Now then, about the Ministry."

"Your Grace," he implored, "I am doing all I can."

"Are you now? It has been almost six months since we agreed to our accord, and what do I have to show for it? Let me see." Sussex took a measured pause in his thoughts as he crossed from one side of Campbell's apartments to another. "Is Doctor Sound still in charge of the Ministry of Peculiar Occurrences? Why, yes—yes, he is. Has Her Majesty dissolved the Ministry? No. As a matter of fact, she allocated more funds and resources to further along the clandestine organisation." He fixed his eyes on Campbell. "And you tell me you are doing all you can?"

"I still have to keep up the deception, don't I?" Campbell retorted. "It's not like I can keep tabs on Sound and skimp on my duties. I still have assignments to fulfil. If you want me to arouse suspicion, I can do that, sure; but then you lose your man on the inside, don't you?"

"So far, I would be getting as much information if I *didn't* have a man on the inside."

Bruce finished his cognac, and stared for a moment at his empty glass. "I need more than time. I need an opportunity. It's a bit difficult when I'm keeping my own cover intact."

Sussex nodded, serving as a comfort to the colonial. "Sir Francis Bacon once said, 'A wise man will make more opportunities than he finds.' Perhaps you can take something from Britain's more regal history as opposed to your rather colourful own."

Bruce's jaw twitched. "And do you—"

"My dear colonial, I cannot do everything for you, now can I?" Sussex picked up his coat and top hat, slipping into both as he talked. "You put forward a valiant argument, and I would agree that yes, I should have considered that maintaining your own deception would be time consuming.

"I cannot wait for results while you wait for opportunity to present itself. So, Agent Campbell, my advice to you is to show some initiative. Make something happen, lest my attention and patience begin to wane. Which, at its current rate, would give you a month."

Campbell took in a deep breath. "And if I don't make my opportunity by then?"

Sussex chuckled. "Oh, is this where you would have me twirl my moustache and present to you some idle ultimatum? I am a gentleman, and a Lord of the Privy Council. I don't make threats. I simply act in the name of Her Majesty, under my discretion." He slipped on his gloves and picked up the glass of cognac he had earlier set aside. He regarded the silent Campbell for a moment and then handed him his own glass. "Consider your next month within the Ministry walls while you savour this nightcap of yours. Good night, Agent Campbell."

Sussex hardly cared what happened once he closed the door behind him. He could have been called a variety of names, or maybe the glass shattered after being hurled against the door. Sussex heard no impact from the inside, even as he descended the steps to the foyer; and that was promising. Could the colonial have been correct about him? Could Sussex be underestimating his mole in the Ministry of Peculiar Occurrences?

Tosh, he chided himself silently. *Of course not.* The man was as common as muck. Sussex was simply reminding his hound about who was master here, and the mongrel seemed to be responding to his word.

A quick rap to the roof of his carriage, and Lord Sussex was en route to his own home. His eyes watched the amber lights of London pass before him, a sight that—if he were anyone else—would lull him into a calm state. This was, however, not his lot in life. Duties to the Empire and to his own family continued to hum and buzz in his head, none of his concerns taking a priority at that moment. This was nothing new or unusual. The higher Peter Lawson climbed society's ladder, and the closer he grew to the throne, the more danger those duties drew to them. He knew the balance between his family's name and the Empire's future teetered perilously. Both his sons showed promise. Yet what good would that promise be if there were no Empire for them to reap its benefits? What he planned would be the legacy for his children. They would take up the reins, and he would watch with pride as his sons carried the Empire further into the next century. That would be their time, not his, and certainly not the Queen's.

Those close to Queen Victoria were dedicated to her. Sussex, unlike many in the Privy Council, looked beyond the crown. The crown was a bobble, a piece of jewellery, like a queen was merely a physical representation of what mattered: an Empire. That was Sussex's true priority.

For my sons, he pledged to himself as his carriage slowed.

The driver opened the door and Sussex entered the warmth of his London home.

"Fenning," Sussex said as he held his arms outward. The coat slipped free of him as he continued, "any callers whilst I was out?"

"No, sir," his butler replied.

"Is the Duchess still awake?"

"No, she retired half an hour ago, sir."

Thank God. He would be getting to sleep early tonight. "Very good, Fenning."

"Master John has been excelling in his fencing. He has been selected to represent his class on their team."

"Excellent news. We must make arrangements for practice time. Perhaps in the dining room. We are not entertaining anytime soon, are we?"

"The Lady did mention the Cartwrights would be visiting next week."

"Oh dear, Algernon and Amelia. I can already hear the scintillating conversation. Reschedule."

"Shall I inform the Duchess?"

Sussex looked over his shoulder, a dark eyebrow crooked

as he stared at his attendant. "Did I say I wanted the Duchess informed? I believe I was clear on my wishes."

The butler nodded. "Very good, sir. Brandy?"

"I will have it in my study."

As he proceeded down the hallway a grandfather clock continued to count away the seconds. Its soft *tick-tock-tick-tock* as well as the time reading a few minutes shy of ten o'clock reminded him of how little time remained of his day. He had the odd matter or two for the Queen still needing his attention. Of late his preoccupation with the Ministry of Peculiar Occurrences threatened to become a distraction. It had even started to take his eye away from goings on in Court. This would not abide. He needed to have that matter taken care of, and hopefully his evening's visit with the colonial would provide ample motivation and inspiration to do that.

He reached his sanctuary—his study. As he turned on the lamp at the corner of his large desk, the shadows retreated, exposing in their wake a solitary parchment, sealed with a blank wax imprint. Sussex's brow furrowed as he picked up the letter, turning the missive in his hands. He reached across his desk and yanked at the bellpull. As he waited, his eyes swept the room. Nothing seemed out of place or disturbed. Placing the letter back on the desk, he checked the drawers. They all remained locked.

"Your brandy, sir," the butler announced as he entered Sussex's office.

"Fenning, I thought you said I had no callers?"

The servant held the silver tray under his arm as he set the snifter by Sussex. "That is correct, sir."

"Then what the hell is this?" he snapped, waving the parchment in his hand.

Fenning looked at the note and then, with no change at all in his expression, stated plainly, "Forgive me, sir, but I do not recall that note being delivered by myself, or being informed of any missive delivered to your office by the staff."

"Really. You're certain?"

"Most assuredly, sir."

The man had been in service to him and his family for well over forty years. He would hate to have to start doubting him, but the butler's resolve did not waver in his eyes or demeanour.

"Very well then. That will be all."

Fenning gave a slight bow, and bid, "Good night, Your Grace."

He watched the butler silently retire for the night. For anything in his London dwellings—or any of his country estates, for that matter—to be out of place would be extraordinary. Fenning would not allow it. If the butler did not recall delivering the letter or was not informed of its delivery, that was the truth of it.

Sussex broke the seal and unfurled the paper. He lifted the snifter to his lips . . .

Peter . . .

The glass tumbled out of his grasp, shattering softly against the fine rug underfoot.

Peter,
I am gravely disappointed in you.

My God, his mind screamed. *He got in here. Into my home. With my boys. My wife.*

No one had seen him. He entered his home—the home of a Duke and member of the Queen's Privy Council—*and no one saw him*? How was that possible?

With his heartbeat thudding dully in his ears, Sussex returned to the letter now trembling in his grasp.

Peter,
I am gravely disappointed in you. We were to
have made progress by now, but in light of recent
events I see I am asking far too much of you.
Need I remind you of how important your control
of The Ministry of Peculiar Occurrences is in
what we are working to achieve?

Sussex wiped the sweat away from the back of his neck. Through the pounding in his head, he could also hear the clock ticking away.

Tick.

Tock.

Tick.

Tock.

The seconds now seemed fleeting. Each passing moment one closer to his own death. His displeasure carried consequences.

We must talk. Either a new strategy is agreed upon, or our relationship must terminate. Permanently.

The clock suddenly sounded much louder in his ears.

My associates will collect you Monday at ten o'clock in the evening. You will not keep them waiting. I look forward to our talk. I do hope you can prove me wrong, Peter.

Sussex stumbled to his office chair, the parchment now crumpling against his chest. His eyes returned to the brandy staining the carpet, the shards of his snifter shimmering in the gaslight. He remembered that he had relieved Fenning for the night. Still, he could call on the man. It was his right, after all, yet Sussex could not move to the bellpull. He could not even will himself to get up from his chair and pour himself a drink.

He had been in here. No one saw him. There truly was nowhere Sussex would be safe. Nowhere.

With one hand still pressing the letter into his chest, Sussex covered his face with his other hand. His body shook as his sobs grew louder and louder in his private office. Thankfully, there was no one there to hear them.

CHAPTER FIVE

In Which a Mess Is Made and
Miss Braun Has Nothing To Do with It

"Once more unto the breach," Wellington grumbled in the stillness of the carriage.

Eliza looked up from the address Douglas has given her. "Sorry, Welly, what was that?"

"Shakespeare. I always recite it just before placing my career in harm's way, or have you not noticed that when we began casually stepping out of Ministry protocol?"

"And here I thought you were whispering sweet nothings in my ear when you were spontaneously breaking out into passages from *Romeo and Juliet* yesterday."

"You failed to notice I was reciting the scene at Juliet's tomb." Wellington snipped, but she got the impression that it was rather wrung from him.

"And yet here you are, following me onward, crying, 'God for Queen Victoria, England, and Saint George,' yes?" She was pleased with herself on that one. "Go on. When you found the case file in your basket—"

"That hardly nullifies my real concern on your vendetta against Agent Campbell."

Whatever his concerns were, they remained unvoiced as

they came within view of the elegant white stone building and saw another carriage just pulling up. When the woman alighted from it, Eliza smiled again. She almost didn't notice the tall young woman who hopped down after the elder woman descended.

The first lady, Kate Sheppard, was wearing a long mauve tea dress underneath a thick fur muff. She was more than fifty but still beautiful and elegant. Her silvered hair was piled atop her head underneath a stylish matching hat. She could have just stepped out of a fashion plate—were it not for the curved brass that covered the left portion of her face.

"One obstacle at a time, Welly." She found herself whispering the words of the young King Hal at the gates of Harfleur. *Stiffen the sinews, summon up the blood . . .* and yet she couldn't. Eliza was overwhelmed with a strange shyness, but that was soon washed away as Kate spotted her.

"Oh my dear Eliza!" she exclaimed, and darted the few feet up the street to embrace the agent. "Oh *kia ora*!" The green light where her eye would have been flared as her smile widened, and she embraced her heartily.

For a second Eliza enjoyed the moment, even though she was aware of the Protector and Wellington shifting in embarrassment beside them. Even among acquaintances such behaviour on the street was a little common.

When she pulled back, Eliza felt herself actually blushing. She shot her hand out and yanked Wellington closer. "Kate Sheppard, I would like you to meet—"

Eliza floundered for a moment as she considered what exactly he was to her. She wasn't about to call him her superior, but her position was so nebulous at the Ministry maybe that was exactly what it was.

"Her colleague." Wellington extended his hand to take Kate's.

Eliza never knew if Wellington intended to turn that handshake into a "gallant" kiss on the fingers (nonsense that Kate would outwardly refute) as the Protector suddenly slipped in between them, one of her hands catching his wrist while the other pushed him back a step.

Ye gods, but that woman was fast!

Kate's own form broke the Protector's hold on Wellington. "For pity's sake, Betsy, do you really believe every man in the Empire is out to kill me?" The Protector shot Kate a hard look, but glanced at Wellington and then at her charge once more. As she stepped back, Kate restored her demeanour to a cheery one as she motioned to the Protector. "This is Betsy Shaw, my own personal virago to keep me from harm."

The tall woman smiled, but didn't say anything. Betsy looked strong but perhaps a little shy of the famous lady she was given the charge of. Eliza knew exactly how that felt.

"Quite," Wellington returned, tipping his bowler to her. "I could say Eliza serves a similar office when it comes to my well-being."

The suffragist's good blue eye narrowed but the bright smile remained. "Such a bold man to consort with lionesses!"

"Boldness? Hardly, Miss Sheppard," Wellington said, turning back to Eliza. "I think it's more of your fellow countrywoman's influence."

"Not surprising," Kate replied.

Eliza had met many committed people in her life—mad scientists, leaders with the glint of power in their eye, and some who were actually committed in Bedlam—but none had ever come close to the steely backbone of this suffragist. She left them all in the dust. If there was one other woman in the whole world, besides her own mother, who Eliza D. Braun admired, it was Kate Sheppard.

Now the suffragist was looking at her for support and help. The last time that had happened, it had ended well for the movement, but badly for Kate.

The older woman took Eliza's arm. "Please give us a moment." She directed her request so sweetly at Wellington and Betsy that neither of them could really complain.

Besides, both had just seen what could happen when Kate Sheppard was cross.

She led Eliza down the causeway a little bit, glanced over her shoulder, and began to speak in a low tone. "So, Douglas found you."

"Kate," Eliza began, her heart pounding in her ears, "I—"

"—am sure you have a great deal to tell me, but considering the circumstances, let's clear the air quickly." The smile widened, and her hand rested gently on Eliza's cheek. "I am very glad to see you again. I have missed you."

The words—everything she wanted to say, everything she implored from her since leaving, every burden she wished to unload—lodged in her throat. In Kate's gentle gesture, it was Aotearoa reaching out to her. She felt *aroha*. She felt home.

The emerald glow in Kate's clockwork eye diminished, and she removed her hand from Eliza's cheek (good thing too, for Eliza could not have held back her tears if it had lingered there). "I wish seeing you were under better circumstances though. We in the movement are in danger every moment. The other day at Speakers' Corner . . ." Kate paused to catch her breath.

Eliza clasped her hands, feeling them warm, even inside the gloves. "This is nothing new, Kate. I uncovered some files at work. There are other disappearances that no one else seems very interested in pursuing."

The women shared a glance. Kate knew of the Ministry—had been exposed to it in rather a spectacular manner back in New Zealand. "A real shame," she murmured under her breath, "but to be expected, I suppose, especially being of Her Majesty's government."

Eliza glanced back to Wellington, who appeared to be trying—unsuccessfully—to strike up a conversation with Betsy.

"Not everyone in the Ministry is all bad," she muttered.

Kate didn't seem to hear her. "I only arrived a few weeks

ago," the elder suffragist went on, "and I can tell you, though the ladies are trying to put on a show of being brave, they are beginning to crack. All of the missing women are very influential in the movement. As these abductions are growing more frequent, it won't last out the year if this continues."

Eliza didn't comment on what she was thinking, because she knew that Kate would be thinking the very same thing: many people in high places would delight in that outcome. It made the list of suspects rather long—including Queen Victoria herself, knowing her attitude towards the suffrage movement. This could serve as a mundane explanation behind the Ministry allowing cases to slide down into the Archives.

Eliza pressed her lips together before asking, "Do you know if there is any other connection between these women?"

Kate's brow furrowed. "I don't, but the woman who lives here might." She pointed to the graceful abode Wellington and Betsy were lingering on the doorstep of. "Her name is Hester Langston."

"The chief secretary for the London movement?"

"Indeed," and Kate's smile went wry. "She is also known as its chief gossipmonger."

The two women shared a secret smile and a quiet giggle.

Kate's tone was somewhat bittersweet. "She is one of those 'sisters' who want to believe themselves progressive but are still a touch set in their ways. After all, an upstart little branch of the Empire getting ahead of the mother country?" She motioned to herself, raising her one remaining eyebrow. "Some of the ladies here are tainted by a bit of jealousy. I'll help where I can, but I am not entirely welcome here. I am a show-pony for success."

She slipped her hand into Eliza's arm as they started walking back to the estate. "Now just remember to look behind you often, Eliza. And keep your pistols handy."

On reaching their companions, it was Wellington who

took Eliza by the arm and removed her from Kate's side. "Eliza, if you please?" he asked, motioning to the back of their carriage.

The crate strapped there immediately conjured for Eliza their adventurous night at the opera; but while the *auralscope* had been slightly cumbersome, this case was an eight-hundred-pound gorilla that had stolen a ride on the back of their cab. It took both of them to heft it off the carriage and carry it up to the open door where, thankfully, a maid waited for them.

Kate eyed the massive case with curiosity and then looked up at Eliza.

"The ways of men," Eliza said, motioning to Wellington. "For some, it is an enigma. With Welly here, it is a mystery for the ages."

It did not go unobserved that Betsy remained in the hallway. Guarding the entrance would have been an excellent tactic, if they had not observed yesterday what they had. The room they entered was a cacophony of styles, colours, and knickknacks. Eliza favoured a certain style of interior décor: oil paintings, mixed in with eclectic items she collected on her travels for the Ministry. She did not like chintz, doilies, or anything that took long to dust. Alice was relieved about less housework but was always trying to get her employer to conform to more current trends. Eliza had lost track of the number of times she'd had to throw some atrocious majolica monkey jug or parrot hat stand out of her rooms.

Alice would have loved Miss Hester Langston's apartments in Hampstead. She would have cooed over every surface covered with lace, pictures and curios. The riot of purple vines embossed into the wallpaper would have sent her into paroxysms of delight.

Eliza, however, felt a little ill.

Still, both agents of the Ministry and Kate perched among it all; Books with great aplomb while Eliza was terrified to move lest she topple something expensive. The only thing of interest to her was a series of long, clear pipes screwed to

the far wall. It was rare for a private house to be connected
to the pneumatic tube exchange, but did indicate that Kate's
description of Hester as the centre of information and gossip
might well be true.

"Mrs. Sheppard." A low, sweet voice made them look up.

The two women who entered the room were completely
different from one another. One was older and had flyaway
blonde hair accompanied by a long Roman nose, while
the other was, like Ihita, a lady of Indian persuasion—or
at least her mother had been. She had a paler complexion
than Eliza's agent friend, and so could "pass" as society.
Only her first name, and occasionally her dress, gave her
away. Eliza knew her by sight at least. Chandi Culpepper
was a well-known and ardent supporter of the movement.
Today she was wearing a sash of deep umber over her very
English walking dress, and a pair of elaborate drop earrings
that looked to be made out of gold. Though she was only at
the most twenty, she and Miss Langston had become great
friends over the right for womens' vote and a shared love of
romance novels, or so the New Zealander had heard.

It was Chandi who had spoken. "And we have guests, it
would seem?"

"Yes, Miss Culpepper." Kate motioned to Wellington.
"This is Wellington Books, a gentleman sympathetic to our
cause."

Wellington smiled awkwardly. "Indeed, miss."

Eliza felt her skin flush slightly as Chandi offered her
hand to Wellington. The smile she gave him was quite brilliant. "How fortunate."

He fumbled a bit before taking it. "Ah, yes, Miss Culpepper. I, uh—I hope I can—" he stammered, and then blushed.
"Quite."

When she turned to Eliza, that brilliant smile beamed
only brighter. "And our guardian angel from Speakers'
Corner. This is a pleasure."

"This is Eliza Braun," Kate said, "and if it weren't for
her, the sisterhood of New Zealand would not have the vote."

Eliza's cheeks burned. "I think Kate downplays her own efforts."

"If your actions the other day are the indication of your character, Miss Braun," Chandi replied, taking her hand in greeting, "I have no doubt you are an ally to keep close." She glanced to Wellington and then winked at Eliza. "At the very least, for the company you keep."

Both ladies turned to Wellington, and now Chandi's smile was more mischievous than cordial.

"What?" Wellington asked, shifting a little on his feet.

Both women gave a slight start when Hester's voice, her manner reflecting the no-nonsense tenor in her words, interrupted. "I believe, Kate, you came here for matters more pressing than introductions, yes? Your message was most mysterious." She turned and rang the bellpull. "Alva will bring us some tea and I hope you can explain."

Kate pulled off her gloves slowly. "I have. Mr. Books and Miss Braun might be able to help us sort out the events that have been plaguing your work here."

The new arrivals all sat, while Chandi examined Eliza and Wellington. It was not a piercing gaze, but it was most curious. "Apart from additional protection, I fail to see how they can help?"

"You must forgive Miss Culpepper," Hester began, motioning to Chandi without looking at her. "She has only emerged into society of late, and sometimes her isolated upbringing lends itself to cynical assessments."

"Hester," the Indian said, chuckling pleasantly, "not cynical. Cautious. Something we all have to be, considering recent events."

A soft murmur of agreement rose from the collected suffragists. Kate glanced at Eliza, giving her a slight nod. The cracks were, indeed, starting to show.

"I've observed you at some of the meetings, dear," Hester said, looking at Eliza with a hesitant smile.

The agent knew a mention of the government would not be comforting to these women; bureaucracy had failed them at every turn. Instead she offered another, equally true explanation. "We're investigators, and yes indeed, we both believe strongly in the cause."

Alva brought in the tea tray, set it before her mistress on a table, and disappeared in a most efficient manner. Alice could never quite manage such silence. Hester leaned forward to pour, but her hands were shaking too much.

"It is all right, Hester, let me." Chandi took the teapot and began to make sure everyone had a cup. It was a full-bodied black tea that Eliza took with relish.

Kate took hers with her usual grace. "Given this week of terrible events, everyone is on edge; but you can perhaps help set things right."

Hester Langston did indeed look a little on edge herself—at least on the precipice of her lavender settee. She had the neck of a swan, and such a delicate manner about her, that Eliza would never have imagined that she had a spine of steel.

And yet she must. On receiving the card from Douglas, Eliza had done some light legwork on Miss Langston. Merely the highlights: a member of the suffrage movement since she was only fifteen, left a large inheritance by her mother, and fighting the good fight with as much determination. Eliza recognised her name from the papers, as well. For the suffrage movement, Hester had suffered police intimidation, including three stretches in prison where she had been force-fed. This woman had been called many things by London journalists, but "shrinking violet" had not been one of them.

Yet now she sat in her overwhelming blue parlour and looked terrified. She held out her hand, and Chandi took it and held it firmly. "Even with the Protectors around, I still don't feel safe, but you trust these people, Kate?"

"Yes, indeed," Kate assured her, smiling warmly, "with my life."

Hester nodded. "I will do whatever I can to assist."

Wellington set down his cup on the thick doily that covered the mahogany table and smiled. "As Shakespeare attested, there are more things on heaven and earth than are dreamt of. In these days of modern marvels that is even more so."

"It's hardly a marvel what is happening." Chandi pressed her lips together, but her voice remained calm. "All those fine women disappearing and no one held accountable."

"My apologies," Wellington replied after a moment. "This is why Kate called upon us and asked us to lend a hand." He glanced at Eliza and added, "Discreetly, of course."

A threat of tears lingered in Hester's eyes, compelling Eliza to press her hand on top of the older woman's knee. She couldn't have borne to see this doyen of the movement weeping. "We're going to get to the bottom of this. You have my word on it. We just need the lists of the people at the meeting before Lena Munroe disappeared—it will give us the starting point."

"And why should we be giving those to you?" The question snapped at them like the crack of a coachman's whip. "You're not a member!"

Wellington's eyes shot up at the vision of womanly ire standing abruptly there in the doorway, but Eliza was totally unsurprised. When she had heard that the Protectors were now guarding the top members of the movement, she had expected this confrontation. The newcomer acknowledged Kate with a little bob of her head, but nothing more.

Eliza heard Wellington flipping through his journal, stopping as he searched, and then he looked up from its pages. "Charlotte Lawrence, the captain of the Protectors, I take it?"

She crooked an eyebrow, her cheeks flaring crimson. "And who might you be?" she asked, her voice surprisingly even.

"Wellington Books, I am with—" And the words stuck in his throat before he continued. "Miss Braun and I represent a concerned party."

"A concerned party?" Charlotte asked, nodding. Her lips

pursed for a moment and then she said, "In the past year we have lost six of our sisters under mysterious circumstances, and *now* you turn up. Your concern is most touching."

Wellington cleared his throat, and then motioned to Eliza. "This is my associa—"

"Good morning, Chaz."

Charlotte Lawrence did not greet her at all but her glare only sharpened on Eliza.

Kate got to her feet smoothly. "I didn't know you knew Eliza, Charlotte."

"A friend of yours?" Wellington asked Eliza. "Or perhaps a lost relation?"

In an instant both of them were looking at him with daggers in their gaze, and he squirmed.

Yet Eliza could grudgingly see why he might get that impression. Since Chaz had been training the Protectors she had instituted similar costuming to the Ministry's standard issue for female agents. Stab-resistant corsets were, despite being a little behind the fashion, still a sensible precaution. The Protectors, dressed in these and simple black men's pants, conveyed the proper measure of menace to men who might otherwise wish the movement harm. Instead of the plethora of pistols and guns that Eliza favoured, the Protectors carried thick fighting sticks that in a pinch could be screwed together to resemble a walking stick. (Handy when police were on the lookout for "those trouble-making suffragists.") Also often carried in their bags were "Indian clubs," smaller versions of skittles. Chaz's own weapons were tucked into bandoliers on her back, poking out from behind each of the women's shoulders like the remains of broken wings. Yet she was not a fey creature. Chaz's strong jawline and muscled body were the virtual antithesis of Hester's fragile strength.

"Mr. Books, do try to keep a civil tongue," Eliza said, tilting her head and smiling disarmingly at this bruiser. "Miss Lawrence, you will find, is most proficient in Bartitsu. In fact a foremost member of the Bartitsu Club in Soho—"

"Oh," Wellington said, nodding appreciatively. It had

been the Ministry of Peculiar Occurrences that brought Barton-Wright back from Japan early to teach his new form of combat to their employees. "Quite the honour."

"—until Mr. Barton-Wright had her barred," Eliza added.

Charlotte barked a dry laugh. "Not my fault old Barty bruises so easily."

Eliza gave Wellington's knee a gentle pat. "I would not recommend taking the last biscuit off the plate until you have checked if Chaz wants it."

"Charmed I am sure," Wellington croaked out, getting to his feet hastily.

It was quite the wrong gesture for this particular woman. "Don't rise on my account," she said, smoothly sliding into the room—all the time keeping an eye on both the window and the door.

While poor Welly hovered between the gentlemanly thing to do and the risk of getting punched—Eliza sipped on her tea. "Left quite a gap there, Chaz. We've been in this room for some time now and you only turn up now?"

The Protector's lips curved. "Actually I have been here the whole time," she pointed to the rear of the parlour, and the agent nodded. A concealed room then.

"See, Wellington." Eliza turned to her partner. "Don't you feel safer already?"

He cleared his throat and then took his seat again—but did not look nearly as comfortable as he had only moments before. "Indeed."

Kate spoke, her voice cutting through the conversation like an elegant knife, "Come now, ladies—we are both on the same side. Charlotte, you surely can't suspect Eliza of involvement in this dreadful business?"

"I was thinking more about your face, Mrs. Sheppard," the Protector replied, "and how it ended up that way."

Eliza swallowed hard. "For your sake, Chaz, I hope that glass house you live in is reinforced."

"Well now, Lizzie, is it the concern or the guilt that suddenly brings you here? Now?"

"It most certainly isn't your competence on the job, now is it?"

Charlotte turned to face her. "Would you care to test that competence now?"

Eliza stood, allowing her shawl to drop free of her shoulders and slip into Wellington's lap. "I promise to make this quick."

"You're both being perfectly ridiculous." Kate's glass eye swiveled between the two of them. "We can't afford to fight amongst ourselves like this."

"Indeed, ladies," Chandi added. "Shall we focus on the matter at hand? Our missing sisters?"

Kate and Chandi were right. If this kept up, Miss Lawrence's delightful parlour would be the next victim of what threatened the Auxilliary. Eliza had already sized up the poker by the fire as a go-to weapon. So Eliza turned back to Hester, her smile soft and sincere. "If we could, please, secure lists of past attendees over the previous year, we can return to our business."

"Naturally," the secretary replied, and then hesitated, pulling at the cuff of her blouse. "Those are quite a few ledgers we've collected over the past year . . ."

"I'll help you, Hester," Chandi murmered.

The secretary left the room, shooting a concerned look over her shoulder. Perhaps she had caught Eliza's eye on the poker, and was now in mortal fear for her décor.

All six of them trailed out into the hall, where Betsy and another Protector were standing guard. Their expressions were serious, but not nearly as unwelcoming as Chaz's.

Kate smiled at her young guardian. "Betsy, would you be a dear and help Miss Langston and Miss Culpepper upstairs with some ledgers?"

"I'll stay here and keep an eye on these two." Chaz's hands flexed on saying that. Eliza pressed her lips together, tempted to grab those fighting sticks herself.

Wellington, no doubt looking for a method of escaping this rather awkward situation, stepped forward. "If I can be of any assistance, Miss Langston, I am a trained archivist and I have brought my portable vellum scanner." He gestured over to the valise he and Eliza had struggled to carry from carriage to foyer.

" 'Portable' is truly a term of endearment with you, isn't it, Welly?" Eliza asked.

"We carried it this far," he retorted.

"You're staying right here." Charlotte actually waggled her finger at the agent. Eliza now recalled that Miss Lawrence had once been a schoolmarm.

Although Wellington Books was technically Eliza's superior and had been tasked with teaching her alternatives to gunpowder as the answer to any problem (which still she had some problems with), it appeared he had also been learning from her. Wellington held his gaze with Charlotte for a time that felt slightly inappropriate, and then glanced at his colleague with quite a furious look. Eliza was suddenly sure if she said the word, or indeed gave so much as a gesture, Agent Wellington Thornhill Books would have barged past Lawrence, or at least given quite the try.

For a second she contemplated it. It might have been very interesting to see how he would fair with Charlotte Lawrence.

Instead, while Kate chitchatted with the grim-faced Protector, Eliza took Wellington's arm and led him over to where Hester had displayed the most insipid watercolour she had ever seen. "We're just here for the names," she whispered to him. "And though I might appreciate your gallant gesture, I can assure you these other ladies would not." She shot him a wicked smile that he returned in kind.

"Quite," he said adjusting his ascot. "Forgive me. A rush of blood to the head."

Eliza felt a saucy reply itching the tip of her tongue; but instead, the two agents waited in silence, the magnificent grandfather clock ticking in the hallway, and Kate kept an eye on the red-faced Protector. Upstairs, they could hear Hester, Chandi, and Betsy moving around. These ledgers indeed sounded heavy, and they were asking for close on a year's worth of meetings and minutes. Three women, with so many records? They were most likely having trouble.

"This is ridiculous, Chaz," Eliza blurted out, and started towards the stairs.

The Protector grabbed her arm, and the agent froze. Eliza noted the wider Chaz smiled, the tighter her grip became. "Give me a reason, Lizzie. Please."

Eliza inclined her head to one side, her eyebrows lifting slightly. "Forget your last sparring lesson with me at the club?"

"Ladies," Kate stepped between them. "Once more I implore you, try and remember who our true enemy is!"

Charlotte held her gaze for a moment, but eventually flicked away Eliza's forearm with a grunt. It was somewhat similar to the sound she'd made when the agent had thrown her to the ground at Barton-Wright's. It had been a most satisfactory defeat, and one that Eliza still savoured. She judged that Hester's hallway was quite large enough to bear a repeat, though some of the paintings might be put askew, and a couple of the rather ghastly majolica items could end up smashed.

From Eliza's point of view that might improve the ambiance.

Then, still from that place on the stairs, an odd scent filled her nostrils. When she looked at Charlotte, the Protector too was scrunching her nose at the sharp smell permeating the air. Screams erupted from upstairs. Eliza had heard her fair share of screams: outraged ones when she shot someone, unexpected ones when an explosion went off a little too close, and ones from Wellington pretty much whenever she did anything sudden. These screams spoke of shock and genuine terror.

Eliza spun on Kate as Chaz pushed past her. "Please, Kate. Stay here."

"Hester! Betsy! Chandi!" Charlotte bellowed as she thundered up the stairs and sprinted for the door. She grabbed the handle before Eliza could warn her, and now Charlotte's scream echoed in the corridor. The strange odour—the same sharp, almost choking tang to the air that had assailed them immediately after Lena disappeared—was now joined by the smell of burnt flesh.

"Miss Lawrence!" Wellington caught Charlotte as she fell back into his arms, cradled one hand with another, sobbing. "Let me help you. I am trained in—"

"Don't you dare!" The Protector howled, spinning away from him. The tears in her eyes were not something she would allow a man to see. "Get in there, you dolt!"

Eliza was staring at the door to Hester's library, now warped in its frame as if it had been punched from inside.

The agent didn't care about the Protector's pride; she was already laying shoulder to the door. The wood protested, and something snapped. It was solid oak, yet it actually buckled under a bare shoulder strike? She wished she had the *plures ornamentum* with her, but all she had was the archivist. "Welly," she asked, motioning to the door, "I could use a spot of help here, there's a good fellow."

"What does this to oak?" he gasped, looking at the dilapidated door.

"Lend me a shoulder and let's find out," she said.

Together they slammed their weight against the wood. A loud snap echoed in the hallway, and then both agents tumbled into the library. Despite the warped condition of the door, there was no fire or explosion in the library. However, it was very, very dry. Eliza had been many times in the desert, and the experience inside a British house on a rather cold, wet day was decidedly odd.

Poor Betsy was on the floor, while Chandi was against the back wall sobbing. Wellington scrambled over to the downed Protector, but immediately recoiled, waving his hands about him in a wild, spastic manner. "Damnation!"

"What?" Eliza asked.

"Her body," he said, splaying his fingers and then balling his hands into fists. "It's charged. Static electricity!"

He looked around the room, and quickly grabbed a small coat tree. He then hefted it and placed it by the fallen Betsy. Still grasping the metal tree, Wellington then gently touched her body. With a small sigh, he bent closer to her.

"She's alive," he gasped, "but look at her."

He turned her head gently, and Eliza felt her breath sucked right out of her. Betsy could be not much over twenty, but her face looked as dry as a sun-baked rock. It would be quite the shock for a young woman to wake and find herself so badly damaged.

Jumping to her feet, Eliza ran to Chandi. The woman was sobbing, clutching at the library shelving. Her immaculate hair was out of place, but she was not as damaged as Betsy.

"Are you all right?" Eliza asked, cautiously taking the younger woman's hand.

Chandi shook her head, her eyes wide and her mouth working around words that would not form. Seeing there was nothing to be immediately got out of the woman, Eliza looked around the room. Papers were lying scattered about the library, and several chairs were turned over—but there was no sign of Hester.

While Wellington continued to try and rouse Betsy, Eliza darted to the window and yanked at it. The sash was down and locked, and when she peered out through the glass, she saw immediately that there was no chance that an assailant had leapt from the window with the secretary over one shoulder. It was a straight drop three stories, and no sign of any drainpipe anywhere near it. She might have considered ornithopters or a mechanised climbing rig, but it had only been a moment since they'd heard the screams, and the window was locked from the inside.

Chandi slid to the floor, wrapping her arms around her head. The sound of her sobs echoed in the crackling atmosphere of the library. Eliza would have gone to comfort her, but her colleague gestured her over to his side.

"She's coming to," Wellington said, gallantly holding the

poor Protector in his arm. Eliza slipped on the opposite side of Betsy and both lifted her to recline into the couch. Eliza, having experienced a milder version of this effect, winced in sympathy. She would have to get a large jar of the ointment from the Ministry for the poor creature . . .

Charlotte kicked the door away from her, causing Betsy's eyes to crack open, and by cracked that was very nearly the case. Betsy's eyes were startlingly blue in her reddened face.

"What did you see?" Charlotte barked, all the while cradling her own hands. "What happened to Hester, for God's sake?"

Besty's mouth worked a few times until she could manage to croak out anything like words. "I saw light. Blue it was. I heard Miss Hester cry out . . . and then . . . then she was just gone." The woman's fingers rose to her face and fluttered there as if she were too afraid to touch herself.

Eliza stayed her fingers. "Best if you don't, pet. Believe me, it will heal, but better if you don't look."

Chandi, who had recovered herself, crawled over to the sofa. "Oh my God," she whispered on seeing Betsy's ravaged face, her own trembling fingers coming up to her own face. "Is that how I—"

Wellington touched the side of her face, and gently tipped it. "No, Miss Culpepper. It seems whatever radius this event has, you were luckily outside of it."

"I . . . I was going to get the last of the year's ledgers off the top shelf." She sniffled.

"You were very lucky." Eliza muttered, her eyes still somehow searching for Hester in the library.

Wellington too was conducting his own examination of the scene. "It appears that whatever happened was as sudden as what we observed on the train earlier." He peered at the carpet, running his hands over the surface. "There is a distinct burning here, but not as if a fire were lit." He glanced up, "Almost as if it were seared off with red-hot scissors."

While Eliza clasped Betsy's hands to prevent them from

touching her face, she thought of all the things she'd seen and experienced in the Ministry. "Have you heard of such a thing, Wellington?" He was the Archivist, and if anyone had a chance of recognising what this was, it was he.

Yet when his colleague looked at her, she felt her heart sink. "I shall have to look in among the case files, run some searches with the analytical engine. This is all very new to me."

They now heard Kate's footsteps on the door outside, followed by the maid who gave a little shriek at the destruction of Mrs. Langston's study.

"Alva," Charlotte said to the maid, not even bothering to look at her. "Get Betsy out of here." Charlotte then looked at her seared hand, and stared at Eliza. "Leave," she hissed. "Leave now."

Wellington leapt to his feet, to protest, but Eliza waved him away. Charlotte was in pain. She'd just had her charge taken, and one of her own badly injured. Eliza had been in similar situations before—she knew they stung. Chaz needed someone to blame.

Apparently, Chaz had found it. "I'll bloody well tell the Council how useless you are."

"Enough!" Chandi pushed her hair out of her eyes, and got to her feet. "It's not your fault, Miss Braun. This was an ambush, and you would not have been able to stop it." Her trembling hands came up to her mouth as she whispered, "No one can stop this."

Wellington crossed over to her. "Did you see anything different from Betsy, Miss Culpepper?"

She passed a hand over her eyes. "Not really. Like she said, a light came . . . it was terrifying and extraordinary." Chandi gave an odd laugh and said, "I think I need another cup of tea."

"Of course," Eliza said, shooting Wellington a pointed look. Just by where he and Chandi stood were ledgers. "Let me help you back to the parlour."

With Kate flanking Chandi, they returned downstairs,

Wellington trailing a few steps behind. Only Charlotte remained. She just silently took in the scene of this latest abduction.

"She's not outside," Mrs. Sheppard jerked her head slightly to the wrought-iron gate outside. It would have been even more unbearable to find Hester impaled on her own fence. The women went into the parlour and took a seat while Eliza fussed over the tea set.

Wellington had remained in the hallway, a good choice on his part. Women's business.

The tea was probably colder than preferred but there was comfort to be found in that room. Eliza glanced up at the ceiling, wondering what Charlotte was expecting to accomplish up there alone.

Once Chandi had a cup of tea cradled in her hands, and Kate's arm around her, Eliza felt safe to slip away. She exchanged a look with her mentor, who merely nodded a quiet understanding. The agent would do what she did, and Kate would hold the group together as best she could. Eliza returned to the corridor where the Archivist was waiting, a ledger—or what appeared to be half of one—in his hands.

"Should we not have questioned the ladies more thoroughly?" he asked in a hushed whisper.

"Welly, we're already seen the event for ourselves. *Twice.* Whatever happened here is obviously the same thing. We gain nothing by tormenting women who have survived quite a shock."

Her colleague was staring at her in some disbelief. "Is that something like diplomacy from you, Eliza?"

The smile his comment engendered was bright and brief. "Maybe I am learning something from you after all, Welly."

They both cautiously returned upstairs. Chaz had taken leave to another room, and she sounded as if she were on some telephony device. Her voice could be heard behind the shut door, and Eliza knew the tone enough not to intrude. It also meant a pocket of time unobserved in the devastated library.

Eliza glanced at the half book in Wellington's grasp. "I am guessing that Hester took some of the ledgers with her as well. That would be just our luck."

Wellington motioned to a few of the scattered pages. Some were only half pages, where whatever had happened had cut ledgers in half. He laid the one he was holding out on the desk and ran a professional eye over them. "This is the most recent ledger, or at least what remains of it. So yes, Eliza, it would appear that is the way our luck runs tonight."

Eliza let out a long sigh. "Well, it was a good idea. Try and find out if any of these women were at the same meeting. I thought maybe they might have overheard something, maybe conspired together—I don't know, eaten the same toffee apples as each other!" She picked up a turned over chair, and then flopped down on it. "Without some connection, then these disappearances are all merely random events, and we have absolutely no way of predicting who is next."

For a moment they were silent. Then Wellington organised the papers into stacks, out of sheer reflex no doubt. "Well, Miss Braun, we most certainly do not give up. What does the Ministry say when a lead runs out?"

She glanced up, knowing perfectly well what her training had taught her. "You go back to the beginning again. Re-examine the evidence. Re-check your assumptions."

"Then that is what we shall do." Wellington sounded remarkably undeterred, despite what had just happened in this very room. "However," he got to his feet and held out his elbow, "not until we get some food and a bit of a rest."

"And Campbell," Eliza stood too. "Do you think we should tell him about what happened here?"

Wellington cocked his head, "Do you really think it would matter if we did?"

That made Eliza smile even wider. She *was* having an influence on him after all.

She shook her head. "No, I don't think so."

"Then we go on as we have been." He gestured to the

door. "Now let's go and get a spot of luncheon and start over. I am sure if we put our heads together we can come up with something."

When he said it in that tone, Eliza quite believed him.

CHAPTER SIX

Wherein Our Heroes Take a Moment To Breathe

Perhaps lunch was a preposterous notion following the events at Hester Langston's estate, but Wellington needed a moment's peace. Surrounding himself with the mundane and the routine reassured him he was not lost in some bizarre nightmare—though one appeared to be unfolding all about them. He glanced around the bustling tearooms, filled with ordinary folk going about their business completely unaware, and sighed.

Three women snatched from thin air, two in front of him and his partner. He recalled the jovial words of Doctor Sound as he said, *"Chaos and mayhem tended to follow them wherever they went."* Of course he knew there was no real substance to these words, but the comment still haunted him.

"Welly," Eliza asked as she poured herself a cup of tea, "are you well?"

He forced a smile onto his face. "This is one of those times when I am reminded of how insulated from fieldwork I am."

Her brow furrowed, she gave a soft "ah" and then poured him a fresh cup. "It's one thing to see these items, read about them, and know what they do, but quite another altogether to experience them."

"Indeed." He shifted in his seat and changed the subject as best he could. "I'm trying to see the correlation between Lena Munroe, Kate Sheppard, and Hester Langston, apart from their involvement in the suffrage movement." He took up his tea, sipped, glanced at the rather weak brew, and then set it down. "Perhaps we could at least take precautions so it doesn't happen again?"

"How do we do that, Welly?" Eliza asked, dropping her fourth sugar cube into her tea. He swallowed back a groan of revulsion as she added cream. "Even if we know who is targeted, how can we stop them?"

"A fair question." Wellington produced his journal and turned to a page dated from their walk to Speakers' Corner. He fanned out the journal and used his pen as a pointer, tracing along the streets of his simple map. "So, exactly what we know: a device of some sort, producing an electrical field of immense power, grabs their quarry, and teleports them to a designated location. Something like our Atlantean æthergates."

"Teleportation?" Eliza shrugged. "What makes you think the women are teleported to another location? They could just as easily have been incinerated on the spot."

"If that were the case, we would have far more evidence to go on." He leaned forward, his voice dropping as he continued. "To incinerate a body completely requires a heat source generating temperatures exceeding one thousand and seventeen degrees Farenheit."

"You're speaking 'science' to me again, Welly, and as we both know, we are certainly not dealing with the rules of everyday science."

"Very well then, Miss Braun. Then consider, if there were any sort of incineration even of a kind wherein there was no residual heat generated, what about the lack of ash? Or perhaps a burn pattern? A body simply does not combust without leaving some sort of residue.

"Besides, in the case two days before, we had a body

appear in an iron gate in Grosvenor Square." He tapped his finger on the small X drawn on his map. "A body that disappeared in the same fashion as previous incidents."

"A sound conclusion there."

Wellington looked up from the map. Eliza took a sip of the milky concoction in her teacup and continued. "We also know that it can capture moving objects. On the train we were moving at speeds say fifty to sixty miles per hour, so the targeting system on this teleportation device can compensate for objects in motion."

He blinked. "I hadn't even considered that."

"Welly, this is all conjecture at this point, but in the cases of Munroe and Langston, we have two women that are snatched from thin air—exactly the same as the other cases Bruce ignored."

She stopped abruptly and his journal disappeared back into his coat pocket when their meal arrived. The first bite of his sandwich revealed exactly how hungry he was.

Dabbing at the corners of her lips, Eliza finished her own mouthful and then continued. "But with Kate at Speakers' Corner, that has all the characteristics of a botched abduction; the electricity jumped to the closest object it could latch on to once I got Kate on the ground."

"Poor Melinda holding the rhino stopper was nothing more than a lightning rod."

"So it would seem, but her materialisation into that gate? That was not part of the plan."

"How can you be so sure, Eliza?"

"Let's say whomever these perpetrators are, they had got to Kate, and she found herself part of the ironworks of Grosvenor Gate. Kate would have been turned into a martyr, and the movement would have galvanised. The horror of it all could have even won sympathy in the government."

Wellington took another bite of his sandwich, turning his glance out of the window where they sat. At the street corner, he could see a suffragist passing out flyers. The movement continued on, even in light of events. How the women would have rallied if, all jealousy set aside, their symbol of success were to die such a horrific death.

"So you are suggesting Kate's disappearance and maybe a ransom would have served our perpetrator better?"

"Looking at the world through the mind of a criminal is a simple task, Welly. It's the truly unhinged ones that take us all by surprise."

He sat up even taller in his chair. "By having a dead body appear so soon after it's snatched, you tip your hand to what your intentions are."

"Nicely played, Welly," Eliza said, a twinkle appearing in her eyes. "You see firsthand with these abductions the panic that is spreading through the movement. By revealing a rather grim fate awaiting those who are stolen, the movement will only rally the troops harder."

"So, staying with this line of thinking, what do you think happened with Melinda Carnes? Could they have aborted the abduction?"

She finished her bite, and then shook her head. "Again, tipping the hand. Also, that would mean an accomplice would have to've been within eyesight of Kate, or perhaps closer to her; and have been in constant contact with a controller at the other end." She now saw the suffragist at the street corner and smiled. "No, I think the gruesome death of Melinda Carnes was an accident."

"How so?"

"A feeling." She held up a hand to hold back Wellington's protestations. "Think about it, Welly. Why snatch Kate, as was the intention, only to have her materialise in an iron gate and make her into a martyr? And why reveal that you possess a teleportation device when you instill far more fear with a device that simply makes you disappear? This feels rather like a clankerton's grand experiment, and something at Speakers' Corner went wrong."

"What, do you think?"

Eliza shook her head. "It could be a number of things.

An interruption during the abduction. A miscalculation of some sort. A sudden loss of power. That is really open to speculation, isn't it?"

He paused just before his next bite. "Between disappearances, there has been a large span of time, whereas now . . ." His voice trailed off. "But surely those behind such technology would have full working knowledge of what it can and can't do."

"Really?" Eliza asked, taking another long sip from her teacup, before asking, "Tell me, Wellington Thornhill Books"—the Archivist braced himself—"do you know everything there is to Lisa?"

"Lisa?" He tried to think of whom she was on about, until he blurted, "My analytical engine, you mean?"

"Welly, it needs a name."

"It is a device. Not a pet."

"Lisa is quite the associate at the Ministry."

"It is an efficient machine, quite apt in the routines I programme into its memory."

"And do you recall its backup battery in case a problem occurs in the intake valves?"

"Of course," he grumbled, "I built the bloody thing."

Eliza smiled warmly. "How long does your battery last?"

He went to answer, but his mouth remained open for what seemed far too long to be proper. Wellington felt a twinge of worry work through him. He had considered a contingency for any problems if the Thames failed to power his creation, but he had never run a test on battery power only.

"You see," Eliza said, her victory displayed quite clearly on her face, "even Lisa has her secrets; and she has been by your side far longer than I."

Wellington surrendered a reluctant smile. "You have me there, Miss Braun. Well played." He dabbed at his mouth clean with a napkin, and sat back in his chair. "You're thinking during the materialisation of Miss Carnes, the device suddenly stopped working?"

"That is the field agent's instinct in me, Welly. Whatever

this device is, it has the ability to transport people through space, from one designated point to another. A machine like that is going to require a lot of power." Wellington went to interject, but Eliza raised a finger. "As far as our technology at the Ministry, we have the Thames to power our operations. However, consider how you would manage if you didn't have an inexhaustible power source such as a river? What if you wished to keep such a device self-contained?"

Again, he went to speak, but again his words never left his lips as movement caught his peripheral. The gentleman approaching was turning heads, in particular the ladies', but the dapper gent didn't notice. His eyes were fixed on Eliza. Wellington immediately reached for his walking stick—just in case violence was in the air.

Eliza caught where the Archivist's attention was directed, turned around, and called out, "Douglas! Whatever brings—"

"I expected you to guard Mother from harm, Eliza. Just what the hell happened at this morning's meeting?"

She straightened up in her seat as she replied, "I would be more than happy to discuss with you this morning's events, provided you lower your voice and soften your tone with me."

"I will address you however I please, particularly when you are enjoying an afternoon's repast and not watching over my mother as I assumed you were doing."

"I did so this morning with my partner here," Eliza replied tightly, motioning to Wellington. The newcomer rudely did not turn and acknowledge the Archivist. Her eyes narrowed as she continued, "We are here, reviewing conclusions and possibilities—"

"While Mother remains a target for whatever infernal device is at work here."

Wellington had quite enough of this posturing. "So you would prefer to make both your mother and Miss Braun targets?"

Douglas turned on Wellington, his eyes sharp and dark as he took a good look at him. "Were you addressed, sir?"

Wellington took a sip of his tea just before his reply. "Well, as you are addressing my associate as one would a truculent child, a manner which I do take umbrage with, I feel social niceties have rather flown out the window."

Douglas glanced between them. He was, obviously, someone close to Eliza and their current investigation; but that didn't change the growing urge in the Archivist to bang some manners into his head.

"If you are quite finished, Douglas," Eliza spoke, somehow still managing to remain calm, "I'd like to introduce you to Wellington Thornhill Books, Esquire. My partner at the Ministry."

He looked at Wellington with a crooked eyebrow. "I don't suppose you have reached conclusions to what is going on."

Oh, this gent was quite the charmer. "Sir, we still have not surmised exactly what sinister forces are at work. We are, however, attempting to draw a logical—"

Douglas turned his back on Wellington and addressed Eliza. "I believed you could protect Mother."

"And we can—"

"Yes," Wellington said, his tone matching Douglas' own insistent one, "we can, just in case you forget I am here."

Eliza took the interloper's hand. "As Wellington tried to tell you, all we have are facts and bits of evidence." Her voice became pleasant, soothing. "I cannot move mountains or change the course of the tides, Douglas, and this is only my first day on the case."

Watching her thumb gently stroke the skin on Douglas' large hand sent a stab of jealousy through Wellington. He forced himself to release his walking stick lest he smack the other man with it.

Douglas took in a sharp, deep breath; and then removed his hat. "Yes, Eliza. You are quite right. I am just a bit—"

"Churlish?" snapped Wellington.

"*Concerned*," Eliza bit back, giving the Archivist a warning glare.

Douglas glanced over his shoulder and grinned at Wellington. "No, no, I think you're right, mate. I did come across a bit rough there just now." He then extended his hand. "Douglas Sheppard."

"But of course you are," Wellington returned, shaking the man's hand. He decided not to present Sheppard with his card. "I cannot think of anyone other than Miss Sheppard's son showing this level of concern."

"Yes, of course." He tapped Wellington's shoulder with the top of his bowler. "So, you are Eliza's partner in the Ministry, eh? Good to know she's got someone levelheaded to keep her straight."

Wellington tipped his head to one side. "I beg your pardon?"

"Well, Eliza's not changed all too much I would assume, always a gal in the midst of the action." He gave a nod at him. "Doesn't hurt a capable girl to have a man providing the facts and strategies that will get her through."

Wellington looked over to Eliza who was pinching the bridge of her nose as she screwed her eyes shut. It was a look he knew all too well.

"Miss Braun is indeed most capable when anyone or anything threatens the Crown. One of many reasons she is such an outstanding agent."

"I have no doubt." Douglas flashed what Wellington could only assume was his most charming smile. "And better for you as you have no need to dirty your hands. Handle the logistics, and send in Eliza for the real work. It must be quite the team you two make."

"Yes," Wellington muttered. "Quite."

"Douglas," Eliza interjected, her voice now—for the first time since the brute's arrival—insistent, "unless you would care for Mr. Books and I to brief you on what little we know, I must ask you to grant us a bit of privacy. The fewer ears involved in our discussions and deductions, the better."

"Oh yes, yes, of course." Douglas smiled and motioned back to Wellington. "I can imagine how tough a time you're having keeping up with this gent's intellect."

Wellington furrowed his brow. He really could not tell if the man was complimenting or insulting him.

"I did want to let you know," he said, returning his bowler to his head, "that Mother is still keeping her schedule. She has a talk in two days at the Olympia Tea Room, and we're expecting a large turnout."

"Even with everything's that has happened?" Eliza asked.

"Particularly in light of what has happened. Mother intends on addressing it directly." He passed along to Eliza a small note. "All the details are there, along with your tickets." He tipped his brim to her, then to Wellington. "Good day, Mr. Books. Do watch our for my little Eliza, if you can."

His parting salutation continued to ring in Wellington's ears; and from the expression that Eliza wore, she too was feeling some sort of sting from his words. Once out of eyesight, she let out her breath and then stared at her teacup.

"This really needs to be something stronger," she finally uttered.

"Beer?"

Her eyes flicked up to meet his. "Vodka."

With a polite chuckle, Wellington looked back to the street corner. The suffragist was no longer there. Dancing in a light breeze, where she had once stood, was a single leaflet. It spun one way and then another, and then fluttered back to the pavement.

His eyes then jumped to a window attached to the corner building. The curtain shuddered, and then went still. He squinted to see if he could make out a form through the lace. Had someone been watching them?

"Welly," Eliza asked, "do you see something?"

"If I did," he said, still watching the curtain, "it's gone now."

"We have two days," Eliza commented, gathering her purse and rising from her chair. "Shall we try and see if previous cases reveal anything?"

"It cannot hurt," he agreed.

His eyes kept going back to the window. Perhaps it had

been nothing. Perhaps it had been a moment's happenstance when a building's tenant looked out to note the traffic or the day's weather. A simple coincidence.

"Coming?" Eliza, now standing next to him, asked.

In the time that Eliza Braun had joined the Archives, things had changed dramatically, and "coincidence" had become for Wellington a distant memory.

"Right behind you, Miss Braun," he whispered, "and very much watching your back."

CHAPTER SEVEN

Wherein Our Colonial Pepperpot Takes Double and Wellington Is Denied a Heroic Moment

The two days (and odd hours between Douglas' visit and their arrival at the Olympia) of case review and investigation yielded nothing apart from possibility upon possibility of what could be happening during these abductions. Up to the moment when the clock on their desk chimed six o'clock, Wellington and Eliza both combed through the neglected cases and their own notes and accounts concerning Lena Munroe, Melinda Carnes, and Hester Langston. They'd looked for any similarities, apart from the suffrage movement. Money. Political influence. Marital status.

Nothing. And now, they were out of time, and they had an appointment.

It was a lovely after-dinner affair with tea, sandwiches, and biscuits offered at the Olympia Tea Room, and there was a surprising number of people present. The lack of conversation and the tense posture of the attendees, however, countered the evening's pleasantries.

"I must admit," Wellington offered as he shut the door behind them, his eyes looking over the attendance. "Those dedicated to the cause are most stalwart."

"These people aren't just dedicated," Eliza returned. "They're curious—they want to see who's next."

Eliza pointed through the crowd. Silently observing the suffragists, a sheen of sweat just visable across their foreheads, was the "gentlemen's gallery" from Speakers' Corner.

With a frown, Eliza motioned with her head towards the podium. "Come on."

As they eased their way through the crowd, the silence around them thickened like a London fog. Mrs. Sheppard, standing in the corner chatting with Chandi Culpepper and Charlotte Lawrence, seemed drawn stiff as a bowstring. Eliza's eyes never left Kate as they finally found some empty seats.

Wellington glanced at his partner and sighed. "I doubt sincerely that staring at Mrs. Sheppard will prevent anyone from kidnapping her. What we should be doing is examining the crowd for suspicious behaviour, behaviour you will miss if you keep you attention trained on—"

"Wellington," Eliza whispered softly, "do you recall what the young lady seven rows behind us, seated in this aisle, just to the left of us, is wearing?"

He scoffed. "Well, no, but why would that—"

"Green dress, leaning more towards a darker shade as it is winter. The hat though is a wide-brim which, for the life of me, I cannot understand. Whoever in their right mind would wear a wide-brimmed hat in winter? The dress is accented by a cream-coloured lace, redemption for the appalling choice of hat, and finally her hands are still cold, seeing as she has not taken them out of the muff she has across her lap."

Wellington whipped his head around to spot the woman Eliza had described, seated seven rows behind them, just to the left.

"I would have gotten her hair and eye colour," Eliza grumbled, "but I think being in the Archives for a year has taken a toll on my faculties." He turned back to the former field agent and received a shrug in answer to his silent question. "No offense, mate, but it's what I do."

He gave a slight sniff. "Don't you mean what you *used* to do?"

Eliza glared at him. "Don't you mean what we are doing at this very moment?"

"Well played, Miss Braun."

Eliza grinned, but briefly as she looked around at the other ladies. "I even recognise a few journalists in the house, far more than usual for a suffragist speech. Word on what has been happening to the sisters, it would seem, travels fast."

"Almost as quick as lightning," he remarked. "Wouldn't you agree?"

She patted his hand. "Why, Mr. Books, is that a touch of levity I hear you attempting? For a so-called proper gentleman, you can be most inappropriate sometimes, you know that?" She winked at him. "Stop playing with me, Wellington."

He could not ignore the sudden surge of heat in his skin. "Now, now, I simply am trying to lighten the mood a little," Wellington blustered. "This sort of anxiety is so heavy, it could very well break the back of the movement."

The sharp look she levelled at him made him realise how foolish he must seem in her eyes. "Don't you think that is the whole reason for the attacks?"

"Oh come along, Miss Braun," he grumbled. "The suffrage movement is far larger than merely its key members. It's a strategy. There are generals, captains, and lieutenants, and victory does not solely rest on the shoulders of one officer."

"True," a voice said from beside them, "but what happens to an army when no one wants to pick up the mantle of the fallen general?"

Eliza and Wellington both gave a start, their seats creaking loudly as they turned to face a dapper gent seated next to them. The spot had been empty only moments ago, a small placard reading RESERVED resting on the middle of its cushion. Neither of them had heard or seen Douglas' arrival. The gentleman regarded Wellington for only a moment before focusing intently on Eliza.

"Ye gods, Douglas," Eliza seethed, slipping the small pistol that she'd automatically dropped into her palm back up into her sleeve holster. "How did you do that?"

"Surely you are joking, Eliza?" He chuckled. "I am used to spending my winters sneaking up on entire lion prides in the Serengeti and whiling away summers doing the same to fur seals in Antarctica. Do you think a suffragist meeting would pose any sort of challenge?"

"You do have your ways, don't you?" she said, and Wellington did not like her almost gentle tone. The Archivist knew very well had he attempted to surprise Eliza in such a fashion, he would have more than likely been rapped on the nose for it!

"As do you," Douglas said, giving her a rakish wink.

When he had met Mr. Sheppard two days ago, Wellington did not care for his company.

Now, he was sure he did not care for this gent *at all*.

"So I am to assume that this is a rally for morale, not necessarily for attention?"

"It is now. After word got out of what happened at Hester's, the Protectors tried to have Mother cancel this talk. She, of course, refused, and insisted that the sisterhood should make this rally a defiant stand, at the very least in memory of Hester. That struck a nerve." Douglas took his eyes away from Eliza—something Wellington was quite happy about—and looked over the crowd. "These Englishwomen are very strange. While they are force-fed and labour under police brutality they cry 'Havoc!' and let slip the dogs of war. A few of their number disappear and suddenly they jump on sight of their very shadows."

"Or perhaps it is the unknown," Wellington blurted, feeling moved to defend his countrywomen. "There were eyewitnesses, and the stories passed through the grapevine have grown more fantastic. However, there is one thread of truth binding them: the fantastic manner in which these ladies are disappearing." He held his chin up a bit higher as he added, "That might be a good reason to take caution, wouldn't you agree?"

"Mr. Brooks, correct?" Douglas asked. He made no attempt to mask his appraising glance.

"*Books.*" Wellington's blood now rushed to his face, and a tingle crept across his skin, reminiscent of the sunburn he had just about recovered from.

"So tonight," Douglas continued smoothly, ignoring the Archivist and motioning to Kate, "my mother is planning to address what has been happening, and—in that fashion we know oh so well—turn it in to a rally that could even persuade Queen Vic herself to join us. She should be starting any moment now."

As if on cue, Kate Sheppard patted the arm of one of the Protectors and then stood. She walked over to the podium and scanned the assembly. There was no welcoming applause, but her smile communicated confidence.

Wellington discerned a few accusatory glares from the women watching her, yet most seemed to be calmed merely by Kate's presence. She did make a striking figure with the gaslight gleaming off her brass-encased jaw as she inclined her head.

"Sisters . . ." And her smile widened as she let that word carry across them all. As she began to speak, Wellington let his gaze drift over the crowd once again. While Eliza was mesmerised by her heroine's speech, he could not afford to be drawn in. He sat quietly and watched the crowd while Kate drew the movement's spine straighter and strengthened it with iron.

He tried not to lose his focus, even as he observed Douglas take Eliza's hand and give it a slight squeeze while her gaze locked with his. A tightness welled in his throat, and Wellington reclined back in his own chair, unable to deny Douglas Sheppard's courage to do what he could not.

"Eliza," the Archivist said in her ear, causing her to jump slightly. "I will go on and check the door, see if anything is amiss."

"Very good, Welly." Eliza nodded. Her hand remained in Douglas' grasp. "I should have a handle on anything that goes awry here."

He glanced at Douglas who, unlike Eliza, was looking at him. The adventurer nodded, giving a blessing at his tactical decision to "take a walk." Wellington eased himself out of the row and strode quietly along the outside of the assembly. While the centre aisle beside him would have been the faster exit, he felt using one of the outside aisles would attract less attention. He had guessed right as no eyes left Kate Sheppard as he made his way to the main entrance.

The cold outside slapped him hard. In truth, this was what he wanted—a bit of fresh air and some clarity on the matter at hand. He did get the fresh air, or at least fresh for this part of London. With the cold, the smells were not as unbearable as in the summer. As far as gaining a touch of clarity, that was proving more elusive.

All he could see was Douglas Sheppard holding Eliza's hand. Such a small thing, and his rational mind knew that. So why was Wellington so bothered by it? Was it the fact that Sheppard was a part of Eliza's past and of her distant home? Was it that he was Douglas Sheppard, the first mountaineer and explorer to reach the summits of Everest, K2, and Kangchenjunga all in one year? Was it that Sheppard was well known for his survival tactics, skills that kept him alive in the Australian Outback for a week when he found himself separated from his expedition? Or was it Sheppard's reputation for being a master chef, hosting his own celebration of another thrilling adventure across the Amazon?

Why would any of those things bother him?

A flash caught his eye, and Wellington turned to the building across the street. All but three of the windows were dark, with their blinds drawn. He walked to the edge of the pavement. Wellington couldn't be certain something was amiss, and yet some primitive part of him said something was not right.

A curtain moved, and someone placed a kerosene lamp by the window. The person disappeared into the room's darkness before he could get a better look at her, but the glance he had stolen was quite disturbing. Perhaps it meant he should go back inside. It was too cold.

Wellington reached for the door handle. His hand recoiled immediately at the sudden shock to his hand. It had been so powerful, he had caught sight of a small blue bolt jumping between the handle and his fingertips. Wellington had not felt anything like that since . . .

He yanked open the door and dashed for the assembly. Kate Sheppard's inspirational words had earned her a standing ovation—so his warning would be drowned out. He just had to reach the stage and get her clear of what was coming. What exactly that was remained uncertain, but Wellington could guess from what happened at Hester Langston's home. Whoever was doing this had decided to have a second potshot at the target that had evaded capture at Speakers' Corner. Just shy of the front row, the smell of electricity— that odd scent of copper or brass heated by a summer sun— reached him, making his mouth grow dry. His foot hit the first step leading to the stage—

His legs were suddenly kicked out from underneath him as his arms also shot forward. Wellington felt an odd, dizzying sensation of flight. Then he realised he was in fact being pulled backwards—it dawned on him—by the collar of his coat away from the stage and Kate Sheppard.

Before he hit the chairs of the first row, before the screams of ladies filled the air, Wellington did catch one word. Certainly not coming from his lips, or Eliza's for that matter. "*Mum!*"

Douglas Sheppard was bounding for the stage. Strange bolts of blue and violet danced between the chandelier's ceiling fixture and Kate's own brass arm and jaw. She looked only startled by the sudden display of electricity rather than

truly shocked. Douglas dove for his mother, knocking her
free of the podium, and sliding with her to the far left edge
of the stage, before tumbling off the edge in a tangle of arms
and legs. Tendrils of energy clung to Kate but dissipated
as she slid out of reach. They disappeared from view just
when a brilliant white claw of energy reached through the
highest windows of the meeting hall and struck the podium
where Kate had been. The bolts angrily danced along and
around the stage as if searching for a victim. Finding none,
the lightning grew brighter and brighter.

Thunder roared through the tearoom. Wellington ducked
and rolled away into the retreating wave of panic as the
podium exploded.

A hand gripped his bicep and pulled him up to his feet.
"Welly?"

The Archivist adjusted his spectacles, looking up to at his
colleague. "Eliza? Are you hurt?"

Strangely, her evening dress appeared only slightly tou-
sled, but her hair was not even out of place. "We must have
been safely out of its range this time."

He nodded, his eyes immediately turning to the stage.
"As were most of the ladies."

Eliza suddenly shoved him aside, her eyes boring into the
crowd. "And there you are again!"

Wellington followed her gaze to a rather imposing woman
of extraordinary height, accentuated either naturally or by
the lights of the meeting hall, with sharp cheekbones, dark
eyes, and golden hair just visible underneath her hat. Before
he could enquire, his colleague shoved herself in the direction of the tall suffragist. A short scream from someone in
Eliza's way caught the woman's attention, and on seeing she
was being pursued, she too began to push and shove her way
through the chaos. Eliza made a strange motion with her
arm, and then she turned to Wellington and made the gesture again.

When she mouthed *"Cut her off!"* to him, Wellington finally understood and worked his way around the fray, now

beginning to die down as most of the assembled had escaped into the night. He had reached the door at the same time Eliza did, her face now red with frustration.

"Damnation," she swore. "She got away."

"Who exactly got away?"

"I don't know." Eliza raised her hand, a warning for him not to say anything. "What I mean is, I don't know who she is, but she was at Speakers' Corner. I can't quite put a finger on it now, but there's something about her I recognise."

"Please Eliza, sometimes you do make it difficult to follow your train of thought. Can you not elaborate?" He followed her back towards the stage.

"I recognise the other suffragists from previous rallies. They also have a carriage suited for such gatherings. They looked like they were supposed to be here." Eliza pointed to the doorway where she had last seen this stranger. "She didn't. Not at Speakers' Corner. Not tonight. And I know her. I don't know where." With a final sigh of irritation, she turned back and strode hotly back towards the stage, "I don't know how, but I *know* her."

Douglas was helping up his mother, while the officers were being tended to by Protectors. Eliza and Wellington joined him at her side. "Mrs. Sheppard," Wellington asked, "are you well?"

"As well as can be expected when one is tackled twice in one week," she grumbled. "Good Lord, Douglas, when do you find time for rugby? Your tackle is terribly fierce!"

"I make time, Mum," he said. "I have to stay fit for when I scale Lhotse next year, yes?"

They both chuckled at that. Eliza examined the other women, all of them still catching their collective breath. "I suppose we must add tonight to a growing list of disasters."

"I beg to differ. We . . ." And Wellington paused, his eyes darting at Douglas. "We prevented Mrs. Sheppard's abduction, and got a very good look at how this device works." Now it was Eliza's turn to pause. "Not only do we catch a whiff of electricity before an event, but there is a buildup in the air. Brush or come close to anything metal, and it can give you a bit of a shock. At first I thought it was a residual of the abduction, but now . . ."

"That's what brought you back in here," Eliza realised.

He looked back towards the door. "Partially."

Her brow furrowed. "Something else then?"

Wellington wanted to tell her what he saw, or what he thought he saw. But, "No, nothing. A trick of light."

They both looked around the hall. Moments ago, there were screams and pandemonium. Now, the silence—aside from the murmurs coming from the officers of the Movement—was just as deafening.

"Well then," Eliza groaned, "I have endured my fill of peculiar occurrences for a day. I'm off home."

Wellington watched her gather up her coat and scarf. Tonight was the first time that he could recall ever seeing Eliza looking exhausted.

The same instinct that urged him to study the building across the street urged him to look back at the Sheppards. Kate was gazing around the empty meeting hall with the air of a general reassessing her resources.

Douglas was watching his mother intently, until his eyes caught Wellington's. The sombre look on his face softened, and he smiled. The man was almost as insufferable as his books made him out to be.

Wellington heartily wished he would go back to the Serengeti, posthaste.

CHAPTER EIGHT

In Which Our Dashing Archivist Upholds His Gentlemanly Upbringing and Our Beloved Colonial Pepperpot Entertains Unexpected Guests

"Stare if you wish, but on this I am firm," Wellington insisted.

He swore for a moment that he saw Eliza blush. He was not certain whether it was in reaction to his words or his removing his coat, but Wellington would not be denied in this moment.

"Welly . . ." Eliza began.

"I will hear no arguments to the contrary, Miss Braun. I will be spending the night here." Her eyebrow arched slightly, until he placed his coat on the back of a chair. "I will be staying on the couch, if you please. Tomorrow we will return to the Archives and search for clues—but after all these goings-on, you have made yourself quite the target, and have been seen talking to Mrs. Sheppard on many occasions."

Eliza fixed her gaze hard on him. "This is *me* we are talking about, just to be clear."

"Admittedly, yes, but even you, the South Pacific Angel of Wanton Destruction and Calamity has to sleep sometime."

A hiss of pistons took Wellington's attention away from Eliza. Alice seemed as if she wanted to interject, but Eliza stepped between them, her smile warm and pleasant.

That unsettled Wellington quite a bit.

"Now, Wellington . . ."

And she was calling him "Wellington" which made him, unexpectedly, a bit wobbly in the knees.

". . . your gesture, while sweet and endearing, is really unnecessary. I think Alice and I can protect ourselves most admirably."

She was being difficult, so he brought out the ultimate argument. "Remember," he said in a quiet voice, "how you felt when Agent Thorne went missing. Surely you would not wish to put me through the same thing?"

Eliza's mouth opened and shut a few times in an impotent search for further argument. Finally, she walked up to him and gave him a hard shove, sending him backwards into the plush couch. He now looked up at her; and with her hands on her hips, lips pursed, and eyebrow crooked as she considered him, she was quite the vision. As he was sitting down, he couldn't tell if his knees were weak but he somehow knew they would be. At that moment he saw exactly why men all over the world couldn't resist the compulsion to grant her with whatever she wanted.

"Stop trying to use logic on me, Wellington Thornhill Books!" Her sapphire eyes trained on his own. "And using Harry is a bit below the belt."

A cool sweat formed on the back of his neck. It wasn't from fear, and that was more unnerving than if it had been.

"However, if you insist." Eliza motioned to her maid. "Be a dear, Alice, and fetch Mr. Books a sidearm. Something fitting for a gentlemen."

"Yes, miss." Alice curtseyed and then walked over to a gorgeous music box. As Pachelbel's *Canon in D* began to play, the maid pressed a hidden button, and produced an impressive firearm from within the still playing device. "The Bulldog, miss? Or may I suggest the Webley Mark I for the gentleman?"

"A standard," Eliza acknowledged. "A fine pairing, Alice. Nicely done."

Wellington shook his head, taking up his walking stick. "No need, Miss Braun. This will be adequate."

She went to protest, but Wellington emphatically held up his hand.

Alice closed the music box and then pressed the *fleur-de-lis* in the same end table. A panel slid back to reveal a small shotgun. "Perhaps, Mr. Books, would prefer something with a bit more stopping power? It's not as gentlemanly to be sure—but who wants to be a gentleman in a tight corner?"

"Good Lord!" Wellington stared at the compact weapon for a moment, and then motioned around himself. "I'm spending the night in a bloody armoury!"

Eliza clicked her tongue and finally spoke. "I would say that this problem you have with guns will be the death of you." She looked him over and gnawed lightly on the inside of her cheek. "Now I worry if it will in fact be the death of *me*." Eliza tapped her fingers against her bodice and shook her head. "Alice, fetch a few pillows and some blankets for Mr. Books as he will be joining us tonight." She leaned down and pressed the tip of his nose, before adding, "Better you stay here anyway. I can't defend you if you're outside playing the gallant and not within eyesight."

"Your faith in my abilities does inspire me as would Helen's visage," snipped Wellington.

"Helen had a thousand ships covering her backside, mate." Eliza shrugged, motioning to him. "I have an Archivist who's afraid of guns. You figure out who has the better deal."

Alice returned with her arms full of pillows and linens. "And with that," Wellington huffed, snatching a pillow and punching a bit of air and softness into it, "I bid you good night, Miss Braun. Sleep easy as I will serve as your first line of defence."

Again, he noted Alice shooting a glance to Eliza. His partner did little to conceal the look of frustration as she turned and made for her own bedroom. She said good night before closing the door.

The couch had looked a good few inches longer when he made the offer to stand for her honour. He was sure it had shrunk in the intervening minutes. With a low sigh, Wellington pulled a pair of blankets up to his chin, and wriggled against the couch. It failed to get any more comfortable.

He reflected on when he had slept on foreign soil while serving at Her Majesty's pleasure in the Transvaal War. This couch was void of rocks, dirt, insects, and any passing indigenous species, and yet he was actually more uncomfortable now than he had been then. He scanned the room for an ottoman of some kind to prop his feet up on even as the shadows began to lengthen and devour the room.

Eliza's apartments now appeared as when he first saw them. Lights of London crept in through the windows, the late-night carriages and calls from the streets creating a constant murmur. His mind wandered to the Archives. *Noise*, Wellington thought as he struggled against the cushions, *can serve as a lullaby in some instances.* Granted, it never did as such in the Archives, but it should have, as the generators there always filled the crypt underneath the Ministry with a low, steady drone. Such noise could lull others to sleep, as he had seen on occasion with Eliza; but it was more of a comforting cadence to him, a reassurance that, yes, he was doing the right thing. From the Archives would he serve Her Majesty now, a destiny he felt far more comfortable with than the one his father had groomed him for.

The soft din from outside was not as comforting. He was "in the field" as Eliza would put it. Hardly familiar ground for Wellington.

More to the point, it had been half a decade since Wellington had known the kind of action that Eliza thirsted for. Sound had assigned her to him to blunt that edge. Now he squirmed on her couch, serving as her protector. *Would I do this for any of the other female agents?* he mused. Agent Ihita Pujari? Agent Kitty O'Toole? Both beautiful women, and based on their previous cases, perfectly competent. No, Eliza was probably right. She didn't need protecting.

But Eliza was different. To him, at least.

Somewhere between the aural backdrop of London at night and his own random considerations, Wellington surrendered to the warm, friendly embrace of Morpheus. His dreams were as they usually were: vivid. However even in the beautiful field of flowers he found himself in, something ominous hung in the air. A repeating displacement thrummed in his ears, sounding as if it were a palpitation of his own heart. He couldn't hear his own footfalls as he ran through the plain of brilliant flowers, and yet something or someone was coming closer with every thud within his skull. In the dream, in the centre of this wide, vast moor, Wellington stopped, his hands over his ears, his mouth open in a scream that made no sound, while high above him the quick claps of thunder grew louder. Louder . . .

And with a start, Wellington was back in the darkness of Eliza's apartments.

"Bloody hell," he whispered as he brought himself up to a sitting position.

He was shaking. How odd. He had to calm himself and remember old habits, as he couldn't afford a sleep as deep as that; otherwise, Eliza would truly be better off without him there. He took a deep breath, trying to slow his heartbeat now resounding in his ears.

Wait a moment, Wellington thought, the grogginess of his odd dream now surrendering to his military and Ministry training. *That's not my heartbeat. That beating is coming from—*

He felt the shower of glass and wood just before throwing himself to the floor, his walking stick now against his chest and tight in his grip. Another window shattered and from his vantage point, two pairs of feet paused and then started coming towards him. Wellington looked behind him to see three others closing on his position. He brought to mind the variety of furniture and fixtures decorating Eliza's apartments. In this sitting room, the three entering in from alley side would have more ground and décor to work around. The other two would be better targets, particularly as they were city side and had the lights of London, few and far between as they might be, behind them.

Why, oh why, could this encounter not have been in Paris with all its grand illumination?

From the coffee table he grabbed a small but solid statuette. (Mercury, or was it Loki?) He pushed the distraction to the back of his mind as he stood and threw the small idol at one of the advancing shadows. As the statuette flew, preferably with Mercury's speed, Wellington launched himself at the other shadow. His walking stick cut the air and impacted hard against what he was hoping was an arm or perhaps ribs.

The way the shadow reacted to his blow, his cane had connected with a shoulder. Who were these intruders? Pygmies?

He could hear footsteps behind him. Footsteps, and pistons firing rapidly in succession.

Wellington brought the cane around, lifting the diminutive intruder off his feet, and then thrust the cane forward, its silver tip catching the glint of the outside light before striking what he hoped was a head. A crunch of glass accompanied the cane's impact into something solid.

"Alice," Wellington shouted as he spun around. "Be—"

He could see the shadows stir and then abruptly stop when the maid stepped into sight; the shattered window frames painting dark, angry streaks across her body. She was still, but pistons continued to pop and hiss angrily while cogs and gears spun so fast they screamed a high-pitched whine that made Wellington grind his teeth. He wanted to believe what he was witness to was a trick of shadow, but he—and no doubt, the intruders opposite of Alice—knew it was no illusion. It all flashed by in a moment: a moment for Alice's left thigh to burst open, a moment of hesitation on the intruders' part, the briefest moment for Alice's right leg to step back; and in the same moment for the maid to pull from her open prosthetic the forearm-sized firearm. Alice's first shot thundered through the apartments, lifting one of the assailants off the ground while sending the other two scattering into the darkness. Another shot exploded from the shotgun's second barrel, but Wellington doubted if it hit anyone.

"Careful as mice," Alice shouted back as she fell back into cover.

Wellington could hear in this brief lull Alice reloading shells and the remaining two intruders closing on them both. Quickly. How were they able to move as deftly as they could?

On hearing the grinding of glass against wood, he glanced at his own felled opponents. One of them was attempting to prop themselves up on one elbow, and that's when he caught sight of pale skin through a shattered lens. Where his cane had connected, the goggles' thick frame had cracked open, revealing a collection of wires, some hanging loose as if they were innards of an animal torn free after a lion's attack.

"Starlight Goggles!" he shouted.

"Bugger all!" Alice replied.

He brought his cane around, but this time his opponent caught it. Wellington twisted the head of his walking stick, and the blade appeared with the lightest of rings. The attacker scrambled back, returning to two feet, standing with knees slightly bent, waiting for Wellington's next attack.

"Never you mind, Mr. Books," Alice called as she fired off a round, shattering what sounded like something made of marble. "I got a mind for these lurkers. You tend to yours, I'll tend on mine!"

Wellington turned back around and cut the air with his sword and assumed a challenging stance.

The shadow's arms dropped sharply, and from its forearms came a hard, loud ring as two blades locked into place.

"Oh, dash it all," Wellington swore.

Blades now seemed to be coming from every angle as he retreated, his own fending off both of the attackers'. There was no opening; and in the near darkness, it was difficult to anticipate any sort of attack. Wellington parried and then rolled forward, closing their gap for a second. He felt the brush of a blade as it narrowly passed above him, and then he heard the impact of something metal digging into the wall. On this, Wellington continued to scramble forward.

The Samson-Enfield roared again, this time finding a target as another attacker fell. Another shot thundered in his ears as he drew closer and closer to what he needed. From behind him came a tearing of gears and fabric. His attacker was now free of the blade stuck in the wall and was coming for him. Wellington couldn't hear the footsteps behind him, but based on the movement and even the damaged Starlight Goggles, his life was now reliant on the next few seconds.

Wellington reached the *fleur-de-lis* and brought the spare Samson-Enfield's Mark III Alice had offered him earlier around to bear. The first shot knocked his attacker back. He immediately trained his weapon on movement on the left—movement far too fluid to be Alice—and rapidly fired another round.

A door from down the hall slid open. Wellington replaced the shotgun back into its concealment and waited.

Behind him came the sound of feet grinding glass and plaster powder into the floor. He immediately turned over, his eyes darting from shadow to shadow. There was still one left.

Eliza came around the corner and fired. One shot. The final intruder slipped out of the darkness in front of Wellington and then collapsed at his feet.

"I do love my Starlight Goggles," Eliza said, stepping into the room. Her own lenses flashed against the incoming light as she lifted them to a resting position on her forehead. "Makes easy work of unexpected callers."

"Get many of these, do you?" Wellington panted.

"Occasionally," Eliza remarked. "Particularly when I'm progressing nicely on a case. Tells me I am on the right track." She looked positively revived, when only a few hours ago she had appeared sunk to the depths of despair.

Wellington took another breath, but his heart simply wouldn't calm down. Continuing to thrum in his ears was a repeated *thump-thump-thump* that showed no sign of slowing.

Then he took another deep breath. The thumping continued.

"Eliza, the window!"

Both Wellington and Eliza went for the window where they both heard the thudding far more clearly. While the moon was half obscured by clouds tonight, they could see gliding over the city the dark shape of what could have been best described as a monstrous bird. The *thump-thump-thump* was distant this time, but the monster climbed higher; and on banking to one side, Wellington could see the lone figure underneath the wings.

"Very nice," Eliza muttered, returning her pistol hammer to a safe position. "I understand those ornithopters are quite the challenge to master."

A set of lights slowly flickered to life behind them. Wellington and Eliza turned to view the five assailants as well as the collateral damage from this visit. The intruders were dressed entirely in black, all of them wearing Starlight Goggles and what appeared to be large haversacks.

And they were all small. Not dwarves, but petite in their build.

Eliza looked closer at one of the corpses. She idly thumbed a large O-ring dangling from the haversack's shoulder straps. "Would you care to wager that all of these ruffians have ornithopters of their own?"

"I know better than to bet against you," Wellington said, kneeling next to her. "Shall we?" he asked, motioning to the mask and goggles of the corpse underneath them.

"By all means."

The cowl and Starlight Goggles slipped free and both of them started. Not even the pistons of Alice, coming in for a closer look, tore their gaze away. The girl could have been no more than fourteen, a row of freckles running across her checks and nose, her hair a sea of blonde curls that now formed a small halo around her head. Her eyes, when they were full of life, would have been beautiful to behold. She could have almost been a younger version of Eliza.

The agent immediately went to the other corpse Wellington had gunned down. She was the same age, her features revealing lineage from the Far East.

"Oh God," Eliza said, her hand going to her mouth. "They're practically children."

"Miss Braun," Wellington spoke gently, "not all unfortunates can be as blessed as the Ministry Seven."

"But why children?" she seethed.

"If you note, they are not carrying firearms of any kind. Only blades. It is a good assumption that in order to maintain flight, they needed to remain light. As they are younger, I'm sure these young ladies possess the proper musculature to endure the rigours of the ornithopters."

Her eyebrow crooked as she looked at him. "Books, how can you turn off your emotions to something like this?"

"The fact that these young ladies burst into your apartments in the dead of night to kill us gives me little reason to grieve their deaths. I will also hazard a guess at something else," he said, removing a blade from the first invader's belt.

Rolling the girl on her side, Wellington sliced into the black top and cut downward, stopping when the knife reached the haversack. He then pulled back the fabric and nodded. "As I thought. Miss Braun, have a look."

Eliza's eyes narrowed on the ornate, palm-sized tattoo decorating the young woman's shoulder blade. The scene, preserved in her skin, depicted a celebration, the revelers enjoying drink, food, and—for one or two—each other. At the centre of this debauchery was a large, brilliant diamond.

"Press gang branding, it appears," Wellington said, motioning to the tattoo. "Any idea to whom claims this moniker?"

"Diamond Dottie?" Eliza was answering his question, but it was more shock than a question. "Now I must admit, Welly, that this case has become truly peculiar."

"How so?"

"Diamond Dottie is a step up from a common thug and brawler, but only barely. I don't see her as the kind of criminal becoming involved in any peculiar occurrence. It's not her style. She's a fence, and the head of a gang of female thieves."

Wellington gave a shrug. "Perhaps this Diamond Dottie is broadening her horizons."

"But why?"

"That is indeed a pertinent question. Why indeed."

"Oh, I am an utter fool!" Eliza slapped a palm to her forehead. "A world-class idiot!" She turned and grabbed him by both sleeves. "I saw her! I saw her at the suffragists' meeting. I knew I recognised the face, but I didn't recall until just now the name to go with it."

Wellington's eyebrows shot up. "Is she a well-known supporter of the suffrage movement?"

Eliza's laugh was short and bitter. "Hardly! Dottie's far more likely to have been scoping out the wealthy women as targets for her gang."

"Miss?" Alice's voice sounded behind them.

The maid was looking around at the corpses and the ruined decorations of the apartments. It was hard to decide what was upsetting her more. Finally, she straightened her uniform and stood taller. "Well, I never did like that wallpaper. It was due for replacement anyway."

Eliza's smile was brief and not deep. "I doubt if any of us will be getting a night's rest, let alone set about redecorating." She stood, looking down at the two unmasked girls for a moment, allowing her eyes to linger on their faces. Perhaps committing them to memory. She swallowed and then turned back to Alice. "I will send an emergency dispatch to the Ministry. They will send a team here to dispose of the bodies. We will have to give statements, all three of us."

"No need to conceal anything," Wellington offered, "as I was indeed concerned for your safety and therefore—"

"I'm more concerned about how that is going to look on a report," Eliza grumbled. "Still, you held your own. Thank you." Eliza motioned to the two that Wellington had shot. "And lovely job on these two, Alice. I heard it from the hallway. I'd first thought you were reloading."

"Thank you, miss," Alice muttered with a quick curtsey.

Wellington's shoulders drooped, and the growing knot in his stomach loosened slightly. "So I suppose we should wait for the Ministry to arrive."

Eliza tightened the belt across her shift, "Just in case it is Bruce again, I'd better change into something less revealing lest he interview my chest instead of me."

He let the crass comment pass. Eliza had most certainly earned the right be a little common after as her inner sanctum had been violated. Wellington wondered for a moment if any of the pieces lost were irreplaceable. Even so, they would be harder for her to replace as she was no longer gallivanting around the world as she once had. As she left him and Alice in the now quiet parlour, Wellington allowed his eyes to roam over the scene. These girls were a tragedy, yes, but they were also sent to kill Eliza. What conclusion were they closing in on that would warrant the attention of a street gang scurf?

Eliza was right. Most peculiar.

"I suppose if the Ministry is on the way, we should put the ket—"

Wellington's words caught in his throat. Alice had not moved from where she stood. Her hands still gripped the Samson-Enfield Mark III, her fingers splaying lightly when his eyes met hers. Certainly there could be no mistaking it: Eliza might still be unaware of his abilities with a gun, but her maid knew, most assuredly.

Alice continued to stare at him in silence, until a voice made them both jump.

"Alice," called Eliza, "would you mind coming in here to assist me? I think Mr. Books would rather make the tea than lace me up in a corset."

"Coming right away, miss," Alice called back. She gave Wellington a little nod, sharp enough to have been mistaken for a kind of salute.

A heartbeat later, and still holding the Mark III at the ready, the maid walked out of the parlour, heading for Eliza's bedroom.

The knot in Wellington's stomach tightened as he wondered just what she would say to her employer.

INTERLUDE

Wherein Madcap Ambition Drives
Agent Campbell Towards Lofty Positions
Within the Ministry

Bruce had considered any and every option before him. Outside of pinning Doctor Sound to his desk, twisting his arm to where his chubby shoulder would lock painfully, and demanding access to the Restricted Area of the Ministry, this seemed to be the opportunity that Sussex was on about. Really the only one he had.

His fingers rapped quickly against his knees as he sat in the doctor's antechamber. Across from him, Miss Shillingworth continued her own work, the *clackety-clack* of her keys he found slightly unnerving. The two half domes with their twenty-six respective keys sprang up and down as she made quick note of what was, no doubt, dictation from the Fat Man. Even though she couldn't see the paper her typography appeared on, something in the way she quickly glanced over the completed sheets told Bruce that her work was error free.

Now this bird, Bruce thought, allowing his mind to wander, *must have been one of the benefits of this lofty office.* Miss Shillingworth was a fine specimen of female, and when she held the paper in front of her face, it afforded Bruce a moment to stare at her breasts. Maybe not as full as Eliza's, but the curvature led him to believe they would be just enough to fill his hand. A pleasant size. The desk between them and her current task deprived him of any sort of glance from the waist down, but what he could see most certainly suggested that it would be fine. Even with the office lacking any windows, her blonde hair wrapped tightly on the top of her head seemed to glow. Bruce could imagine himself very easily removing the hairpins, watching with delight as it fell to tickle the small of her back.

The quiet, bookish ones, he thought, his head nodding gently as he watched her type. The librarian in Scotland. The receptionist in Paris. And then there was Greta, from the Frankfurt mission. He remembered Agent Dinsdale telling him, "I don't envy you. There's not much to do in Frankfurt."

Poor sod had clearly not met Greta.

Miss Shillingworth was that same sort of woman, he wagered—icy on the outside, until you got them into bed. All that pent-up desire, hiding behind a façade of civility. Bruce loved that in a woman. A good reason why he himself enjoyed the wives of respectable gentlemen. Those poms spent so much time working on their respectability, they would ignore their fine fillies at home. *I bet you are a goer,* he thought darkly towards the secretary.

Leaning back in his chair, Bruce flashed a smile at Miss Shillingworth. "You make that look easy."

He felt the air grow heavy when her fingers stopped, but it was the look she shot over octagonal spectacles that made him shift nervously in his seat. Her glacier blue eyes locked on him, and Bruce felt as if he were in danger. *Hold on, did she catch me staring at her tits?* He immediately dismissed the notion as he was a trained field agent and she was just a secretary.

Then, considering this place, what if she wore a necklace or a ring that gave her the power to read minds?

With the slightest of twitches at the corners of her mouth, Miss Shillingworth returned to her typewriting.

He was about to excuse himself when the door leading to the hallway opened. The Fat Man had never been a more welcome sight.

"Good morning, Miss Shillingworth," Doctor Sound said. He gave a small start when he saw . . . "Agent Campbell? Well now, this is most unexpected."

"Yes, Doctor, I know—"

When Shillingworth spoke, Bruce felt himself stiffen like ice had been poured down his back. "He had no appointment this morning, Doctor."

"Yes, sir," Bruce began once more, "I know you were not expecting me, and I wasn't sure if you would have previous commitments so—"

"And so you took in an early repast and have been waiting here for, what, fifteen minutes? Thirty minutes?"

Bruce blushed. "An hour, sir."

Doctor Sound gave a cheerful chortle as he clapped Bruce on one of his massive shoulders. "Well then, it is I who have been keeping you waiting, haven't I?" As Doctor Sound guided Campbell to his office, he called over his shoulder at his secretary, "Miss Shillingworth, a spot of tea for us both. An Assam would be lovely . . ."

"Oh, Doctor Sound," Bruce said, every instinct in his body screaming for him to run for the door, find his own, modest desk, and hide under it as the secretary's eyes drew down on him. "There's no need to put out Miss—"

"Oh stuff and nonsense, Agent Campbell, your fortitude has earned you at the very least a good cup of tea."

The mere moments between crossing the threshold of Doctor Sound's office and taking a seat before his massive desk were more like a languid dream where Bruce might have taken a month, or a year, or perhaps a decade to cross from one point of his beloved Outback to reach the other. Walkabouts, they were called back home. Instead, he had only taken a few seconds to reach his destination, a comfortable, cushioned chair with ornate carvings in its handles. The dock sounds from outside were muffled in here, turning the Director's office into an oasis from the clamour of the City.

Then he became cognisant of the clock behind him. His mind reached for a memory: 1890, spring. His first meeting with the Director, only hours off the airship. He should have tried to get some sleep but he was ready to get cracking, whether it was his own knuckles or another man's jaw. Bruce was itching for a fight in the name of his country, Australia. He remembered the mantelpiece behind where he sat, and there was a clock. It kept perfect time . . .

Tick . . .
Tock . . .
Tick . . .
Tock . . .

He'd wanted to smash that clock against the ground in 1890. Six years later, along with Sound's office, nothing had really changed.

"Were you intending to wait in silence for the tea, Agent Campbell?" Doctor Sound asked, snapping him out of his reverie. "Or did you have something more urgent to talk about?"

Bruce's head whipped forward on hearing the Fat Man's voice. He gave a nervous cough as he shifted in his seat. "Sorry, Doctor Sound, I, uh—" What the hell was wrong with him? He'd faced dozens of madmen, boxers, and brawlers twice the size of Sound, and yet here he was ready to shit himself! "I, uh, don't really know where to begin."

"The start." Sound winked mischievously. "I've always found that a good place."

"Right." Bruce nodded, cleared his throat, and was about to begin when the Director interrupted him.

"How are things coming along with the Edinburgh hypersteam case?"

He was suddenly caught in mid-syllable, his mouth locked in an odd pucker that made his lips feel queer. Bruce leaned forward and asked, "I'm sorry, sir?"

"The case you are currently working on, concerning the

134 PIP BALLANTINE & TEE MORRIS

suffragist that disappeared in—oh, goodness me . . ." Sound turned his eyes to his desk, and then began to rifle through a small tray at the corner.

Bruce felt a cold chill run up his back. The tray Doctor Sound was looking through was labelled ACTIVE.

"Ah, here it is! Yes, let me see, how was it described? Ah yes—the witness claimed the woman disappeared 'in a dance of light and show of a Yorkshire summer rainstorm.' What a colourful description," he said, giving a slight chortle. "Witnesses can be rather dramatic when describing what they see." Sound held up the paper before Campbell. "This is my copy of open cases currently being investigated by Ministry agents. At least, the United Kingdom. The most basic of notes, you understand."

"Of course." Bruce tugged lightly at his tie. That tea was taking forever, and he was thirsty. Very thirsty.

"So, how goes the progress?"

"Slow." Bruce had lied to the Director before, in communiqués and closing reports; but face-to-face made him uncomfortable. "Very slow, sir. I've got a few more leads before it becomes a concern, so I'll press on."

"That's a good chap." Sound beamed.

"Thank you, sir," he replied.

"Do let me know when your progress picks up a pace, yes? I find communication is key in running an effective, efficient, and successful ministry, not that I have experience in running other branches of Her Majesty's government apart from this one." He chuckled. "But I doubt my day-to-day administrative goals are hardly of interest to you, a field agent of your outstanding calibre."

And there it was—his opportunity. "Well, Doctor Sound, that is why I wanted to talk to you this morning."

Sound's eyebrows raised slightly. "Oh?"

"Yes." Bruce straightened in his chair slightly, the clock's incessant ticking now fading as he took the lead. "I'm coming up on my sixth year here at the Ministry."

"Good Lord," and Sound gave another small, short laugh

as he added, "has it really been six years? Jesu, the days that we have seen, Master Harry."

Bruce furrowed his brow. "Beg your pardon, sir?"

The Director merely waved his hand, dismissing whatever nonsense he had just babbled. "My apologies for interrupting. Do go on, Agent Campbell."

Bruce took a deep breath, drawing from that confidence he'd possessed when he spoke these words to an empty chair back at home. "Since accompanying you to York, I have been thinking a lot about my job. My place in the Ministry, as it is."

"As it is?" Doctor Sound scoffed. "Agent Campbell, you are one of this agency's most outstanding representatives. I can name several impossible exploits that you have undertaken that go well above and beyond the expectations of myself and Her Majesty. Are you finding your work tedious, of late?"

Bruce blinked. "I'm sorry, Doctor Sound?"

"Well, agents of the home office, I am well aware, are part administrative in their duties. We watch over the satellite offices and are called into action when our brothers and sisters abroad are in need of assistance. We only directly become involved when the situation calls for the elite of the Ministry's finest, or if the case is within the boundaries of the Isles." Doctor Sound leaned forward, his eyes narrowing on him. "Before you came here six years ago, you were serving in the South Pacific branch, and used to immediate employment. You have enjoyed your fair share of assignments here, but it has been a change, hasn't it?"

This was not going well, and rapidly heading in the wrong direction. "No, Director." That wasn't true, and the Fat Man saw right through that. "Well, yes, sir, it has been a bit of an adjustment."

"A six-year adjustment?"

The man's inability to stay quiet and let him speak started chipping away at Bruce's determination. Practicing in front of the chair had been a lot easier.

"No, Doctor Sound, I'm not bored in my position here

at the Ministry. I'm considering—" Bruce had to make this convincing. He gave a slight shrug of his shoulders and finally said, "—a different approach to the Ministry."

Doctor Sound sat back in his chair, his gaze remaining on Bruce. "I see. And our trip to York brought this about?"

"This has been building since I worked with you locating Agent Thorne." Bruce hung his head low. "When we found him in his frail state of mind."

The Director's expression darkened, and his gaze wandered away. Sound was staring out of his large window overlooking the Thames, perhaps trying to find solace or even vindication for his decision that day. "Yes. Rather nasty business, that."

"When you asked me to give a hand in York, I was thinking the same thing I was that night with Harry Thorne: Why me? Then I noticed the gap Harry left behind, and the toll it took on poor Eliza . . ."

"Hmm," and Doctor Sound's gaze suddenly returned back to him. "I think you underestimate your cousin from the Southern Hemisphere. 'Poor Eliza,' as you call her, is performing her current duties as Junior Archivist quite admirably by all reports."

Bruce gave a slight snort, but wiped the smirk off his face when noticing Sound's crooked eyebrow. He pressed on. "Director, and please, begging your pardon if you consider my next words as a slight, I have been given a glimpse of your world, of your responsibilities as Ministry Director. Responsibility that I believe you can no longer shoulder—"

"I crave a pardon, Agent Campbell?" Doctor Sound's tone went from affable to stern in an instant.

Bruce held up his hands as he immediately added, "Alone."

Tick . . .

Tock . . .

Tick . . .

Tock . . .

Tense moments passed between them, and then—had

Bruce taken a breath, he might have missed it—Doctor Sound asked, "Alone, you say?"

"Yes, sir. I see you taking on a great deal. In particular, dealing with the death of one of our own—"

"Death is nothing new to the Ministry, Campbell."

Why did he insist on interrupting him?

He could hear a slight warble in his voice, a control he could feel waning, "Considering the *manner* of Harry's death and the difficulties you face up here, day after day, alone . . ." Bruce straightened in his seat, and said, throwing every ounce of conviction he had in him. "I'm ready to shoulder more responsibility, sir."

Now it was Doctor Sound's turn to blink. Bruce felt a muscle at the corner of his mouth twitch, but he fought the urge to smile. He was pleased with himself. The Director was the type that was hard to surprise.

"Perhaps it was your concern cloaked in an insult, or perhaps I am growing old and my hearing is blasted to hell, but are you telling me that you are interested in an *administrative* position in the Ministry?"

Now he let his smile shine. "Yes, sir. I am."

"You?" Sound asked again. "In *administration*?"

Hearing the disbelief in Sound's voice made him flinch. So he was a man of action. Bruce knew that about himself. That did not make him thick as this pom's clotted cream. Did Sound regard him as some kind of lummox? It was bad enough that Sussex regarded him so dismissively. He did not need that from his superior as well. After all, the training that Ministry field operatives were subjected to tested more than just personal mettle. There were tests of literature, mathematics, and the sciences. True, Bruce had just managed to squeak by those trials, one or two of them yielding to his charms.

Campbell's building tirade was interrupted by the door opening. Miss Shillingworth appeared, pushing a small trolley of a contraption resembling Mad McTighe's automated tea butler, but this model was smaller, less intricate.

His eyes scanned it quickly for the coat of arms of the McTighe household, but he could see no identifying craftsman's crest.

"Ah, the tea!" Doctor Sound beamed at Miss Shillingworth. "Cassandra, your timing is—as always—impeccable."

Bruce started at what he saw next. Miss Shillingworth *blushed*. "Thank you, Doctor."

"Help yourself, Agent Campbell," he said, motioning to the apparatus.

"Yes, sir." Bruce leaned forward and added, "Thank you, Cassandra."

His finger was about to press the service button when his instincts lurched into "flight" mode. He looked up.

Miss Shillingworth's charming blush had disappeared. Completely. Through her spectacles, she shot him a cold, deadly gaze.

Bruce swallowed. "*Miss Shillingworth*," he said gently.

With a heartbeat of a pause, she turned back to Doctor Sound. "Your next appointment is at ten o'clock. It's Sir . . ."

Her voice trailed off as she looked over at Bruce, now watching the contraption's small arm extend, grab a cube of sugar, and then repeat, as the dark liquid poured out of the spout closest to him.

"Go on, Miss Shillingworth," the Director said, motioning with his free hand to continue, while his other was helping himself to tea.

The secretary turned away from Bruce, and continued. "It's Sir William Christie."

"Oh?" His eyebrows raised at the man's name. "Things amiss at Greenwich?"

"He's been noticing odd volcanic activity on Mars."

"Oh dear," Sound muttered, his face darkening slightly. "Ten o'clock, you say? Very well. That will be all." He waited until his secretary left the office, and then turned back to Bruce. "So, what do you think?"

The cup had just reached Bruce's lips when Sound's

question was put to him. He set his cup back on the saucer and shook his head. "Sorry, Doctor, but I was never much a bloke of the sciences. I know Mars is a planet. It's red. And it's not made of cheese, like the moon, eh?"

The tea was a jolt to him. Two sugars barely blunted its sharpness.

"No, I mean what do you think of the life you are considering." He motioned to the door. "You got a taste of it."

Bruce set his tea on the trolley and leaned forward. "I'm sorry?"

"I will admit, the Ministry—even on its limited funding and resources—has grown exponentially in the past decade. Perhaps it is the impending turn of the century that has brought said peculiar occurrences to the forefront of people's minds or perhaps the House of Usher is preparing a dramatic move against the Empire. Who knows? I have noticed, though, more demands upon my person, and I have actually considered the need for an assistant director in the home office.

"You, however—and now it is my turn to ask for your pardon if you take this as a slight—were the last person I would expect to ask for such a promotion, if that is how you would regard such a position."

He felt his pride recoil from that blow. Far from Bruce to back down in a fight. "I assure you, I could handle this job without a fuss. No worries."

"Could you now?" Doctor Sound laced his fingers together as he asked Bruce, "Could you settle for using protocol instead of pistols? Could you commission instead of call on combat? Could you, a man of action, settle for a life in administration?"

What Bruce had planned following Sussex's visit suddenly came to roost, and the undercurrent of panic he had been feeling since taking a seat to wait for the Fat Man now swelled inside him. He was about to give it all up. The travel. The adventure. The women of all fashions, all cultures. All that, gone . . .

. . . and in its place: paperwork, delegation, and meetings with various hoity-toity types.

"One benefit, I'm sure you have considered, is there is considerably less travel involved." Sound smiled warmly. "I suppose this means more time at home with your wife and children. You could finally bring them over to join you here in London."

He hadn't thought of that. *Good Lord, what the hell am I doing?*

Campbell felt his head give a slight nod, but that was the only thing in agreement with Sound. The rest of him was silently insisting that he gather himself together, apologise for a brief moment of madness, and then go back to the field and pick a fight with a group of complete strangers.

Bruce kept at the front of his mind the image of Sussex. The man had a hold on him, and promised to end a life-style that Bruce had grown accustomed to. He continued to remind himself that this was not a permanent assignment. Sussex assured him he would be needed in this new branch of the government that he wanted to helm. Even if Bruce didn't fulfil Sussex's wishes, assuredly someone else in the Ministry would. The difference would be Bruce would be without the Ministry, without his wife and children, and back in Australia. This would truly be . . .

" . . . quite the departure for you, Agent Campbell."

Had Sound been talking to him? Bruce took in a slow, deep breath, and then shrugged with hardly a care showing on his face. "I never blink at a challenge. This opportunity would be a much needed change of pace for me."

"And what of your current case load?"

"Oh that shouldn't be a bother," Bruce said, waving his hand dismissively.

"Even the Edinburgh hypersteam case?"

The Fat Man caught him on that one. "Ah, yes, well, I can easily look into that case while understanding my new responsibilities. As people like to point out, these are massive shoulders. I can handle it."

"Perhaps, Agent Campbell." The politeness seemed to drain from his face the longer he looked at him, and then finally: "I will think on your offer."

Doctor Sound then turned his attention to another folder in the "Active" bin, and continued to sip his tea as he reviewed the notes of whatever case was now before him. Bruce couldn't tell at a glance if the notes were from an agent in this office, or from one of the Ministry's remote offices.

"Doctor Sound?" Bruce asked.

"I'm sorry, was there anything else?"

"No, sir."

He looked up from the open report and smiled. "Very well then. Off you go. As you mentioned earlier, you have leads to pursue."

Bruce nodded and made his way for the door. He stopped just shy of the door handle, and turned back to the Director's desk, his mouth open, ready to offer more inducements to Sound.

"I said I will think on it." He didn't look up, but his voice was even and controlled. "As I consider your proposal, you will serve at the Queen's Pleasure as you have most admirably done in these past six years."

And that was the end of their discussion.

"Thank you, sir," Bruce muttered.

The door latched behind him and now he was back in the waiting area of Doctor Sound's office, Miss Shillingworth's fingers once more dancing along the keys of her Hansen Writing device. His stomach grumbled a bit. Perhaps he could sneak out for a quick snack somewhere close. He snorted, remembering he had the entire morning as Doctor Sound believed he would be out and about chasing leads on a case Bruce had already sent to the Archives.

Bruce then considered, provided he could hold off for an hour or so, if Cassandra would wish to join him for a light repast.

The typewriter keys then stopped. Miss Shillingworth's

head turned slightly. She was not looking at him, but she was regarding him. Somehow, Bruce knew that.

Bruce cleared his throat and passed by the desk, his invitation to Miss Shillingworth for elevensies abandoned. *Hastily.*

As the lift descended to the main offices of the Ministry, Bruce felt himself relax more and more. The seed was now planted and Doctor Sound would think on it. Something in his demeanour suggested he would take the bait. What overworked civil servant would not?

A soft laugh rumbled from his chest. That stuck-up toff Sussex had been right, and he was one step closer to the Restricted Area.

CHAPTER NINE

In Which Eliza and Wellington
Meet Up with Old Friends

Wellington tried desperately not to stare, but he could not help himself.

Pistons pumped and miniature boilers hissed within the inner workings of Alice's prosthetics. Truly modern marvels they were. While granting her walk a bit of pronouncement, the artificial limbs allowed Eliza's maid incredible mobility, her managing of fine delicate tea settings or china finery through an application of push carts. This morning presented more strenuous work as Alice was single-handedly attempting to restore Eliza's apartments back to order. At least the "Caretakers," as the Ministry referred to them, had tended to the tragic corpses, leaving in their wake the remains of what had once been an immaculate dwelling. The Caretakers had also delivered a missive from the Director granting both archivists a day to gather their wits. Eliza, instead of taking advantage of the reprieve as Wellington expected her to do, was out early in the morning. Wellington had somehow managed to sleep through her repast and departure, waking up to the smells of a late breakfast and reminders of Eliza's late-night callers.

Now around this delightful wonder of fortitude and science was Eliza D. Braun's domain, a domain that appeared to be maintained and kept by a staff of four. Only Alice reigned here; and in the short time between his breakfast and joining her in the parlour, she had restored a good portion of Eliza's luxurious apartments to their pristine and fine appearance. These apartments stood as a testament to the public persona that the one-time field agent now archivist-in-training wished to maintain, as well as the skill of her chambermaid.

"Pardon me, Mr. Books," Alice said suddenly as she polished a brass statue of Athena. *Most appropriate for them both*, Wellington thought in passing. "But you're doing it again."

"Beg your pardon?" And that was when he noticed Alice's reflection in the statue. "Oh. Yes. I told you to remind me of when I did that, didn't I?"

"Yes, sir," she answered, nodding as she finished with the Greek goddess.

"My apologies," he said.

"No need for that," she chided lightly. When Wellington had first met her, Alice's speech still carried hints of the past Eliza had rescued her from. Now and again she would slip back to that, but only in moments. In the brief time he had known her, she had come far. "I understand my enhancements put off some."

"Just the opposite, Alice," Wellington returned. "I find them utterly fascinating. While I now know that in your leg you are carrying an impressive firearm, that bit of trivia hardly warrants my impropriety."

Alice turned to Wellington, her smile quite sincere and disarming. This was another unique trait of Eliza's semi-clockwork housekeeper: she was not a fixture or addition to the household. Alice was a breathing entity, and she had a voice.

"Mr. Books, the mistress insists that when I have a question of her, I should ask. If I may be so bold, sir, might I make the same insistence upon your person?"

He unlaced his fingers and rubbed his hands against his knees, considering Alice's kind offer. "Would you mind?"

"Sir, I am flattered by your concern, but really, it might be for the best if you had a question, you might wish to ask it of me as I'll feel much better."

"Better?" Wellington considered that for a moment. "Better in that you answered whatever question I deemed inappropriate to ask?"

"No, sir," she replied. "Better in that you wouldn't be staring at me."

"Ah."

He noticed Alice's eyes catching the sunlight and an odd smile formed on her face. "But sir, would you mind after you ask your question that I ask a question of my own?"

"You? Ask me a question?" He chuckled. "It is not so much improper as it is unexpected, but certainly."

"Very well then. We have an accord." Alice grabbed a broom and started sweeping where shards of glass remained from the shattered window. "Ask me a question."

Wellington finished his tea and set the cup and saucer aside. Then came his first query. "Do you tire quicker? I would imagine manipulating the weight of your limbs carries a toll."

"It did, at first." She moved to the nearest fireplace and began her dusting, sweeping into a small pan remains of figurines no doubt brought back from Eliza's escapades. "Eliza and that clever gent, Mr. Axelrod, were most patient in teaching me how to work with, not against, the . . ." She paused, her brow furrowing. "Oh dear, what is that funny word Mr. Axelrod used? Started with an 'm,' I believe. Mo—"

"Momentum?"

"That's the word—momentum. It was Mr. Axelrod who taught me how to use only a bit of myself and let the momentum carry me along. Like those dandies on the bicycles, you know?" She gave a little chuckle. "He is quite amazing in the sciences."

Wellington sniffed. "That's one word you could use."

"Since then, I've been able to work a bit longer, not that Miss Eliza likes it when I do. But when the spirit moves me, I like to get more things done. Less of a burden on her."

He nodded, and then picked up his cup and saucer. "Tea, Alice. Two lumps?"

"Certainly, sir," she replied, giving a hiss-accented curtsey before moving towards him.

Wellington noted that when Alice quickened her pace, her limp disappeared. Perhaps it was easier for the maid to sprint and run rather than walk. The "cyclist" analogy was making more and more sense.

"So, if needed, you can move quickly."

"Indeed, sir," she said as she pushed the tea cart closer to Wellington. "I am a housemaid, sir, but I also must see to the apartments."

"You mean, as a caretaker?"

On that, Alice afforded a wry smile. "Yes, sir. Something of the sort."

She took the cup, placed two cubes at the bottom of it, and then began pouring.

"Does Miss Braun—"

"Pardon me, Mr. Books," Alice interjected, keeping an eye on the tea. "You did promise me a question of my own."

Wellington opened his mouth in protest, but his mouth shut as Alice pulled away from him. His cup was full, but he could not partake just yet.

"Very well then, Alice." Wellington set his brew aside and sat upright in the couch. "Quid pro quo."

Alice kept her eyes cast down for a moment. Then she shut them, took a deep breath, and when her eyes flicked open they fixed on Wellington Books. It was a look that made him start lightly. Had he been holding his tea, he would have added to the mess Alice was still tending to.

"Last night, one of those harpies had you. Had you dead to rights." She was still as a statue, her eyes never faltering from their gaze on him. "And last night you handled that Samson-Enfield Mark III as if it was God's divine gift bestowed upon you since your birth, sir. The first shot was an easy kill. The second? Sir, that lass was in full concealment. Based on a footfall, you were able to train your firearm on her and execute a lethal shot. There was no luck in that."

Wellington took up his tea and savoured a sip. It did little to soothe him. "And your question, Alice?"

She took a single step forward. "If what Miss Eliza tells me about you is true—and she has never given me reason to doubt her honesty—you and guns are not on friendly terms. What's your game, Mr. Books?"

"A valid question." Wellington's tea and saucer never clattered as he held it before him. He couldn't understand why he was so calm, seeing as his secret was no longer secret. "As much as you want Miss Braun to walk through that door safely every evening, I wish the same thing. I would not hesitate to lay my life down for her. Not just out of duty to the Ministry, but because I . . ." His mind suddenly went blank. Why would he do this again? ". . . because I choose to do so. We are partners. While life in the Archives moves at a more pedestrian pace than her previous exploits, it is that *other* life I have caught glimpses of in our brief time together that has made me feel . . ." And his voice trailed off again.

"Alive, Mr. Books?"

He nodded appreciatively. "Well put, Alice." He took another sip of tea, and then continued. "What is 'my game' then?" He paused, considering the question. "Alice, I have no simple answer to give you other than this. You have seen a glimpse of what I am capable of. So, ask yourself this question—why am I not in the field, but in the Archives, a place that no doubt your mistress has shared her displeasure for spending time there?"

She gave a little shrug, a most curious smile crossing her face. "Well, for the most part."

He inclined his head to one side. "I'm sorry?"

"There are some things in the Archives that have caught Miss Braun's attention."

"Really?" Wellington shook his head. "Damned if I know what they are."

He waited for Alice to recover from the sudden giggle that had overcome her before continuing. "It may not surprise you that I was influential in our escape from the Havelock estate this previous summer."

"No surprise at all," she said, returning to her duties in reclaiming the parlour. "I found it a bit unlikely that Miss Eliza couldn't recall a firefight. She has a mind for such things."

"So why would I, possessing such skills of marksmanship and survival, be down in the Archives, except by choice?"

That question made her pause in her duties. "By choice?" Alice's furrowed brow then relaxed, and her hand went to her chest. "Sir—"

"I wish to serve at Her Majesty's pleasure, but on my terms."

The maid nodded. "I understand."

And what struck Wellington so deeply was that she did. Completely.

"The mistress," Alice began. "She doesn't have an inkling, does she?"

"Your mistress is a superlative field agent, but this secret I have managed to keep from everyone at the Ministry, including our Director." Wellington gave her a warm smile. "I will tell her. When I'm ready."

Alice glanced at the door, and then said, "Beg your pardon, sir, but would you mind if I spoke freely?"

"I have no objection."

With another quick look at the door, she turned to face Wellington, but suddenly she seemed to have a difficult time looking him in the eye. "Miss Eliza is quite special. You can trust her."

"I know." Wellington took a sip, but he still felt cold, even with the drink's warmth in his stomach. "When the time is right."

"Considering what you and Miss Eliza do in secret," Alice said, motioning around them both, "time is not to be taken for granted."

Wellington was impressed with Eliza's tutoring of the young girl. For a house servant, Alice was quite savvy. He could not imagine the anguish she had suffered on losing her legs, but perhaps it had been a blessing in disguise.

He watched her clean for a few minutes longer, and then asked, "Does Eliza ever share mission details with you?"

She gave a bark that Wellington assumed was a laugh. "If I may be so blunt, I dress, sometimes bathe, and—as you now know—stand watch over the mistress when she sleeps. With such intimate knowledge, what do you think?"

He gave a nod. "Well, Miss Braun is hardly one to stand on Ministry policy." Wellington smiled, as he could now, at least for the moment, relax a bit and enjoy his tea. It was, as per usual, perfect. Alice had needed only a few tries before finding exactly how Wellington took it. "She is hardly your average employer, is she?" Wellington asked, setting aside his cup. "She has encouraged from you a rather forward demeanour with her house guests, wouldn't you agree?"

"No, sir, just with you."

He nodded, his lips pursing as he did. "I see."

"In private, though, Miss Braun has welcomed me to speak my mind, be bold in my heart, and remain confident in my abilities."

"Of that, I have no doubt," he said. "I'm curious about what you intend to do if something were to happen to her."

She continued to sweep shards of wood and glass up into the dustpan as she asked, "Whatever do you mean?"

"The risks we are taking . . ." Wellington leaned forward, keeping his eyes fixed on hers. "The Ministry does not know we are investigating this case. As far as they are concerned, we are in the Archives. If they were to find us in the field . . ."

His voice trailed off on that thought. He meant to say,

"If they were to find her in the field . . ." but it had instead come out as it did. They were partners, after all. He had lied for her, and she would—without hesitation—do the same. The little side jobs she carried out while they were away on official Ministry business were easy to cover, but now they were at it again with this case. Or in this situation, *cases.* They were both daring the devil with this little confidence game of theirs.

"I shouldn't worry, sir," Alice said, returning to her dusting by the fireplace. "If Miss Braun were to find herself without need of my services, I have her recommendations and accolades to find me work at another house."

That jarred him back to his original question to Alice. "I'm sorry. Another manor?"

"Well, yes."

"But what about all the choices you have in the world, choices that Miss Braun is encouraging you to explore?"

Alice snorted. "Mr. Books, this is who I am."

A strange dichotomy, Wellington pondered as he watched her return to her work. The girl possessed a voice in this house, under the wing of his partner Eliza D. Braun. His spirited cohort was, no doubt, stressing to Alice the importance of having a say in society and making sure it is heard. As Wellington had observed earlier, Eliza was hardly the average house mistress.

It was a sweet voice Alice was finding, and it would be silenced at any other manor. Even if the women were to receive the vote, the right would never befall on Alice as she was—as his father impressed upon him—merely a contrivance to the manor that, if for any reason was showing counter-productive behaviours, would be replaced. Alice was a house servant, more invisible than a roomful of privileged women all demanding an equal vote in the government. Idly, Wellington wondered if those same women would insist the same right be extended to those "sisters" who cooked their breakfasts, tended to their estates, and served their tea.

"Besides, why would I worry about all that?"

He blinked. She was cleaning up remnants of a full-on assault from assassins using ornithopters, and she didn't find that worrisome or concerning?

Alice, as if reading his thoughts, smiled and said to him, "She has you. I have your promise you'll look after her, make certain she comes home."

Wellington smiled. "Naturally, Alice."

"Well then, there you are, right as rain."

The commotion at the door made Wellington's head turn, and over his shoulder Eliza's face appeared at the door. Her eyes made contact with his, but her greeting was lost in a small "*Whoops!*" as two rows of grime, filth, and boundless energy snaked on either side of her into the parlour of her apartments. The serenity that Wellington had been waiting in was now supplanted by the screams and calls of children. Street urchins very familiar to him, as a matter of fact. They called out to one another in wonder and amazement as they surveyed what little damage now remained to Eliza's flat.

"Children! Children!" Alice called out, clapping her hands over her head. "Line up!"

It brought back memories of his days in the cavalry when he would inspect his regiment. The Ministry Seven, without hesitation, lined up in front of Eliza's fireplace, ranked by height. Little Serena stood to the far left while Christopher stood to the far right. Between them, apparently organised by height, were the others. Wellington looked at the urchins, his eyes going back and forth.

It seemed that this morning was a morning for asking questions.

As Alice reviewed the troops, Wellington joined his partner in the foyer as she hung up her heavy winter coat. He whispered, "Eliza, I have been meaning to ask . . ."

"Oh? Has this been on your mind for some time, Welly?" she whispered back.

His head tipped to one side as he eased into his query. "More like a revelation. Eliza, when are you going to let your Ministry Seven know that they have been dramatically misnumbered?"

Eliza looked at the Ministry Seven, and smiled. "Just noticed, have you?"

"Well, usually I was distracted by something, mainly assuring that my wallet did not take flight while in their company."

"Fiddlesticks, Welly, I told you that your person was completely safe around the Ministry Seven."

"All *eight* of them?"

She gave a sigh and brushed her finger quickly on the tip of his nose. "If you must know, the Ministry Seven have always been, in fact, the eight children you see before you."

His brow furrowed. "And these eight children were able to somehow make you and Agent Thorne see seven where there were eight?"

"In a manner of speaking." Eliza was now looking over them all, a gleam of pride in her brilliant sapphire eyes. "Harry and I discovered that while we did hold out a bit on the Ministry Seven early on, they were not entirely open with us either. Things came to light for us all on one particular case, a haunting that seemed legitimate."

Wellington's eyebrows raised slightly. "A *legitimate* haunting? Really?"

"Hard to fathom, I know; and Harry and I were not entirely convinced. We had set the stage for an exorcism, the nine of us. In the middle of our little sting, the mark got the jump on us."

"Bad luck, that."

Eliza winked at him. "Wait for it. So with all Ministry Seven and their chaperones present and accounted for, our mark—Frederick Fellowes, travelling under the alias of Count Zanzibar, professional medium—called for his men to sever a few gas lines, leave us for a few hours, and then return to untie us, make it appear as death due to unexplained circumstances.

"That was when the spirit awakened. It was their spirit, a

trick of light, smoke, and mirrors, but Fellowes and his fellows were accounted for. I will not lie to you, Welly; Harry and I were both a bit alarmed. The children, however . . ."

"Dare I ask?" Wellington asked.

"We noticed they were grinning. Like Cheshire Cats, the lot of them. Fellowes and his men buggered out double-quick, leaving us to the shrill screams of these illusions. Then the phantasms disappeared and out from behind a set of curtains from where Fellowes worked his magic popped Jonathan."

"And this is significant because . . ."

"Welly, Jonathan was already with us, bound as we all were."

He blinked. "I'm sorry, Eliza. You lost—" and then his eyes fell on the twins. "Just a moment . . ."

"And that was the night Harry and I met Jeremy, the backup who was told by the others to stay in the shadows in case Harry and I called the crushers on them. As Jeremy saw us all in a tight spot, he decided we were indeed loyal to his friends. We found the Ministry Seven as a moniker still appropriate, seeing as we have two for one with the twins."

Wellington clicked his tongue. "You and Agent Thorne must have made quite the incorrigible pair."

Her smile was dark. "You have no idea."

He felt a slight pang on that saucy comment of hers.

They both joined Alice and the Ministry Seven at the fireplace, their expressions a little dismayed at seeing Alice's concern.

"Mistress, these children could be eating better."

"Oh?" Her eyes went to Christopher. "Been sneaking a quartern or two from the *Hunter and Fox*?"

Christopher looked down and away from the others. His shoulders shrugged.

"Rotter," Liam mumbled.

Christopher went to strike him but Eliza stopped him cold with a look. All the children noted Eliza's stern expression, and any mirth they possessed coming in to her apartment, disappeared.

"Gentlemen," she said with authority. "Serena."

No smile of hero worship. The child remained completely still.

"I have asked you to take a few chances with me in the past. This time, things are very different. As you see by the mess, we were attacked last night. And we know who was behind it." She took a deep breath, her eyes touching one of them before she continued. "Diamond Dottie."

Little Serena's hands went up to her mouth, quickly silencing the gasp she made. The boys either shuffled nervously or leaned forward to where Eliza stood, their jaws dropping.

Christopher, the eldest and one closest to Eliza, stood a hint taller. When the boy spoke, Wellington thought his voice sounded a bit deeper than usual. "Are you sure?"

"I wish I had a reason to doubt, but yes, I am most certain."

"And she's the cause of your trouble?"

Eliza opened her mouth to answer, but Wellington interjected. "She's a constant in this case, but that is the extent of it. Nothing more."

A single eyebrow of Eliza's crooked up in a silent reply. Wellington didn't flinch.

"Diamond Dottie sent five of her girls here last night to call upon me. I was fortunate to have Alice and Books standing watch last night." Eliza walked down along the length of the children, speaking as she did. "We are in need of the Ministry Seven; but unlike other jobs you have taken for your Queen and Country, this one may carry consequences that could haunt you in the streets."

Serena and the twins raised their hands.

"A consequence is the result of your actions, such as when a crusher grabs you for nicking a purse," Eliza said.

The three nodded in understanding.

"We're asking you to take on a job against someone who could make your lives very uncomfortable. I cannot ask you all to take that risk without understanding them. If this job has the outcome I think it will, you will have to protect one another when you all are together. If you ever find yourselves alone, you will either be casting glances over your shoulders, or hiding here. Survival is nothing new for you all, I know this; but it's a different sort of life you will live from this day forward. Do you all under—"

"That will do, Miss Eliza."

She looked up into the gaze of Christopher. Wellington could read in the lad's face a deep regret and in his eyes a silent plea of forgiveness. "You have been nothing but kind to us. You've taken us in. You've fed us. You didn't turn your back on us when the rest out there considered us coopered." He looked at the other children, all their eyes on Christopher, and then he turned back to Eliza. "Diamond Dottie's a bludger, to be sure. She and her gang tried a caper on you though. That's a caper against the lot of us.

"Doesn't matter the job, Miss Braun. With the Ministry Seven, you have an accord."

The boy was from the darkest parts of London's back streets, and here he stood with the other urchins, speaking with their voices, pledging their lives in service to Eliza. Wellington felt the smile on his face widen. She did test his limits and try his patience, but she also inspired all kinds of people.

He looked to Eliza, her own hands up to her mouth, her eyes sparkling brightly. She too was moved by the gesture. After that, anything seemed possible.

CHAPTER TEN

In Which Agents of Derring-do Dare a Lioness in Her Den, and Wellington Books Is Slightly Distracted by a Jewel of India

"Show me the note again," Wellington insisted.

He could feel his usual calm wearing completely away. He did not like being dragged out of bed—especially after so much excitement at Eliza's apartments the previous night, or being pulled awake by a rather grubby street urchin. Wellington made a quiet note to himself to begin work on better locks. The fact that the boy had been able to locate his home, and gain access to it with such ease, was terrifying.

It was not as disturbing, though, as what they were about to do.

The note that had been delivered to Eliza's apartments earlier that morning, now in Wellington's possession thanks to one of the Ministry Seven, had been penned by the Protectors' captain, Charlotte Lawrence. She was requesting an audience.

Perhaps that would have been stunning enough, but that shock paled in comparison to where the meeting was to be, where Wellington found himself. His mind could do nothing but process what he witnessed.

Before Wellington and Eliza were a cluster of women wearing nothing more than a hodgepodge of bloomers, corsets, underthings, and even outfits similar to men's boxing leotards, as they sparred in a small dojo located above a perfumery in the heart of London. When he and Eliza had stepped into the confines of this threadbare training facility, he'd immediately felt awkward. As their physical activity grew more ferocious, Wellington felt in desperate need of a bath. A very cold one.

"Welly," his partner cooed, "are you blushing?"

"I could be," he responded, his voice cracking lightly.

Eliza tilted her head and watched the women for a moment. "I suppose that in a real sense they are sparring in their underwear. Surely that isn't causing you distress—I mean you must have seen women in the altogether before?"

Now the Archivist could feel his face flush scarlet. How on earth had their conversation drifted this way?

She snapped her fingers. "Of course you have. At the Phoenix Society on First Night."

He paused, cleared his throat, took in a quick breath and spoke. "My experiences are neither here nor there, Miss Braun, and hardly relevant to present manners from Miss Lawrence's Protectors."

"You claim to be open-minded, but when it comes to the matter of the female form you're quite prudish. Aren't you?"

"Not prudish," he protested. "Old-fashioned. While the Protectors' present dress and demeanour I find—" He watched as one woman gave a sharp cry, picked up her opponent, and dropped her to the ground. Both ladies' corsets were performing well beyond any expectations. "—rather immodest, the training is necessary. But even this much immodesty is a bit much for a gentlemen to take."

"The Sultan didn't complain," she muttered under her breath, though which escapade she was referring to had to remain a mystery, because just then they were interrupted.

"Mr. Books? Miss Braun?" came a smooth voice beside them.

They both turned to see the striking Chandi Culpepper. Wellington felt his breath catch in his chest as her dark gaze jumped between them both. He hoped his appreciation for the beauty she engendered did not show outwardly. He swallowed, trying not to flinch at the dryness in his throat, and cast a glance back at the women practicing Bartitsu.

The lady, or a small den of tigers. Wonderful.

"Miss Culpepper." Eliza, thankfully, oblivious to his awkward admiration, accepted the suffragist's hand and shook it. "A surprise to find you here."

Miss Culpepper motioned to where Lady Francis Pethick stood with another pair of young ladies intently watching the Protectors' training session. "I am merely taking care of our president—it's part of my duties."

"Indeed," Wellington said.

"And you? What brings you to our training session?"

"Not really sure, if you must know." Eliza's mouth tightened for a moment. "Chaz called us here."

"Really?" Chandi nodded as she turned back to the women training in the studio. "With no offence intended, I'm a bit surprised that Charlotte would reach out to you."

"None taken, Miss Culpepper," Wellington said, his mouth twisting into a wry grin. "I think we are just as flummoxed."

The Protectors all let out a collective yell that caused the Archivist to jump. Just as quickly a silence fell over them. Their instructor, the formidable Miss Lawrence, inspected their ranks like a military leader reviewing the troops before a push. It was an intensity Wellington was familiar with, but he'd never seen it coming from a lady.

Chandi gently placed a hand on Wellington's shoulder and said to them both, "Good luck on this unexpected collaboration." Then she joined Lady Pethick and her seconds, reviewing their notes.

Charlotte Lawrence turned about and caught sight of

Eliza and Wellington. Her expression hardened as she strode over to them.

"Come for a rematch, have you?" she asked, looking down at the diminutive Eliza.

"Is that what your invitation to us was? A reason to get me back on your mats?" She glared back. "If you feel the need to be reminded of it, no need to stand on ceremony with me."

"I crave a pardon," Wellington interjected, making both their heads snap in his direction, "but the lingering feud between you ladies can wait. I will assume the invitation was more concerned on the present: protecting the suffrage movement?"

Charlotte and Eliza stared at him for a moment, before taking a step back.

"I did send that invitation, didn't I?" Miss Lawrence asked aloud, considering them both. "Mr. Books, would you care to know more of the Protectors' initiatives concerning these disappearances?"

"Rather," he replied emphatically. "I believe if we can assist one another, maybe combine resources—"

Charlotte threw a towel over her shoulder, and motioned for Wellington to follow as she walked to an isolated corner of the studio. Water ran from the corners of her mouth as she gulped from a tankard, her quenching ending with a long, deep sigh. She turned back to the two agents, using the towel as a napkin as she said, "Sorry, but I tend to get a bit thirsty after working up a sweat."

"No bother, Miss Lawrence," Wellington said, attempting to loosen his collar. "We are at your disposal at present."

"Excellent." She bent down to where she had picked up her tankard, and handed him a narrow, round tin. "There you are. The abduction of Hester Langston."

Eliza looked at the tin, then back to Charlotte. "You recorded the abduction on film?"

"*Yes*," she hissed, her eyes warning Eliza. Wellington followed Charlotte's nervous glances over to Chandi and her fellow officers present. "The disappearance of committee members is not new to us, as you can well imagine. The Protectors began filming meetings, both public and private committee-only ones. We've been doing so for some time now."

"How bloody long have you daft bints been sitting on these rather crucial pieces of evidence?" Eliza still managed to snap at Charlotte, even though her volume was barely above a whisper. "It would have been ducky if you had shared this little detail with us earlier."

Wellington sighed as he considered the tin in his hands. "Rare as it may be, I agree with my partner here."

Charlotte folded her arms. "We couldn't."

"Why ever not?" he asked.

The Protector's head tipped down, as a deep shade of scarlet appeared on her cheeks.

A slow, lingering dawn of understanding crept across Eliza's face. "You didn't tell anyone they were being filmed." Both Charlotte and Wellington turned to her. She merely shook her head. "Isn't that some cheek?"

Charlotte pinched the bridge of her nose and rubbed her eyes for a moment. Finally, she looked to Eliza. "Miss Braun, my charge is to protect the committee and their guests, guests like your countrywoman, Kate Sheppard. And my orders are most clear: by any and all means." Eliza's snort made the imposing woman flinch, but she continued. "It is not as if we recorded anything that was said. Merely . . ."

"Merely meetings of the highest in power of the suffrage movement, and the other women supporting them." Eliza's lips pursed tightly together as she closed the distance between them. "You didn't have a care for any of those women who may have wished to remain anonymous, who would— and still could—pull their support from the movement knowing that you have preserved their involvement with us."

Charlotte peered down the length of her nose at the colonial. "I did what I felt was necessary for the good of the cause."

"Is that what you're calling placing people in harm's way these days?" Eliza bit.

"I believe the ethics of what Miss Lawrence has done is of little consequence, Miss Braun," Wellington chimed in.

Charlotte pushed the last of her sweaty hair out of her eyes. "As long as this investigation is all you use the reels for, and your eyes are the only ones who see them. Braun does have a point—there are influential people at our meetings."

"I assure you," Wellington gave her what he hoped was a trustworthy smile, "we will be most discreet."

With a slight nod, Charlotte turned away and disappeared with Chandi and the executive assistants behind a door labeled CHANGING ROOM. What they would be doing once there was something Wellington could not linger on. It was the subject of far too many scandalous kinetoscopes.

Instead he looked down at the canister in his grasp. The most powerful women of Old Blighty's suffrage movement had no idea they were being filmed. He turned that over and over in his head for a moment. He held in his hands something the authorities would love to have in their possession.

"Charming bitch, isn't she?"

With a start Wellington turned to Eliza. "I beg your pardon?"

"We've been running like chickens with our heads lopped off," Eliza said, pointing at the door, "and Lady Pethick's lead watchdog here enjoys the show until one of the brass boaters suddenly disappears."

Close on her heels, Wellington regarded the tin. "Can't we just be grateful that we have what could be the key to this mystery?"

"And ignore that fact?" Eliza asked, turning to face him. "The reality that she is doing it to make up for failing to protect Hester and the rest?"

He tilted his head. "Does it really matter why she is doing it?"

She glared at him for a moment, and then down at her shoes. "Perhaps not."

Her admission would have been impressive, perhaps monumental in their personal history together, but something else had caught Wellington's attention at that very moment. Was it happenstance that a delicate lace curtain draped in the window across the street suddenly fluttered, catching his eye? In that instance, he could make out suggestions of movement. Then a glimpse of sunlight struck the glass curve of a telescopic device of some kind, and Wellington could make out a pale hand working the lens into focus.

The window he stared at was in line of sight of the studio's other window, to his left. Whoever was over there was not interested in them, but rather in someone else in the dojo.

"Welly?"

Wellington blinked and looked at Eliza, surprised that she was standing so close to him.

"Did you—" Wellington glanced at the window, to Eliza, and then back across the street. "No, I suppose you didn't. You weren't facing the right way."

She frowned. "Everything shipshape?"

Wellington tapped on the pane of glass as he stared at the lace curtain now drawn completely. Someone was definitely moving behind it though. He was certain of that. "We are being watched."

"Oh?" Eliza asked, "You mean the telescope across the street?"

"You saw it?" He exclaimed, somewhat disappointed he'd not caught her off guard.

She was fighting the urge to smile. "While you were enjoying the Protectors, I was taking stock of our neighbours across the street. Third floor, two windows from the right?"

"Yes, but—" Wellington looked out again.

Eliza's fingertips gently took hold of the Archivist's chin and turned him back to her glacier-blue gaze. "A bit of training you didn't receive being in the Archives."

Wellington nodded slowly. "We're not the ones being watched?"

"No, but we should not act hastily."

"Did you catch a glimpse of anyone behind the telescope?"

"Afraid not. Not quite close enough." Eliza pressed her lips together. "That lace curtain must have been a reaction to you at the window." Her eyes narrowed as she considered Wellington. "Did you see anything?"

"I thought I saw—" Wellington swore inwardly. He wasn't really certain enough to share with Eliza. "It was only a glimpse."

"Welly, anything you see, even fleeting, could be useful—if not now, then later." She stepped closer to him. "What did you see?"

How he hated when Eliza did this. When she kept her distance from him, it was far easier to remain focused on the facts, the investigation, and the puzzle itself. At present, all he could see was how very blue her eyes were. He could now enjoy the curve of her mouth as well as the curve of her figure. And filling his nostrils was her scent, a lovely medley of tea, rosewater, and copper.

"Copper?" he whispered.

Eliza's brow furrowed. "What?"

"Do you—" but the question stopped abruptly as they both felt it crawl across their skin. Simultaneously.

Above their heads, a soft crackle echoed in their ears.

"Chandi!" Both agents raced for the door.

Over their footfalls, pops and cracks of electricity could be heard coming from behind it, along with the cries and shrieks of remaining Protectors. Wellington's hand had just touched the doorknob when the final flash blew the hatch outwards. The wood pushed Wellington and Eliza back with a great force that left them gasping. They gathered themselves up and stood stock-still as the door now swung back and forth idly—beckoning them both to enter. At their own risk.

Wellington and Eliza decided the risk was worth taking. Stepping into the small public bath, they both expected the smell of perspiration rather than perfume as this was a changing room for athletic women. What assailed them instead was the scent of warm copper, blood, and charred flesh. The moans of those still alive were soft, but their volume did not necessarily reflect the amount of agony they were experiencing. Wellington's stomach roiled at the carnage. Even the ones who had been shielded by other sisters were trapped under blackened and blistered corpses.

Both he and Eliza searched for the suffragists' sergeant at arms. He felt his hope slip, until a repeating whimper of "They took her," made them both turn.

Eliza knelt by the fallen Protector and felt her forehead.

"They took her," she sobbed again.

Eliza shook her head.

"She means Charlotte," Chandi Culpepper murmured, her own voice quivering lightly as she pulled herself back to her feet. "Charlotte Lawrence is gone."

CHAPTER ELEVEN

In Which Mr. Douglas Sheppard
Springs a Surprise

After the shock of Chaz's disappearance, a spot of tea was definitely called for, as well as a marshalling of the troops. Wellington suggested they regroup at Eliza's apartments—since they were close.

"But how will we get word to the Ministry Seven?" asked Wellington.

Eliza pulled out from her breast pocket what looked like a modest compact, but his eyes went wide when she flipped it open.

"Isn't that—"

"Yes, it is," Eliza said, pressing a large red button within the small interface where makeup would normally be found. A small red light blinked rapidly. "I had Axelrod make me one on a private frequency. Originally it was for Harry. Now it's for the Ministry Seven."

"They are creatures of the back alleys and the streets, Eliza," Wellington said assuringly. "I'm sure they will be perfectly fine."

"I just need to know where they are," she murmured.

Wellington chose not to chastise Miss Braun for her unauthorised use of the Ministry's wireless ETS. The concern in her voice was authorisation enough. It was a maternal instinct that he rarely saw and, he hoped, was not wasted on street urchins. For reason that eluded him presently, this compassion touched something deep in him.

Up the lift and through the door, and there was Alice with her Samson-Enfield Mark III trained on them both. She let out a sigh and replaced the powerful sidearm into her thigh, whispering a silent prayer to God as her leg hissed shut.

"Thank goodness you are all right, miss," Alice began, relief pouring over her face. "When I received the missive—"

"Have the children arrived?" she asked quickly.

"Not as of yet, miss."

"Put the kettle on," Eliza said removing her coat and cap. "Hopefully, we will all be present and accounted for by the time the tea is ready."

Barely had they sat down in her parlour and Alice put the kettle on, when the doorbell chimed. As a trained agent of the Ministry, Eliza did not jump, but Wellington noticed her hand slip under the pillow of the sofa. Goodness alone knew what she kept in there—but it undoubtedly went bang.

Alice hurried off to answer it, Eliza's fingers still dreadfully close to the small silk pillow. When Serena thundered around the corner, Eliza stretched her arms out and wide, allowing the small, grubby blonde girl to run into her tight embrace. She stroked the child's hair, rocking her back and forth while Serena returned the gesture.

"When I saw the red light go off," the child said, motioning to a small button sewn on the inside of her scarf, "I got scared, mum."

"It's all right," Eliza whispered, her eyes welling up with tears, stroking the child's hair over and over again. "It's all right."

The remaining Ministry Seven appeared, and Wellington found himself taking in a sigh of relief at finding all eight of Eliza's street informants present and accounted for.

"What the game, mum?" Christopher asked.

"All is well now, children." Wellington caught Christopher flinching at that, and he failed to understand why. This was *good* news. "It is time, I believe, we let you all know exactly what we are investigating."

While the children scoffed back biscuits and Eliza silently drank her over-sweetened tea, Wellington recounted the disappearances, the repeated sightings of Diamond Dottie, and what could happen to the suffrage movement if Kate Sheppard were to disappear.

"Blimey," Colin whispered. "So no one knows what has happened to these birds what's disappearing?"

Eliza shot the lad a look. "If you mean the ladies that have disappeared without a trace, yes. We have no idea what their fate has been. All we know of for certain is Melinda Carnes."

"So this is Diamond Dottie's caper—snatching big bugs?" Eric scratched his head. "Doesn't sound like her kind of caper at all."

"Eric's right," Callum said, spraying biscuit crumbs all over Alice's tea setting. "She's usually all about screwing, in and out all quiet like. Maybe sometimes she throws a blag."

"And that would explain what happened here with her girls." Eliza spoke over her shoulder to Wellington. "A blag is a smash-and-grab theft."

"Ah," and Wellington returned to his tea.

Jonathan—or was it Jeremy?—leaned over to his doppelgänger and whispered something in his ear. The brother then leaned over to Callum and whispered something to him. "Jeremy says it wouldn't be the first time a kidsman's tried something off the path."

Wellington pointed to the twin closest to Callum. "What makes Jeremy say such a thing?"

Callum shook his head. "No, Mr. Books, that's Jonathan." He then motioned to the other child, identical to his brother in every way, to Wellington; but clearly, Callum could see the difference. "That's Jeremy over there."

How can he tell them apart?

Eliza's hand gently patted his shoulder. "I'll explain later, Welly." She then motioned to Jeremy. "What makes you say that, Jeremy?"

Jeremy leaned over and whispered to Jonathan. Jonathan then whispered to Jeremy, and Callum nodded to them both. "There have been some capers around town we've been hearing about. They all have signatures of skilled cracksmen, but the marks are all wrong."

"I think, if I am accurately deciphering your street gibberish, you're saying the burglaries are out of character for the thieves in question."

"Pretty bright for a toff," Liam snorted.

"Mr. Books is right," Serena piped in. "What about that caper at the museum with all them bones and rocks?"

Wellington's brow furrowed. "The Museum of Natural History?"

"We all had a right laugh about that one at the pub," Christopher said. He ignored Liam's scowl as he continued. "Seems that Fast Nate pinched a fancy ol' rock from the museum, and there we were having a pint with him, and he's all, 'It was such a clean mark I don't remember doin' it.' Fast Nate's more for the manor jobs, you see."

The Archivist shared a glance to his partner. "Interesting. Perhaps, Miss Braun, we should charge the Ministry Seven to ask about, see if there have been capers going unclaimed by Britain's underworld?"

"But what about Dottie?" Eliza asked.

"When one crime is out of character, I would believe it to be a delinquent reaching for something more. If what the children are saying is true, this is not coincidence, but an outside hand. Perhaps Diamond Dottie's, perhaps not." Wellington turned back to Christopher. "Do you believe you could find out if there are other crimes being attributed to confidence tricksters?"

"I think so, yeah," he answered.

"Then while the Ministry Seven look into that," Wellington said, turning back to Eliza, "you and I look at the kinetoscope reels on loan from the Protectors, perhaps dig into that theft from the museum as well. I'd like to know exactly what was stolen."

"Then we have our duties for tonight, yes?" Eliza said, looking around the table.

Nods and soft utterances of "Yes, mum," came from the assembled children.

"Excellent." Eliza then rubbed her hands together as she started to pace behind Wellington. "In the meantime, we should be thinking of getting closer to Diamond Dottie."

"Infiltration?" asked Wellington.

She shook her head. "No time. I was thinking of a visit to her dwellings. A social call, just without the social aspect of it."

Before she could continue, the doorbell chimed. All of them, save for Wellington, immediately went quiet and looked toward the door. He sat in wonderment. Did they really believe Diamond Dottie would ring the doorbell before attacking?

Alice returned to the parlour with Douglas Sheppard in tow, a small bag and what looked like a slender box half the length of his forearm cradled against him. They all relaxed—all except for Wellington who now tensed. Douglas' courageous rescue of his mother—or at least the motivations behind it—still gave him pause, even two days later.

"Good morning, Douglas," Eliza said, rising and smiling.

"Not for poor Charlotte Lawrence," he blurted out, setting the items before him. Then Douglas suddenly became aware of his hat, which he quickly removed. "I'm sorry, Eliza—a dreadful thing to say, but the movement is in quite an uproar, and I am even more certain the so-called Protectors can do nothing to protect my mother."

"Yes," Wellington muttered, "I would have thought that was obvious at the last meeting."

He shot Wellington a look, and then cleared his throat. "When I heard you had been at the dojo earlier this morning, I immediately asked where you were. I was so worried, Eliza."

Wellington watched her earlier demeanour of strategist and field agent melt away.

"Oh, before I forget—" He scooped up one of the trays of biscuits and dumped the remaining few onto an empty plate, then grabbed the small bag which he proceeded to turn upside down.

"*Lollies!*" squealed Serena.

As the younger children dove and reached for the assortment of confections, Douglas chortled and said, "I think we all need something to lift our spirits in such a gloomy time." He then turned to Christopher. "But you, lad—"

Christopher, who had in fact started to reach for the small pile of sweets, paused and looked at Douglas with apprehension.

"When I was your age, boy, I had already taken down my first big game. A Siberian tiger. I remember it as if it were yesterday. I was armed with a bow, a quiver of arrows," he said presenting Christopher with the box, "and this."

Christopher looked to Eliza for a moment and then back to Douglas. He was clearly at a bit of a loss. Wellington, on the other hand, was ready to burst.

"Well, go on!" Douglas motioned to the box. "It won't open by itself. It will need a bit of help."

The eldest of the Ministry Seven pried open the box and then froze. The other children followed suit as Christopher produced a long, menacing hunting knife. One side of the blade had been sharpened to the finest of edges, while the other side sported teeth that could make easy work of any tough material. He noticed in the hilt a small button which he pressed. With a sharp ring, two stilettos shot out from the hilt, making a deadly *V* extending from the base of the double-edged blade.

"I'm sure being a child of the street you need to defend yourself and your fellows assembled here," he said cheerily, motioning to the stunned, silent children. "If that is good enough to help me take down a Siberian tiger, I'm sure it can handle an unwanted thug or two."

Christopher's eyes never left the blade. "Thank you, guv."

"If you like, I can show you how to use it properly. That way, no one will liberate it from you, eh?" He motioned to the box. "The scabbard is in the box."

"Just what every lad needs," Wellington said, his voice piercing the unexpected silence amongst the gifts, "a weapon that could either get him arrested or killed."

"As these children know, Mr. Books, these are dark times. We need to defend ourselves and the ones we love. Which brings me to the reason I am here." The explorer's eyes turned to Eliza, and the sight of her, even in her masculine wear, seemed to rattle him. He smoothed out the front of his suit, checked his watch, and then hooked his thumb in the vest pocket as he began. "In light of what has happened, what with the Protectors now without their captain, we need to regroup. We both know Mother will not surrender, but I believe today's events leaves the responsibility of protecting her to us." He gave a shy smile and asked her, "Would you care to chat with me about my mother and her well-being say, over dinner? Tonight?"

Eliza blinked.

Alice blinked.

As did Wellington and the Ministry Seven.

"Dinner?" Eliza finally stuttered.

"Let's call it meal between old friends. The topic of conversation, of course, being the well-being of Mother. It would mean a great deal to me, knowing your mind on this matter."

Eliza looked back at Wellington, and then back to Douglas. "Well, I—"

"—have reservations tonight at the *Bird's Eye View*, at six."

"The *Bird's Eye View*?" Eliza gave a nervous laugh. She was the only one in the room finding anything remotely amusing. "But it's close on nigh impossible to get a table there."

"I have a few connections in London. To be frank, my books have opened more doors than Mother's causes."

The man was growing more arrogant by the moment. Wellington remained glued to his seat, even as this little tableau played out before him. He barely noticed when Alice topped off his tea.

Then, as his fingers searched for his teacup, as he waited for Eliza to explain that she already had previous plans for the evening, Wellington watched in horrified wonder as Eliza D. Braun blushed. She actually *blushed*!

"I would be delighted, Douglas," Eliza murmured. "I can't think of a better way to discuss pressing issues of Kate's security."

"I can," Wellington's mouth blurted out. The Ministry Seven remained stock-still, silent as a collection of grave robbers.

Eliza ignored his comments as she took his hand and nodded.

Douglas replaced his hat, giving his lapels a light tug. "I take it, as per usual, you won't let me pick you up at your apartments?"

"I haven't changed that much—I'll meet you there."

"I hope one thing has changed. I hope Ministry business won't keep you away from our appointment?"

"Certainly not, Douglas."

Wellington stared down at the teacup. It looked as if he would be reviewing those secret reels tonight. Alone.

"Children," Eliza said, her voice lighter. "I think you all should have a good hot meal tonight. Seeing as I will be otherwise engaged this evening, I'll have Alice serve up something nice for you all. We will talk about the matters concerning Diamond Dottie another time, yes?"

No one answered her.

"Capital. If you all will excuse me then, I need to change for the impending evening." Muttering what sounded like a preparation list for a grand night out, Eliza disappeared into the corridor Wellington knew led to her bedroom.

The silence felt thick and oppressive—at least to the Archivist. Wellington polished off his tea, and then collected his walking stick still propped by the couch he had slept across on the fateful night. A night when he had defended her in secret. "Well then, I suppose I will be off to the Archives, seeing as I have some evidence to tend to."

His hat suddenly appeared in front of him. He looked up to Alice. Not secret to everyone, he recalled.

She looked back to where Eliza had disappeared and then turned back to him. "Is there anything you'd like me to convey to the mistress?"

"To be frank, Alice," Wellington said, taking up his bowler and slipping his winter coat across his back, "I doubt if she would hear anything clearly right now. When she is more focused, tell her I will be more than happy to review a strategy with the Ministry Seven and Diamond Dottie. Until then, I will be retiring for the night. Alice, children . . ." He placed his bowler on his head, lightly tapping its crown. "Good day."

"I'll see you to the door, old chap!" Douglas chimed cheerily.

Oh, Wellington thought to himself, *Lovely. I do hope there are no Siberian tigers between the parlour and the door.*

The Archivist slapped on a final smile for Alice and the Ministry Seven before heading to the door with man-of-the-world Douglas Sheppard at his side.

They remained quiet while waiting for the lift. Once Douglas shut the gate and pressed the button for the main floor, Wellington spoke up.

"The gifts were a very nice touch."

Douglas looked confused for a moment, but then that same smile Wellington had seen the night he rescued his mother appeared. "They were. Weren't they?"

How he wished he had his auralscope with him. It was apparent Wellington was now enjoying an audience with the real Douglas Sheppard. "So how did you know about the children?"

Douglas gave a soft laugh. "Well, I have spent many days and nights tracking big game, so it would stand to reason that I would do the same for someone I still treasure."

A chill passed though him. "You have been watching us?"

"No," he said, his smile bright and honest, "I've been watching over my Eliza. I need to, seeing as no one here can. Believe me, neither you nor those guttersnipes upstairs really know her. You just don't." The lift shuddered to a halt. "But cheer up, Mr. Books. Tonight you have nothing but time to take care of the investigation. No need for my little Eliza to trouble herself with all that bloody fact-checking." Douglas opened the gate and saw himself out. "Be seeing you, old chap!"

Wellington Books remained in the lift, the silence threatening to smother him. It would be his word against Eliza's past, and Douglas Sheppard knew it.

A pang of regret formed bitterly in his mouth. He had finally found a chess player worthy of his own skill, and that opponent was a right bastard rivaling that of his own father.

"Dash it all," he swore, his words echoing in the hollow space around him.

CHAPTER TWELVE

Wherein Old Lovers Hold Old Secrets

$\mathcal{D}$ouglas always wanted to pick her up at her apartments, but Eliza couldn't quite trust herself. Like in the Ministry it was best to arrive early and choose your ground. What Douglas might mean by asking her to dinner in such a public way she could not judge.

As she got ready for the evening out she felt as if she were preparing for battle. But she was not buckling on her armour alone.

"The *Bird's Eye View*," Alice murmured to herself as she laid out a dress on the bed for Eliza. "Very grand, I am sure." Her clockwork leg chattered to itself as she went to the dressing table to open the drawer of jewellery. "I wish I had a fancy gent to take me out on the town."

Eliza was already in her underthings, soft silken garments that made her feel genteel and feminine. It almost matched her pensive mood.

"Ah, Alice," Eliza said, smoothing out the midnight blue satin of the dress, "I know you have your own set of admirers who'd be willing to take you wherever you like."

Her maid snorted. "Billy can't afford it, and I swear I'd never let Frank get what he'd want if he took me to such a place. No, Miss Eliza, I shall stick to my eel-jelly or fish and chips and be happy about it. Still . . ." she began as she pulled out the velvet jewellery box, undid the clasp, and flicked it open, "I can enjoy you going there, eating your fill and telling me all about it."

Their relationship was certainly not typical of a mistress and her maid, but then neither of them were exactly typical. Eliza with her clandestine work in the government and her love of explosions made her anything but an average woman. And Alice, with her poor upbringing and her clockwork prosthetics.

Yet, Eliza knew, they were a perfect pair—and she did enjoy sharing her goings-on with Alice. She had very few lady companions in London, and none that could be as discreet as Alice.

"I shall tell you of every morsel that passes my lips," she said, undoing the buttons on her sleeves.

Alice nudged her, "Oh, I wouldn't go that far!" and then broke into a gale of giggles. "Mr. Douglas Sheppard is quite the dashing gentleman—and he did make quite the impression on the children."

Eliza knew she was blushing.

"Now tonight, don't you fret about them." Alice bent and briefly lifted her skirt to reveal one gleaming brass leg. Alice's fingers brushed by the handle of the pistol sheathed in among the clockwork. "I am always prepared for whatever the world may throw against us."

As Eliza slid a tiny pistol into her garter belt, she said, "As am I."

"Expecting trouble from this gent then?"

"Not from him," Eliza smiled, "but I have found in the life I live that it always pays to prepare for the worst—at the very least a street thug might appear."

"I think you are going to the wrong end of town for that, miss." Alice helped her step into her dress and began the task of doing up all its tiny pearl buttons.

"Such high society is not my usual environment," Eliza

reminded her. "My parents are still pulling pints at their hotel—and honestly I wish I was back there many times."

Alice pressed her lips together—Eliza had told her this often enough. "You are lucky, miss—to know where your folks are." Her hands fumbled on the buttons, and Eliza felt like a fool. She had rescued the younger woman from the poorhouse where she had been placed after her own parents had abandoned her. Alice's accident had seemed to be a stroke from a cruel god. Eliza had taken it upon herself to remedy that.

So she turned about and squeezed Alice's hands. "Once the Ministry Seven have finished their dinners and left, take the night off." She slipped a coin into the maid's hands. "And how about *you* take Billy somewhere grand. It's a new age after all, Alice."

The younger woman's smile was broad and wicked. "That it is, miss." With a hasty bow she took her leave.

Eliza looked into the mirror at what they had created. She was still young, but not as she had been when last Douglas had taken her to dinner. The midnight blue dress she had picked with care—he had always admired the colour on her. She still recalled how he had whispered that it made her eyes blue pools that could drown a man.

Back then, such compliments had made her blush and stammer. She wondered how she would react should he say the same tonight. In New Zealand there had been such sweetness to their courtship, but back then she had been quite a different person. Still a little reckless, but in the way of a young woman not yet as familiar with black powder and explosions.

Looking directly into her own eyes she spoke softly, "Bloody fool!" Then she smiled. Douglas might have surprised her with his invitation to dinner, but she had a surprise waiting for him in turn. It simply would not do to dare being alone with the paragon of New Zealand manliness. No, not indeed.

Then, snatching up her tiny jewelled purse, she made for the door.

The *Bird's Eye View* was quite the newest way to see London—and though she didn't say it, Eliza was impressed that Douglas had managed to get a booking at such short notice. Four small airships bobbed in their moorings, quiet and awaiting passengers. These were pleasure craft meant for local journeys, with room enough for only twenty or so people in the accommodations beneath.

Eliza jumped down out of the carriage and stared up at them. The trepidation growing in her chest was not their fault, but they did give her something to focus on.

"Quite a sight, aren't they?"

She spun around and glared at Douglas. "Have your customs changed so much that you enjoy frightening women?"

He tipped his hat to her. "As if anything so minor as my voice would scare the redoubtable Miss Eliza D. Braun."

She was just about to reply when she heard her name called from a little distance. At the sound of Ihita's greeting Douglas' eyes widened.

"I hope you don't mind," Eliza whispered. "Since you said it was a dinner between friends I thought to invite a couple of mine." It was quite insulting, but then she felt in need of some backup.

Ihita, wearing a breathtaking tangerine sari accented with gold threads and what appeared to be tiny medallions, practically skipped up to them. The perfect gentleman, Douglas regained his balance quickly.

"Ah yes," he smiled. "I recall you were with Eliza buying sandwiches. Any friend of hers is indeed a welcome addition to our party."

"A party is it?" Agent Brandon Hill appeared on the other side, and Eliza couldn't help the small smile of triumph sketching itself on her lips.

The second time Douglas did not look surprised, but Ihita's cheeks flushed red and her gaze shot to Eliza. Brandon was dressed in an exquisitely tailored evening suit, his car-

riage making many of the ladies turn and take notice. The
Inverness overcoat was a very nice touch, Eliza found, and
made the eccentric agent look exceptionally dashing.

Eliza winked at her friend, and hoped she recalled that
she'd promised not to interfere. As she made another round
of introductions between the men, Eliza congratulated herself. In one step she had taken care of one of Ihita's problems and one of her own. Her friend pined after the curious
charms of Agent Hill, and Eliza was no longer alone with a
man whose charms she knew very well.

"We shall make quite a jolly group," Douglas' recovery
was almost superhuman. No one looking on him would ever
guess that he had not planned the whole thing.

"Only four is it, Eliza?" Brandon whispered to her. "You
said it would be a party when we spoke this afternoon." His
eyes were pretending to be stern, but twinkled with a barely
withheld enjoyment. Agent Hill was much like her—he enjoyed the rush and the excitement of fieldwork. Yet he'd been
stuck in London for the last month going as quietly mad as
she was in the Archives. Inviting him along tonight had
served multiple purposes, but it had also been a kindness.

"Maybe my mathematical skills aren't all that," she murmured back. "But I think the company will make up for it." In
response he glanced over at Ihita. She did look lovely tonight.
Eliza began to reconsider her earlier judgement. Maybe Brandon wasn't as blind as she'd said, because when he turned
and looked at Ihita no one could mistake the slight lifting of
his lips. He knew full well how beautiful and charming Miss
Ihita Pujari was. It had not escaped his notice.

In the midst of all these strange disappearances and con-
fusing feelings, Eliza was glad that someone was moving
towards happiness.

"Indeed." He tipped his hat, and walked over to join the
conversation between Douglas and Ihita. They really did
make a striking couple.

The four of them set off towards the gangway. Ihita took
Brandon's offered arm, and Eliza did the same with Douglas.

Her fellow New Zealander smiled wickedly. "I recall how you used to watch the airships from your father's house. You used to say you would ride one when you were older."

"I said a lot of things back then—I was an exceedingly foolish girl."

"And the most beautiful in two hemispheres." Luckily he did not mention that he had said the same thing when he'd proposed.

Brandon and Ihita were polite enough to drop back a little.

"Oh, Douglas," Eliza whispered. "You are exaggerating. You thought my sister Anna was far prettier than I."

"Nonsense!" He looked positively outraged. "She might be considered the most lovely girl in Auckland by many, but I never held with it myself."

"I should very much like to meet your family," Brandon chimed in. "The stories they could tell of the young Eliza Braun? It would be most . . . educational."

"Are they all like you?" Ihita squeezed her arm.

Every one of them laughed, and she felt the sting of it. At the mention of the family she had so rashly lost, Eliza felt a pierce of grief. Letters were not nearly enough.

"Mr. Hill, I could tell you plenty of stories!" Douglas began, but before he could elaborate, Eliza tugged on his arm.

"Come along—I am ravenous!"

All four of them trouped up to the small craft with the name BIRD'S EYE VIEW written on the keel in flowing golden letters. The captain at the prow tipped his hat to them as they entered, and looked ready to leap to service immediately. Still they were civilised beings, and took their time entering this luxurious dining establishment.

Thick red velvet drapes framed the large windows while jewel-coloured Turkish rugs spread over the teak floor. Over each of the white-draped tables gleamed a crystal chandelier lit with the newest sealed electric tubes.

"Delightful!" Ihita breathed, and from the child of a

raja—even one that had run away to join the Ministry—that had to mean something. Douglas went over to the imperious-looking maitre'd and had a whispered conversation.

When he strode back to the other three, there was the hint of a smile in the corners of his lips. "They're able to accommodate our new party, but unfortunately only at two smaller tables."

Check and mate, Eliza, his gaze told her.

She crooked her eyebrow at him, but would not kick up a fuss. Instead she turned to Ihita and Brandon. "I hope you don't mind."

The look Hill shot her friend made Eliza suspicious that perhaps he was starting to get the point of the evening. "I am sure Miss Pujari and I can find many topics of conversation." He held out his arm and gestured towards the table that a waiter was indicating.

Douglas and Eliza were taken to a nearby table, close enough so that they were within polite eyesight of the others, but not so close that they would easily overhear each other's conversation.

As the waiter placed the pure white linen napkins on their laps and handed them the menus, the ropes were released and the *Bird's Eye View* slid up into the sky. The agent felt the familiar dip of her stomach and the slight racing of her heart. She loved air travel—and found it the closest thing to taking wing herself.

They were seated near one of the tall windows and for a few minutes they were lost in the transformation. The distance stilled London's noise, and smoothed away the chaos of the great city. Even the Thames was beautiful from up here; going from unforgiving purveyor of sewerage and trade to a glistening silver ribbon. She had seen it before many times, but each was like the first. The lights twinkled and the city became a fairytale place. Eliza and Douglas watched as London rolled out beneath them. If either of them had been a poet, perhaps they would have been able to create words to match the moment.

"Quite a grand sight," Douglas finally murmured, his eyes still on Eliza.

"The grandest the Empire has to offer." If Wellington had been there she definitely would not have said that. She preferred him believing she was totally miserable in both her new city and her new position in the Ministry. It was far more fun that way.

The waiter gave a demure cough, and they took the very subtle hint. It was time to order. Douglas examined the menu, before offering, "The menu by necessity, is limited— but quite marvellous. We had the fish here last week, and I would highly recommend it."

"What? The son of New Zealand's leading suffragist trying to tell a perfectly capable woman what to order?"

"Oh tosh," Douglas leaned towards her across the tiny table. "Mother would never forgive me if I ignored all my upbringing and didn't at least give you my opinion. I confess I believe civilisation would fall if we had to give up proper behaviour. You may have the vote back home, Eliza, but you are still a lady."

She pressed her lips together at that. Across from them, Brandon and Ihita were engaged in animated conversation, laughing, with their eyes fixed on each other. Eliza recognised that look and the accompanying feelings. It felt so long ago.

In the awkward silence, Eliza and Douglas ordered lobster bisque to be followed by the roast beef, and she was grateful the entree arrived so quickly. It was served in fine porcelain bowls and smelt delicious. As she dipped in her soupspoon, from back to front as she'd been taught by Kate, she wondered how many details about that last dreadful incident in New Zealand the suffragist had imparted to her son.

Eliza enjoyed the soup, which was perfectly prepared and beautifully seasoned; and as she took her time with the first course, she examined Douglas closely, covertly. Time had not really changed him, and that made her smile. She wondered if she looked any different to him.

"I was in the Bull and Bear shortly before we departed." His sudden revelation caught her by surprise and she dropped her spoon into her plate with a clatter. Douglas slid an envelope across the table. "I nearly forgot about it, truth be told, but your mother gave me this since she was somehow positive we would run into each other."

Inside was a picture of her family: Mum, Dad, Grace, Gerald, and Nora. The only people missing from it were Herbert, still locked away in the asylum, Anna who was happily married and living in Napier, and herself. Eliza swallowed hard. Though there were regular messages from her parents, and even the odd photograph, this was a new one. Nora, only four when she had been cast out of New Zealand, looked so grown-up. Would she remember her sister Eliza?

"Thank you, Douglas." Eliza, swallowing against the tightness in her throat, tucked the photograph into her purse. "I can't tell you how much it means to me that you took the time for that."

Finishing his soup, he dabbed at his mouth. "I go in there quite often actually. It is still the best pub in Auckland after all. Your father keeps a well-ordered establishment. In fact he's talking about getting one of those McTighe bars in, and buying another place further south . . . maybe in Christchurch."

"Oh yes, he says Auckland is getting too big for him—but I don't think he will ever do it." Eliza smiled. "Unlike myself, my father really doesn't like change."

Douglas leaned back and the waiter cleared the soup course. "Well, it's a good thing that you do. Otherwise this whole escapade would be quite unbearable." He waved his hands to include the airship, the food, and all of London. "And the movement would have lost one of its greatest champions."

It was quite a statement, but one Eliza knew was not entirely true. "Champion? Come now, most of the English suffragists can't stand me, and most of the New Zealand ones never even knew what I did to help your mother."

Douglas' eyes met hers. "But she does, and Mum believes you can help find these women, and who is behind these abductions."

"Yet she must keep her distance as my own reputation within the ranks of the London suffragists precedes me." Eliza folded her hands on her lap. "I understand."

They paused their conversation while the waiter refilled their crystal glasses with good Spanish wine, and served them roast beef and potatoes. Eliza could detect hints of rosemary in the sauce, but at that moment the food did not have her attention.

Douglas didn't notice, too busy looking uncomfortable, but eventually he met her gaze. "That is the nature of your personality, isn't it, Eliza? We both know that you make people uneasy. You enjoy it, in fact." He took a sip of his wine and waited with one raised eyebrow for her reply.

Her thoughts darted once again to Wellington. "Maybe. But by doing that, sometimes it moves things along. Poke someone enough and they reveal truths they prefer were hidden."

Douglas gave a slight chuckle, and nodded. "No, my sweet Eliza, you have not changed that much after all, now have you?"

A shudder passed through her when he called her "my sweet Eliza," and she could feel her cheeks burn at his words. *No, I haven't changed that much, but I miss home. I miss it so,* she thought in earnest.

Eliza looked at where his hand rested. It was so close. She felt her fingertips itch.

"So, what can you tell me about your investigation?" he asked suddenly.

The itch subsided. Taking up the glass of wine in the hand wanting to feel Douglas' own, she leaned forward and asked, "Do you know a person called Dorothy Bassnight? Or Diamond Dottie?"

Douglas frowned. "No, I think I would remember someone with such a dramatic name."

"Well, if she didn't tell you her proper name, you probably remember seeing her. As tall as a man, and excessively dressed even at a meeting—silks, furs, and enough jewellery to sink a ship?"

Her former lover was not so much of a dunce that he missed such a brilliant creature among all the deliberately dowdy suffragists. "Oh yes, her! Quite the strapping woman. She could probably give even me a good go in the ring. Do you think she has something to do with this whole mess?"

Eliza finished her wine, and then placed her silverware on the empty plate that had held her very excellent dinner. The waiter with his eagle eye immediately cleared away her plate. "Well, she is one of the most powerful women in the city. She runs a huge gang of female thieves and thugs known as the Elephants. They in turn are part of an even wider criminal organisation that takes in all of London. A very strange woman to be attending one of these movement meetings, wouldn't you agree?"

"Perhaps she is interested in having a say too," Douglas offered.

"More like scoping out the territory. At the very least she could be sizing up the ladies there as marks for robbery—at the worst she could be involved in something that the larger gang has planned."

"This is delightful, Eliza." Finally Ihita found her voice. She leaned over and spoke slightly louder than was polite. "Thank you so much for inviting me . . ." She cleared her throat. "I mean . . . us."

"Don't mention it," Eliza replied. "Excellent food is only improved by excellent company." It was something she'd heard Kate say often. Douglas grinned a little at that.

At least someone was having a good time. Apart from their surroundings, Eliza felt as though she'd been balanced on a knife's edge throughout dinner.

Douglas raised his hand slightly, and the waiter brought over the dessert—a trembling plate of blancmange. It looked both sinful and erotic to Eliza, and she managed not to giggle. This was, after all, serious business.

"So you'll question this delightfully named Diamond Dottie?" He leaned closer to her over the table, his smile a bit rakish. "Perhaps enquire about some fashion tips?"

For a second they were both back in New Zealand, trading little jibes. She stuck out her tongue at him—a reflex gesture that hearkened back to her childhood. She swallowed after doing it, and felt herself go red again. "I don't think that I will be taking advice from Miss Diamond. Her tastes are far more extravagant than my own—and besides, she is not someone you just go up to and question. She tends to have her own bodyguards about."

"Armed men?"

"No." She smirked a little. Even this son of a leading suffragist leapt to the default position—when he had so much experience of how things could be. "Think more of the movement's own protection."

"Ah." He was perhaps imagining the sticks, the yelling, and the rather fearsome results those ladies were known for. "I can see that might be a problem for you. Does that mean you'll need to call in people from the Ministry to assist?"

Eliza raised her finger. "I still have some mysteries, Douglas, and though you may know a tiny bit about my employer, I think it best I not share all of its secrets. They tend to frown on that sort of thing." She thanked the waiter for the topping off her wine and smiled at Douglas, taking the glass up. "Let's say that I have a plan or two that should do the trick. I imagine within the week we will have an answer as to what has happened to the women."

Douglas smiled. "You always were so very sure of yourself, Eliza."

As the sip of wine settled in her stomach, she began to wonder about how true that was. "Not all the time . . . not when it came to you."

Once the waiter had done his work and retreated to the

sideboard to stack the dishes, Douglas leaned forward in his chair and held out his hand to her. "We all have regrets in life, Eliza. What is important is that we don't look back, but keep moving forward."

Moving forward. A quaint notion, Eliza thought, taking his hand, *but I want so very much to go back*.

This time, they both turned their attention to the grand window, and she felt his hand tighten over hers. She cleared her throat, staring out at the lights, but not really seeing them. Her heartbeat was erratic, her thoughts in chaos.

She shot a glance over her shoulder and observed Brandon promenading with Ihita on the other side of the deck. What had meant to be a jolly dinner party had somehow turned into an intimate evening for two couples. Her best attempts to scupper Douglas' plans had certainly not worked out. This would not do at all.

"In order to move forward I must solve this case, and I must make arrangements between myself and Miss Bassnight. Can we land please?" She knew she was snapping and really didn't care.

A dark look washed over Douglas' handsome features but he nodded. It was a simple enough thing to do; one quick conversation with the pilot through the brass mouthpiece attached to an articulated hose, and the *Bird's Eye View* tipped her nose down.

"All good things must end," Eliza spoke as brightly as she could while walking towards her fellow agents. "Perhaps for the better. Some urgent Ministry business . . ."

A slight frown crossed Brandon's face—surely he was wondering what sort of "urgent business" could originate from the Archives—but he did not comment.

"I should be going too," Ihita broke in, her face slightly flushed. "My landlady is quite the dragon about me arriving in late."

The four of them watched in an awkward silence as the airship began its circling descent.

"Can I see you again, Eliza?" Douglas finally whispered into her ear, and by his tone she could tell he was feeling the same stream of odd emotions. The feeling of his breath on her naked skin sent chills scampering down her spine.

She bit her lip, and thought about replying, *What would be the point?* but something stopped that answer. Instead she nodded. "Once I have Diamond Dottie's story, that would be lovely."

"It's a strange world," he said, his hand tightening on her waist, "that brings us back together under such dire circumstances."

She shot a glance at Ihita and Brandon, but they were sharing a few intimate words themselves. "You always were the optimist, Douglas."

The *Bird's Eye View* released her ropes; and its patrons watched as underneath them, ground crew scurried about as dancers in a ballet and tied her off. Powerful winches then began to pull the airship into her dock. Together the four of them walked down the gangplank and back towards a rank of hansoms, settling into slightly uncomfortable pairs.

"Let me at least see you to your apartments." Douglas' dark eyes sparkled from beneath the brim of his top hat. Eliza was remembering other things about Douglas. His passion. His strength. Pleasant as it might have been to dive into that pool once more, she knew from experience that there were plenty of rocks lurking in those depths.

"That's very sweet of you." She patted his arm. "But I have some work to do tonight. I will get my own hansom, thank you."

"And what about you Miss Pujari—would you like me to accompany you to your redoubtable landlady?" Brandon's voice held none of the seductive lilt that Douglas' did, but Ihita still stumbled over her next words.

"No, no . . . there's no need for that. I found my way from India to London well enough. I can make it home by myself." She went to hail herself another hansom, but her hand froze just as it reached eye level. She then turned to Brandon and smiled, "But I do know of a place where we can, perhaps, enjoy a lovely nightcap. Would you care to join me?"

"Oh, that sounds delightful!"

"And Eliza," she began, holding a stern finger at Eliza that was tempered by a delighted smile, "Thank you for a lovely evening."

"My thanks too." Brandon tipped his hat, offering Ihita his arm. "A fine night of dining and"—he winked—"opportunity." Then they both strode off into the night, apparently intending their evening to continue until they were done with it.

A corner of Douglas' delightful lips lifted, but he knew better than to argue. He tipped his hat and gave her a little bow before hopping into the closest hansom. "Then I shall see you soon. As always, it has been a delight."

As she watched him drive away she smiled herself. She did not want this evening to end.

Sadly, she had to remember where she was. Not Auckland or Wellington. But London. "You can come out now, Christopher."

There was a moment of silence, and then the oldest member of the Ministry Seven appeared from behind a stack of barrels, looking deeply unhappy about being spotted. Eliza's network of street urchins might be unkempt and living rough, but they also saw and penetrated a side of the city that even she could not. Christopher was perhaps fourteen years old, but he was a fine pick-pocket and knife fighter—if it came to that. He was not the best at concealment.

"And where's Eric?" She tried now to hide her smile. "I know you two partner up most times, and he *is* a bit better at making himself invisible than you are."

The younger boy popped up from under a stack of tarpaulins. Just how he had managed to wriggle in there without her noticing was the great unknown. His gap-toothed grin said he wouldn't be revealing any secrets today.

"Blimey, miss—how long have you known?" Christopher grumbled.

She touched his shoulder. "I saw you slip on the back of a cart as we turned the corner in our carriage. But don't feel ashamed . . . I was looking specifically for you."

Eric darted up pulling off his cap. "But you didn't see me, did you, miss? I was on the same cart, but underneath."

His older colleague scowled even deeper and stuffed his hands into his pockets.

"Now tell me." Eliza's voice grew sterner. "What are you doing following me?"

The boys shared a glance before Eric blurted out, "It was that bloke you was with, mum. We wanted to keep an eye on you—in case you got into trouble."

"What? Douglas?"

"He comes in the middle of our meeting, giving out lollies and such." Christopher then looked around and unsheathed the imposing hunting knife Douglas had bestowed upon him. "And do you have any idea what the bloody crushers would do if they found this on me?"

Eliza shook her head. "Lads, that is hardly a reason to distrust Mr. Sheppard."

"What about his invitation after you agreed to work with Mr. Books tonight?" Eric asked. "We was thinking he had some sort of, you know, one of those peculiar devices what tinkers with your head."

From the mouths of babes. She *had* promised Wellington to work with him this evening on the case.

"I tell you what, lads," she said, dipping into her purse and pulling out a few shiny pennies. "I will make my apologies with Mr. Books first thing tomorrow, but this is for your trouble and assurance that you will not follow me in such a manner again. Agreed?"

The boys' smiles were wide, and the coins were whisked away so quickly it was as if they had never been. "You're the governor, Miss Eliza." Christopher tipped his hat, in the same way Douglas had. Then the two members of the Ministry Seven disappeared into the darkness.

Eliza sighed. She had tried many times to get the urchins

to move in with her, like Alice—but they loved the freedom of the street and were fiercely proud of their independence. She could understand that, but hated to imagine them enduring the daily dangers that London streets offered.

Still, that was where she was going; down into the dark after Diamond Dottie, Queen of the Thieves.

Wherein Sussex Is Called Before the Maestro

$\mathfrak{B}$y the time the second note arrived to remind him of his appointment, Sussex had almost convinced himself that his tormentor was in fact ready to leave him alone. He had taken luncheon with Her Majesty on Saturday, driven his boys to the ice skating in Regents Park immediately afterward, and even accompanied his wife to a totally dire dinner party at Lord Childs' City apartments that evening.

That was until he was getting ready to retire for the day. Ivy had already retreated to her own rooms, complaining of her usual headache brought on by far too much exertion. His valet was unfastening a fine pair of silver cufflinks when Fenning knocked at the bedroom door. Valet and master shared a shocked look. Disturbing Sussex's evening ritual was something that the redoubtable butler had never done before. A moment after that realisation, the Duke of Sussex immediately remembered the dreadful note.

Even before Fenning entered, Sussex had turned to his valet and demanded the return of his jacket. When the butler finally held out the silver tray with another little note sitting on it like a drop of poison, the Duke was so numb that he snatched it up without even a word to the butler.

Fenning was trying to explain, mumbling, stuttering.

Something had terrified the old, experienced butler beyond his usual iron discipline. Sussex could see he was shaking.

"I am so sorry, m'lord"—Fenning's eyes were wide—"this strumpet just came in the front door. James the footman tried to stop her, but . . ." He paused, and looked around the room as if he could find the right words lurking in the corner. "I have excused poor James for the rest of the evening. He's not used to being manhandled by anyone—let alone a woman."

Fenning kept talking, but Sussex was no longer listening. If the Maestro had sent her, then there was at least a chance for redemption.

Quickly he flicked open the note written on the most expensive embossed paper.

Best hurry. I don't like waiting.

"Is she still downstairs?" he managed to croak out, as his valet slipped his jacket over the Duke's shoulders.

"Yes, m'lord," the butler rocked back on his heels. "But you cannot go down there. We can call for the other footmen, or the constabulary or both!"

"Go to hell, you doddering old fool," Sussex growled, spittle flying between his clenched teeth and lips. "Long before that she will come up here and then we will all be dead. I'll go down, and you won't tell a soul what happened." He then whirled on his valet, directing his building rage at the innocent. "If either of you do, I can assure neither of you will ever find another place in service."

Both men dropped their gazes to their feet, their countenance like statues as Sussex strode from the room. Somewhere between passing Ivy's chambers and the boys' bedroom, he paused. The world seemed to teeter slowly. A buzzing sound rose in his ears. Sussex, recognising the attack, stopped and recalled his doctor's commands: closed eyes, deep breaths, and images of serenity. The pounding in his head threatened to bring on the migraines that usually accompanied his fits, but the image of walking with his wife last spring through Hyde Park filled his mind's eye. That was the serene moment he always counted on. Tonight, with the vivid memory of his darling Ivy looking at him, her smile simply perfect in the brilliant noonday sun, the memory restored his demeanour. His mind was still numb with this dreaded appointment before him, yet he managed to descend the stairs with his composure once more intact.

Then he felt it crumble slightly on seeing his unscheduled caller.

"There you are," the woman standing in the entrance hall cooed. She was a pretty little thing with a sweet Italian accent. She should have, by rights, made him think of taking her to bed; but he knew what she was, and all she engendered in the breast of Lord Sussex was a deep and deadly fear. Taking a snake into his arms would have been the safer option.

For a start, her outfit was most outrageous. Her hair was tucked under a leather cap that a boy selling newspapers on the street might have owned, and every inch of her womanly curves was bundled up in a thick worsted jacket that was the twin for the one Sussex's coachman wore. Around her neck was a pair of goggles that could have been stolen from an aviatrix and made no sense to the Duke at all. On her small hands was a pair of bright red gloves—not silk as a lady would have, but chunky leather. The whole affair was finished with a pair of stout workman boots and a pair of thick woollen trousers—only confirming her common nature. Though there was a little part of him that realised her delightful female form was thrown into stark relief by the very masculine nature of her attire.

For a moment he was struck dumb. The woman laughed, throwing back her head as if it were the greatest joke. When she stopped she fixed him with a sharp look, one that really should never have been seen on a woman's face. "You didn't think he had forgotten, did you? Or perhaps you believed if you pushed it out of your mind it wouldn't happen?"

Sussex cleared his throat. He was most certainly not used to be talked to in such a common manner by a woman, in his own house. The trouble was, it was not the first time it had happened. Luckily his wife had never found this pert, attractive, yet completely unsuitable woman berating him thus. "Perhaps I hoped that," he muttered, his voice hoarse from the anger that had torn at it earlier. "But it seems I am proven wrong."

"Then we can go," she gestured to the door, and followed up behind him as he made for it. "You know," she commented in an offhand tone, "I do believe your footmen's tooth ruined the knuckle of one of my gloves. I shall have to send you the bill for a new pair."

Outside a dark carriage waited. It had no distinguishing features at all, and looked like a dozen other ones already on the street. However, there were two things that marked the scene as different. One was the hook-nosed imposing bulk of Pearson standing by its door, doing his usual glower that seemed to threaten violence at any moment. Sussex knew his name all too well from previous encounters. The other item was something of a mystery, it had two wheels, one in front of the other like a bicycle—but it was far bulkier than that. In between the wheels was a collection of valves, pistons, and flywheels. They were spinning and chuffing away, causing quite a racket on the elegant street. It was leaning to one side with a small iron bar acting as a third leg. More disturbing of all was a narrow tray at the bottom, tucked deep in the machine, that flickered with blue flame. It looked like something the devil himself might have invented.

Despite Pearson's disapproving look, the Duke spared a moment to examine the contraption. He knew his lip was curling. He was all too happy with advances in modern life, as long as they stayed out of his. He'd flown on airships to the Continent, but that was about the sum of his use of what his father had always called "infernal contraptions." They seemed so noisy, so insistent, and so damn inelegant to his eyes.

"Like my lococycle?" the woman's voice purred with the kind of avarice he usually only heard from the fairer sex when diamonds were in the offing. She ran one finger over the bars at the front of the device, that resembled nothing as much as a pair of bull horns. Then the Italian wrapped her hands around them tightly. "Our employer is most generous with his gifts." Her expression took on a touch of whimsy as she added, "And he can be just as generous with his punishments." She let go of the bars long enough to apply a pair of bicycle clips around her trouser legs and pull her goggles up over her eyes. Then while the Duke watched in horror, she swung one leg over the device and sat upon it.

For a moment he was unable to move. He had seen ladies on push-bikes before, but they were genteel pursuits compared to this vision. She looked terrifying and arousing, clad in men's attire, atop a hissing, chugging machine. "I'll see you there, Your Grace," she shouted over the roar of the machine, while examining the row of dials which now sat between her knees. "Don't be tardy."

Sussex, despite everything he knew about the woman and the machine, felt an embarrassing twitch within his evening trousers. A wave of guilt swept over him. Was he really so weak?

As a consequence he stood stock-still, while the Italian pumped the levers, kicked back the third leg, and sped away. She had to be going at least twenty miles an hour, considering how quickly she sped out of sight. Sussex and Pearson were left in a cloud of steam watching her. The manservant said nothing, but his gaze, like every man's on the street, followed after her.

"She has her ways," was the only comment Pearson made as he gestured Sussex into the carriage. He sounded almost admiring.

The Duke took his seat in the carriage without a reply. He was fighting to regain control of certain parts of his anatomy, but luckily, Pearson sat with the driver rather than in the carriage. For the second time this evening, Peter Lawson had to pull himself together and focus on the more pressing concerns of the Maestro.

Once they left Mayfair and began to roll into less salubrious parts of the capital, Sussex pulled the blinds down over the windows. Like last time, on the opposite seat he found a cloak waiting for him. Neither he nor the Maestro wanted it to be known what a peer of the realm would be doing in the East End.

Not that he would have been the first of his ilk to seek more debased pleasures there—but the Duke of Sussex had never been one of them. He wasn't about to start now.

By the time they pulled up at their destination, Sussex had wrapped the cloak around himself and calmed his churning stomach as best he could. He had not heard the roar of the lococycle, so he was sure that the Italian had arrived in considerable advance of him.

Pearson opened the door, and the Duke, without looking at him entered the warehouse by the usual path. The backdoor was reserved for servants, so it was only fitting that was the way he went in. The strumpet was waiting inside, holding a lamp before her—the only light to be had in this cursed place.

With a smile and an inclination of her head, she handed it to Sussex. "He is waiting for you upstairs." As he moved past her, the woman actually let her naked fingers drag lightly against the Duke's cheek. It was an impertinence that nonetheless fired his loins again. The damned woman had done it for that very purpose—to unsettle him for what was to come.

After ascending the stairs, he opened the door into the room that had once been the warehouse's office. It smelt musty and felt empty, yet unfortunately it was not.

A single light shone against a lonely chair. It was the type a schoolboy might use in a classroom. It was hardly fitting for the Lord Privy Counsellor to the Queen, but Sussex knew this was where he was meant to sit. There were only shadows surrounding the chair. He remained by the doorway, his grip tight on the knob.

"Sit down, Peter."

The voice had come from every darkened corner around him. Even in its gentleness, the voice demanded compliance. He felt an invisible grip on his throat, but Sussex would not cry out, would not give in to the emotion that welled inside him. He swallowed back a sob, and shut the door behind him.

He was now trapped in the Maestro's web. Completely.

Every step hurt. His calves and thighs stung; and the chair waiting for him drew more and more of his will away from him the closer he came to it. When he finally surrendered to it, there was no comfort to be had. He felt far too big for this rickety thing. It was a place meant for a disobedient, petulant child.

Then he understood.

And at that moment of comprehension, the single red eye flared to life in the darkness directly in front of him. It shone bright enough to catch a glare off the brass mask it was affixed to. Sussex felt his head swim in panic, but flight would have been pointless. He would have been cut down in a moment. Quickly. Cleanly.

The malevolent eye dimmed slightly, and Sussex forced himself to straighten.

"Peter," the unseen monster wheezed, "you know why I have summoned you."

"Yes, Maestro."

Sussex thought his voice sounded off. It was detached somehow. The command and authority were gone. He cleared his throat, hoping it would help him sound less frail.

"Peter, why are you testing my patience?"

"I don't mean to." Clearing his throat had done little. His voice sounded pathetic in his own ears. "The man I have on the inside is not producing the results that I had anticipated."

"Is this the colonial you employed?"

"Yes, Maestro." Sussex ran his sweaty palms against his evening trousers and took in a deep breath before continuing. "My spy has recently assumed a role in the Ministry that should, in theory, get him closer to Doctor Sound. If this gambit plays true, I should have evidence to back my own suspicions."

"Your suspicions matter very little to me." Sussex tried not to flinch on hearing the gasps, the gears, and the quick *clickity-clack* of small pistons that allowed the Maestro to have a voice. "What does matter to me is the Ministry's downfall. From what I have seen and heard, Doctor Sound still holds the Queen's favour."

Sussex felt his heart stop for a moment. "How do you know of the Queen's mind?"

The harsh laugh caused him to shift in the child's chair. "Do you believe I have ascended to my position without followers of influence? I know a good many things, and were it not for my present condition I would stand at the right hand of the crown. Until such a time, I must work in shadow." He paused with a gentle hiss of steam. "Your colonial contact—what have you threatened him with should he fail?"

"Loss of the lifestyle he has become accustomed to."

The red eye flared again. "A strong motivator."

Sussex allowed himself a smile. "There is something my man has eluded to. It could prove of value to your own agenda. There is something the Ministry is hiding within the Archives."

"I know."

His reply caught in his throat. "Maestro?"

"What I want is in the Archives. It is a device of unimaginable potential, and I must have it under my control. Otherwise, it will continue to stand against me. The weapon we have recently commissioned is nearing completion. Once in our possession and the Ministry disbanded, I will be able to help myself to what I desire."

"Why not send Pearson after it? I know the Archives are tended by only two agents."

A hiss of steam, and the eye appeared to take on the semblance of fire. "Ask *Signorina* del Morte about their head archivist, and what happened to the House of Usher on attempting direct interference." He took in a hollow breath, and added, "We must proceed covertly, and therefore I need you, Peter."

Sussex nodded, his fear slipping away, surrendering to a brief moment of hope. The Maestro was fixated on something in the Archives, evidently something gathered and catalogued within the numerous shelves Campbell had told him about.

This meant that the secret of the Restricted Area could be used. A secret that eluded the Maestro could prove to be a means of escape for Sussex.

"That need keeps you alive, Peter. I hope you do not take that for granted."

"Of course not, Maestro." He let his eyes drop for a moment, as if to study the barrier of darkness between where he sat and where the monster remained hidden. "I believe the man under my employment is growing closer. You will have the fall of the Ministry before the end of March."

A soft hiss from the darkness was his only reply. The red eye remained constant as the North Star.

"Maestro, I know you would prefer—"

"I insist that you produce results before the end of this month."

Two weeks. Sussex felt his muscles seize, his heartbeat quicken. "Maestro, please . . ."

"Now, Peter," the monster chided from the darkness, "you know how I find grovelling common."

The Duke shut his mouth with a light snap.

"What I need to progress further is kept within the Ministry, and I will not allow this artifact to simply gather dust and rot in the Archives. I suggest that your colonial pushes, finds what evidence you need to denounce Sound, and then takes action." A rush of air and a pop of pistons, and then the Maestro continued, "I am counting on you to succeed. If you cannot, then I am afraid I will have no further need of you."

"Maestro—"

"I would also advise you to manage your time carefully.

While my desires are certainly a priority, I would suggest you make time for your sons. If, by some misfortune, you are quick to depart this mortal coil"—and then the eye began to pulse, mimicking the beat of a heart, but accompanied instead by a cold, metallic *click-click* undulating—"they will have fond memories of their father in his final days. Good night, Peter."

Sussex leaned forward in his chair, his mouth opening as if to speak; but the red eye had disappeared into the dark.

When the light above him went out, Sussex let out a small yelp.

Before childhood terrors he had once long forgotten could threaten to resurrect themselves, Sussex heard a creaking from behind him. He looked over his shoulder to see the door slowly swinging open.

"Good night, Peter," the shadows whispered again companionably.

It would never be good again as far as the Duke was concerned.

CHAPTER THIRTEEN

In Which Mr. Wellington Thornhill Books Takes a Role in the Racket

"This is the house of Diamond Dottie, the scourge of upper-class London?" Wellington looked from across the street at the white stone building, with its Doric columns, on a tree-lined street in Mayfair. "Are you absolutely sure, Miss Braun?"

Eliza shrugged. "She has delusions of grandeur, and thanks to the success of her thieves she can afford it." She was glancing up and down the street, looking as he was for the Ministry Seven. "You're not going to back out on me now, are you—just because we're in a nice neighbourhood?"

"This isn't any common or garden area," Wellington hissed. "For goodness sake we are only streets away from where several peers of the realm reside. I cannot believe the queen of the London underworld is nearly rubbing shoulders with them."

"Believe it, Mr. Books," a little voice piped up from behind them.

Both agents spun around and saw no one.

Then they looked down.

Neither of them had observed Serena coming since the street urchin appeared totally unlike her usual self. In the first place, she was clean and washed. Secondly, she was wearing a charming little blue dress, complete with bonnet and fine wool coat. She looked like some child of the aristocracy that had momentarily slipped away from her nanny. The only oddity was a tin case she carried. Its contents, Books wondered, could have been anything from a sandwich to a severed hand. No one could really tell with that little scamp. When Wellington tried to get a closer look at the item, Serena shot him a wicked look that did not help put his mind at ease.

Instead he examined her clothing more closely. "Goodness gracious, what has happened to you?"

Serena inclined her head to one side, her eyebrow taking a very purposeful arch. "I can hardly go turning up 'round here like I usually do. Bloody peelers would be on me before you can say Jack Sprat."

The Archivist could see the sense in that, but knew somewhere a privileged child was looking for their pretty bonnet, dress and coat. He wondered if they had received a black eye in exchange.

Meanwhile the child took Wellington's hand, who instinctually recoiled at Serena's proximity, but the girl held fast.

She glared up at him. "We've got to hurry," Serena began. "The shop is opening soon, and we don't want to be seen legging it along the street. It has to look all natural like." Her brown eyes bore into him as she said, "So act like a *proper* daddy."

Wellington glanced over at Eliza, who had nothing to offer but a shrug. "I'd listen to her if I were you. She's the child with the plan."

"You cannot be serious." His eyes returned to Serena. "Oh dear Lord." Switching his glare from the street urchin to his partner, Wellington whispered tersely, "You failed to mention this part of the plan!"

"Which part, Welly?"

"The part where the toddler is in charge!"

"Watch it, ya toff!" Serena hissed back.

Assuming the role of a family on a morning's stroll, the three of them slipped into the shared park. As there was only a slight nip in the air, many of the couples and families from the surrounding homes were also taking in a short walk before lunch. So Wellington found himself out amongst the elite, pretending to be father and husband. As they proceeded in this charming fashion around the square, he could feel they were drawing glances. A pair of old women, bundled up in furs, smiled at them. A chimney sweep crossing between the streets tipped his hat and wished them a fine day. Even a policeman walking his beat couldn't help grinning. Though Serena stiffened a little at this last one, apparently they made quite a convincing family.

This scheme was getting more and more outlandish. "Now that I know this idea is that of a child—no offence intended, Serena, I assure you—may I once more voice my displeasure."

"Welly, I and the elder boys are handling Dottie's home. The longer you keep her preoccupied the more time I have to find out her interest in disappearing suffragists." Eliza looked over to Wellington as a couple walked by, bidding them good morning. She returned the salutation, and then continued in her light, casual tone. "Just follow Serena's lead, and you should be fine."

"Follow *Serena's* lead?" Wellington asked, struggling to maintain his composure.

"Just as it says in the Good Book." Serena offered her "father" a wide smile. "About the child leading and all."

Wellington took in a long, slow breath as they proceeded through a private garden between luxurious townhouses. He had to trust Eliza. She knew these children.

To calm his nerves, he took in the vignette the three of them created; and for a moment he considered what he had never had: walking down a street, the hand of a little girl in his, a beautiful woman on her other side. Glancing across at Eliza, he wondered if she was feeling the very same thing.

Their eyes met. She was playing the part. It was his presumption that Eliza did not want to have children, but now, catching a glimpse of the small smile on her face, he began to wonder if that had been far too bold of an assumption.

She lifted a single eyebrow at him, and he suddenly realised that was where Serena had picked up the mannerism. "And what are you smiling at, Wellington Thornhill Books?"

A hotness flared in his cheeks, and he cleared his throat, turning away from her gaze and catching the child's. She too was preserving the illusion; but behind her sweet, innocent eyes was a silent mandate. *Don't cock this up, guv.*

Ahead was a narrow alleyway where a dapper young man in a fine morning coat and top hat waited. Around his neck a pair of brass-rimmed goggles dangled. *Christopher?!* Wellington thought quickly as Eliza spoke, "And here is where I must part company with you."

"Have a care," Wellington urged. Colin was far from the most careful, and something about those goggles made him a little nervous. The idea that any of the Seven were tinkers had never crossed his mind.

"Now where is the fun in that?" And with a devil-may-care of a wink, Eliza followed Colin into the shadows. Wellington fought the urge to watch her disappear, but attracting attention to that alleyway was the last thing she needed.

He felt a tiny pressure against his right hand, and he was again looking into Serena's eyes.

"Mummy will be fine."

Mummy? Wellington thought, then he realised she was keeping up the façade far better than he was.

"Of course . . . sweetling . . ." That didn't sound right at all in reference to this savvy street urchin. "I cannot help to worry about Mis—er, Mummy."

"I worry too, Father." And that sounded even more peculiar, coming from Serena. "But Mummy can take care of herself. She is a very special lady."

"That she is," he replied.

"I love Mummy very, very much."

"As do I."

They proceeded for a few steps in silence, until Serena whispered, "I knew it."

The Archivist glanced down. She looked as if she were the happiest child in all of Christendom. Wellington didn't quite know what to say, so he hurried the girl on.

Ahead, a shop window was being loaded with a variety of breads and rolls, and the baker's assistant looked most familiar.

Liam?

Now Wellington's gaze swept across the street. Jonathan or Jeremy had to be nearby. Then again, would he even see the twins? Their talents, after all, were infiltration.

He then caught the flash of a young boy in a smart pea green suit with a dandy's top hat adorning his fresh face. Jeremy (or perhaps Jonathan?) was looking left and right. When he met Wellington's gaze, he loosed a wink.

Perhaps it was for the best that the Archivist did not know the particulars of Serena's confidence game.

Obviously, they had arrived at the place. Wellington checked his watch. It was quarter to ten o'clock in the morning. Before he could ask, Serena pulled at his hand, urging Wellington down to her eye level. The child's finger fussed on her bow, a subtle cue for Wellington to "do something fatherly." Her expression turned sour as Wellington, visibly flustered, wiped at her cheek. Presently, he was as comfortable with this ruse as he had been when Eliza had invited him for a weekend with the Phoenix Society.

Serena actually rolled her eyes, but then stopped mid-huff to stare at something behind Wellington. He didn't need to look over his shoulder to know their objective had been spotted. A calm washed through his body, and when their eyes met, it was not father and child nor Archivist and street urchin. They were now fellow operatives.

"Get ready," Serena whispered.

He should have felt his heart skip on that, but Wellington was ready. Perhaps he was growing accustomed to this lifestyle Eliza was introducing to him.

He had finished fluffing one side of the bow on Serena's dress when the little girl darted around him. Wellington spun about to see the blur of blue and white heading for a footman securing the door of a rather ornate coach. The mêlée that ensued looked positively awful from Wellington's point of view. The footman toppled over Serena in a most spectacular fashion; arms flailed and legs lifting from underneath him, giving the tall man the semblance of a child's rag toy being tossed in the wind. Serena's own entanglement with the footman looked as if broken bones or at least a skinned knee would have resulted. The Archivist winced in sympathy.

Then, in a strange, surreal moment, Wellington caught the grin on the girl's face just before hitting the ground. This was apparently not an unfamiliar trick.

That realisation provided comfort as cold and bitter as a winter across the Yorkshire moors though, when the shrill piercing cry of a child drowned out the drone of morning activity and shattered the peace of Mayfair.

Serena's scream could have come out from a banshee; and though he would have usually stuck a finger in each ear to shut out the sound, the Archivist instead shouted the first name that came to his mind.

"Angela!" he called out, pushing people aside, "Angela, sweetling!"

Of all the names, a voice in his head hissed, *you chose hers?*

That particular ghost, had it anything more to add, went unheard as Wellington finally reached Serena. All the blood had run out of his face, and Wellington felt the icy hand of panic grip his heart. What would he need to do if she really had injured herself? Should he take her in his arms? No, no—wait. He recalled in his Ministry training that he wasn't supposed to move a fallen agent until the injuries were diagnosed properly, otherwise he could cause—

Oh sod it all, this was a child! Children are supposed to be more resilient, but they are still human, though much smaller, for that matter, making them more susceptible to—

As his head buzzed with thought over interrupted thought, Wellington grew increasingly aware of how totally inexperienced he was in the ways of childish wounds.

Serena's wailing increased in ferocity and volume, a true triumph to abilities that should have attracted a stage manager or choir director from the London Opera; but in her petite fury, Serena spared a fleeting, frustrated glance at Wellington. *I can't carry this tune forever, Mr. Books. You better join in.*

Yes, even if she never did birth children, Eliza D. Braun would leave her mark on the next generation.

"Sweet Angela! What happened?" Serena began to cry into his shoulder. Placing his walking stick by the child, he gently started rocking her back and forth. She wailed even louder into his coat as he held her. "Daddy's here."

"Shove off!" a voice barked from above them.

His head shot up to look at the footman, covered in dirt and muck from the streets, towering above. He was uninjured but showed no concern whatsoever for either child or father.

Wellington heard over Serena's sobs the mutterings of the growing crowd. Could inciting an angry mob be this easy?

"Are you the cad that did this to my sweet little girl?" Wellington bellowed. He knew from shouting commands in the battlefield that his voice could carry; but in the serenity of Mayfair, he wondered if anyone in Ipswich heard him at present.

"The brat ran into me!" he barked back.

"Brat?!" Wellington was on his feet now, bringing Serena up to her feet as well. "I'll have you know, sir . . ." and then he felt a nudge at his side. Serena was still continuing her cadence of crying, while simultaneously handing Wellington his walking stick. He stopped, took the cane in his hands, and now wielded it as an extension of his arm, emphasising his points as he raged. "I'll have you know, sir, that my little Angela here is my light. She is all I have since her mother abandoned us for a life in the arts, chasing the coattails of that illusionist Angier!" The gasps from the audience he found most satisfying. "Yes, we have faced hardships, but we are honest folk." He pointed his silver-tipped walking stick at the footman, shouting, "I saw you *push* my sweet Angela!"

Show concern for the child.

Give onlookers a tragic story of adversity.

Release child just enough so her cries are not so muffled by the waistcoat.

Allow the crowd to simmer.

I say, creating a riot is much like whipping up a lovely beef stew, Wellington thought.

The footman flinched at the quick *rap-rap* coming from the carriage. He took a step forward, but made sure his voice was heard clearly. "Piss off, ya' toff. I didn't push no one."

Serena's sob subsided, giving Wellington ample room for his voice to carry across the scene. "Are you insinuating my child is a liar?"

Tension, Wellington knew from meetings with the Director and the odd social engagement, was more than an emotional state. With the right amount of stillness, tension could become a tangible, palpable thing. At present, it was more than that. It now bore weight. Neither one of them moved, and with a good crowd now gathered, it seemed as if even the smallest of sounds were amplified, ringing in Wellington's ears as would the brass-heavy finale of Tchaikovsky's *1812 Overture*. Someone now had to make a decision of fight or flight.

However there was another option. It presented itself when the carriage door opened. Serena's sobs immediately stopped. Wellington willed his feet to remain put.

Dorothy "Diamond Dottie" Bassnight towered over her coachman, Wellington, and most men present in the audience. Her extraordinary height accentuated her hardened face of high cheekbones, dark eyes, and light peppering of freckles across her nose, all this topped by a thick mane of golden hair. In his peripheral vision, Wellington noted that most everyone gathered around them took a few steps back. Her coachman froze immediately, the colour draining from his skin now providing sharp contrast to the black garments he wore. Quickly, he took his hat off and bowed his head, scuttling back as would a dog facing a harsh disciplining from their master. Her gaze of dark ice now fixed on Wellington. She looked at the Archivist as if he were a fish at market and she a skilled monger about to slice into him.

Then she smiled at him.

"Sir," Dottie spoke gently, but Wellington could hear an undercurrent of menace. "Is there a problem?"

He had to keep her talking.

"Madam, this does not concern you," Wellington snapped at the giant of a woman. "This is a matter between gentlemen."

He managed to meet the coachman's eyes on "gentlemen," expecting the ruffian to snort or scoff in disdain. Instead, Wellington saw nothing but pity in his eyes.

"Really?" cooed Dottie. "Well, as you can see, my carriage isn't moving. I am somewhere I do not wish to be, I am nowhere nearer to my destination, and you, sir, are wasting my morning. Therefore—" And she took a step closer to Wellington. Was it his imagination playing tricks, or did she just grow another inch or two? "Your argument with my coachman does concern me."

"Then perhaps, madam, you should choose your staff more carefully. This gentleman," Wellington said, motioning to the meek monster in black, his head still hung low, "not only struck my child down, but also called her a brat."

"So I heard." She looked at her footman. "I find myself at an impasse, Mr. . . . ?"

Dash it all. What is my alias?

"Smith," he blurted. "John Smith."

"John Smith? Really?" She tilted her head. "Well, Mr. Smith, you have me at a disadvantage. I have just met you and your . . ." Dottie paused, and her cold gaze fell on Serena. Wellington felt the girl's grip tighten around his leg. " . . . charming child here, so I know nothing of your background or intentions; but outwardly they appear to be quite honourable.

"My man here has been with me for quite a long time. If memory serves me right, Gregory has served and tended to my needs here for close on five years. So you see I have a history with him, and I know him to be a man of his word. So as—"

"And how much did you see from your carriage, madam?" Wellington raged, and his grip tightened on his walking stick. *Dammit*, he chided himself silently. *Let the woman finish. Make every moment count.* "You were not witness to my sweet angel being struck down."

"Indeed. So I will have to simply rule this unfortunate accident as just that—an accident." She turned away from him and ordered Gregory, "Pay the man."

Wellington's silver cane top touched her bicep. When she turned to look at him, her eyes were no longer attempting to be kind or even civil. He swallowed, pushing back that itch to run, and returned his own cold stare.

"Madam, do you find me so easily bought?"

He half expected the footman to step in, but he could see Gregory cowering back further.

Her eyes went from the cane—"If you would rather not have your offspring in an orphanage"—and then flicked back up to Wellington's face—"then I think you should reconsider your morals."

"For the sake of my child," Wellington insisted, "I demand satisfaction."

"And payment is not enough?"

"I demand an apology from your footman and from you," Wellington insisted. "It's the least Serena and I deserve."

"Serena?" Dottie's brow furrowed. "Who is Serena?"

Bugger. Wellington craned his neck to one side, trying to catch a long, deep breath.

That was when he heard the tiny click at his feet. From the tin box Serena kept on her person came the cheerful children's tune that he remembered as one of his most cherished of memories . . .

Half a pound of tuppenny rice,
Half a pound of treacle.
That's the way the money goes,
Pop! goes the weasel . . .

"Wait a moment," Dottie said, her eyes narrowing on the two of them, "You're the bearer up, aren't you?" Dottie looked around her for a moment, catching sight of the baker's assistant watching intently from the window. "He's the bludger, I take it." The woman's skilled eyes immediately pegged Jeremy across the street. "There's your crow. That must make me—"

Every night when I get home
The monkey's on the table . . .

"—the Mark."

Take a stick and knock it off . . .

On the moment of "Pop!" Serena tossed the tin box to the closest back wheel of Dottie's carriage. The clown figurine leapt up from its hiding place. Immediately after *"goes the weasel"* played, the box exploded, causing shrieks and screams from the onlookers to rise in the air and Dottie's carriage—now one wheel short—to topple over.

Wellington rolled to one side, and Serena emerged from underneath him. Her angelic appearance was now a vision of dirt, horse shit, and street muck. She sent a piercing whistle of two quick chirps and third long note that cut through the crowd's cries of panic. From across the street, Wellington could see Jeremy (or possibly Jonathan) begin to tear down the street.

The whistle above him ripped his attention from the lad to the Amazonian looming over them both. Dottie let out a piercing call of her own—two long, shrill bursts of sound—immediately followed by a quick pumping of her arm in Jeremy's direction.

"That's the crow!" she screamed at the gathering of on-lookers across the street. "Get 'im!"

She shot Wellington a look that would have rooted him on the spot, had he not spent nearly a year under Eliza's glare. Dottie attempted to set off, but his walking stick worked its way underneath the loose fabric of her dress, catching the point of connection between foot and ankle. With a jerk, Dottie toppled over.

"Time to go, Ser—"

The child leapt and pulled, and had it not been for Wellington's training in the army, he would have wondered what game the child was having with him. Instead, the hard tug on his coat told him to roll towards the carriage, which is exactly what he did. Two shots rang in his ears, and he didn't stop moving until his back hit the carriage.

Nowhere to go.

When he looked up, Gregory had a bead on him, and the hammer clicked back to a firing position.

The loaf of bread that knocked the gun off-target must have been several days old as it hit the weapon with such force that the bullet struck high on the carriage wreckage. Gregory was also visibly in pain, and by the time he recovered, Liam was in full stride, resembling those brave souls Wellington saw charging across the barren battlefields of Africa. Those men had fallen dead, but this soul—in a battlefield far different and closer to home—was smarter. He couldn't take a full-sized man down except by diving for the man's knees. Based on the scream erupting from Gregory's mouth, it would be a miracle if he ever walked again.

Wellington and Serena drew themselves back up on their feet, but sadly at the same time as Diamond Dottie.

Perhaps the woman was one of the underworld's most lethal and cunning minds, but she hardly dressed the part. His stern father would have approved of a woman wearing this particular outfit, but not in its present state. Her once delicate and delightful dresses of bows and finery were caked in mud and filth. She was looking at her dress and gloves, the initial shock manifesting itself in a wild anger.

Movement to his left. Wellington saw two ladies emerge from the crowd, wielding small clubs. Across the street, two other ladies of the same fashion and demeanour broke ranks. This pair of bludgers, Dottie might have called them, were coming for Liam.

"Girls," she seethed, "make this messy, if you please." And with a rustle of fabric, Diamond Dottie was on the run, as much as her current footwear allowed. Any poor sod who got in her way was cast aside.

The first woman stepped forward with a headshot. Wellington went to deflect, but the feint had worked brilliantly. Air rushed out of Wellington as her club hit his stomach instead. The blow was enough to send him backwards, but thankfully not high enough to connect with any ribs. He could just make out blurry forms closing on him. With a breath that sent an ache through his torso, the Archivist tucked tight into a ball. He heard one club miss his skull, but the second he felt across his back. He kept rolling forward, finally stopping and pulling himself up to his feet. He was able to take in a gasp of air, and that was all the time he truly had as a blur holding a darker object advanced. He was able to feign distress well enough—not that it was a complete challenge to do so—that he saw Dottie's muscle drop her weapon a fraction lower. He had to wait for one more—

The club was rising as something akin to an uppercut, but Wellington spun away from what would have been a jaw-shattering blow. Following this spin, his arms brought the fine silver-topped cane around, its solid sphere impacting the back of her skull, sending her forward into the crowd. He planted his feet and glanced over at Liam. The two ruffians were trying to corner him, but the boy continued to evade them.

It was only an instant, but enough time to give the other woman a chance to get in a swing. His walking stick, of a much better and sturdier make than its predecessor, caught the blow, but now Wellington was open for fisticuffs, which is exactly what he felt against his chin and lips: a hard fist that sent him back a few steps. He managed to keep his balance, but just barely. She should have come in for a club-assisted backhand, but she didn't. Why?

"Serena!" he heard someone scream.

Process of elimination: Liam. Serena was in danger. *Pull it together, man!*

Wellington righted himself and caught sight of the woman trying to grab the small child now attached to her back and biting whatever she could. He took one step forward, and that was all Wellington managed before Dottie's thug exploited a momentary advantage.

The woman's hand found purchase in Serena's long blonde hair and her fingers dug in deep. Wellington heard the girl's growl as well as the woman's scream, but Dottie's woman still pulled. The child's body peeled off the woman, and a small spray of red erupted from where the thug's earlobe had been. It would have been a victory for the street urchin had she not landed facing her opponent. Dottie's woman reeled back and then brought her club around. The force of the blow lifted the child off her feet. Wellington hoped Serena was unconscious as he watched the diminutive body land hard against the cold dirt.

The club came up again, but this time it was in reaction to Wellington closing on her. He said nothing, made no announcement to his opponent on who he was or whose honour he represented. Nor did he issue an apology. His manners and etiquette were now totally abandoned. His walking stick shot out like a cobra springing from his hand, and the woman's head wobbled on the first strike. It snapped back on the second. She was fighting to keep her balance, but Wellington refused to wait. The third strike was with the head of his walking stick, the solid silver sphere smacking Dottie's woman in her jaw, a jaw he knew would never work again without clockwork assistance.

His cane-blade rung clearly in his ears, and then he sliced

his blade across her neck. However, this victory was followed by bad luck. One of the thugs grabbed Liam.

The last of Dottie's ladies twisted her wrist and grasped the pistol that popped into her palm. She pulled the hammer back and placed the weapon's muzzle against the lad's temple.

"*Stop!*" she said, pressing so hard Liam winced. "Don't think I won't put a ball in this chi—"

She was so focused on the crimson-kissed blade that the sheath—the actual walking stick itself—went unnoticed. It struck her in the temple. Liam easily slipped free of her as she righted herself and attempted to draw aim on Wellington. He swung the blade around in an arc that ended at her wrist. His cane sword was hardly of a build or girth to take her hand off, but it was enough to dig in. On feeling contact with her flesh, Wellington gave a twist, and that served as ample motivation for her to release the pistol.

Wellington still saw in his mind Serena lying in the mud. *No,* he thought as he pulled the blade back, *this is not enough. They could still hurt her.*

And much as he hated repeating himself, Wellington slit the woman's throat.

He heard no calls for constables. He heard no onlookers swooning or crying out in alarm. He was, for a brief instant, smothered in a thick silence.

"Mr. Books!" cried Liam.

He turned towards the screams but he knew it would be his first attacker, emerging from the crowd where he had sent her sprawling at the beginning of this dance. He would never be able to clear the distance between the two of them, and he was in the open street. Nowhere to dive for cover. If she missed him on the first shot, he would assuredly be hers on the second. His grip tightened on the hilt of his cane sword. No time to react. No time to think. He only had time to die.

How would he explain this to Eliza?

The single bullet found its target without fail. Centre of the brow.

The woman took two steps back before dropping. A few seconds later, two women shrieked on noting their lovely morning dresses were covered in blood. *Poor things,* Wellington lamented silently. *Those* stains will never come out.

"What happened?" Liam asked, looking back from where the shot had emanated.

"I don't know. I would say divine intervention," Wellington said, staring at the dead woman, "but I don't recall God ever smiting His enemy with a rifle."

"Not His style, sir," the boy agreed.

Wellington started and spun around, dropping his sword. "Serena?" he called, sliding down to one knee over the child.

She had not moved from where she had landed. Her eyes were closed, and her sweet face was now starting to swell on one side. Wellington's hands didn't know where to touch first. Should he pick her up or should he send Liam for a doctor, or should they grab a hansom and make for the closest hospital?

The girl was in his arms as he stood. "We have to get her to a surgeon."

"No, Mr. Books!" Liam snapped. "No doctors."

"Good Lord, Liam, look at her!"

"Serena there is deathly afraid of doctors. Afraid if'n they treat her, the doctors will call the peelers. Send her off to the workhouse right smartish."

The piercing call of a constable's whistle suddenly filled the air. He was across the street, and alone. The policeman was looking over the carnage as he blew his alarm, and then ran up the street. They had moments, if that.

"Liam," Wellington hissed, "we need help."

The boy's hand tugged at Wellington as he pulled him through the parting crowd. "Take her to Miss Eliza's. Alice will know what to do." The boy's head shot left and right, and on seeing the standing cab he reached into Wellington's coat and pulled out the coin purse. "I'll get word to Miss Eliza. Let Miss Alice start care of Serena."

"But—"

"Just. Do. What I say, Mr. Books."

Wellington nodded. His instincts told him to trust Liam.

He knew he was overpaying the driver, but Wellington held the man's gaze for a moment longer than would be considered polite. The driver nodded, and then looked ahead, waiting for his fare's command. Wellington tucked Serena next to him, his arm around her holding her close as a father would with a daughter. He was about to give the rap against the cab's roof and deliver Eliza's address to the driver when the low rumbling of a combustion engine caught his ears.

Across the street, from the wide alley, a two-wheeled metallic monster emerged, its motor's roar parting the crowd before it. Wellington's eyes narrowed on the pale-skinned rider, a svelte, curvy creature she was, decked out in leather and a thick riding jacket, no doubt to stave the chill when she picked up speed. A long, slender case rested across her back. Her face was partially concealed by her riding goggles, but the resemblance was uncanny. Not to mention impossible.

"Eliza?" he whispered.

Then her head turned, revealing a long ponytail of raven-black hair. When she glanced back, their eyes met; and when she smiled at him, Wellington felt a chill in the deepest part of his stomach.

It was most definitely not his colleague.

Get to Eliza's, Wellington's mind screamed as he watched Sophia del Morte accelerate away on her lococycle. Thankfully, in a direction opposite to where he was headed. *Right. Bloody. Now!*

CHAPTER FOURTEEN

In Which Eliza Dares a Dance with Diamond Dottie

They gathered in the nearest alleyway—though because this was Mayfair it was the tidiest one Eliza had ever seen. Still, the police around here were more plentiful than in the East End, so they had to be quick about their business.

"Are you ready for this?" She eyed Christopher, Callum, and Colin sternly. Christopher, the eldest, she knew could handle himself. But the younger boys had never accompanied her on a break-in before—not that she laboured under any illusions that this would be their first.

"Cor, mum." Colin blinked up at her. "We're as ready as a ladybird is for gin."

"You can trust us," Callum said, a little more seriously.

She took a breath. When dealing with the Seven she began to feel old—even worse, she realised she was perilously close to sounding like her mother. "It's not that, lads. It's the fact that we are breaking into the inner sanctum of the queen of the London underground. She commands a lot of ruffians, and if we get found out—"

"We've caught it from Diamond Dottie's gang before."

Christopher scuffed his foot on the ground and glared down at it. "Couple of weeks ago two of them put the screws to Jonathan and Jeremy. Reckoned they'd messed up a job on Regent's Street."

"But we is always careful to keep away from the Elephants—they give us a hard time about Serena and all." Colin trailed off as Christopher shot him a filthy look. Naturally the marauding groups of women and those of the children clashed from time to time. Eliza was aware the Ministry Seven were part of a larger organised group of children, and they were natural enemies of Dottie's Elephants. Often, the Elephants tried to lure away the girl children to their gang— and if that didn't work they could use more unpleasant methods.

Christopher, seeing the agent's face go white, patted her on the arm, "It's all right, mum. We would never let them have her."

Eliza's throat was so tight that for a moment she was unable to reply. Instead she simply nodded.

"And the twins are just topping," Callum assured her, "with just a couple of scrapes and such to show for it."

Eliza winced.

"So ya see"—Christopher's fingers tightened on her sleeve—"we don't mind a'tall doing a bit of pannie with you. Might even say that we've been looking forward to it."

After a long look at all the boys, Eliza nodded. "Very well then, lads, it's a big house and we need to be quick about it."

"There's only two maids." Christopher grinned. "We did some poking around yesterday. Dottie might be all high and mighty, but she's a skinflint when it comes to hiring help."

"Busy servants will be a real blessing this morning," Eliza pulled off her fine morning gloves and replaced them with sturdier leather ones. "Now, as for the door—"

"Chris has got that sorted," Colin piped up.

"Oh, really?"

"Something special." Christopher grinned and tapped the tin container he was carrying. "Mr. Books gave me a bit of a hand with it."

Something from Wellington? This was, indeed, something special. "Let me see." Her fingers darted to the tin, but Christopher brushed them away with all the art of a master pick-pocket.

"Not just yet—it has to be a surprise."

"I am not entirely sure I like the fact that you are colluding with Wellington," she muttered. "But we'd best be getting on with it."

Cautiously, she led them through the alleyway and to the rear of the street. Here was where the tradesmen and the servants entered the house, through a basement doorway that led into a kitchen. Unable to use either door, there only remained the windows or French doors as points of entry. Yet as she looked up, she realised the builders of these houses were not without their cleverness. Each possible entrance on the exposed side of the townhouse was not only on the third story, but also had a large balcony on it, that in essence acted as a stout defence. The smooth surface of the stonework had no anchor point for a grappling hook, and there was no convenient drainage pipe to make use of.

She looked down the street, but Callum whispered back to her, "No need to fret, mum. Jonathan and Eric are playing the crows today. Jeremy to Jonathan, then Johnny to Eric."

Christopher tugged her over, and all four of them crouched on the ground, backs against the wall of the house. Anyone in the early-morning mist would have the hardest time seeing them this low.

"Time for my peace day resistance." The eldest boy, who was usually a little more reserved than this, grinned. She didn't have the heart to correct his pronunciation.

Eliza watched bemused as he opened his tin and pulled out three objects. The first was a shiny grappling hook; the second appeared to be a spiderlike automaton, and the third was a box with half a dozen tiny levers on it. The agent blinked in genuine surprise, "How did you—"

"I didn't much care for Mr. Books at first like, but he's kind of grown on me." He handed the spider creature to Eliza. She turned it over in her hand. It was quiescent now, its eight legs tucked in tight against its brass body. She was surprised at its relative lightness.

"Wellington bought this?"

"No, mum, he made it."

Her eyes shot back down to the device cradled in her hands. She knew from their night at the opera together he was a bit of a tinker; but unlike the auralscope he had revealed to her, this device had an elegance and sublety to it. This was a device tailored for fieldwork. Had he made this with her exploits in mind?

Christopher tapped its domed body. "And he said he made a few modifications to it just for today's caper." The look on the young boy's face was a pleasure to see. The Seven, along with the rest of London's homeless waifs, had very few toys to call their own. That Wellington had given into Christopher's care such an amazing, shiny, and new device was a wonder to the boy. He fairly glowed with delight and responsibility.

"Did he now?" Eliza settled back. "I am entirely in your and Books' capable hands, it seems."

Callum had under his coat a tightly wound coil of half-inch diameter densely-woven rope. It must have been tucked under his armpit this whole time. It always amazed her how the Seven could make rather large objects disappear into their clothing—a survival skill on the streets. Taking the curiously silky-looking rope, Christopher attached it to the grappling hook with a knot that would have done a sailor proud. Then taking the spider back from Eliza, he placed it on the ground next to the rope.

"Now comes the magic," he whispered, waving his hand in a dramatic fashion before the wide-eyed other boys. Then he slipped his goggles on and picked up the box of levers. Eliza guessed what was coming, but still she jumped, as did Colin and Callum, when the spider suddenly unfurled his legs, clamped the two front ones around the grappling hook, and set off for the wall. The rattle of its tiny steam engine was, thankfully, swallowed by the fog—yet still sounded unusually loud to Eliza. She was glad that Wellington was not present to witness her surprise.

As it was, the two young boys jammed their fists into their mouths to keep from oohing and aahing like they were at a fair. Yet, she had to agree it was an amazing sight. The spider, with Christopher working the controls like a master, scuttled quickly up the wall, dragging the grappling hook with it, the rope trailing after like Rapunzel's hair.

Eliza, Colin, and Callum all waited with held breaths, while their companion worked his magic. Finally, he slipped the goggles off his face to perch them once more on the top of his head.

"Sorry," he whispered, "I had to get the little blighter to work the lock open. Took a bit longer than I thought, but it's done. Your turn, Colin."

The youngest of the boys scampered over to the rope, and with the practiced touch of a professional, flicked it around his wrist and then into his grip. Then by virtue of twisting it around his leg, began to wriggle his way up it. He looked so fragile climbing up so high on something so thin—like a caterpillar on a trembling stalk.

"Don't worry, mum," Callum squeezed her fingertips. "That there rope is made by Mr. Lowe. His work's the best, and our Colin knows how to climb like one of them African monkeys. I saw one last week, down on Marylebone."

"Get off it," Christopher growled to his younger companion, "Mum doesn't want to 'ear about that." The two boys glared at each other until Eliza thought she might have to separate them, but luckily at that moment Colin dropped another thicker rope down.

The agent was quite relieved. Callum might have plenty

of faith in Mr. Lowe's work, but she was wearing her Ministry issue corset under her finery, and thus she weighed considerably more than any street urchin. Still, there was one way she had to lighten the load.

Quickly she undid the buttons on her very proper skirt and dropped it to the ground. The boys blinked at her in alarm, until they realised that beneath she was wearing trousers. Eliza's pistols were tucked into the small of her back and secured with specially designed holsters, while the legs were decorated with an array of pockets for the tooling she currently needed. Her fashion was something that they were very familiar with, but the make and cut of these trousers were highly unusual. The fabric looked sturdy, but it stretched and moved easily with Eliza's form. *Very* easily.

She happened to look over her shoulder and noted the two boys staring inappropriately at her backside. Yes, they were boys. Boys quickly growing up to manhood.

"Now you two see why I don't wear these around Agent Campbell," she quipped, playfully tapping the curve of her rear. "These particular trousers I had made for me the last time I visited San Francisco. Quite innovative, those yanks at Levi Strauss."

The boys just nodded. Their eyes were no longer blinking.

Eliza snapped her fingers, knocking them out of their stupor. "I'll go first, lads," she said, and now it was her turn to grin. "But I shall go up in style." From one of her side pockets she produced a gadget of Axelrod's, a sort of multitool for the operatives; and even though she wasn't theoretically classified as a field agent at the moment, the clankerton had not seen fit to change the lock on the armoury door since they'd gone out for dinner last year. It was really his own fault, and this was how she could strap the long metallic box to her forearm with no real twinges of remorse.

It had taken her quite some time, and no few number of minor injuries, to work out what the gadget did. One thing she had mastered was the rope ascender. Turning the dial on the side popped out a sturdy loop of some kind of shiny metal. Placing that around the rope, she turned the dial the other direction, and locked it around the rope Colin had dropped. Then it was merely a matter of flicking the lever and she was being lifted along the rope by the arm.

Truthfully, Eliza had never tested this in a proper situation—more with a five-inch piece of rope in her living room, and that just to work out the feeding mechanism. A full application of the contraption out in the field, though, yielded very different results. With Eliza's full weight and several stories above her, the device chugged alarmingly, and Eliza contemplated that it would be ironic to have lived through all those gun battles, explosions, and assassination attempts merely to splatter on the ground in Mayfair.

She felt her breath return as the balcony loomed into view out of the mist. Eliza flicked the lever off and grabbed hold of the stone lip. One jerk and she was standing next to the smiling Colin.

"Excellent job." She couldn't help ruffling his hair, and he bore it very well, considering. The little spider creature sat on the railing of the balcony by the grapple, ticking away to itself. It had to be impossible but it did seem to radiate some kind of contentment. Surely Wellington had not made it with a personality?

In a few moments the other two lads joined them. Christopher picked up the waiting spider, while Callum went to the French doors and examined the lock.

"Looks cheap," he commented over his shoulder, his hand already reaching under his jacket for tools.

It was quiet Colin who stopped him. After running his eye over the inside and outside of the frame, he pushed back his cap and scratched his head. "There's some kind of mechanism between the door and the wall. Smells like clockwork."

Eliza frowned at the strange comment, but Christopher merely nodded. "One more trick from Mr. Books then." He put the goggles back on, and began to play with the levers again. Eliza knew that the boy could only have had a day or two at most to learn how to use the little device—yet he had mastered it with great aplomb.

The spider rattled over to the door, raised itself up on its tiny claws, and then held out its front right leg. When the boy cranked a little knob on the side of the control box, a tiny clank sounded and along the outstretched claw slid a whirling bright blade.

Within a short moment, the spider had cut a decent sized hole in the bottom pane, set down the circular piece it had made, and then hopped inside.

Underneath his googles, Christopher beamed with success. He walked the spider around the corner and out of sight. "There's the off lever," he muttered, and then a tiny bell chimed and the sound of the door mechanism came. "Blimey, but I do owe Mr. Wellington a pint. This bit of clockwork is genius."

Pushing down his goggles, the boy pushed open the door and sketched a bow. "Won't you please come in." His accent suddenly sounded like it belonged in Mayfair.

As she passed him, Eliza tipped an imaginary hat. "Why, thank you, sir." His wicked grin gave her the distinct impression that Wellington was never going to get his device back, and she wondered what other trouble the boys could use it for. It really didn't bear thinking about.

Cautiously, all three of them entered the room. Christopher bent, scooped up Wellington's spider, and gave it a little pat on the head like it was a puppy. This appeared to be a medium-sized guest room—but apparently Dorothy did not have many of those, because it smelt musty, and there was no fire even built under the mantel. Christopher gestured, and Colin ran to the door and eased it open. Nothing but silence was on the other side. The young boy slipped out, and they followed in his wake. The corridor was long and narrow, with a set of stairs at either end. The smaller set must have led up to the servants' quarters under the eaves, but also down towards the kitchen area. However, the one at the other end was far grander and must be the one the mistress of the house used.

Together, the three boys and Eliza checked the third floor, but found nothing except guest rooms and storage. One whole room was devoted to furs and fine clothes, and for a moment Eliza was stricken with fashion jealousy.

"Caw," Colin rubbed his cheek, thankfully, clean, on a dress of fine Chinese silk. "This is like water."

"But not likely Dottie's," Eliza said, running her hand over the rows of hanging treasures. "I'm surprised she's got them all here."

Christopher scowled. "Too big for her britches she is, mum. Forgotten where she come from, and too sure the peelers will stay off her."

"She pays 'em good." Callum darted in among the clothing. "You sure we couldn't—"

"No, we may not." Eliza sighed, turning back to the door. "This isn't why we came here. Let's move on. We're looking for a study of some kind."

They dared the front stairs, since they were far less likely to run into any staff there. The second floor seemed like a better chance for finding things, since the first room they'd opened there was immediately obvious as Dottie's inner sanctum.

Even Eliza was unable to find words in the first moments after they entered, but Callum's comment was remarkably accurate. "It looks like a flower shop threw up."

Indeed the chaotic swirl of pinks, lavenders, puces, violets, and every shade in between produced a kind of stomach-churning reaction. No person who loved fashion even a jot could be moved to anything but horror. It was the kind of visual assault Eliza was totally unprepared for. Dresses, jackets, underwear, scarves lay scattered on all the furniture. It was apparent that the mistress of the house liked to keep her fair share of the Elephants' haul—the most garish and outlandish portion. The boys were standing near the door, and they looked very much out of their depth.

"Well," Eliza whispered, "I think Dottie might need to hire herself a lady's maid." She then considered the various mismatched garments, and added, "One with a tight lip and loose morals, it would seem."

They had probably never seen so many, or such intimate, pieces of ladies' apparel. Colin was beet red, and muttered, "I'll keep a look out, mum." He then escaped into the corridor.

Poor Christopher and Callum stood shifting on their feet, while Eliza proceeded into the room. "Come on boys," she hissed, "You've stolen plenty of clothes in your time."

"Not ladies'." Christopher jerked his head. "*Things* like this . . ."

For a fourteen-year-old who had lived over half of his life on the street, the boy's attitude surprised her. But then thinking on it, the women he'd probably seen had most likely never had many underthings anyway.

"Never mind," she replied breezily. "There is always time for education." And with that she dived into rifling through the treasures of Diamond Dottie. After a moment, and still rather red in the face, Christopher and Callum joined her.

Once she had cleared a path through the scattered clothing, Eliza honed in on the furniture. Dottie had several fine pieces from the French revival, including a lovely armoire. While the boys searched through her wardrobe, Eliza picked the lock and whispered, "This is more like it." Notebooks, with lines and numbers scrawled in them. Price and value of things probably, though there was no notation to reveal that. Eliza picked up another notebook, and this was a little more understandable.

It contained addresses. Addresses of women. Eliza felt her heart begin to race as she trailed a finger down Dottie's neat handwriting. She knew these names, names of those in the movement.

Just as she was about to spin and tell the boys what she had found, Colin barged into the room. "There's someone coming down the stairs! Running!"

Eliza gestured to the boys to make themselves scarce. The footsteps were fast approaching the bedroom. She herself slipped behind the door and waited to see what would happen.

A shape burst into the room, and Eliza reflexively grabbed it by the back of the jacket and whirled it around. Luckily, she managed to hold back her punch for a second.

"Douglas?" she gasped, as her former lover's eyes focused on her upraised and clenched fist. "What the hell are you doing here? And how in the blue blazes did you get in?"

As Colin, Callum, and Christopher emerged from their hiding places, Douglas straightened his coat and ascot. "I am here to help you, Eliza. I followed you up the rope you left dangling since I knew that you were up to something ridiculous."

The agent lowered her arm, but kept a sharp gaze locked on him. "No, *you* are the one being ridiculous! How do you think I have managed all these years with you in New Zealand and me in London? Do you think it is sheer chance that I have somehow survived without you and your bull-headed chivalry?"

Douglas looked very much hurt, as if she'd slapped him in fact—then he looked a touch perturbed. "Bullheaded chivalry? Considering your ill choice in professions, I have no earthly idea what you have been up to since leaving New Zealand, nor do I grasp what you are doing presently. I only know I want to protect you if I can."

"Protect me?" Eliza could feel the heat rush to her cheeks. "You must be mad! I am in no need of protection—not even when you knew me back home. For the son of a suffragist, you really are a cutup."

"Mum?" Colin tugged on her arm.

"In a minute." She flapped her hand at the lad. Her ire was up, and part of her was enjoying putting Douglas in his place. "I doubt Kate knows you are here, does she, Douglas? Perhaps you are a world adventurer and you can cross a desert valley, scale a cliff face, and serve a high tea all within a weekend, but here you're a civilian, while I am *a trained agent*. Having you here makes things worse."

"But, mum . . ." Now Colin was wriggling about like he needed to go to the toilet. She took no notice.

Douglas was flushing red as he gestured to the three members of the Ministry Seven. "Now, just a moment—these boys are barely in long trousers, and yet you've let them accompany you . . ."

"Hold on a minute, guv," Christopher grumbled, more than a little annoyed by being considered child when he was creeping up on manhood.

"These boys are experts of a jungle far different from any you've conquered, Douglas," Eliza snapped. "Now, before you are spotted—"

"Bleedin' Nora!" Colin stamped his foot, and yelled so loud that everyone else in the room jumped. "Would you look at that!"

Elzia spun around to where Colin stood, looking even angrier than Douglas, and felt a scolding on her lips until she followed to where the lad pointed. Christopher had put the spider device on top of the armoire. It was doing a fair impression of a vaudeville dance—jigging around and waving its tiny brass legs. Christopher, his goggles still dangling around his neck, had shouldered its controls. The device, it appeared to everyone, was working on its own accord.

"Eric!" Christopher whispered, his eyes widening. "He's got the panic switch."

"The panic switch?" Eliza asked.

"Eric's the third crow, mum, remember?" Christopher quickly motioned to Colin and Callum to head out into the hallway. "Mr. Wellington made this thing called the panic switch. Works on a wireless. Eric's gotta to be telling us she's coming back."

Eliza didn't know how long the spider had been doing its danger dance, but she knew they didn't have long. She'd hoped to get her hands on something that would tie Dottie to the disappearing suffragists, but it was more important to keep the boys safe.

"Nommus!" Christopher barked, scooping up the still wriggling spider and stuffing it back into the tin container. All pretence was abandoned as they ran out of the bedroom and back up the stairs to their entry point.

Colin and Callum met them in the stairwell. "The grappling hook—it's gone!"

One of her pounamu pistols slipped free of its holster. "No other choice," Eliza turned about and gestured them out of the room, "Front door or nothing." She fixed her eyes on Douglas, but addressed them all as she said, "Follow me. Quiet as church mice. No rash moves."

They had all made it halfway down the corridor, but unfortunately, never made it to the stairs. Diamond Dottie emerged from the first-floor landing, a coil of rope and a grappling hook swinging in one of her hands.

"Apparently I will have to increase my security measures." She flexed her fingers, so that the diamonds flashed, "But first I will have to take the rubbish out." Her voice, though trying its best to be posh, still held an underlying rasp of the East End. Her outfit was as garish as her wardrobe might have suggested—yet it was not in the best of condition. Her hat was askew, her cuffs and shirt decorated in mud, and the skirts torn. Eliza presumed that was not how she had gone out that morning.

Still she was not about to poke fun at Dorothy. The boys were frozen in fear—even Christopher. They were, after all, faced with their nemesis. The one who made their daily lives on the street that much more difficult, and now that she had seen them there would be even more to worry about. Colin looked like he might bolt like a rabbit, but his escape route was blocked.

The weight of the other pistols on Eliza's person tempted her, but if she shot Dottie into next week then she might never find those missing women.

While she was contemplating her options, Douglas took

an unfortunate initiative. Stepping forward, he swung his fists up. "I don't want to hit a woman, so you'd better stand aside."

Dottie, who at nearly six feet stood eye-to-eye and toe-to-toe with the man, tilted her head, her eyes darting over his shoulder to meet Eliza's. "Is he having a laugh?"

"Douglas," Eliza hissed, her gun now pointing to the floor, "did you fail to heed my warning about rash moves?"

Clearly, when Douglas cleared his throat, he had. "I said step aside," he repeated.

This was more than enough encouragement for Dottie. Up until now she had probably been holding back, but she did no longer. Grabbing hold of the New Zealander's shoulders, she pulled him down onto her upraised knee into a most vulnerable spot between his legs.

Douglas let out a muffled groan, while the boys winced in male sympathy. Eliza could tell that this was not the first kick to the bollocks dealt out by Dottie. The underground queen pushed the wheezing Douglas out of her way, tossed their rope aside, and stepped towards Eliza.

The agent sized her up, sheathed her pistol, and then shoved the boys behind her. "Once you get an opening, down the stairs, lads. I'll keep her busy."

Dottie looked down at her and grinned. "For a spell, love." Dottie remarked, tossing her purse to one side. "Aren't you a pretty little wisp of a girl."

"Enough of a 'wisp' to handle your angels sent from on high."

"Yes," she said, "about that—"

And with speed rivalling a mule's, Dottie's kick lifted Eliza off the ground and sent her sprawling into the boys.

Eliza gave a hard, harsh cough as she stood. With a quick glance to the three boys, she strode back towards Dottie. The tower of a woman remained stock-still; so when the punch came for Eliza, it would have taken her by surprise.

Eliza, however, was not Dottie's average opponent.

The moment her arm flinched, Eliza evaded and grabbed

Dottie's extended limb and threw her into the adjoining room they had previously searched. Dottie's feet caught on a pile of clothes, sending her to the floor. With the thundering of footsteps behind her, Eliza followed her opponent into the gaudy parlour, and promptly clocked her in the chin with a quick uppercut. Dottie stumbled back which Eliza was fortunate she didn't see her waving her hand. The woman's skull must have been made of granite.

Dottie staggered to a small end table. From the drawer she pulled a pistol and checked the cylinder. She stopped though, giving a slight wince on trying to stand. "Well now," she said, rolling her foot a few times before saying, "fancy that—you are wearing a reinforced corset. Expecting trouble, were you?"

"Perhaps," Eliza wheezed, still trying to catch her breath from the first kick. She looked down to see the clear imprint of Dottie's sole and heel in the centre of her stomach. With the muddy impression against the bright colours of her dress, the outfit looked somewhat comical.

"Oh dearie, that stain isn't going to come out," Dottie chided.

Eliza motioned to both their dresses. "Seems to be a new fashion, doesn't it?"

Dottie looked down at her stained, destroyed outfit. "You'll be getting a bit more than the cleaning bill."

"Mud stains, I have no doubt. Blood stains though . . ."

Dottie clicked her tongue while cocking the pistol. "I can replace the carpet."

Eliza felt around for some kind of shield and saw a tea service set out for later use. She swept her hand across the serving dish, sending the cups off in one direction while she held up the tray. The bullet slammed hard against the metal but stopped there. Eliza immediately threw the tray at Dottie, its edge connecting nicely with that annoying protrusion commonly known as the funny bone. The shock caused Dottie to release her gun.

In the brief time before the tray struck the taller woman

and Dottie looked up from where she dropped the gun, the Ministry agent was on top of her.

Eliza's fist came down from a high angle, the coffee table supplying ample altitude, which she needed to compensate for Dottie's height. Her brief descent helped with the fist's momentum but instead of the temple, she caught Dottie's jaw, driving her down and away from where she was landing.

"I'll give you this, dearie," Dottie groaned, catching herself on the back of a couch and giving a begrudging nod, "you do know how to punch."

"From you," Eliza said, stepping back to assure herself a good stance, "I'm taking that as a compliment."

The tall woman's signature, a row of thick gold rings studded with diamonds on each hand, caught a glint of sunlight. If she were to land a punch with that anywhere on her person, it would turn flesh into minced meat. When Dottie's left hand came around, Eliza grabbed her forearm and slipped underneath the attack. Dottie's greater reach could threaten to catch her, so Eliza drove her elbow deep into the woman's ribs. The punch intended to return the gesture of Dottie's earlier kick merely caught the woman off balance.

With a hard shove, she bent Dottie over the small end table where she had fetched the gun. Eliza twisted as she lifted, but kept her eyes on the table as well as Dottie. This house offered too many surprises for her liking.

"You're my kind of lady." She chuckled. Eliza wrenched the arm harder, but Dottie still laughed. "It happens that I've got some openings in my gang, thanks to you."

"That's enough, Dottie!" Eliza hissed into her ear. "Where are they?"

"Where are who?"

"The suffragists! Where are they," and she leaned in even closer, "and why do you want Kate Sheppard so badly?"

"Oh dearie," the woman purred, "you shouldn't have done that."

"Done what?"

"Leaned into me," she said with a slight gasp. "Now *you're* off balance."

Dottie then turned into her trapped arm, teetering Eliza further forward as she pushed hard against the table. The agent stumbled back, fists up, as her opponent whirled about and charged. A wild left hook cut the air in front of Eliza, followed by another right hook that she batted away. At least Dottie was angry enough. Perhaps that would serve her when another opportunity presented itself.

Eliza shuffled back. In fact that was all she felt like she was doing. By the gods, Dottie was tall!

"Come on, just a step or two closer," she taunted, slowly circling with Eliza to one side. "For someone who fights like you, retreating wouldn't be your style."

"And wind up like your other dance partners?" Eliza said with a tiny laugh now peppering her own words. "Unlikely."

Dottie glanced at her fists, the tightly clenched fingers sporting the finest specimens of diamonds and sapphires.

Eliza lowered her guard only by an inch. "I'm going to ask again—"

"You can keep asking, but whatever makes you think I would tell you anything?"

"Is that how you want to play this little game then?" Eliza countered.

"Right now I'm following your lead, dearie." Dottie's gaze darkened. "At least, I was."

Dottie took one step—one confident, wide step forward—and Eliza's wrist disappeared in the woman's two-handed grasp. Damn that reach! Far longer than she had anticipated. Eliza found herself flung aside, her knee and foot catching a couch that she landed on hard, causing both it and her to tumble forward. She rolled back up to her feet and reassumed her defensive crouch, but felt a clamminess creep over her skin as she saw Dottie calmly cross over to her discarded gun.

"This is a disappointing stalemate, dearie," Dottie lamented, "because as much as you want to know about disappearing suffragists, I want to know who you are and why you are rummaging through my place. Something I do not take kindly to."

Eliza felt her jaw twitch. She couldn't reach Dottie in time, not before the bullet reached her; and there were no fine tea trays of any sort now within reach.

"I take it," Dottie began, still closing the distance between them, "you're not going to tell me who you are then?"

"You sent ornithopters to my house, and you didn't know who I was?"

"All I knew was that you were some privileged bint what's taken an interest in me," she said, waving the gun lightly, "and a rather unhealthy one at that. You seem to know all about me, except for something to do with me and suffragists."

"Dottie—"

"No," she said, shaking her head, "I really don't care."

The gun reached forward, and she pulled the trigger pulled just as the poker struck the base of her skull.

Dottie's gun went off, and the bullet did fly, but both gun and bullet were dreadfully off target thanks to the bullheaded chivalry of Douglas Sheppard.

"That woman," he wheezed, dropping the poker by her body, "was not very pleasant, I'm telling you."

Caught in the moment, Eliza ran up and kissed him. She meant it as a gesture of thanks, but the longer she stood there, the more her lips lingered.

She also wanted to enjoy the kiss, but something was niggling at the back of her mind. Perhaps that they were in a dangerous woman's home and that Diamond Dottie was merely knocked out?

Yes. That was it.

"Let's go," Eliza said.

Douglas took a deep breath, giving Dottie one final look. "With pleasure."

The boys were waiting in the foyer as Eliza had anticipated. They may have been of the street, but there were some loyal undercurrents in these children's hearts.

"Well, that could have gone better," Eliza huffed as she and the boys burst from the doors of Dottie's fine home and out into the streets.

"Could have gone worse," Christopher retorted.

"Speak for yourself, mate," Douglas winced. "I'm still trying to catch my breath."

"Where to?" asked Callum, his eyes looking up and down the street.

Christopher gave the anxious boy a nudge. "Go on then, what are you looking for? Bluebottles?"

"It's all right, Callum," Eliza said, her eyes also sweeping the outside. "I doubt if we'll have any crushers to contend with. It's Dottie's lot I'm more concerned about. If they think she's in a spot, they'll descend on us." Then she recalled the ornithopters from the previous night. "And I do mean that literally," she said, casting a glance upwards.

"Miss Eliza!" came Liam's voice from up the street.

Eliza prided her Ministry Seven in their field training, or at least the training that she and Harry had been able to bestow on them in their time together. They were children, but wise beyond their years. Clandestine operations were best kept quiet, particularly when talking to one another in the streets of London where ears were everywhere.

For Liam to be calling out to her, something was wrong. Very wrong.

He was short of breath when he finally reached her, but Liam managed, "Serena. She's hurt."

Eliza's heart sank. "Serena? Where is Wellington?"

"Mr. Books—" he gasped, took in a hard gulp of air, and then started again. "I told Mr. Books to take Serena to your house. You know Serena and doctors . . ."

Eliza shook her head. "Foolish girl." She waved down a cab, and then nudged her companion. "Hail us a cab, darling. We need to go home."

CHAPTER FIFTEEN

In Which a Fallen Angel Is Given a Hero's Welcome and Our Dashing Archivist Takes the Higher Road

Serena had only gotten worse since arriving at Eliza's apartment. While Wellington had treated men in the wilds of Africa, those were wounds earned in the heat of battle. Here and now his mind was blank, a strange numbness that bothered him. Even when his special talents surfaced, Wellington's brain was in a heightened state. All sensations were at peak. He could calculate trajectory and acquire targets as if the world were a parchment and he could sketch coordinates, angles, and mathematics in the air around him.

All that was gone at present. Nothing.

"Mr. Books," Alice asked, looking up from Serena. "Are you well, sir?"

"Alice," Wellington said and forced a smile that he didn't expect to be convincing. In fact, the smile hurt. "I am the least of your worries."

This was entirely different. This was a child.

"You did the right thing bringing little Serena here," the

maid said while placing the chilled cloth on her face. "Considering all the scrapes and bruises that I've had to tend to of Mistress Eliza's and Mr. Thorne's."

"So you've had some practise on this sort of thing?"

"Not this severe, but you did right, now don't you worry." Alice positioned the large chunk of ice against the cloth and Serena's face. "These little angels often come here after they have been through some rough and tumble, so we always have on hand whatever they need."

She wouldn't pander to him. Would she? Wellington rubbed his face, trying to find his composure.

"You have entrusted me with your secret. Continue to trust in me now. Serena needs you to be strong."

"But . . ." he began, his voice dry and hollow. "I am a stranger to her."

"No, you are Mistress Eliza's new partner. The girl understands that." She held out the wrapped ice. "You are her family now."

Following Alice's instruction, Wellington gingerly placed the packet underneath her lips. With the dressings now surrounding half of her face, Serena looked a full stone heavier. The red was spreading across most of her face, and darker hues of purple and black were creeping from underneath the dressings.

The tiny brow furrowed, and she flinched ever so slightly. Alice leaned in and shushed Serena as would a doting mother over a child sick with fever. "It's all right there. Mr. Books got you back to Mistress Eliza's."

She took a long, slow breath, and while the right eye was now swelling shut, the left eye fluttered open. "For now it is just Alice and myself." Wellington cleared his throat and added, "Liam told me about your concern for doctors, so I did as he told me and brought you here."

Serena gave a tiny nod. She then motioned for Wellington to come a bit closer. He gave his stained and soiled coat a futile smoothing-out with his hands before taking a place by Serena. Her hand continued to motion for him to come closer. Wellington placed his ear at her mouth and waited.

"Good. Job," Serena whispered. "Mum would. Be. Proud."

He looked back at the little girl who was forcing her swollen mouth into a smile.

"Tosh, child." Wellington squeezed her hand lightly. "You are a brave girl, indeed, speaking for Miss Braun like that. I did so once, and I thought she would skin me alive on the spot." Wellington looked up to the maid who gave him a wink. "A rather amazing adventure, that weekend in the country. And a valuable lesson learned."

"Now, Serena dear," Alice spoke gently, "you have some nasty bruising on your face. I've got the ice doing its work, but you must lie still. A little miracle in itself, to be sure, but it's what you need to do."

Wellington went to stand, but the girl's grip tightened on his hand.

"Seems she would prefer you to stay." Alice placed her hand gently on Wellington's shoulder as she said to Serena, "A glass of warm milk would help you rest, and rest is what you need. How does that sound?"

The girl nodded, wincing as she did so.

"Very well then." Pistons pumped and hissed as she stood. "And I'll put the kettle on while I warm the milk."

"Thank you, Alice."

The brass-enhanced maid had only taken a few steps when the door burst open. From outside came a chaotic whirl of people, all of them grim and silent.

Eliza raced to Serena's side, gently taking the child's other hand into hers. The agent of ordinance and action looked very different now.

"Serena?"

The girl gave a little grin. "Miss Eliza . . ."

"Shhh, that's enough from you."

"You. Should. See." Serena paused, took in a slow breath, and continued. "The *other*. One."

Wellington wondered if Eliza's brashness was countered presently by an equally stronger, less self-destructive force. Compassion.

Alice gave a nod and said, "I was just getting the kettle on." She started to leave, then turned to look upon the scene. "I wouldn't say no to some help. Colin, Eric, Jonathan, Jeremy, you're the cleanest of the lot, do come along."

The four boys quietly preceded Alice to the kitchen, the sounds of her hydraulics getting fainter until finally a quiet settled in the parlour.

"Did what you. Told me." Serena closed her eyes, swallowed, and then managed a smile. "Fought. To survive."

Wellington's brow furrowed, and he looked up to Eliza.

Her eyes never left the girl. "When the Ministry Seven came to pass, I taught them the difference between fighting to win, and fighting to survive." She enveloped Serena's hand in both of hers now, but no tears were falling. Wellington concluded she was not going to show anything other than determination or fortitude in front of the child. "I taught them to fight in such a way that their opponents, if they walked away, would never want to cross paths with them again." Eliza leaned closer to Serena. "What naughty thing did you do?"

"Bit off. Her ear." The remaining boys and Douglas all flinched.

He wanted to give Eliza more time. There never seemed to be enough of that when in the field with her. "Eliza?"

She slowly sat up and then her eyes flicked to Wellington. The compassion there dissipated.

"I won't be far, Serena. I need to talk to Mr. Books."

"Wait." Serena gave a little whimper, but she creased her brow and then squeezed Wellington's hand. "Mr. Books. Did. Good."

Eliza looked back at Serena, and then returned to the Archivist. Wellington let go of the child's hand and went to where Eliza had motioned. Instinct was telling him this little chat between himself and Eliza was going to be most unpleasant.

"What the hell happened?" a man's terse whisper came from behind him.

When he turned around, the unpleasantness increased a thousandfold. Douglas Sheppard was standing near his partner, his hand resting gently on her shoulder.

"I'm sorry," Wellington asked Douglas, "but I believe I am having a discussion with my partner here. May I help you somehow?"

"The way you helped that little girl back there?" Douglas snorted in reply. "I doubt it."

"I suggest, sir, you change your tone with me."

"And I suggest that the both of you stuff the cock of the roost routine before I become testy," Eliza broke in.

Douglas blinked. "What? You're not testy now?"

Eliza and Wellington replied in unison, "This is agitated."

The odd colonial out looked at them both. "I'm sorry, Eliza, but what did I do?"

She slowly turned to face Douglas. "Did I ask you to accompany us on our intrusion of Diamond Dottie's sanctum?"

"Well . . ." And he stopped, his lips puckering as if he were a fish out of water, taking final gasps of water that was not there. "Well, no."

"And there is your answer to what you did, Douglas." Her eyes shot back to Wellington. "What happened, Welly?"

"I made a mistake, if you must know. A slip of the tongue."

Eliza started, her mouth open as if to loose a barrage of insults; but instead her hand slowly ran down her face, stopping at her mouth. She stared at him over her palm and then, and then lowered her hand as she asked, her voice a thin veneer of calm, "A slip of the tongue?"

"The deception was moving at a pace until our target grew more insistent on leaving. The woman she set upon me had a club. I had a cane-sword. We had eyewitnesses. Not the best of combinations."

"Wellington, it was a simple operation. Delay her—"

"And I did, but then the plan began to unravel. I did the best I could."

"You call this your best, mate?" Douglas snapped. He pointed back to Serena.

"Douglas, I am more than capable—"

"As a gentleman," Douglas continued, "it is your responsibility to assure the child's safety!"

"Douglas . . ." Eliza warned.

The tall man stepped forward, looking down at Wellington. "How can you call yourself a man if you fail to protect a child properly?"

"Douglas!" Eliza whispered tersely.

"Miss Braun!" another voice snapped.

All of their heads turned to where the scolding had come from. The children and Alice stood, surrounding Serena. It appeared that Alice had reached a breaking point of her own.

Alice's voice pierced them all as a sharp, cold blade. "That. Will. Do!"

Wellington looked again at Douglas, or at least the back of his head. He hated to admit it, especially in front of Eliza, but, "Yes, Mr. Sheppard, you are quite correct." Both Douglas and Eliza turned to face him. "I did fail. I failed both Eliza and Serena. While I have been assured by Alice that the child will heal, the burden of this falls upon me."

Eliza's gaze kept hopping between Douglas and him. She went to speak, but Wellington lifted his hand, shaking his head. "Please, Eliza. The truth is that yes, my mistake put all this into motion. Now we are compromised, and I must bear this responsibility. Therefore, I humbly ask for your pardon and will trouble your investigation no more." He gave a nod to Eliza and walked around Douglas, saying nothing to the Ministry Seven or Alice as he went to the door.

"Books—"

"I have done enough today. Perhaps in this case, you are best working alone." He cast a glance at Douglas. "Or perhaps with a man more suited to your talents and particulars. Good day, Miss Braun."

The door closed behind him, and Wellington made his way down the staircase. Once outside, he took in a breath of air, hoping it would clear his mind.

One more failure to add to today's list.

Wherein Doctor Sound Retires to the Archives for Research on a New Project

Tick...
  Tock...
Tick...
Tock...

Sound watched the clock as would a big game hunter waiting patiently under camouflage. He was waiting. He had to wait.

Tick...
Tock...
Tick...
Tock...

Miss Shillingworth had poked her head into his office and bid him good night with a smile and a wave. He knew few in the Ministry would have believed his secretary could smile. In reality she was a very pleasant woman. He waited until he heard the lift gate shut behind her. Now there were only the muted sounds of the dockside to keep him company.

He flexed his fingers as the clock continued in its futile service. Every second, every minute—lost forever for what?

To sit? To remain static? Losing time was truly a shame, if not a tragedy.

But this would not be time wasted. He was a rogue of many colours, but he had made his honest pledge to Queen Victoria on assuming this office. He would not fail her, and the secret he kept would only remain secret if he was patient.

Tick . . .

Tock . . .

Tick . . .

Tock . . .

Thirty minutes. Perhaps that would be long enough. Agents rarely wished to stay in the offices any longer than necessary. That was their nature, after all. The incredible men and unique women of the Ministry's ranks preferred the wide, open spaces of the world. Their theatre. A grand theatre it was, too. The lush, smothering forests of the Amazon. The open barrenness of the Kalahari. The harsh, untamed savagery of Nepal. The agents faced danger as part of their day's work, and some of them fed off that.

Yet here he was, standing at his desk, his eyes fixed on the dossier of an agent asking for a change of pace. Quite out of character. Quite out of place.

With a final long, deep breath, Doctor Sound looked at his own pocket watch, walked over to the clock at the mantelpiece, and set it accordingly.

Then it was out into the receiving room and to the lift. When it arrived, clattering and rattling, he stepped in, pulled the cage door shut and set the Chadburn to take him down.

As it descended, Sound looked down into the gap between lift and walls. Below in the shadows of the shaft, he tried to make out any sounds from the Archives; but only the lift's motors whined and groaned in his ears.

Reaching the bottom, he opened the lift gate and walked down the small corridor to the iron hatch. When he wrenched it open moments later it moved with a grating, high-pitched whine. Before him lay the Archives—the history of the Ministry of Peculiar Occurrences and its many adventures throughout the Empire and the world. His footsteps echoed around him, a light counterpoint to the rumble of the massive generators powered by the strength of the Thames. He continued down into the darkness, its heaviness pushed aside by many gaslight globes suspended from the shelving units marked by year. Sound paused on reaching the archivists' desk. No cups of tea or morning newspapers present. Some signs of work, but nothing extraordinary. Clutter present on either side of the desk caught his attention. His eyes narrowed as he studied the details.

If he were to describe the mess on Books' and Braun's shared desk in a single word, it would be *intentional*.

Perhaps tonight's personal project would take a little longer than he had anticipated.

Doctor Sound continued along the shelves, casually noting the years as he stepped further and further back in time. Reaching Year One, he turned right to see the heavy iron door marked "Restricted Access." Withdrawing the two keys from his inside breast pocket, Sound inserted both into the hatch's locks and turned them away from each other in one fluid motion. The latches released with a hiss and then the Director pulled the door open. With a final look behind him, he removed the two keys from the hatch, slipped the keys back into his pocket, and stepped into the soft sapphire glow.

The hatch hissed shut behind him, and the low hum and dark shadows of the Archives were replaced by the warm blue light and slightly higher-pitched thrumming of the Ministry's Restricted Area. Doctor Sound continued further along the metal grating of the walkway, looking around as he was prone to do when he first entered this deepest of the Crown's secrets. He smiled every single time. *Perhaps you never got too old for wide-eyed wonder.*

Sound walked up to the terminal at the end of the walkway and, from the vest pocket opposite of his pocket watch, produced a small brass key, which he inserted into the keyhole and turned. Twice, anti-clockwise.

"Now then," Doctor Sound said aloud, rubbing warmth into his hands as he watched the screen before him flicker to life, "let's see what we can discover about our ambitious agent Bruce Campbell."

CHAPTER SIXTEEN

Wherein Eliza Sees Things She Shouldn't and Learns Things She Didn't Know

Douglas was having a hard time keeping up with Eliza, and apparently also having some difficulty understanding her motivation. They had taken a hansom in silence, but finally, as they were walking down the street towards Wellington Thornhill Books' house, the New Zealander could take no more of it.

"Remind me why we are going to apologise again?"

"Not 'we,'" she said, poking him with one finger. "Me. I was very rude to Wellington, and perhaps, just perhaps, he is . . . right."

At that Douglas jerked to a stop. "By Jove—did hell itself freeze over or did Miss Eliza D. Braun say she was wrong?"

He was trying to be funny, but she realised that he did perhaps have a point. However, she was certainly not going to admit it, so she now wagged the finger she'd assaulted him with in front of his eyes. "Ah . . . I said he was right, *not* that I was wrong!"

"Ah well," he sighed theatrically, "still the same old Eliza then."

"I am not going to dignify that with a reply." She tucked her hand around his elbow, while with the other she withdrew the scrap of paper with Wellington's address on it. In all their months together she had never actually seen the Archivist's home, yet he'd been to her apartments many times. It was curious . . . and that bolt from the blue made Eliza increase her pace. She was actually pulling Douglas along with her.

Hampstead was a nice enough location—even if it was not very metropolitan. The houses here though did have their own small gardens, and oozed a certain gentility that spoke of good money earned in good time and not too rushed. Tree-lined streets and tranquility. It was not the place she would have imagined her colleague to inhabit. He'd always seemed so much part of the Archives.

Living a life in Hampstead said that Wellington was doing well as an archivist. The thought idly crossed her mind that perhaps she should ask for an increase in her own salary.

"This is it." As Eliza spoke, she examined the redbrick building sitting behind the ironwork fence, and then the small garden. "I would never have considered that Wellington would like topiary."

Douglas stared at the neatly carved hedge leading up to the door. "Seems a bit of an odd bird, Eliza."

"In the best possible way," she shot back as she unlatched the gate and pulled him up the gravel path, "Now let's go in and apologise."

Wellington answered the doorbell himself—no maid, clockwork or otherwise. His jacket was off, his collar loosened, and a patchwork apron tied around his waist. There was something endearing about actually catching him, the amateur tinker, in mid-work. This was more like it— exactly how she imagined Wellington Books off the clock. Also it was one of the few times she'd seen him in a state of undress—excepting the time they had masqueraded as husband and wife. That had been quite a different kind of exciting experience all together.

"Miss Braun." It was not lost on her that he had retreated into some formality. "I was not aware you knew where I lived."

She waved the piece of paper before her triumphantly. "Even Shillingworth has to take tea sometime. So I managed this feat yesterday. You didn't notice as you were still punishing yourself."

Her colleague's shoulders slumped. "I suppose I should have paid better attention." He spotted Douglas. "And I see you've brought company—fortunately, I just put the kettle on." He opened the door wider and ushered them in. Once formality had been dispensed with, he led them to the front parlour.

It was not what would be called formal, or indeed tidy. At least at first glance.

Douglas waited until Wellington had disappeared down the hallway before muttering to Eliza, "I told you so—an odd bird."

Carefully she strolled around the room examining every piece of it, like it was a crime scene. Tidy piles of papers were stacked against the wall, none of them standing higher than her knee. Every surface on the dressers and table was covered with cogs and gears, or half-assembled pistons. Pinned against the walls were diagrams and schematics. She was no expert but this one looked like some kind of heavy cannon assembly. Presiding over all of this was a huge, fluffy tabby cat. He sat atop the largest stack and watched these two interlopers with bright yellow eyes. His expression precluded Eliza from daring to pet him, but as she passed by he began to purr as if to comfort her.

In between all this strangeness were semblances of a normal life. The room was littered with plenty of tiny framed landscapes. She recognised the Isle of Skye and Brighton—as well as some representations of places that could only be in Africa.

Finally at the conclusion of her reconnaissance, Eliza reached the fireplace. Hanging above the iron grate was a magnificent portrait—its grandness totally out of place in the simple room. It was the only image of a person on display. It showed a beautiful lady, her back turned to the viewer, her face caught in profile. Around the ornate gilt frame was hung black ribbon. Eliza didn't need any plaque to tell her what she could recognise immediately. This was Wellington's mother. He had the same strong nose and her hazel eyes.

While Eliza was contemplating that, she heard her colleague's footsteps in the hallway. Quickly she spun away. Douglas, apparently to feign indifference or to cover up his awkwardness, went to pet the huge cat. When it flattened its ears and hissed at him, he fairly leapt back.

"Don't mind Archimedes." Wellington came in balancing a tray with the accoutrements of tea making, "He makes a lot of fuss and bother, but he wouldn't hurt anything bigger than a rat."

The tabby stared at them as if to deny that reassurance. The Archivist laid out cups and saucers, and began to pour. Though he might have little care for the décor of his house, Eliza noticed that the tea service was of the finest bone china.

"I even managed to locate up some biscuits." Wellington shoved the offerings nearer, and then poured some cream into a saucer and put it down on the floor. Archimedes dropped down and began drinking with the elegance of a member of the aristocracy. The Archivist looked oddly nervous, and it seemed that perhaps Eliza had not made the right choice in coming here.

Finally, she could no longer take it. "Look, Welly, I didn't go to all this trouble to track you down to make everything difficult for you. I needed to tell you something and I couldn't wait until Monday."

Somehow in his own house Wellington was more formidable—far more so than in the Archives. He waited while she considered the best words to use. However, there were no others. "So perhaps you were right."

He kept silent—tilting his head and concentrating on stirring.

"All right then—you *were* right. I don't think Dottie did it."

Barely were the words out of her mouth, than Wellington's house rocked. For a second the thought crossed her mind that her admission had changed the fabric of reality. The piles of work in progress tilted alarmingly, and the pictures on the walls slanted. Archimedes looked up from his careful drinking of the cream, blinked, and then resumed his snack. The rest of the occupants of the room were not nearly so blasé about it.

Douglas leapt to his feet. "By Jove, what was that?"

"No need to worry!" Wellington exclaimed, in a tone that had the completely opposite effect, and then bolted out of the room and back down the hallway.

"Stay here," Eliza barked to Douglas as she darted after her colleague. "In case this whole thing goes pear-shaped."

The house was settling back on its foundations like a lady with a bad case of indigestion, but now there was smoke oozing up through the floorboards. Eliza shouted out his name, but Wellington snatched up a bucket of something and dashed down a set of stairs.

Eliza followed in his wake, though she had to take care because the smoke was so thick in here she could barely see where her foot was going. A whirring sound filled the house now, like the engine of a dirigible. As she stood poised on the last stair, the haze began to clear and she could finally see where she was.

Strings of yellow lights hung suspended from the ceiling, which gave the underground space the air of a mining operation. Which it somewhat was, by the look of it. Thick iron beams held up the house above them, and that was surely not an original feature to the property. Once again there were stacks of paraphernalia and a laden desk, but in addition there were a number of curious-shaped objects under oilskin cloth.

While Eliza marvelled at that, Wellington was busy in

front of a whirring fan device that was responsible for sucking the smoke out of the room. Since he was preoccupied, she decided to pad around the room instead, and find out what she could about her co-worker. It didn't seem like he had even noticed she'd followed him, and the rattle of the machine drowned out the sound of her footsteps.

Eliza knew that the Archivist had an interest in tinkering, but had always assumed it was a gentlemanly hobby. The scale of what she saw now disproved that little notion. The downstairs workshop was packed full of tools that the clankertons at the Ministry would have been proud of. They might have considered Wellington a novice, but they would have been wrong.

As she examined the workbench she found a real surprise: a half-assembled Gatling gun. Eliza shot a look over her shoulder but Wellington was still working the levers of the fan device. "Quite the contrary man," she muttered to herself before moving on.

Against the wall she found a small shelf where a row of medals hung. At first she thought they might have been his father's or grandfather's, but she read with some surprise that they were for the Boer War. She even recognised the Queens South Africa medal—though she was not well-enough versed in military regalia to identify the various clasps on it. In previous conversations he had touched on the fact he'd been in the army, but she understood his reluctance to discuss it. However he certainly had not continued military neatness.

Her gaze travelled on across his workbench. It was scattered with papers and notebooks. On them were the kind of mathematical workings and formulas that she'd seen in the research division, and on Blackwell and Axelrod's desk. Wellington had been hard at work on something. None of it made any sense to her, but she was impressed anyway.

In the centre of the room was a large lump of a device that took up most of the space, and running in front of it was a ramp angling up. Whatever Wellington was creating down here, he wanted to roll it to the surface at some stage. Cautiously, she lifted the corner of the oilskin. She caught a glimpse of a wheel and the front of some kind of velo-motor when she ran out of time.

"Eliza!" Both of them jumped when Wellington's hand clamped down on her wrist. She dropped the corner of the tarpaulin. "What are you doing here?"

She shrugged. "Forgive me—but when a house shakes like that and smoke starts coming from every orifice I think you might need a helping hand."

"Oh tosh." Wellington waved at her. "It was a little experiment I left brewing—that's all. No need for alarm."

"I am so glad you don't 'brew' experiments in the Archives."

The smile he shot her was both wicked and rather enjoyable. "As far as you know." He turned back and flicked off a row of levers. The fan shut off and conscious thought was once again possible.

"This is quite impressive, Welly." Eliza tucked her hands into her pockets, lest she be tempted to touch more things. "You should bring Axelrod and Blackwell down here." Naturally, she was messing with his mind, but this whole downstairs revelation had shaken her, and she needed time to acclimatise.

As an answer Wellington snorted. "I really don't think they would appreciate it."

"Well, you are certainly beavering away on your off hours. And by the by, I thought you disliked guns! Have you been withholding information from me?" She pointed accusingly to the dismantled Gatling on his workbench.

"I dislike *using* them," he corrected her tartly, "that doesn't mean I don't like the engineering challenge of working with them."

Her fingers trailed over the remaining pieces he had laid out. They were the mountings for the gun to be attached to a vehicle. "A Gatling gun on a velo-motor? Remind me not to cross your path when out on the town."

"Please, Eliza." He produced another oilskin and threw it over the pieces. "This is my domain. I don't come into your house and poke about."

"No, you do worse than that—you make a mess."

In the low light it was hard to tell if Wellington was blushing, but he turned away.

Perhaps she had taken her ribbing too far. Eliza placed a gentle hand on his shoulder. "I'm sorry, but it seems to me you are in the wrong place, Welly. You should be in Research and Design—not the Archives."

Her colleague fixed her with a hard look. "I did originally apply for the position of junior inventor, but was not successful. The Director said my talents were best served belowstairs." It didn't take a trained field agent to hear the trace of bitterness in his voice. It certainly explained a few of the barbed comments he had directed in Blackwell and Axelrod's direction. "Besides," he went on, "did you think the creation of the analytical engine was a one-off event?"

A shrug conveyed her confusion. "Truthfully, I thought it was something all Archivists could do. I never claimed to be knowledgeable in these things."

His laugh filled the workshop. "I never imagined I would ever hear that! Miss Eliza D. Braun admitting she was wrong. I wish I had some recording device running."

"So what exactly are you doing down here, Welly?" She waved her hands to take in the full scope of his endeavours.

"Several things at once. I like to work that way." The Archivist pointed to the workbench strewn with papers. "I'm working on some calculations on how much power it would take to snatch a person out of thin air, and from there I should be able to determine the range of a device."

Eliza cocked her head. "How can you possibly do that when you don't know what kind of machine they are using—or if they are using a machine at all?"

When he touched his nose in a conspiratorial fashion, his grin was blinding. "Let's just say that being the Archivist at the Ministry of Peculiar Occurrences gives me access to a few pieces of research that make all the difference in the world." He frowned. "Still, it is giving me some difficulty, but I think I am near a breakthrough."

Then Wellington pointed to the still smoking test tubes. "That is my own private experiment into . . . well, it's not connected with the suffragist case."

When Eliza opened her mouth, he waved his hand to include the large velo-motor. "And these things too—but this"—he tapped the circular device—"is allowing me to examine the film the Protectors were kind enough to provide. I must say that despite your dislike for Miss Lawrence, she has done an admirable job of filming the occurrences."

"A pity she has not done nearly so well when protecting the ladies." Eliza sniffed.

"Please—put aside your dislike for Miss Lawrence," Wellington snapped. "Especially since she possessed the wherewithal to covertly film these committee movies." He waved in the air towards his massive worktable as he turned to what appeared to be a modified kinetoscope. "Now have a seat and watch what I've discovered so far."

Eliza grabbed a nearby stool and waited as Wellington fiddled with the carnival attraction. "Exactly how am I to watch the footage when I am over here and the kinetoscope is—"

Her words caught in her throat as, in the centre of a bare patch on the workshop wall, materialised shimmering images of London's suffragist leaders.

"Bloody brilliant, Welly," Eliza whispered as the figures moved silently along the wall.

"Not as hard as I thought, modifying it to project an image on a surface. A bit like a phantasmagoria, if you get the light source just—"

"Welly, hush," she said, watching the film intently.

She watched as the women continued their discussions, any of their gestures appearing faster than normal. Then their expressions changed, one or two seeming to sniff the air. Then bolts of electricity flashing about, a blinding light, and then, a committee member suddenly gone. With no sound, the pandemonium ensuing afterward made the hair on the back of Eliza's neck stand on end.

The image then slowed to a halt. "This is marked as the disappearance of Mildred Cady. She was the Treasurer." The images then suddenly reversed. Eliza noted Wellington slowly turning a crank connected to the kinetorama. "I have to do this slowly lest the film snap. I have to keep an eye on the film's tension and temperature."

"Of course," Eliza said, nodding slightly. She couldn't hide her fascination with this creation of Wellington's. Ingenious.

The film started again, and Mildred Cady—a woman of short and stout build but, as seen in the footage, quite a formidable speaker—took the floor. Perhaps she was speaking her mind on a motion made during a previous public meeting or between the committee members themselves, but she held the ladies' rapt attention. Then came the distraction. Eliza assumed it was the smell just before the abduction. The lightning. A flash. And Mildred was gone.

The images then recessed back as Wellington spoke, "I have timed it in each of the abductions where someone reacts, obviously, to the smell of electricity. It's roughly thirty seconds between that tell and the incident." He began playback and then paused the film. "I need more time to review the footage, but I have noticed something already." He stepped into the projected image and tapped on a seated image of a dark-skinned individual. "Miss Culpepper is present at every meeting."

"That's all? Welly, most of the committee members are there at every meeting. I am there practically every meeting too—am I a suspect?"

"This is different." Wellington turned and looked at the wall with the flickering image from Cady's capture. "There's something . . . wrong about her though. I can't quite put my finger on it."

Eliza was used to working on listening to her instincts—or

had been when she'd been a full agent, not some half-baked paper shuffler. If this were Hill or Lochlear or even Campbell, she might have put more store by it. Wellington Thornhill Books was not a field agent. He was an Archivist, very good at his job, but not a field agent. So, she patted his arm. "We'll need more than that to arrest a vaunted member of high society."

He nodded slowly. "Yes, I can see that. Like everything the Ministry does, it must be based on facts. Once I have delivery of the new equipment I should know more. It is a slow process." He rubbed the bridge of his nose, pushing his glasses off them for a moment. He looked grey and tired.

Eliza plumped herself down on the stool he had near the workbench. "I'm sorry, Welly. I wasted so much time on Dottie. I just hope we can catch the perpetrator before any more women go missing."

"It's not your fault." He took her hands in his. "Diamond Dottie is a nefarious underworld figure, and the kind of person that could well do such terrible things."

Eliza let out a long sigh, and slumped a little. It wasn't the first mistake she had made in an investigation, yet this one stung the most. These were her people, and she took it deeply personally that the Ministry had failed to find the perpetrator of such crimes. She'd been happy to jump to a conclusion.

Wellington's thumb was rubbing the spot between her thumb and her forefinger gently as she considered these bitter facts. It was rather pleasant.

"Is it safe to come down?" Douglas' head appeared around the doorjamb from the staircase. Eliza and Wellington jerked their hands apart.

"Certainly," Eliza smoothed back a curl of her hair.

"Quite the cave you have here." Douglas came over to them, but showed no curiosity, as Eliza had, to look beneath the oilskins. He put his hand on the back of Eliza's neck.

"Thank you." Wellington smiled. "It's my sanctuary."

"You should get out more," the other man joked, and then

seeing the Archivist's brow furrow, he put both hands up and added hastily, "I mean no man should be shut away in the darkness like a mole all the time."

"Wellington gets out." Eliza found herself defending her co-worker. "With me."

"Oh come now," Douglas twirled a spanner on the work-bench and chuckled. "That hardly counts, dear lady." He stopped, spun around and pointed at the Archivist, his lips quirked in a slight sneer. "I know. You should come to the rugby game with us tomorrow morning. I take it you played at school at least?"

"At Harrow I was in the first Fifteen."

"Excellent," Douglas slapped him on the back. "Then you'll play for Mother England, against our colonial team. It should be fun."

Eliza watched with a confused expression on her face. She prided herself on knowing men, but she was unsure about this dance Wellington and Douglas were doing. Were they trying to be friends, or manoeuvering each other into place so they could stab each other in the kidneys? Part of her said that allowing them to meet on the rugby field was a very bad idea indeed, but another part said perhaps allowing them to let off some steam regarding their rivalry would not be a bad idea at all.

Wellington smiled slightly. "It has been a while since I played . . . but we are in the middle of a investigation I really—"

"Go on, Welly." Eliza stood up. "Your eyes will go square looking at all those flickering images. Take a moment for yourself. Besides," she pointed her fingers at both the men, "I could do with some entertainment myself."

CHAPTER SEVENTEEN

Where Wellington Books Takes Some Offence

Wellington set off from his home early Sunday morning, forgoing church and even tea at eleven. In his satchel he carried his rugby boots. Though it had been a very long time since he'd played, he was confident he would not let his English teammates down, nor embarrass himself in front of Eliza.

The teams were warming up on the field. The Englishmen were in a variety of clothing, while the New Zealanders were standing around in rather simple, black shirts. Over to one side was Eliza, her back towards the Archivist, talking to Douglas.

Heat rose in Wellington's face. Here, on this cold field of battle, a primal urge to play for her attention rushed unexpectedly to him. He paused a moment to regain his composure.

"Wellington?" Eliza had come up on him unannounced—as she was wont to do. As if in deference to the menfolk around her, she'd dressed simply this morning: a dark blue walking dress with a boater whose spare decoration was a straight emerald green feather that pointed behind her like a horizontal exclamation point. The only jewellery she wore was a cameo with a unicorn engraved upon it. Usually Eliza liked to enlighten him on which raja or viscount had given her such trinkets—today, she did not. "Are you all right to do this?" Her brow furrowed.

Really, she was somehow more lovely without any adornment, Wellington mused.

"Welly?" Now she squeezed his arm.

"Pardon?" The Archivist jerked backwards.

"I said, are you sure you should do this?"

He straightened up to his full height. Sometimes it felt as though she doubted his masculinity. Well, today he would change all that.

"Indeed I am." He stalked over to the bench where a few chaps were chatting. After inserting himself amongst them, and thinking he had shaken her off, Wellington began changing his shoes.

He should have known better—Eliza did not give up that easily. She elbowed her way through the press of men and continued to berate him with her concerns. "It's just that these aren't any old rugby players—they're the New Zealand team. Douglas went to school with several of them, and he might have meant well asking you, but I worry."

Those were words Wellington could not recall ever having heard out of her mouth. It was so unusual that he paused lacing his boots and glanced up. He'd seen his colleague in firefights, confined at the whims of madmen, and throwing explosives left and right—yet never had he read as much concern in her eyes as he did now.

Surely, she didn't think him that much of a coward.

"Stuff and nonsense," he said, jerking the laces tight. "There is absolutely no reason for any such emotion."

Before she could say any more, he got up, tucked his spectacles into his street shoes, and strode forward onto the pitch. He did now notice that the men about him were of a considerable size and musculature. How the jerseys could contain them was somewhat of a mystery. Wellington swallowed hard, but steeled himself. He was, after all, surrounded by Englishmen. It wasn't as if he were going on the field alone.

Douglas, who was wearing a dark blue jersey, laughed and joked with his countrymen. Wellington found himself rather hastily introduced to his fellow players, who all seemed good solid chaps, but whose names all went past in a blur. A tall Yorkshireman, who had taken on the role of captain, sized up the Archivist with a practised eye. "How's your speed, old man?"

Wellington glanced back at the sizeable New Zealanders. "Pretty up to snuff, I think you will find."

"Then you'll do fine as our outside centre." And that easily it was decided.

However, there were some unusual formalities that the visitors had to get out of the way.

First the New Zealanders lined up in a row. When they began chanting in Maori and slapping first their thighs and then their chests, for a moment he was not sure what delusion he had fallen into. And then he remembered reading about something called the *haka*. A war dance he recalled—one that he'd read about while perusing a tome on native customs. Several of the New Zealanders were Maori, but all of them set to the dance with a great deal of gusto.

Glancing from side to side, the Archivist noted that his interest was not the prevailing attitude of the English. It was mostly confusion with a confident few chuckling at the display. Wellington, however, considered something more ominous: if they were performing a savage dance, then they could most likely play savagely too. Such an energetic dance would fire the blood. Perhaps Eliza should do it before going into a gunfight. He grinned at the thought—and consequently missed the kickoff.

One thing he did notice was that Douglas Sheppard was playing in the position of wing. Usually such players were light fellows, meant for running the ball and scoring a try. Eliza's paramour was anything but small, and though Wellington hated to admit it, he did not suffer for it. He was fast on his feet, and a terror to try and tackle.

Douglas' so-called "friendly" game was far more brutal than Wellington expected. This he figured out when the first of the opposition backs took him down with a solid tackle from one side. The rest of the game proceeded in much the same light, and Wellington was very glad to make it to half-time with only a few bruises.

Tea was served by a gleaming clockwork mandroid, its collection of tiny wheels on a rotating track easily gliding it over the beaten field. Eliza was standing on the other side of the pitch, talking with her countrymen, but her attention turned to him and her expression went from jovial to concerned. As she made her way over to him, he tilted his chin upwards. "Lovely day for rugby, Miss Braun," he said, forestalling her as best he could. "Partaking in the manly arts truly makes one feel alive."

His colleague's gaze trailed from muddy boots, along soiled shorts, and beaten jersey, to his face. Wellington wiped at it self-consciously, but there was no getting away from the fact that he'd taken his fair share of tumbles into the wintery puddles.

Eliza's lips pressed together. "You've proved your point, you know. You're as tough as any man here, and they all know it. Even Douglas is talking about you." She pointed back in the general direction of the other team. "They're impressed, so now you can graciously bow out of this, and tomorrow—provided you can walk—we can head back to the Archives and do what we need to."

"On this point I shall not be moved. I started this game, and by Jove I shall finish it." Right on cue, the referee blew his whistle and the game was back on. Placing his cup back on the top of the mandroid, he got up and walked back to his position without a second glance at Eliza.

The second half was even more painful. Wellington ran the ball several times, and the English even got a try thanks to his efforts, however the New Zealanders scored three times. Douglas scored two of them. Their offensive line was brutally efficient and nothing seemed to stop them.

Eliza was standing among the crowd at the halfway line, and her glare seemed to be aimed squarely in Wellington's direction. It was most insulting, and the little knot of anger in the Archivist's stomach began to grow. It was, after all, not his fault that he was here. Douglas Sheppard had asked him, taunted him really, and he'd responded in kind.

All of this Wellington simmered over, while running back and forward on the pitch, chasing, tackling, and endangering himself. His anger seemed to reach real steam when the ball found itself in his hands. The feel of leather, the winter crispness in his nostrils, and the raw determination in his teammates' eyes, snapped something inside the Archivist. Some mad, competitive demon grabbed hold of his primitive emotions, and he barrelled forward, rushing towards the goal.

Ahead, he saw Douglas running towards him, positioning himself for a legal side tackle. The proper thing to do would have been to increase pace, or with some fancy footwork elude his attack. None of these things mattered to Wellington, however—all he saw was a chance to knock Douglas down a peg or two. Literally.

Pushing off from his left foot, he lurched to the right, and into Douglas. Wellington's shoulder collided with the New Zealander's chest with a resounding thump. The impact shuddered through the Archivist's body like he'd run into a brick wall. It was most satisfactory.

The New Zealander flew backwards and landed in the mud, the breath knocked out of him. Wellington paid him no heed, racing up the pitch to place the ball squarely between the goalposts. The Archivist put his hands on his knees and sucked in a good few chilly breaths.

When he glanced over his shoulder, he caught a glimpse of Douglas still on the ground, surrounded by his teammates. Everyone else, including Wellington's own side had stopped in their places, and the air was full of the referee's whistle. For a moment they stood there, frozen in to the spot, all the players steaming in the winter chill.

The cold voice from his past echoed in his head. *Bloody good show. You've made me very proud.*

Yes, indeed his father would have enjoyed this moment. Wellington felt a little twinge of pride that he'd managed to knock Douglas down like that. One of the English backs, who was standing nearby, shook his head. "What the hell was that, Books?"

The tone in his voice was embarrassed. Eliza was running onto the pitch, heading towards Douglas, but the look she shot her colleague was terrifying: it was the chill gaze of a stranger. The shock had worn off the New Zealander players, and they began shouting and pointing at the Archivist. Only the English players holding them back stopped them from explaining to Wellington how much they didn't like his kind of play.

Suddenly Wellington didn't feel proud. He had broken no rules, but that did not absolve him. The hit was intentional and hardly sportsmanlike. As Eliza bent over Douglas, he turned and strode off the field, collected his things and left. His father's training had never left him, and by forgetting that, he had endangered a fellow gentleman. (Regardless if that gentleman was a cad.) Worse, he had acted terribly in front of Eliza when he had only meant to make a good impression.

Well, there was one thing he was still good for. He'd go back to where he was comfortable—back to his basement, back to the investigation to look for answers.

CHAPTER EIGHTEEN

In Which Eliza D. Braun Must Confront Ghosts of New Zealand Past

"**W**ellington should not have bowled you over like that," Eliza growled, while taking a bowl of steaming water from Alice.

"It's part of the game." Douglas shrugged, wincing as he did. "Just a bit of rough and tumble."

"It was most certainly not," Eliza glared at him. "It was absolutely shameful."

"Maybe so, but I am fine."

She knew full well that he was not, and Eliza wondered exactly what she would find when she got his shirt off. Once there had been a day when she'd not been concerned about that—in fact it had been her main goal.

Alice snorted, breaking her recollections. "And who is looking after Mr. Books?" she snapped, dropping a stack of towels on Eliza's parlour chair. "Do you think he has a pretty lady to care for his bruises?"

Sometimes her maid completely forgot the line between employer and employee. It was entirely her fault for never pointing it out. Neither could she now. "I don't give a jot what Wellington is doing. He caused this whole thing, Alice."

Her bow-shaped lips pressed together. "Yes, miss. I know he did—but still, after all he has done . . ." Her voice trailed off as her gaze wandered to the recently papered-over bullet holes.

Alice had the ability to cut anyone, even Eliza, down to size. Quite impressive considering her curly red hair and impish appearance.

Douglas looked from one woman to the other in pain but still dumfounded by this little exchange.

"Yes." Eliza pursed her lips. "Wellington has done quite enough. Including breaking the rules of the game quite terribly."

"He didn't break the rules," Douglas corrected. "He just directed his passions on me."

"I am sure he had plenty of reasons." Alice put her hands on her hips, before reluctantly adding, "Miss."

Then when her employer shot her an aggravated look, she finally took the cue and stomped out of the room to the accompaniment of pistons hissing. Eliza noted that though her prosthetics always gave Alice a heavy step, this time they were even louder.

Douglas tilted his head and watched her. "It's hard to imagine you with a maidservant, Eliza, but somehow that one seems to suit you."

"You mean with her prosthetic legs?"

"No." He grinned. "With her attitude."

"Yes, well, Alice was not exactly born to service." Eliza rummaged around in her cupboard until she found a large jar of the company-issue ointment. Unscrewing the lid she peered in. "Oh dear, I think I have only a little left." She glanced up and gave him a somewhat sheepish smile. "I do tend to go through rather a lot of it."

"I can imagine." Cautiously, Douglas felt his chest. "I'm no expert but I think I may have at least a bruised rib or two."

"Well then," Eliza swallowed, trying to find the next few words—but there really were no two ways about it. "Take off your shirt."

Douglas was looking at her with those ridiculously bright blue eyes, but she wouldn't meet his gaze. She heard rather than saw him do as he was bidden. Miss Eliza D. Braun had seen her fair share of naked men's chests; she had caused not a few of them to get that way. She could certainly not be considered a wallflower, and yet memory made this quite a different situation. Perhaps she should have let Alice and her relentless efficiency do this part.

Steadying her nerves, she dipped her fingertips into the mint-smelling cream and began to smear it on. She did not hurry.

"This reminds me of how we first met." She could feel Douglas' voice, low and entrancing, through her flesh and bone. "You were less gentle then."

Eliza swallowed hard but could not avoid the recollection. She'd been only a mere slip of a thing working at her father's pub. She'd been used to the cursing and the occasional intimate suggestion when her dad had his back turned. When a sailor fresh off a whaling ship offered to show her his harpoon, a tall stranger had leapt to her defence. The resulting brawl had been one of the more spectacular the pub had ever seen, and had required Eliza's father, brothers, and naturally, herself to get involved. When she'd slid over the bar and leapt into the melee, she hadn't really taken much notice of her defender.

It was only later, when she'd helped him get up off the floor, that she'd felt a flash of heat. Even nursing an amazing shiner, Douglas had been handsomer than any man she'd ever met. While her father wasn't looking she'd poured him a beer, and fetched ice for his wounds.

Eliza flinched. "I didn't know any better. I've amassed a lot of practice since then." She leaned over and picked up the roll of bandages next to the jar of ointment, but Douglas stopped her hand.

"I know things are different now"—he paused—"but I never forgot you. There's no one quite like you, Eliza." Now it was his fingertips that brushed her skin, skimming over her face, and there was the ghost of remembered caresses that went with it.

She'd loved him. He was her first love, her first everything. She'd thought she'd lost him, and now Fate had played her a kindly card—he was here again, with her. Everyone at the Ministry thought she was as tough as nails, impulsive, as brave as any man. Yet, she had not always been that way, and a small part of the agent wanted to go back to that place where she had been young, full of hope and possibilities.

When Douglas shifted, slid his arms around her, and pulled her onto his lap, she let him. He smelt warm and intoxicating, the exertion of the rugby bringing out the musk, and she was positive that his skin would taste like salt should she put her tongue to it. Exactly as it had when Eliza had first let him hold her. Douglas' hands slid over her shoulders and tangled in her hair.

"You haven't forgotten, have you?" he whispered against her neck, the warmth of it sending shivers along her spine.

Turning, she looked him in the eye, their lips only scant inches apart. It had been a heady few days, and Eliza could feel her heart racing in her chest. It was impossible for her to forget him, the long antipodean summers, lying in the sand dunes, their hands on each other. Civilisation quite forgotten in primal sensation.

"No," she replied softly, "I have most certainly not forgotten."

Then Douglas Sheppard smiled and kissed her. His lips and tongue on hers were sweet, like a memory of sunlight. He tasted of sweat, loss, and melancholy. Still, such things could stir passion, and Eliza wrapped her arms around him, feeling his warmth kindle hers. As his hands pulled her tighter, she knew they would end up in bed. She'd wanted him so badly after her exile to London. She'd dreamt of him and of this moment.

Yet, as his fingers slid up her thigh and his teeth began

to describe sharp little circles on her neck, a sudden thought nearly stopped her enjoyment of this moment. Wellington had broken the rules. Wellington lived for the rules.

Douglas' fingers brushed the top of her stocking, sliding under it. The stab of lust brought a gasp to her lips.

Wellington had only ever broken the rules for her. Dammit, these thoughts were getting in the way.

"There are far too many clothes between us," Eliza growled, tearing off her jacket and fumbling with her blouse. She heard a few buttons clatter against the floor. The cool air felt good against her skin.

"Now *that's* the Eliza Braun I remember," Douglas cooed. "My sweet, little Eliza," he whispered kissing the tops of her breasts.

Beneath her corset, she could feel her skin warming, her body wanting . . .

Even as her mind screamed over and over again, *Wellington broke the rules* for me.

Suddenly, when those blue eyes looked into hers, her warmth dropped away, and a chill sadness descended. They should have been hazel.

Eliza slipped off Douglas' lap, tearing herself away from his hands, and stood up suddenly. "Eliza?" He was a little *breathless* too.

This is quite ridiculous, she told herself. In her first year in London, she'd dreamt of this very moment. When alone in the privacy of her bedroom, she'd shed tears over this man, all the time hoping he did not hate her. Now, here he was, half-clothed, kissing her the way she yearned to be kissed, and yet it was completely the wrong man.

She began to understand why men thought of her sex as fickle. Yet, as she turned around and looked down at Douglas she understood that she was not that girl who had slid across the bar to stop the proud son of a good family being beaten to an early grave. Too many experiences separated her from that person.

"I'm sorry, Douglas." Slowly, and with long breaths to calm herself, she began buttoning up her clothing. At least, where buttons remained.

"Sorry?" Those blue eyes were glazed with confusion and desire.

"This isn't something that I can do. Not now."

He cleared his throat. "I am sorry too, Eliza. I know our relationship in New Zealand was not exactly . . . proper."

Rolling around in the sand dunes, making love recklessly as young people are wont to do. Despite all her jibes aimed at Wellington, she only fell into bed with men she loved—and she had not loved that many. One of them was here in the flesh, before her. Another had been killed in Bedlam without her ever telling him, nor doing anything about it.

In this moment of clarity she regretted many of her sharp-edged jokes aimed in Wellington's direction.

"No," Eliza sat on the chair opposite him. "It was perfectly improper, yet at the time I enjoyed it."

"As did I," he leaned forward, his arms on his knees, "But now it is time to confess something to you." Despite her confused thoughts, she was intrigued, but she let him continue. He cleared his throat. "When Mother declared she was coming to London, I insisted on coming with her. I wanted to see you."

"And why was that?"

Douglas pressed his lips together, and appeared to be searching for some words. The *perfect* words. Eliza waited patiently. "I've been on adventures all over the world. I've sailed up the Ganges, and climbed the Alps. Through all that I couldn't get you out of my head."

"Of course you couldn't," Eliza replied in a flat voice. She was trying her very best not to be excited by this.

"I need you in my life." Douglas took her hands into his, and pressed the palm of her hand to his lips. "Come away with me. Explore the world."

Visions of adventures in exotic places around the globe

popped into her mind. Safaris in Africa. Camel caravans over the Khyber Pass. That was certainly preferable to her servitude in the Archives.

"And if we are determined, maybe we can sort out that little problem in New Zealand. Please, let me take care of you."

"Take care of me?" she murmured, a little distracted by all the other images crowding her brain.

"Yes," he pressed, "I want to do that above all things. I think you need that too."

That was like an ice bucket of water over her. Whatever her realisations about Wellington Books might have been, she was shocked by Douglas' expectations.

"I think you had better leave," she stated, jerking her hands free of his. "I appreciate you trying to take care of this poor, weak woman—but I think you should know the time for that has long passed."

His eyes cleared, and then he flushed red. "What do you want of me, Eliza? I'll have you know, Mother has introduced me to so many eligible young ladies I've lost count, but all I can think about is you."

"And that is somehow my fault?" Eliza paused, feeling a new sensation warming her skin, but this heat was not out of wanton desire. She took a deep breath and continued. "Douglas, I am sorry that I preoccupy your thoughts in such a way, but that Eliza Braun isn't me anymore. A lovely memory of days of innocence, certainly, but that wide-eyed girl no longer exists."

"Given time, I'm sure you will come back to your true self," Douglas implored. "You just have to put this English nonsense behind you, is all."

Nonsense? Did this prat know how many times she had saved the Empire from imminent danger? *Nonsense?!*

"Eliza, I have summited Kilimanjaro and Everest," he said, his eyes growing deep and piercing as he confessed, "but I know now I am closest to Heaven when I am with you."

Her head dropped to one side, an eyebrow crooking sharply. "Seriously?"

Douglas' brow furrowed. "What?"

"Is this the part where I come running into your arms, and then clothing flies in all directions?"

He stammered. Apparently, this was not the Eliza Braun he had known in Aotearoa. "You used to love hearing me say such things."

"I was young and foolish back then," she stated. "Now I'm old and foolish."

"Not that old, Eliza," Douglas replied.

She knew he meant well, but suddenly she wanted him gone.

Eliza got up and walked to the window. Outside, a rain shower had cleared, and the hint of a sun was peeking over the tops of the buildings. It had taken her a long time to get used to the cold; the snow her town never saw, and the clawing fog that she could already see rolling in from the river.

Melancholy thoughts for lost times and feelings had taken her over ever since she'd encountered Douglas again. Understanding that was the first step in clearing her mind. "I'm glad you came to London, Douglas. To help your mother. Yet I wonder why you never did that for me—not in three years." Her voice was calm as she turned back to him. "You see, I've spent that time thinking it was my fault. That I had destroyed everything, but *finally*, I've realised something. I wasn't the one that could travel. You were."

He blinked.

Now her melancholia was being replaced by anger. It felt much better—more familiar. "All that time you were conquering mountains and hunting game all over the world, you never once stopped in London. You never once sought me out."

Douglas frowned as he slipped his shirt back on. Obviously he knew that no more clothing was coming off, but she recognised the signs of his growing anger; pressed lips, and teeth being ground. He didn't say anything, but made for the door.

He tugged it open, but the answer he shot over his shoulder to her was as harsh as his kisses had been sweet. "Did you ever think, Eliza, that maybe it took me that long to forgive you?"

And then he was gone.

it was possible to get, and yet Ihita had a warmth she was nursing. It was not one her parents would have appreciated or condoned, but she'd learned to be her own woman. She was a long way from the little girl growing up in the splendid wealth of a raja's palace. Wrapped in silks since birth, she had long ago traded them in for wool and tweed. Now she was an agent of the Ministry, and tonight she was going to meet another.

Agent Brandon Hill had taken notice of the blush he caused in her cheeks at dinner with Eliza and Douglas, and had asked her to take afternoon tea with him. Alone. Not everyone in the Ministry thought Hill entirely sound of mind, but working with him in the last month, she had seen another side; a kind, shy side not hidden beneath the bravado of his tall tales.

As she walked down the street her footsteps were muffled by the fog and her view of the streets around her was limited. It was somewhat akin, she imagined, to being a blinkered horse. Not many people—let alone women—dared the streets on days like today, but romance wouldn't wait for something as silly as fog to clear. If she didn't get to the hotel Brandon would think that she had stood him up.

The mere thought made her increase her pace. She passed a dockworker, who whistled to her, but he was nothing more than a blink in her perception, and the fog ate up the sound in a moment. She was very nearly there when she ran past someone that she knew. A lady. Ihita only caught a glimpse of her face, and the flash of the suffragist's badge.

Normally the young woman was a stickler for formalities, and in any other situation she would have stopped and greeted her fellow sister—but now she was in a hurry. Besides, the other woman only glanced at her, with not a flicker of greeting. At the strangeness of that, Ihita stopped and looked back over her shoulder. She had only caught a flash of the woman, and recognised her, but could not put a name to the face. She stood there a moment, her handkerchief still clamped over her nose, and thoughts of Agent Hill disappeared in curiosity—because she had noticed something else. The woman had been wearing a pair of tinted goggles around her neck. What could be the reasoning behind that, by the river and at this time of day?

For some reason a chill ran down her spine and settled in her stomach. Turning, she began to walk quickly away. Within another few seconds she was not walking, she was half running, an unreasonable fear driving her on. At first Ihita thought it was her rather vivid imagination, tricking her within the swirls of the fog, making her hear the *rap-tap* of footsteps following after her.

No matter how fast she ran, the footsteps came after. Even when she stopped, whirled around, yanked out her pistols and pointed them in the direction of the footsteps, she could see nothing. The sounds stopped abruptly. Ihita's heartbeat sounded in her ears, and her breathing rasped over her teeth. It had only been ten minutes since she'd set off so confidently from the Ministry's front doorstep, but she really had no idea where she was, and the familiar line of shops and warehouses had been swallowed completely.

"Brandon," she whispered to herself. If there was a more competent agent in the Ministry she had not heard of him. Hill had wrestled polar bears and fought evil in all corners of the Empire. If she could just reach him, then this madness would be sent howling on its way.

Ihita turned and ran. It was a dangerous thing to do blindly in a London fog—there had been plenty of people who had fallen into the Thames, or run off the ends of piers in such circumstances. She didn't care, because there was now a feeling in the air that had nothing to do with the stench off the river. It filled her nostrils and almost choked her.

She turned the corner, and in a break in the fog, she could see a line of lights that signalled the front of the Empire Hotel. It was going to be all right, she was going to make it. Her hands flew to her head, as it flared with sudden pain. Dimly Ihita heard her weapons rattle on the ground as the air tightened about her, and a bright web of light snatched her up. For a heartbeat she could only see the blue glare. The agent was held suspended out of time and place.

Suddenly Ihita was dropped to the floor, and only barely kept her feet under her. One heartbeat. One frozen moment with her at its centre, a strange, captured butterfly held pinned by the light.

The glow was coming from all around her, from dials, levers and tall tubes. It was as if someone had captured lightning and made of it a net. Someone was standing at the machine. Ihita caught a glimpse of the woman looking over her shoulder. Even in profile Ihita could tell it was the same woman she had seen in the fog. How could that be?

Her mouth opened, to cry out in anger or for some kind of pity. Then the light grew bright again, searing her eyes, and choking back any sound she might have made. She was thrown into emptiness, and lost her place.

The rush of information to her brain suddenly caught up. Nothing below her windmilling feet. No ground. She was back in the fog. It was cold.

The one fact that tore all these other strange ones away was the noose around her neck. Her lungs wanted air and there was none of it to be had. Ihita's eyes bulged, and she wanted to scream but could not. Even as panic started to wind itself around her, Ihita recognised where she was: hanging beneath the Tower Bridge, by a rope. She thought of home, her mother and father, and wondered if they would hear of her death and be sad.

Painstakingly, she managed to get the very tips of her fingers between her neck and the rope. It was not much, a moment to drag a gulp of breath and look around. Here the fog was thinner, and she could see right along the river. Lights flickered, alternatively being revealed and disappearing into the murk, the tops of the buildings appearing above it like half-seen animals. It was a beautiful scene that many not-so-unfortunate people would see.

Ihita determined that she would tell Agent Hill about this scene; tell him when he saved her. She held on to that fact as she heaved with her arms and flicked herself upside down. It was impossible to kick her boots off, but she did manage to get one of her legs twined around the rope.

She could breathe—by all that was holy she could breathe. Tiny gulps filled her lungs with a little air, and even at the small amount, she found herself sobbing with relief. The breeze caught her, swinging her like a reverse pendulum, and her heart leapt with new fear. Even wriggling her fingers, she couldn't quite get enough pressure off her neck to loosen the noose.

Only one choice remained. She had to hold on. If she panicked and her leg slipped from around the rope, she would fall. If she waited long enough then Brandon would find her. He had to be wondering. A scrambled and terrified brain would hold on to anything, but Ihita held on to that belief.

The wind was picking up from the sea, racing along the Thames to scatter the fog. The citizens would be pleased, but it swung Ihita around on her rope.

Her thighs twitched, already beginning to ache. She could hold on. He would find her.

CHAPTER NINETEEN

In Which Our Dashing Archivist Finds Himself in a Most Uncomfortable Situation

Wellington felt his body protest as he plodded up the stairs of Miggins Antiquities. He needed sleep, but he was not in a position to get any. Back in the safety of his home, Wellington's kinetorama array was nearly done. Another hour or two to complete the rigging and test it, and then he would be ready to review the footage entrusted to him by the latest victim of this electrical abduction, Charlotte Lawrence. Somewhere in that surveillance footage was what he and Eliza needed. Of that, he had no question.

He did question his sanity on reaching the Ministry's doorknob. Wellington didn't want to go in there. Eliza could have chosen this morning to be there before him. To have words, in private, with him about his rugby tactics.

Then again, could he blame her for being outraged by his behaviour? Wellington had gone well beyond poor sportsmanship. He'd allowed his emotions to get the better of him, and he had blatantly broken the rules. For what? For his own personal gratification? It had felt good to take that arrogant prat Sheppard down a peg. What shocked Wellington all the more was that it *still* felt good, even as he stood in front of the Ministry's façade. However, the cold truth remained: he had caught a glimpse of the monster his father created and his country wished to cultivate.

Shaking his head, Wellington Thornhill Books opened the door and took what felt like the longest walk between foyer and lift. With each step, he wondered what pulled him into the depths of despair more—disappointing himself, or disappointing Eliza.

When he felt a twinge in his chest, he found his answer.

He had just reached the lift gate, absently noting the movement from the other side of frosted glass, when a voice stopped him.

"Books." Wellington turned to see the imposingly tall Bruce Campbell walking towards him. The Archivist glanced back at the windows and saw quite a few agents in the offices this morning. Was there some sort of meeting going on he didn't know about?

"Agent Campbell," he said, giving a polite tip of his bowler to the fellow associate. "Can I help you?"

The Australian continued to advance on him, so that he was compelled to take a step back. Campbell was well within reach, and Wellington did not care for that sort of closeness. From Eliza, it would be somewhat welcome, albeit maybe not this morning, but he could barely stand being in a room with this brash man.

"You look tired, mate."

Odd start to a morning's conversation. "Well, I was up late. Working on"—Wellington paused, and then licked his lips before continuing—"a personal endeavour at home. It started innocently enough but now it has become a bit time consuming."

"A personal endeavour?" Campbell repeated.

Please, don't press upon what it is, Wellington thought quickly.

"What have you got cooking in your mad laboratory, Books?"

He chortled, fishing out his key to the lift. "Oh I doubt it would be of interest to you."

"I think it would, seeing as I have assumed the office of Assistant Director. Part of my duties is the well-being of my agents, and that includes what they are up to."

Assistant Director? Campbell?! *Good Lord,* Wellington exclaimed inwardly, *we are isolated in the Archives!* "First, my congratulations, Age—er, Assistant Director Campbell, on your new office. You must be quite—"

"Bugger greasing me up. I need to know what you're doing."

Wellington's head tipped to one side as he considered his new superior in the Ministry. "I beg your pardon?"

"Sound appointed me Assistant Director for many reasons, and one of them is control. He's been slipping in that respect. For quite some time. He needs to gather up the reins a bit and get this mare back on the straight and narrow," Campbell said, motioning around him, "and that begins with me now. I'm kicking things off with you."

Bruce Campbell, disciplinarian of the Ministry of Peculiar Occurrences? And this "new order" was beginning with the Archives?

Perhaps he should head outside and start this day all over again.

"Assistant Director Campbell," Wellington began. Not only was that an absolute mouthful to say, it did not sit right with him. "I fail to see exactly why what consumes my own time is of any interest to the Ministry."

"Well now, that really is not your call to make. It's mine." Wellington assumed the smile Campbell dealt him was supposed to chill his blood. It did just the opposite. "So, I'll ask again—what is this personal endeavour you are undertaking after hours?"

"Well, it's an endeavour," the Archivist stated, his voice never faltering as he added, "and it is personal."

Campbell straightened up to his full height. Wellington

remained still, refusing to let the Australian's size intimidate him.

"So this is how you want it, Books?"

"Actually I would prefer if you dropped the posturing," he bit back in reply. "I find it tedious."

The man's massive shoulders shrugged lightly. "Suit yourself."

Wellington felt the lift grate grind into his back as he was shoved suddenly against it. Campbell's hand seemed to cover his chest, but the Archivist told himself it was nothing more than his vivid imagination. His exaggerations of reality did not in any way lessen the pain rippling across his back. Campbell kept a hold on Wellington with one hand while jabbing him lightly with the other as he spoke.

"I don't know what your game is, but it ends now. What fiddle-faddle you cook up down there may all be part of the daily operations to Doctor Sound. I see it as something else." Campbell ran his fingers through his hair as he took a breath. "Differences aside, Eliza was once a fine agent. One of the best."

"She still is," Wellington muttered, taking the opportunity to ease himself away from the painful spot.

Quick as thought, Campbell's hand came at him, pushing him once more into the metal. He followed it up with a light, condescending slap.

"I am not done with you yet, Books."

His glasses were knocked askew. With trembling fingers, Wellington straightened the lenses resting on his nose. He breathed softly, deeply, taking note of Campbell's size, his proximity to either wall and his stance.

"You have your own little world down there, don't you? Dank and miserable as it may be," the Australian added as he peered at Wellington. "You think that you can side-step the Fat Man and do as you please? Well, Books, it's time you did a little work for Her Majesty like the rest of us around here."

"And that work is exactly . . . ?" Wellington began, but Campbell merely stood there, his smug expression carved deep into his face. Wellington shook his head and said plainly, "What are you expecting?"

"Full access," Campbell stated. "I want to know what all them trinkets, baubles, and such do, and how we can make them work for us in the field." He straightened up a bit before adding, "And 'full access' also includes the Restricted Area."

That earned a raised eyebrow from Wellington. "Campbell, it is called the Restricted Area because it is restricted. Even from me. Only the Director can—"

"I couldn't give a toss what the Fat Man tells you," Campbell barked, jabbing his finger into Wellington's shoulder. "That falls under your department, so you're getting me access to it."

Wellington shook his head. "I could more easily grant you the cypher to Stonehenge—provided you could understand Ancient Druid glyphs, which I sincerely doubt. I will repeat myself: I don't have access to the Restricted Area."

"Then as your Assistant Director, I am giving you a direct order to find a way to get access. Play dirty." Campbell chuckled and looked him over. "After all, that's something you're good at, ain't it?"

Wellington's brow furrowed, and suddenly Campbell's ire made sense. Could Bruce had been those phantoms haunting him since the beginning of their investigation? "Are you following me?"

"I am looking into concerns that threaten the well-being of this organisation," he retorted. "And you and Braun have become a concern, in my judgement."

"You're *spying* on us, then?" Wellington asked.

"It's not your place to question me, Books," he snapped.

"Considering the amount of unsolved cases bearing your name cross our desk, perhaps I should."

The Australian's skin paled a bit on that threat. It was clear that Campbell knew what they were up to; but on the other hand, they knew what Campbell was up to as well.

Yes, Wellington had been caught breaking the rules, but it wasn't Campbell's role to put him in his place.

"My priority is this agency," he replied, but Wellington found no sincerity in the man's words. The more Campbell spoke, the more Wellington's anger fumed. "And I don't care to see some bookworm undermine it, or its agents."

That struck Wellington harder than Campbell's earlier slap. "Come again?"

Campbell's face twisted into an ugly smile. "You don't think in my investigation into your dereliction of duty I missed how you regard your partner? She's not cut of your cloth, mate. That much Eliza made clear the other day when she brought that Sheppard bloke back to her apartments. Poor sod looked a little flushed after a turn or two with her."

Wellington had heard more than enough.

"I do not have to entertain your—"

He was for the third time thrown back into the grate, and this time Campbell's slap was harder. Much harder.

"You do, Books, seeing as you have forgotten your place here. Eliza is not just a field agent. She's a sister. A kissin' cousin, if you will, an' I'm not gonna have some stuck up toff like you getting ideas that he shouldn't have."

A part of Wellington was strangely flattered that Campbell would regard him as such a cad. The rest of him was more than done with this lummox.

"Would you mind," Wellington said, trying to calm his wavering voice, "stepping back?"

Campbell instead moved forward. Wellington could feel the man's body heat. "Why would I do that?"

Wellington did not really need to administer all the power he dealt to Campbell's kidney. He was close enough that a punch at half the force would have been enough to knock the Australian back a few steps. His sudden strike drove Campbell back a few steps and down to one knee.

"That's why," Wellington replied.

Campbell gasped for breath, but then lunged upward. It was an attack Wellington would have been more surprised by if he hadn't tried it. As he slipped out of Campbell's way, his hands caught the man in a bind and in a moment the Australian's arm was locked against his back.

The advantage was not his for long as Campbell's head snapped back, catching him in his cheek. Wellington's lip rapped hard against his lower teeth, closely followed by the metallic tang of blood. There was little pause between Wellington letting go of Campbell and the fist clocking him against his temple. Somewhere, Wellington heard the clatter of glasses. At best, one of his lenses would have a crack.

He couldn't clearly see Campbell, but he could hear the man perfectly well. His opponent was a brawler. He knew as much. There was also the problem of the man's mass and brute force, which he now felt in full as the Australian picked him up off the floor and tossed him against the wall. Even with his compromised vision, he could see a few rivulets of blood splatter against the white spiral pattern of the foyer's wall.

"This is a real shame, Books," he heard Campbell grunt. "Ministry representatives, squabbling like a pair of drunkards, but this was your decision," he said, moving in for another round, "not mi—"

No matter the size or girth of an opponent, there were certain vulnerabilities everyone despite their carriage shared. For this one brief opportunity, that vulnerability was the nose. With a dash of extra power, Wellington spun about and drove his fist forward, his angle, stance, and delivery of attack all based on where he heard Bruce's voice. His fist connected low on the bridge of Campbell's nose. He felt and heard a most satisfying pop on impact, and the punch sent his opponent stumbling back. He hit the wall opposite of him, rattling the frosted window in its pane.

Wellington slid down to the floor of the foyer, and his outstretched fingers found his spectacles. They were indeed cracked, but he put them on anyway. Campbell, his own laboured breaths punctuated with a soft laughter, sat opposite him, gently cupping his nose. He nodded, and then gave the bleeding appendage a hard shove. Wellington winced as he heard the cartilage surrender a dull snap.

"Nice punch," Campbell said. Wellington was surprised at the Australian's sincerity. "But you know I'm not done. I'll make sure that by tomorrow you won't have a job here."

"Neither will you."

He barked a laugh, but the mirth faded from his face as Wellington kept his gaze on him.

"When I show them the cases you've submitted to the Archives under 'Unsolved,' including the case of Lena Munroe, we will both be sent packing."

"You think so, Books?"

"No, I don't think so." And with a huff, Wellington gave a smile, flinching a bit at the sting from his bottom lip. "I know so."

The door to the main offices opened and Agent Arthur Townsend appeared, giving a start on seeing the two men on the floor.

"S'all right, Townsend," Campbell slurred, "this was . . . personal. A misunderstanding, right then, Books?"

The Archivist kept his eyes locked with Campbell. No, this was far from over.

"I just need to get myself cleaned up, is all."

"Well, be quick about it, the both of you," Townsend muttered, his gaze darting between them. The tightness in his voice sobered Wellington up swiftly. Something was wrong. Dreadfully wrong. "Doctor Sound has called in all active London field agents."

Now it was Campbell's turn to pause. "All of them?"

By Townsend's guilty look it was easy to see he knew more than he was revealing. "Not my place to discuss it. Doctor Sound will explain everything." He looked at them both again, and shook his head, disgusted. "You have five minutes. For God's sake, pull yourselves together."

Wellington knew whatever news awaited him on the other side of the door, Campbell's enmity was assured. Everything had just changed for the worse.

CHAPTER TWENTY

Wherein Agent Books Makes Assumptions and the Agency Mourns

Eliza had felt trepidation heading to work on Monday morning before—yet never for this particular reason. She was not worried about seeing the Director, though once again they were working on a case instead of filing in the Archives. Neither was she worried about a run-in with Bruce and his crass comments on her attire. No, this time she was concerned about seeing Wellington.

Self-examination was not something she was very good at, which is why she seldom did it. Things happened, people passed through her life, and she made the most of every opportunity that came her way. Wellington Thornhill Books and his hazel eyes was a complication she now understood. More than she had realised until the moment she sat on Douglas' lap.

So when she went into Miggins Antiquities her mind was fully occupied with what these revelations could mean for the future. The instant she entered the ground floor and saw all agents assembled, such concerns were washed away. The usual clatter of the cover workers here was stilled. Instead they stood in small groups, talking in low voices. This could not be good.

As she contemplated what could have happened, Dominick Lochlear appeared at the head of the stairs. His tanned and creased face, usually an emotionless mask, contained hints of sadness and rage. Eliza's hands clenched. She knew that expression—the only event that could reach the chill heart of her colleague. Somewhere an agent had died.

Dominick caught up to her, and they silently shared confirmation that one of their own had indeed fallen. Together they entered the offices. Eliza swallowed hard as they pushed through the collection of agents. The Ministry had many divisions, all over the Empire, but there were not many people in London at present. So whoever it was, she would know them.

When she stepped inside Eliza felt herself shiver. The current agents packed the room, the tension thick and heavy. She was not the tallest member of the group, so she could only glimpse the Director between the shoulders of others. She spotted Wellington over by the window. She noticed his spectacles were cracked and, completely out of character, his suit looked dishevelled. If she'd had to guess, she'd have suspected he'd been roughed up. Curious as his appearance was, she didn't care. Of course she had questions; but concerning the present news, she just wanted to be near him.

Eliza wriggled her way between the strapping men of the Ministry to stand next to her colleague. Wellington glanced her way, but she immediately saw she was going to find no comfort there. Behind the Archivist's broken glasses, his hazel eyes were hard and still.

"Miss Braun," he spoke tersely.

"Wellington, what hap—"

"We can discuss it later." He turned his eyes back to where Sound waited.

Wellington had looked at her in so many ways—in surprise, relief, exasperation (quite often), and occasionally with a grim sort of humour. Now she regretted some of the impish pranks she had pulled at his expense, teasing him with stories of supposed trysts with rajas, counts, and cowboys. In that brief exchange, she knew whatever had happened to Wellington had something to do with her.

He looked more than physically hurt. It should have made her happy that he cared that much, but in this setting such feelings got all muddled up. Yet she knew of only one reason he could possibly be this annoyed. Before she could explore that possibility, Doctor Sound's voice broke through the silence.

"I am sure some of you can guess what has happened," he began.

Through the ranks of her colleagues she saw Brandon Hill, his face white and set. Eliza abandoned Wellington and worked her way through the agents towards him. As she did so he passed a shaking hand over his face. He was not crying, but he might as well have been—for this was the most emotion she'd seen the quiet agent display. Suddenly that knot of worry was washed away in a wave of comprehension. Now her fingernails bit into her palms, and the world became a distant blur.

The words the Director said next fell into that stillness like hard stones. "One of our own has been taken. Last night Agent Ihita Pujari was kidnapped. We activated her tracking ring, and that was how we found her hanging beneath Tower Bridge.

Eliza stopped where she was and squeezed her eyes shut while grinding her teeth together lest she let out a sob. Everywhere was stillness. Around her many agents hung their heads, crossed themselves, or shuffled their feet. It was not the first time they had lost one of the Ministry—it was an occupational hazard—but Ihita had not been on field duty. She'd been cycled back to the London Headquarters to act as a liaison and aide to Brandon.

Doctor Sound paused before looking up and pronouncing. "We will find who did this and bring her murderer to justice. You have my word on that."

By the gods, Eliza thought, *she'd been so young and kind. So full of life, and so looking forward to the future.* She choked back a sob, and listened with horror as Brandon took a spot next to the Director.

"Agent Pujari was coming to meet me at the Empire," he said, his voice low and his eyes on a fixed low point. "When she was late, I knew something was wrong. It was on my way home I found one her pistols against the pavement. I got a small shock when I touched it. I . . ." He paused and gathered himself before trying again. "I couldn't reach her in time."

The Director patted him awkwardly on the back. "We will start an investigation immediately. Campbell, assemble a team—"

"I want to be on it," Brandon broke in, his voice like gravel. "I will be on it."

Doctor Sound nodded. "Campbell, please stay behind, the rest please go back to your work. Agent Pujari's memorial service will be on Wednesday before her remains are returned to her family."

Eliza filed out with her colleagues, though she was numb. She made it as far as the doorway, and then stopped. Everyone else lined up for the lift, but they really didn't matter.

As she stood there swaying, a gentle hand grasped her shoulder. When she turned, blinking back tears, Shillingworth's beautiful face was anything but stern. It was a reflection of Eliza's own. Ihita had made a lot of friends during her short life.

They embraced, and Eliza let a few tears escape. She would do the rest of her grieving in private, in her apartments.

"Agent Braun," Wellington's voice was soft. He'd waited behind after all.

Eliza straightened and stepped away from Miss Shillingworth, brushing her eyes. The secretary nodded in a silent greeting to Wellington before heading to the lift where Sound and a handful of others waited.

"I'm sorry about your friend." Wellington pushed his glasses up on his nose. "She was a fine agent."

"And a good person."

"That too." They stood staring at each other, or rather at the ground between them, before he cleared his throat. "I'm going back home. I need to start looking through the film Miss Lawrence provided."

Eliza didn't know what to do with herself. To reach out to him seemed to be the wrong choice right now—an insult to Ihita. So she said nothing . . .

"We know one more thing, Miss Braun. Whoever is taking these women has a machine of great accuracy, to do . . . to do what they did to Agent Pujari."

"Just you make me a promise, Wellington." She felt her rage begin to boil under her grief. "We'll find them."

"Yes," he said. His hand went to take hers, but he stopped. Seeing his hand awkwardly held between them, Eliza noted, was something she deeply regretted. Wellington cleared his throat and pulled his hand away. "We will find them. I swear it."

He gave a weak smile and then left Eliza standing there.

Wellington was upset, but perhaps not solely for the fate of Ihita Pujari. And it appeared he had no intention of sharing his mind with her.

This was the last thing she needed at present—yet another mystery to solve.

Wherein There Is No Honour
Amongst the Wicked

Chandi Culpepper could feel the gentle tendrils of sleep creep along her skin. The excitement and anticipation had reached a fever pitch so intense today that she screamed at one of her servants for tending to her needs too intently at dinner.

This would not have upset her so had the servant—like all of the clockwork servants in the house—been sentient in some way. The servant reacted to the tenor of her voice, as it had been built to do; but why had she screamed at it?

A silly thing to do, Chandi thought. *I must remain calm, pray, and be led.*

She made her way downstairs to the servants' quarters—though there had not been any living servants there for quite some time. It was now given over to spare parts for the clockwork valets, her own keepsakes from travel around the world . . .

And the shrine.

The shrine like no other—but the first of many yet to come. Down here there was no gaslight, no electricity, so

Chandi went down holding a candle before her, penitent and open to the universe.

It was in the room where once the servants had eaten their meals. Now it served her holy purpose. Chandi set down the candle before the sideboard, and began to arrange the offerings before the altar. Her eyes immediately went to the top of the shrine. The ivory cross, representing mother and son, appeared to shimmer in the firelight of candles that she proceeded to light.

Mother. The woman paused, as always thinking of her own mother. A beautiful flower of the East, her father had called her, but one who had not flourished beneath an English sun. She had worn a cross similar to the ivory one against her dark, nut-brown skin; and she had been punished for doing so under the lash and stones of her fellow Indians.

Chandi took her newest offerings from her pocket and laid them before the altar. Jasmine blossoms for the mother. As for blood for the son, she cut her finger with a tiny silver knife she kept by the shrine for that purpose. This fresh offering was given at the tips of the cross, to signify where the Holy Son her father had pledged his life to had bestowed His gift. She then touched a spot on her forehead, and then finally spread it in a long line before the tableau.

The ivory cross was one her father had kept above the mantelpiece at the estate, but he had only had it partly right. Chandi, years ago, made the connection, and therefore implemented a sacred correction. Now, the mother was present, for the son could not be raised in the Light without the mother. She felt tears well in her eyes at seeing in the flickering candlelight the shadows of Kali intertwined with the cross.

Their combined shadows, a prefect union. A proper union. The best of India and England. Just like she was.

Chandi leaned back on her heels, pressing her hands over her eyes, and reaching out to the two of them. Their plans were so close to fruition and her oath nearly complete. The great mother and the burning son. She would be like them.

She would destroy the world to create it anew, and then bestow upon this brave new world, in sacrifice, her undying, eternal love. The coming of the mother and the son. She was the hand of the god.

Tonight belongs to us.

Chandi was jerked from her prayer as a distant rumbling reached her ears. It was the throaty roar of an engine that was very familiar.

No! Her head jerked up and her eyes flicked open. *No, not now!*

Chandi scrambled to get upstairs, and snatched a pen from the desk in the hallway. Even with the shock, her handwriting remained neat and impeccable:

She is here. Get downstairs. The usual place.

No time to be creative.

The engine snarled just outside, and then went silent. All Chandi heard now was the rattle of the clockwork servant standing poised by the door.

Now, she darted into the parlour, slammed the door shut, hastily rolled up her missive and thrust it into the cylinder. She opened the pneumatic tube; and with a quick hiss, her message disappeared into the private network from her house. Her eyes darted back to the hallway. The first knock came when she replaced her right earring. She had reached the door by the time her left earring was secured.

Through the peephole in the parlour door, she saw her clockwork automaton at the front one, addressing the unexpected visitor.

"My mistress is not at home," it spoke with Chandi's own recorded voice.

Chandi heard Sophia reply with, "I am not expected, but the business I bring to your mistress is most important. Please, do inform her I am here."

"It's all right," she called from the parlour. "Let *Signorina* del Morte enter."

The automaton stepped back and then replied in a similar, tinny rendition of Chandi's voice, "Good evening and welcome to my home."

Chandi entered the foyer, and there the assassin stood, decked most scandalously.

"*Buonasera*," Chandi offered.

"Most considerate," Sophia del Morte replied. "I do apologise for arriving at this late hour." She paused, her brow furrowing. "Have you cut yourself? You are bleeding."

Chandi gave a start and immediately fished out a kerchief. "Oh, it is quite all right." She moistened the tip of the fabric and cleaned her forehead free of her blood. "A bit silly, really. Pricking of the thumb while at needlepoint, and then rubbing out a slight headache." She gave a meek smile and asked, "Would you care for a brandy, to stave off the chill?"

"No, that is fine. I would prefer not to drink while I am tending to matters for the Maestro."

"Please," she said, motioning to the parlour. "Come join me by the fire."

Sophia gave a light sigh, her head ruefully shaking left and right as she walked into Chandi's inviting parlour. Chandi watched as the woman she feared as equally as she detested walked around her home, seeming to inspect her paintings, her décor, and even the quality of the marble mantel above the hearth for approval. *Every aspect, every detail,* she seethed. Chandi silently thanked her foresight for desiring only the light of the fire tonight in her sitting room. The odd shadows cast would make her own features harder for Sophia to read.

"Due to the hour and my business, I cannot stay for long," Sophia said, her inspection of the room seeming to reach an end as she unbuttoned her heavy riding coat.

"A shame. Fire and brandy do make for lovely companions on cold nights like this. Perhaps another time," Chandi remarked, motioning to various pouches hanging from her belt, "when you are not engaged in your professional pursuits?"

Sophia looked at Chandi with no readable expression. "Doubtful." She stuffed the riding gloves and goggles into her leather cap, tucking the bundle under her arm as she added, "I rarely make social calls. The Maestro wished me to attend him once our appointment has concluded."

"No rest for the wicked," Chandi said, a light laugh decorating her words.

Yes, the woman being here terrified her, particularly after that little admission. Chandi also knew that God and Kali—in their own way—protected her. This mistress of death would not shove a knife in her back or wrap a garrotte around her neck. She was safe for the moment, tenuous as that safety may be.

The chair was still warm, thanks to the fire. She gave herself a moment to relish the way the chair embraced her. Her father so loved this chair, so loved what she was doing right now. Contemplation by firelight. Privilege personified. Perhaps even part of the order of things. *An order that should be preserved by any and all means necessary,* she could still hear him say.

Chandi opened her eyes and looked at Sophia standing before the mantel, her hand well within reach of the poker. This woman was a monster through and through, and she was now in her home, in her very parlour. She must remain on her guard.

"The Maestro has sent me for the weapon," the Italian said.

Chandi blinked. "I am still trying to understand the power source and test the limits of output. Otherwi—"

"No," interjected Sophia. The smile brought a chill into the room that Chandi swore had not been there before the assassin's arrival. "The Maestro is no longer interested in testing. From what he has seen, you have effectively solved the earlier problem of power stability." Her head inclined towards her, the pride practically making her face glow. "I stole the solution for you after all—please don't forget that."

Chandi felt her muscles tense. She needed time. Only a moment or two longer.

"It's not perfected yet," Chandi stated flatly.

"Not perfected?" Sophia's laugh made her flinch. "Oh, I do find feigned humility most trite, particularly when it comes from the likes of uppity English, or whatever you consider yourself. Perhaps the humility comes from your mother's side?" Her thick Italian accent added venom to those words. When she stepped closer, Chandi felt her grip on the brandy snifter tighten. "You claim the weapon is not perfected, and yet you took that poor suffragist from a moving train, and the fate you dealt a sister from your own homeland—"

"She was an insult," she spat, hoping her venom matched Sophia's. "Do not dare presume that we were cut from the same cloth simply due to our origins." When she saw Sophia lift a single eyebrow at her, Chandi folded her hands demurely in her lap, and cast to the assassin what she hoped was a softer gaze. "She needed to be made an example of."

"And you did," Sophia agreed. "In doing so, you have successfully proven the accuracy of the weapon's targeting system. The Maestro was impressed. So was I."

"It was—" Chandi's voice caught in her throat. She wanted so desperately to indulge the scientist in her and proclaim the truth, but she could not part with the device. Not yet. "—a mere instance of random variables that yielded a favourable outcome. I don't know if the conditions could be replicated."

"Are you saying, in so many words, that you got lucky?"

Chandi could feel her skin burn with resentment. What kind of scientist would dismiss their work as a mere stroke of luck? An utter *clankerton*.

She rose from the chair, but walked over to the window, parting the curtains to look over the quiet streets of London. Her eyes went up and down the lane before her house as she continued.

"We are just scratching the surface of its potential. We must continue testing all variables, thereby guaranteeing that your Maestro is satisfied with its capabilities."

"My dear star of India, what makes you think that we are not impressed with your progress since granting you patronage? Or have you forgotten?"

Chandi turned to see Sophia talking to her over the back of the chair, one foot on the floor, one knee tucked in the seat. Her fingers laced together as she rested her forearms against its high back. "Your starting point with us was the poor condition in which your own father was found. Thank goodness within that mass of organs and tissue, a hand still wearing a wedding band was intact.

"In the past year, you have managed to capture and deliver a mark without complication, capture and deliver while on a moving train, and then we have the death of that sweet Indian agent. That is more than progress in our eyes. That is accomplishment."

It was, and now they were so close. So very, very close.

"*Signorina*, this was not what we agreed to," Chandi insisted. "When we agreed on help from your Maestro, we were promised that once our uses for the device were done, we would then hand it over to you. We are closing in. You taking the device this early in our agenda was not part of our agreement."

"Agendas and agreements change." Sophia shook her head, her sigh heavy and tired. "The Maestro will have his weapon. Tonight."

A moment's silence, save for the light crackling of the hearth, and then Chandi's answer seemed to fill the room, even when spoken just above a whisper. "No."

Sophia started. Chandi found the assassin's surprise delicious.

"Forgive me, *Signorina*," Sophia began. It surprised Chandi how controlled and polite her tone was. I think your previous tactics were better executed, not to mention smarter."

"Be that as it may, my answer will not change. No, you shall not have the device. Not yet. Your Maestro, as we agreed, will have the device . . ." Chandi took in a breath and said with finality, " . . . when our work is done."

The metal delivery tube striking the pneumatic delivery glass interior across the room made both women jump. Chandi gasped slightly as the firelight caught a glint off the knife's edge that had suddenly appeared in the assassin's hand. She had not seen Sophia produce it, nor had she spied it anywhere upon her person. Where had it come from?

Sophia bent her wrist back, revealing a slim open tray, part of the gauntlet's mechanism. The knife returned with a snap, and then retracted back inside Sophia's coat.

She smiled at Chandi and resumed her earlier thought. "Do consider your next words carefully."

Chandi shot a quick glance at the pneumatic tube where the sealed cylinder waited, but she already knew. She tucked a loose curl of raven-dark hair behind her ear, and gently squeezed the teardrop jewel hanging there. Now came the hard part. "Please, while we have come forward in so many ways, we have some unanswered questions. In particular, there is one variable we have not tested . . ."

"This game bores me," Sophia seethed. "The device. Now."

"One crucial challenge that we have not tested yet."

The assassin growled in her throat, stepping out of the chair and casually removing a pistol from its holster at her back.

Chandi smiled as the scent of electricity tickled her nostrils. "Distance."

CHAPTER TWENTY ONE

In Which Our Dashing Archivist Discovers How Patience and Persistence Are Both Virtues, but Loses Himself in a Flash of Inspiration

Somewhere in here, Wellington knew, was what he needed to prove his theory right. Somehow, Wellington knew that Chandi Culpepper was connected with these disappearances.

I just have to find it in this footage, he thought to himself as he started resetting the four kinetoramas.

Wellington passed his hands over the brass plates of the first projection device. Inside, he could see the gas flames burning steadily. He'd put his mother's quilts up against the windows and the doorway of the guest room to provide the best viewing environment, however it was also making it terribly hot and stuffy. The heat was in danger of melting the evidence the Protectors had "graciously" loaned him. So he propped aside a corner of one of the quilts, and opened the sash window beyond. A small square of sunlight intruded on the dimness of the room, but it also let in enough of a small breeze to keep the celluloid from sizzling in the warmth that the machines generated.

The Archivist had already looked over the footage of the last two disappearances and was certain these two new reels also held something that he was missing. Wellington adjusted the starting point of the second, backtracking the footage approximately ten minutes from the point of disappearance. The lack of sound made the whole process somewhat eerie.

Wellington shook his head as he wound back the footage from Kinetorama Number 3. The Protectors had certainly given him a dose of what it was like to be a woman in this society. It was as if his voice, far more educated and knowledgeable than theirs, had no merit or say at all. No wonder they fought against that sort of injustice. Still, he would have preferred they didn't dish the same out to him.

He now shut the fourth kinetorama, and then passed his hands over the previous machines as a final check for their heat circulation. Satisfied, he slowly brought the switch up that fed them power. The four images began to shimmer and move until finally Wellington had reached the point where the kinetoramas mimicked relative human speed. Apart from the odd hand wave and perhaps one or two ladies smoothing out the creases of their dresses, this footage could hardly be described as "gripping." Reaching underneath his spectacles and rubbing his eyes, Wellington watched the same ten minutes he had been watching for the past two hours. Focus was becoming more and more elusive.

Instead he was thinking about her. Eliza. He'd been working on a sketch of her in his idle moments. He could finish it, but then what? Present it to Eliza? Perhaps as a bon voyage gift for her return to New Zealand on the arm of Douglas Sheppard. Eliza would have her old life back. Wellington would have the solitude of his Archives. When she'd first been reassigned it had been what they'd both wanted.

So now why did the idea of being alone in that glorified cellar terrify him?

"Oh dash it all," he muttered. At least seven minutes had passed during his idle wonderings, and his fixation on Eliza and her reuniting with her lover had meant he'd not taken any notice of the film. Nothing for it, he would have to start again.

As Wellington went to slow down the kinetoramas, he caught a moment in Kinetorama 2's playback. He immediately threw the switch to the "Stop" position, and stared at the frozen moment in time.

Have a care, he told himself as he stared at the golden-hued image of Chandi Culpepper.

His hands trembled as he glanced down at the small wheel underneath his fingertips. He only had to step back a few seconds, a minute or two at the most, and this hand crank allowed him to reverse or advance all four kinetoramas simultaneously. He could not do it quickly or for long periods of time for fear of tearing the footage. Turning the crank anti-clockwise, Wellington began a steady progression back before this tiny, insignificant moment he caught in Kinetorama 2. He counted softly to himself, feeling his heartbeat race in his chest.

With a deep breath, Wellington applied power. All four kinetoramas gradually resumed playing their respective footage. Wellington now watched the projection from Kinetorama 3. In a moment . . . in a moment . . .

There!

The switch disengaged, and now Kinetorama 3 showed Chandi Culpepper in the same position as he had seen her in Kinetorama 2. Two different days. Two different meetings. The exact same gesture at the exact same time.

Then he looked at the images from Kinetoramas 1 and 4. Her fingers were also hidden behind her ear. The exact same gesture.

Wellington took the kinetoramas back a few more seconds, popped open the square cover of his pocket watch, and then applied full power.

Chandi nodded in Kinetorama 1, while in Kinetorama 3 she smiled brightly. How did he miss this? In Kinetorama 2 she was still as a statue; and then across all four projections, like ballerinas flawlessly following the rhythm of their accompanying orchestra, the multiple Chandis reached up with their right hands, tucked a wayward curl of hair behind their ears, and tugged lightly on their teardrop earrings.

Wellington's eyes now hopped to his watch. After two minutes, all four projections flashed white and amber, and then what followed would be pandemonium.

He cut power, and then hand cranked the footage back, careful not to turn the wheel too quickly. He went to each kinetorama, quickly checking its temperature. He looked over the footage's tautness. Well within safe limits. He took another deep breath. He was having difficulty remembering to breathe—a sure sign he was onto something.

The switch under his fingertips snapped softly into place, and the footage played once more. Chandi tucked her hair behind her ear. She tugged on the earring. The quality of the film was not fine enough to tell, but he guessed there was some kind of miniature device there allowing her to focus the kidnapping mechanism. Wellington noted the time. Thirty seconds, one minute, one minute thirty, one minute forty-five, Two minutes . . .

Flash.

He backed the footage up once more, checked the reels, and then paused the kinetoramas. Now he needed to fetch Eliza and show her this.

Whatever this quaint device of transportation and electricity was, Chandi Culpepper served as some sort of visual cue for it. The mannerism captured on film was too precise, too purposeful, to be dismissed as merely a habitual gesture. It had been the same at each meeting, with a two-minute window between the gesture and the abduction. This would also mean that the visual cue had to have been seen by an accomplice.

Wellington nodded and smiled to himself as he emerged from the dark room. *Ah yes, an accomplice.* It would mean someone else in the inner circle of the suffrage movement. Not all of the abductions took place during meetings though.

They took place at rallies, at administrative meetings, in the streets of London, on the Edinburgh express . . .

They had been daring kidnappings at various locations, so that meant the device had to be portable. In addition, the accomplice would have to be someone Chandi could trust implicitly. Someone very close.

Then it made sense. All those tricks of shadow and light made sense. "My God!"

If Eliza thought the idea of making Chandi Culpepper their prime instigator was a far-fetched theory, she would laugh in his face at who he believed her accomplice to be. With what he had seen, though, it made a rather twisted kind of sense.

Archimedes' sudden hiss made the Archivist's head whip around. Wellington's brow furrowed.

"Mr. Sheppard?" Wellington called, stepping out into the foyer.

He could hear the birds outside singing gaily in the tree-tops. His feline friend would have to be in the parlour's bay window, a favourite sunning spot for him. Wellington stood in the hallway for a moment, listening for anyone at the door or perhaps in the house. Nothing creaked. No sounds of footsteps.

"Mr. Sheppard?" Wellington asked again, half expecting a reply. "If you have lost track of Miss Braun, I assure you she is not here."

His only reply was a grating feline growl from the par-lour. Wellington proceeded down to hall to find his friend was circling in place. The fat cat's yellow eyes were looking into the vaulted ceiling. In turn, the Archivist glanced up to the modest ceiling fixture hanging overhead, and then back to his agitated housemate.

"Good sir, I assure you"—Wellington patted Archime-des' head—"that tiny chandelier has done nothing to earn your ire."

Then he felt the hair on his arms stand up, and the smell of electricity tickled his nose.

Archimedes bolted out of the parlour as Wellington scrambled for the small notepad and pencil by his game in progress. How much time did he have? Two minutes? Or was it a matter of seconds after catching the smell of electricity? He grabbed the white and black queen, and then cleared the board with his forearm, scattering pawns, rooks, and other pieces across the room's centre rug and hardwood floor. Wellington quickly jotted down three words and then placed the note under the two queens.

Now what?

Get out of the room, he thought quickly. *Remember the heat?*

Wellington scrambled up to his feet, nearly taking a dangerous tumble as chess pieces caught under his foot. *Don't panic. Eliza will understand. She's your partner, after all.*

He stumbled into the foyer, and could just make out the figure on the other side of the door. Even through the curtain and etched glass, she was a beautiful-looking woman. He knew that.

Something lifted him, and his vision filled with an incredibly brilliant light.

When the light changed, he saw her.

Wellington had wished he had been wrong for once. His wish, he realised as the white light filled his sight again, had not come true.

CHAPTER TWENTY TWO

In Which Eliza Finds Both
Unexpected Friends and Enemies

She should have been back at the Ministry, sitting at her desk with the pretence of being a good little junior archivist—but the time for that was long past with Ihita's death. What use was the Ministry if it couldn't protect someone like her—someone within their very ranks?

It was also something she had to alert Kate Sheppard to. The escalation in disappearances made Eliza deeply aware that her friend and mentor was a prime target. Whatever the kidnapper's—or perhaps murderer's—motives were, the presence of an influential suffragist would be too juicy of an opportunity. Eliza knew what she would do if she were that person.

So Eliza got dressed as she did for work, allowed Alice to do the one hundred brushes of her hair she insisted on every morning, and went around to where the Sheppards were staying.

She really did not want to run into Douglas—but Kate's safety was more important than any awkwardness Eliza might feel.

The young maid, smartly turned out, met her at the door.

"I'm sorry Miss, Mrs. Sheppard is not in. She is at the meeting."

"Meeting?" Eliza's hand clenched on her umbrella. "I didn't hear there was a meeting today."

The maid's lips pursed, then she replied with a touch of smugness—as if she were part of some inner circle of knowledge. "It's an emergency one. Called it last night."

Now Eliza's mouth was dry. She spun about without another word to the maid and began running down the street. It started raining but she didn't bother with the umbrella, throwing it aside so she could pump her arms. She almost ran in front of a packed bus and its four horses as she turned the street corner.

The meeting hall was not far, but it felt like an eternity. As Eliza approached it, she scanned the exterior. No one was lingering outside, the doors were shut, the windows all shuttered and locked, and as far as she could see there was no one on the three-storey structure's roof. Taking a deep breath she entered as calmly as she could manage.

The atmosphere inside was far less convivial than the last time she'd been here. A midday meeting was unusual for the movement, yet today it was packed. Many of the women still wore their raincoats, so obviously it had been called in some haste. Up on the stage Lady Pethick and a gaggle of the other remaining committee members were talking to Kate. They were waving their hands and looked nothing like the calm, collected women she had seen last time.

News of Ihita's death had reached the movement then. Eliza was not really surprised. She was not the only suffragist in the Ministry. She had suspicions that Miss Shillingworth harboured an affiliation. If it was she who had alerted these women about what had happened she couldn't be faulted for it. They needed to know.

At the edges of the gathering, she saw the darkly dressed Protectors standing at the shuttered windows, their clubs strapped to their backs and out in the open. Betsy Shaw was there, the raw burn marks on her face somewhat faded, but she inclined her head to Eliza when their eyes locked.

Eliza tried to work her way towards the stage, but the press was thick, and not many of the women inclined to move out of her way. The snippets of conversation she caught were panicked. These were women who were prepared to die for a cause in front of police, or to be locked up and force-fed through a tube. Those were known and expected things, but the possibility of being snatched into thin air at any moment was something else entirely.

This was when Kate stepped forward. Brushing away the chatter of the committee, she took the front of the stage. "Ladies," her voice cut above the chatter and she did not have to repeat herself. They stilled and, as one, turned to her.

Eliza smiled, because she recognised this Kate: the person she had first heard as a girl of not more than fifteen, who had inspired her to put her tomboy talents to good use. One who had helped her understand the wider world and what needed to be done to make it better. For a moment, Eliza quite forgot about the danger and the risk.

Kate's white hair gleamed in the sun coming down through the skylight, as she stood tall and straight before the crowd. "Ladies, I will not insult your intelligence by telling you falsehoods. Here, in the centre of our great endeavour, all must be truthful, for if we cannot trust our fellow sisters, then all is lost."

Eliza glanced over the assembly, and felt them take a collective breath.

"It is true," Kate went on, clasping her hands together, "that we have lost many of our sisters, and that yesterday one of them was found dead, moved by some unholy hand to a place of hanging."

A stifled sob came from near Eliza and she could feel her own throat seize up. The image of Ihita swinging under Tower Bridge consumed her mind, even though she had not seen it for herself.

Kate continued. "We must keep our grief and our anger for the loss of our sisters tempered with the knowledge that they are still with us in spirit. They were taken from us, but our path must remain clear. We cannot afford to stray from it, otherwise all the efforts of those here and those gone will have been for nothing."

Her voice was clear and lovely in the meeting room, bringing some of the women to tears, and straightening the spines of all. Eliza was reminded of the power of such charisma, how it was even more dangerous than dynamite. With a start, she remembered her purpose here, and it was not to draw strength from Kate Sheppard—it was to protect her.

She began squeezing and wriggling her way towards the front. Then she tasted it in the air—the sharp tang that burned the nostrils.

"No!" Eliza yelled, her voice breaking through silence, and then, "Get down!" Everyone spun about instead, but no one dove for the floor. In fact it became harder for her to get to the front as all the women were frozen like statues. Out of the corner of one eye, the agent saw Betsy having the same problem.

Kate was standing up on the stage, her clockwork eye focusing on Eliza, while her remaining eyebrow drew down. She held out her hand, perhaps to remonstrate with Eliza, perhaps to call for people to let her through—but whichever it was no one ever found out.

Previously Eliza had only caught a portion of the kidnapping events. She'd seen Lena outlined in light in the doorway, and seen the devastation after. What she had never experienced was the full force of it in daylight. The air became sharp and so dry it was painful. Everyone flinched back. Not fast enough though, not fast enough by far.

The ball of blue lightning snapped into existence on the stage, engulfing Kate Sheppard in an instant. The nearest committee members were knocked off their feet as a ring of displaced and heated air fanned out from the sphere. Those on the floor nearest the stage were also pushed back, screaming in shock. Eliza, twenty feet away, felt the air brush her, but managed to stay upright.

The lightning was only there for a heartbeat, and then it snapped once more out of existence, taking Kate with it. Eliza turned to her left and saw her. Chandi Culpepper. She was conveniently at the edge of where the effects of the sphere ran out. As she had been in Hester's library.

Wellington Thornhill Books, that annoying yet brilliant man, had been proven correct. Eliza would have to tell him that when she next saw him, once she had secured that lying bint Chandi Culpepper. She had been hiding in their midst like a poisonous snake, with no one the wiser. On exchanging glances with Eliza, comprehension slid over her face. Her eyes went wide.

The jig was up.

As Eliza leapt and dodged groaning women to get to her, Chandi did not linger for discourse. Instead she darted for the closest door. Everyone was stunned and horrified, except for Eliza, and a few steps behind her was Betsy. They followed her out of the main room and into the stairwell. Chandi was young and fast, pelting hard up the stairs; but the other two women were only a single flight behind her.

Eliza was already thinking about what she would ask—and if left alone with Chandi, do—once in the interrogation room, because she knew there was no escape off the roof. The meeting hall stood apart from the rest of the nearby houses. Chandi had not expected to be caught, not expected anyone to suspect her, and now the blind panic of that all happening was going to catch up with her and bite her rather hard on the rear. The agent would happily follow it up with a kick. They'd have Kate back before dinner.

Chandi burst out onto the roof, the door slamming into the wall in her haste to get away. Eliza and Betsy were hard on her heels. The roof was not entirely empty. The agent didn't get a good look at the odd device on the roof, but feared it was an ornithopter such as the children who had attacked her apartments had used.

"Betsy!" she yelled, but they were both running a fraction too slow. Chandi launched herself at the device, so that she and it toppled over the edge of the building. Her two pursuers scrambled to the side, but they were not lucky enough to see her splattered on the ground.

Chandi, her body clamped in straps, spread across a flying machine the like of which Eliza had never seen in action, or indeed in reality. She had, however, seen *cornuretorta* as a concept on a drawing board in the Ministry. Two spinning, screw-shaped wings buzzed above the narrow frame that shuttled the traitorous bitch away from them. Wellington would have loved to see such a thing, but Eliza found nothing to enjoy about the moment.

"Shoot her!" Betsy yelled as they watched the device spirit Chandi away.

"If I do," Eliza growled, "then we will never get Kate back. Think with your goddamn head!" She slammed her fist against the brickwork of the ledge. What was her next move going to be? The image of Ihita under the bridge would not leave her alone, yet she couldn't afford to let it paralyse her. "I have to go get Wellington," she said finally. "Betsy, you'd better round up the remaining committee members, and get them to a windowless secure location. Just in case Chandi wants to complete the set."

The other woman nodded, her hands tightening on her sticks. "I'll take them to . . ."

"Don't tell me," Eliza cut her off. "Keep as few people aware of the location as possible, and don't make it any of the usual safe houses—there's no telling how much information she has on the movement."

"And Mrs. Sheppard?"

"I'll get her back." She turned and fixed the Protector with a hard look that left no doubt she would not stop until that had been accomplished. "Leave it to me."

CHAPTER TWENTY-THREE

Wherein Eliza Discovers Loss and More

Eliza would have tried to flag down a velo-motor on the street, but such things were incredibly rare, and a hansom still so much more at hand. So she grabbed one the instant she got out of the meeting hall. Betsy would have to deal with the frightened women, and those who were injured, since the agent was now working against the clock.

"Double the fare if you get us there in half an hour," she called, holding her money aloft through the hatch in the roof.

The driver cracked his whip at this incentive, and set a cracking pace through London. Never had a journey seemed so interminably long. She tapped her feet on the floor of the hansom, and thought about what she would need once she and Wellington set off to find Kate. The Archivist had been right, and she'd just have to right out and say it—even though apologising twice in one week for her was unheard of!

They pulled up outside Wellington's house. Paying the driver a generous amount, she shoved open the hansom's door, then the gate, and raced up the path to the door.

"Welly, Welly!" She didn't care if she was making a scene in his well-to-do neighbourhood. When she touched the door handle she jerked back. The door was ajar. While a chill spread within her belly, Eliza took out her pistols from

the small of her back. Poking her head into the house, she
listened for any signs of life.

Nothing. Wellington's home was silent. Eliza slipped
off her boots and entered on gentle feet so as not to break
the almost funerary atmosphere. When Archimedes, sitting
in the middle of the stairs, meowed, Eliza's pistols came
around, their hammers pulled back. The cat tilted his head
and glared at her with yellow eyes; and she gave a long, low
exhale, giving the pet a slow head shake.

Still the agent was not about to call out for Wellington.
Instead she padded down the corridor, glancing to the right,
and left to the second set of stairs that led to his workshop.
She could see the door to his den was ajar. A strange fluttering noise could now be discerned along with the slight hum
of an engine, but it was not coming from down there. It was
coming from her right. Yet it was not the sound that frightened Eliza, it was, again . . . a smell. It was not as strong as
it had been at the meeting hall, but the faint whiff of it was
enough to make her heart race.

"Oh no," she gasped, giving up all pretence at stealth. She
dashed down the hallway towards the noise.

It was quite a sight. Wellington had obviously been working hard, because this set up of four cinematic machines was
quite different from that she'd seen in his workshop. The
strange noise was coming from all four circular machines
that were placed facing a white painted wall.

She strode over to examine them. The strange rhythmic
fluttering was from all four devices which each had a length
of film, the sound being small fans keeping the machines
cool. It must have been. Flicking off the machines at least
quieted that noise. For some reason the fans grated on her.

"No, no, no!" Eliza muttered to herself turning around
in the room, eyes darting over everything. Her heart sank a
little when she found his Ministry ring lying on an end table
by the door. It would have been such a doddle to locate him
with its signal—but she imagined he'd taken it off because
he was working.

"Dammit, Wellington," Eliza twisted her own on her finger, "I don't like it either, but I do wear it . . . most of the time."

She couldn't think that he might be hanging under a bridge, perhaps next to Kate, no she most certainly could not afford that now. He was alive. Yes, he was alive and she was going to get him back. In the process someone was going to get a right thrashing.

Quickly she took the stairs down to Wellington's workshop. The room was a mess, but it had been last time she'd been down here. An ordered mess, but one nonetheless. She poked around as best she could, but it was impossible to tell if anything was out of place. Only Wellington would have recognised that.

Looking up, the little half windows she'd taken notice of before were not as they had once been. The layer of dirt on the outside surface that had effectively acted as a screen had been rubbed clean in one spot. Eliza's imagination filled in the gaps, and she could see that evil little bitch clearing it, spying on what the Archivist was up to.

Now here she was, doing the same. The stack of papers and calculations was still here, but it was nothing more than a collection of numbers and notes.

Eliza paused suddenly aware that her emotions were getting the better of her. She needed to look at these notes as a field agent, as evidence in an investigation. She let out a long, deep breath, then looked at the collection of notes once more.

Eliza gathered up the top five sheets and spread them out across Wellington's central worktable. The last one she placed was the oldest one—it was best to remain logical. She narrowed her gaze on them. The numbers themselves were a tad intimidating, but their accompanying notes told a different story.

"Location of Speakers' Corner, location of Melinda Carnes," Eliza read aloud. "Note theft and Case 18820502AURZ Location of Empire Hotel Location of Ihita Pujari."

Attached to this notation was an article cut from a news-paper. It was about the museum heist the Ministry Seven had mentioned, and the item stolen—a geological curiosity that, one scientist claimed to have been investigating and believed behaved similar to . . .

"A lightning rod?" Eliza whispered.

Now her eyes darted around the pile of notes, and there it was—a case file from the Archives. She flipped it open and scanned the summary for the 1882 Australian anomaly known as the Rock of Zeus.

She jumped back to the most recent page of Wellington's notations, a map with words written on it in a large triumphant hand. Wellington had obviously been very pleased with himself, and so he should be:

No more than 25 miles

This proclamation was written under a hastily drawn circle encompassing London.

A smile spread on her lips. Wellington had cracked the enigma of the snatching machine's operation range. Just in time.

"*Quod erat demonstrandum*, Welly," Eliza whispered.

Yet he was gone. She stood there in the midst of his workshop and felt her throat tighten. This place was so very, very him. It was like standing in the centre of the man's imagination. If he died, then this would be all that was left of him.

"No," she spoke loudly, as if by doing so Chandi Culpepper would hear her. "That is not going to happen." Eliza folded up the calculations and stuffed them into her jacket.

As she went back upstairs, her mind was whirling. She'd have to track down the traitor some other way, find out what property she owned. Damn it, that would take time, and scouring through Archives. Something Wellington would have been very good at—were he not in deadly peril himself.

Sometimes fate was a cruel bitch with a rotten sense of humour.

Just as she was about to leave, Archimedes twined around her feet. He wasn't purring. Even a cat apparently needed to be comforted now and then. Eliza picked him up and held him facing her. "If only I could have seen what you did."

She was about to put him down, when her eyes drifted to the door frame that led to the parlour. Then she noted the step Archimedes had once been on. It, and others near the foot of the landing, were the same. The warped and twisted wood was immediately apparent. "So it happened here," Eliza muttered. She was standing directly in the place where Wellington had been snatched. Putting Archimedes on a nearby chair, she poked her head into the parlour. The sun was bright for a winter's day, and fell on the room she'd seen before. However, there was one thing very different. A table set with chess pieces she'd noted previously was now in disorder. The pieces were scattered all over the floor, except for two.

Eliza walked a little closer. How was it possible for the game to have been upset, yet the board and two pieces standing proudly on it remained on the table?

It wasn't.

"Very clever, Welly." She smiled to herself. He must have taken advantage of the gap between the smell and his abduction. Eliza's hands dropped to the two chess pieces remaining. Two queens. Black and white. She could understand the imagery of one queen perhaps—a confirmation that Chandi was involved as he had theorised. But why two queens?

While she was contemplating that, she slid the note out from under where it rested beneath the white queen. Wellington's handwriting on this note was decidedly cruder—he must have been in a much greater hurry. *Turn them on*, was all it said. Eliza looked around, and saw nothing nearby that needed turning on. Then she made the leap of understanding.

Quickly making her way back to where she'd already been, into the room at the rear, she stared at the four machines lined up facing the bare wall. It took her a few moments to ascertain that she needed to light the little filaments within the boxes. When she did that, four still images of four suffragist meetings appeared in a grid of two by two.

"Four of the kidnappings," she whispered. "Now Welly, show me what you saw."

Luckily she had seen a few kinetoscopes in her time, so knew the basics for those smaller versions of these larger machines. It appeared that Wellington had rigged them to work in tandem. By virtue of cranking the lever to the right, the images started to pick up speed, eventually going at a lifelike pace.

And there it was. Chandi Culpepper tucking her hair behind one ear, and then, unmistakably tugging on one of those earrings. A tell.

Just to be sure, Eliza pulled back on the lever, reversed the film and played it again. "No mistaking it," she stopped the celluloid and stared. "Evidence."

That was simple enough, but the meaning of the two queens escaped her. Eliza didn't consider herself stupid, but without Wellington she did feel lessened. She had to get back to the Ministry. Once there she could talk with Hill and the Director. The time for pretending was long past, and there was no way she was going to put Wellington's safety over the secrecy they had been working on in the Archives. Doctor Sound could kick her out of the Ministry, as long as the Archivist was returned safely.

Clutching the two queens in one hand, Eliza shut down the array. She then ran down the corridor, opened the front door, and found herself at the wrong end of a dozen gun barrels.

"Eliza D. Braun." Diamond Dottie sat astride a lococycle. "A pleasure to see you again." She must have turned the huge machine off and rolled in on it, so as not to alert the agent. Her ring of minions must have come in by some other

means. It would have been comedic in any other circumstances. The thieves were all beautifully dressed, but held
their pistols with a steady grip. None could doubt that if they
shot, they would hit.

Eliza cleared her throat and smiled. "Dorothy, lovely to
see you again, and so . . . unexpectedly too. Unfortunately,
you have caught me at a rather inopportune time." Her gaze
darted among the women, but she could see there was no
real way to draw on any of them and not be filled with lead
herself. Only now did Eliza wish that she'd stopped at the
Ministry to grab a few extra pieces of armament. With only
her pistols it was like being out naked.

"I am sure you are busy." Dottie tapped her fingers on
the brass covering on the lococycle. "But dearie, we need to
have a talk. A really serious girl talk."

One glance around told her that refusal was not an option.

CHAPTER TWENTY-FOUR

In Which Eliza Makes an Ally of a Most Multi-Faceted Nature

℗erhaps things weren't as bad as Eliza thought. Diamond Dottie hadn't tied her up and bundled her into a hansom. Instead she'd slid forward so that the agent could take a place behind her on the lococycle. The machine hissed to life beneath them, and Eliza was jerked backwards as they accelerated away from Wellington's house. She was forced to grab the queen of London's underground around the waist rather hastily. The rattle of pistons and the tremendous hiss of the boilers did not exactly make for a calm ride.

Despite all that, Eliza yelped with delight. "Dottie, this really is a most marvellous method of travel. I've never seen one of these before. Where ever did you get it?"

Dorothy's laughter was loud enough to rise above the cacophony of the engine. "Why, I stole it, dearie—but let's save that story for now."

Their journey returned Eliza to Mayfair, and ended where Eliza had never expected nor hoped to see again in her present or future lifetimes—the home of Diamond Dottie. She was no longer the fly lured into the spider's web as she once had been, but she was being given a proper escort and formal invitation to its very centre.

Once the lococycle rumbled still before the house's main door, a hard reality hit Eliza: she and Dottie were alone. Her Elephants were trailing far behind, leaving their leader alone with a mark that had survived a full-on ornithopter assault.

"Before you think you got a cokum," Dottie began as she stripped off her gloves, "take a look at the second floor window, to the left."

Eliza looked over to the indicated window. It was a chilly day but regardless, it was open to the elements, even though its curtains were drawn. Peculiar to any passerby, but to Eliza it made perfect sense. Especially when she saw the thin rifle barrel protruding from the part in the fabric. "I've got two maids in the house, and both can part a man's hair with a single shot." She then gave her a hard look. "We got to settle our hash."

Eliza stood there for a moment. Was there any point in running? The bullet would cut her down, and Dottie could spin any tale she desired on who she was and why she had been gunned down in her front yard. There was no choice in this matter. Eliza steeled herself and followed Dottie.

She glanced out of the corner of her eye. The barrel followed her all the way to the front steps.

When the door opened, she was welcomed into the house at gunpoint. The second maid had picked up where her counterpart left off, and slinked back silently as Eliza now entered the foyer she only saw during a mad dash out of Dottie's home. The lady of the manor was hanging up her own coat and then outstretched her hand to take Eliza's.

"You'll have to forgive my maid," Dottie said with a shrug. "She's currently preoccupied."

Eliza slowly slipped her own coat free, her eyes never leaving the gun-wielding house servant. When she finally looked away, over to Dottie, she was astounded at the woman's demeanour, her outward confidence. She had something to say to Eliza, and remained more than assured that Eliza would hang on her every word.

"Right then, Eliza Braun, is it?" Dottie asked, looking her over. "Follow me."

Their first few steps to Dottie's library were in silence, but Eliza finally snapped, "I really don't have time for this!"

"You will make the time, missy."

"My partner has gone missing and I'm going to get him back."

"You'll be needing all the help you can get then, now won't you?" Dottie turned back to look at her. The smile was neither sincere nor menacing. Contemplative. "After what you said last time you paid me a visit, I did some poking around for you."

London's most feared gang-leader? Doing leg-work for the Ministry of Peculiar Occurrences? *Unbidden?* Dottie could not have surprised Eliza more if she had offered to teach the secret agent how to knit.

Particularly in light of their personal history. "Why the hell would you do that for me?" Eliza scoffed.

The courtesy Dottie was extending to her disappeared into the æther, her polished character switching from Kensington to East End in a moment. "Oi, watch your tone with me, you jammy bint! I is doing you a favour!"

"You tried to have me killed in my apartments!"

Dottie took a step closer to her, her finger raised in the air as if she were going to retaliate with another barrage; but her finger remained suspended there. Then, she inclined her head to one side, and her reply was even as she gently tapped Eliza's shoulder. "That was my misunderstanding. You were making an effort to get to me when you saw me at that meeting what went all possessed like. Thought you were with the blue bottles." She then motioned for Eliza to follow her into the library. "Then you broke in here. Saw that little bob you used to get into my house. Then all your prattle about suffragists? Definitely not with blue bottles. So

I thought I'd help out a fellow sister—especially since you have a passable left hook."

"Get to the point then," Eliza seethed. She knew she needed to proceed more cautiously, but every word shared with Dottie meant another moment keeping her from going after Wellington. Still, she needed to know. "Why would you want to help the movement at all?"

"Maybe I think women should have a say in 'ow this rotten world is run. Or"—her look turned crafty—"maybe those committee cows are my main source of income. Always buying pretty things, always leaving the 'ouse to do 'good works.' Nice juicy targets they make."

Eliza's hands tightened into fists, but she said nothing.

"So I asked around my girls. Asked if they seen anything strange." Dottie leaned back in her chair. "'Course, them ladies are pretty strange as it is, but they's always out of their 'omes when we call. Except for one."

Now she had the agent's full attention. "What do you mean? All the committee ladies attend every meeting. I've even seen one half-dead from pneumonia drag herself there."

"Not Miss Chandi Culpepper. Every time one of me Elephants goes 'round to pay her a call, that cow is there. Never leaves."

Eliza pulled out a chair and sat down opposite Dottie. This made no sense. "Chandi is as studious of attending as anyone. As far as I know she's never missed a meeting."

"Then you've got poached eyeballs. My girls ain't been able to lift a single thing from her 'ouse, not never."

In Eliza's pocket the two queens started to weigh heavily. She slipped her fingers around them and pulled them out. Wellington had been trying to tell her more than just his discovery of Chandi Culpepper. She rolled the two pieces in her palm. She recalled a friend in the music halls, one who had performed the most amazing magic acts, and exactly how he had done it. Even Jonathan and Jeremy. *It made perfect sense.*

"Twins," she whispered. "One to target whatever device they are using, and the other to activate it."

"Blimey—that does explain a thing or two." Dottie's eyebrow shot up, but she nodded. "Twins have a right ole advantage on the street. Got a couple myself working all the angles."

Eliza's stomach twisted as she thought of Jonathan and Jeremy.

"Whatcha going to do now?" The older woman's gaze was sharp. "Take 'em down?"

"Absolutely."

Dottie grinned and then eyed her sharply as if sizing her up for a dress fitting. Apparently the agent met inspection, because the tall woman stood and gestured her over to the grandfather clock that stood in the corner of the library. She moved the hands around, to the sound of clicks like when a safe was cracked. Dottie glanced over her shoulder and shifted her stance, keeping her broad back deliberately to her guest. Eliza would have had to step around her to make out what she was actually doing; and considering all the professional kindnesses she had already extended to the Ministry, that seemed just a little rude.

Still, Eliza was not surprised when the clock began to open, folding on itself like an accordion until there was an opening that even her host could slip through into a small room beyond. The agent followed the tall form of Diamond Dorothy and blinked. Eliza D. Braun had never seen such a pretty secret lair—and she'd seen her fair share.

Dottie lit a small gaslight, and the yellow illumination gleamed over hundreds of little of pieces of glass. It appeared the queen of the London underworld had taken apart chandeliers and hung them all over the room.

The agent decided not to comment on her host's choice of décor.

Instead, she craned her neck about, and examined the pieces of paper pinned between the gleaming crystals: photos, scribbled notes, maps, lists, and plans.

"Why are you showing me this?" she murmured, a little afraid of the response.

Dottie smiled shrewdly. "I know a like soul when I sees it. Besides I gets the feeling you and your man are all on your own with this one."

Not for long, Eliza thought quickly.

"I know how that is," the criminal mistress continued, "and you can't afford to make no trouble neither. Workin' in secret, you is."

"And if we take care of Chandi Culpepper, a bit of professional pride restored, isn't it?" Eliza asked.

"I don't like being played as a mark in my own game." The taller woman tapped the side of her nose. "Now come have a gander at this." It was a map of London and the south of England that occupied the central position of the room. "Now here's that little bint's townhouse," Dorothy laid her finger on a tiny flag. "When I got word that the Culpepper house was clear, I went there myself. She's already cleared out of there. Even her clockwork servants were gone."

Eliza saw that nearly every neighbourhood in London bore a marker in various colours—obviously the Elephants were keeping a very careful eye on their targets.

"And what are these?" Eliza asked pointing to a scattering of smaller flags beyond the city.

"Country houses," Dottie said, flicking one. "Always pays to know how far away your mark is when you're doing a little robbery and don't want to be interrupted like."

The colour of each flag matched the townhouses of their targets. "So this must be the Culpepper estate." Her finger fell on a spot near Barking.

Wellington's note. He'd calculated no more than twenty-five miles, and this house at Barking was well within that.

"Not that she ever goes there," Dottie commented, tapping her fingernails on her teeth.

Eliza was taking note of the exact location. "Things have become too tricky for her in the city—and a fox will always bolt for its hole when things get tight."

Eliza's mind was racing ahead, calculating what she might need. "I'll need to stop at my apartments and then head to the Ministry to rouse the troops first though."

"You'll be needing to move sharpish then." Quickly Dottie got up and led her back to the foyer. "You best take my lococycle. Probably the fastest thing in the city."

It did not take long from acquisition for the queen of the underground to claim ownership, Eliza noticed. She nodded. "Thank you Dorothy, much appreciated."

The grin that spread over Dottie's face was broad and as wicked as a wolf. "No skin off my nose, dearie, and it might rub Chandi Culpepper's into the mud."

"How so?"

"Lifted it from outside 'er 'ouse."

The laughter they shared felt good, felt welcomed. The understanding they had quickly built between them remained even to the door where they said their goodbyes and Dottie even wished her *"Good hunting."* When the lococycle rumbled to life between her legs and the goggles came across her eyes, Eliza looked back to the doorway. The maid was watching the street now, and Dottie was watching the agent depart with a grim, yet satisfied expression.

It was better to have Diamond Dottie as an ally, Eliza mused as she pulled away—especially since her enemies usually ended up in the river. The Thames was deep, murky, and hardly as warm and inviting as Dottie's private library.

CHAPTER TWENTY-FIVE

In Which Our Dashing Archivist
Finds Himself Cut of a Different Cloth

The pain ebbed and flowed over Wellington like a great tide—but it was not that which brought him back to the world of the living. Not even the queer vertigo he was struggling against could do that. Nor even the nausea, migraine, or the ringing in his ears caused him to stir.

What brought Wellington Thornhill Books, Esquire, back into the waking world was the smell. He knew it right away—he was all too familiar with this particular stench.

Anyone passing alongside a slaughterhouse during the summer becomes familiar with the smell of rotting meat. Wellington had different experiences. He knew that under the heat of an African sun, the human body can produce exactly the same stench. Now it was assailing him.

What made this horror even worse was he didn't even have a clue where he was. His eyes were open, but still he saw nothing. The darkness was thick, absolute, and worse—deathly quiet. Wellington knew he wasn't alone. Judging by the smell, there had to be at least three corpses lying nearby.

Rather than take a deep breath, as he might have wanted to, he instead had to take short gasps through his mouth.

Feeling around with his hands, he recognised that he was sitting upright, and his back was against something like a wall. Wellington slowly extended his legs into the darkness. Even when he wiggled his feet he felt open space, so there had to be some depth to this darkness. He then raised his arms up along the wall behind him, flat and flush against . . .

His head inclined to one side—the wall was curved. He felt, most definitely, the slightest of curvatures.

"*Bene* . . ." The voice spoke softly, paused, and then gave a delightful bell-like laugh. "Well, that is a question. Do I bid you a good evening or a good morning? 'Tis all the same here."

Good Lord, Wellington prayed, *please tell me my mind is playing tricks.*

"Shade your eyes, *Signore* Books, as the light may be a bit blinding at first."

Something rapped against stone, and slowly the darkness peeled away to an eerie green glow. The exotic beauty shook the vial in her hand, which made the glow brighter. As it did, the deeper Wellington's heart sank.

"I must say, *Signorina del Morte*," he began, trying desperately to ignore the thudding in his chest, "I am feeling quite torn right now in finding myself here with you."

Sophia gave a soft sigh. "I would have thought you would be happy to see such a resourceful girl as myself here with you." A wicked smile flickered over her lips. "Would you be more grateful if you knew that I used one of my last three illuminati for your benefit?"

"Are you going to tell me that in the darkness you knew who had just arrived?"

She winked. "So then call me lucky as well as resourceful." Sophia then turned back to the darkness behind her and called to it as if there were a lost kitten hiding in the shadows. "Come along. This is a friend. No need to be bashful."

The woman sliding up alongside Sophia looked exhausted, hungry, and in the late stages of dehydration; but Wellington could still see determination in her eyes. Willpower could only take a person so far, and she was nearing the limit.

"Lena Munroe?" Wellington whispered. "Is that you?"

The suffragist blinked. "Do I know—" And then her eyes widened. "You were on the hypersteam express!"

"Wellington Thornhill Books, Esquire, ma'am," Wellington said, pulling himself up to his feet, "of the Ministry of Peculiar Occurrences."

Lena's brow furrowed. "Ministry of . . . what?"

That evoked a laugh from Sophia. "Sometimes, it is difficult to be in our chosen professions, seeing as we must exist in shadow."

"You're not going to tell me you feel at home here?" he quipped.

The assassin merely smiled as a reply.

Wellington crossed his arms and lifted an eyebrow. "Now here's a thought—are you familiar with our captors?"

Sophia gave a very unladylike snort. "She is an associate of my current employer. Chandi Culpepper is her name." Her eyes narrowed. "You don't seem surprised. You are acquainted with her, yes?"

"One of them anyway."

Sophia's head tilted as her eyes widened. "One of them?" Wellington waited, watching with some delight the realisation dawn across her lovely face. "No . . . that cannot be . . ."

"And now you see how Miss Culpepper—or at least Chandi Culpepper—got the drop on us, as those in your profession would put it."

"That abomination," spat Lena. Her voice trembled, growing colder and harder with each word. "I saw them together when in Scotland. I wasn't supposed to see them, of course. She was supposed to protect our officers, our future; but I discovered their secret."

"And that was why you were taken," Wellington said. "It was to preserve the secret."

"Chandi had told us her sister died in India with her mother," she muttered.

"Just a moment," Sophia interjected, grabbing Lena by the arm, "you knew that bitch had an identical twin?" She released her with a shove. "Why did you not mention this to me earlier?"

"I thought you knew, seeing as you are here." The laugh she gave chilled Wellington. She was not only teetering on the edge of starvation. She was also teetering near madness.

Sophia, however, was hardly moved by the woman's odd behaviour. "Lena, dear, I suggest you gather your wits once more. Remember what happened to your lovely Protector when she tested my patience?"

The suffragist nodded quickly, taking in a deep breath. That simple feat amazed Wellington as, even with his small, shallow breaths, he could barely tolerate the smell.

Wait a moment. Lena's Protector? "Is there someone else in here?" he asked.

Sophia looked over her shoulder, and when she turned back to Wellington her face seemed almost as sallow and sickly as Lena's. "Yes. A rather imposing figure of a woman."

Wellington felt his stomach sink. "Charlotte Lawrence?"

Lena gave a short nod, but her eyes were cast downward, not looking at Wellington, and not daring to look at Sophia.

"I suppose, but she's back there." Sophia tried her best to sound offhanded, but even the Archivist could tell the difference. "With the others."

"Others?" Then he looked around him. The stone wall extended into the darkness. No signs of light. The smell. The smell that seemed to grow stronger the more he deduced. "How many?"

"It is hard to tell," Sophia said.

"Five," Lena spoke. "I counted."

"My God," he whispered, looking around him, his face twisting in shock and revulsion. "An oubliette?"

"Yes," Sophia sneered. "Charming, isn't it?"

His eyes immediately jumped back to Sophia. "And you added Charlotte to this madness?"

"Sadly, the aggressive *Signorina* Charlotte fell to my

darker talents. I appeared here, lit an illuminati, and that was when she attacked me. She thought me the enemy, the thick bitch. As if the enemy would trap themselves in the same dungeon as her! I warned her to unhand me. She only tightened her hold." Sophia gave a sigh and a small shrug. "I had to defend myself."

"So you killed her?"

She clicked her tongue once. "Regrettably, yes."

Wellington straightened his jacket as best he could and then looked up at the wall. "Sophia, might I see this illuminati of yours?"

"Certainly," she said, handing Wellington the glowing stick.

He turned the brilliant emerald device in his hand, noting the way the fluid flowed back and forth, bending the shadows around him. "Phosphorus?"

"It remains dormant inside the glass until it is given a hard rap against something. The outside glass keeps the vial intact." Sophia chuckled as she motioned to the device. "I would love to chat with you about craftsmanship, but our light is already beginning to dim. I have two remaining. We should make them last." She then looked to her right and fixed the nearly imperceptible form of Lena with a stare. "Lena dear, do stay close please."

"Yes, miss."

Wellington pushed aside his disgust at Sophia's opportunistic nature, and looked up, holding the illuminati in his hand as high as he could. He hoped to catch a glimpse of the top of the oubliette, but the bricks simply continued into a void.

"Along with these illuminati, did you happen to come armed with any other quaint devices?"

"If you must know," Sophia said, opening her coat, "I was working late when I was . . ." and she pursed her lips, shaking her head.

"Caught off your impenetrable guard?"

"No need to mock a lady," she lightly scolded.

A lady was the last thing Wellington would have called Sophia del Morte, but he decided discretion would be better than valour in this predicament. "Perchance you wouldn't have a grappling gun conveniently strapped upon your person?"

"A grappling gun?" She gave a little laugh. "For what I do?"

Wellington looked back up to the darkness overhead. "Yes, I suppose that would have been a bit too *deus ex machina*, now wouldn't it?" He glanced at the illuminati in his hand. "We need to know how much height we have to compensate for. Judging by the echo, I am guessing well over thirty feet."

"Wellington, dear, do you not think I have considered every avenue of escape?"

He turned around to face her. "Perhaps you have. I am choosing a more . . ." He gave a small chuckle as he said, " . . . opportunistic approach. You are going to have to trust me."

"Am I?"

"If you don't, we all die down here. We both know that." He glanced behind her towards the frail Lena Munroe.

Sophia considered a moment, and then nodded. "What do you need from me?"

"A knife."

From behind her back, Sophia produced a menacing weapon, curved, smooth and clean. In the emerald glow of the illuminati it was impressive and terrifying.

After a moment she extended it, handle first, to him.

Wellington cleared his throat. "Have those other sticks ready. We will need the light to work by." He motioned for Sophia to join Lena. "Stay here. I shan't be a moment."

Wellington proceeded forward into the darkness. He did not take long steps as the actual depth of this oubliette was still a mystery, and considering Chandi Culpepper's use of it, there could be a number of macabre surprises waiting for them. It felt as though the oubliette stretched forward for far too long. He looked to either side of him, but there was nothing but void. The illuminati's light could not even reach the opposite wall.

Then, ahead of him, a shape began to resolve itself. If he hadn't known better, Wellington would have thought it was a pile of laundry or perhaps some seasonal gardening equipment set aside for the winter and then concealed from view by a tarp.

Sadly, Wellington knew better.

The body slumped over the five decaying corpses could not have been more than a day or two old. She had been haphazardly tossed on the rotting remains of the others. Charlotte Lawrence's neck was quite broken.

Wellington did not pay the stench any mind now. The Archivist had acclimated himself to this familiar smell, and even thought to himself, it could have been worse. Far worse. He recalled, as he rolled Charlotte free from the others, how the African sun tended to speed up infection in the wounded, and decay in the dead.

The blade slid cleanly through the dress. He tried not to think of the body within it. In the African bush he'd been forced to use the dead as camouflage. Another time they'd used their slaughtered friends to stand watch while he and the survivors of a failed push safely made it back to base camp.

His task was made more difficult as the light dimmed, casting more and more shadow around his grim works. Wellington paused cutting and shook the illuminati, the phosphorus glugging quickly as he worked the glass light back and forth. The glow flared, but not by much. Time was running short, and so he grimly kept cutting. He promised himself to head back once the light began to dim again. Another long strip fell at his feet. Then another, and another.

This was about survival.

He needed as much as he could carry, but this served him no comfort as he cut the dress free of the second corpse. If their supply started to dwindle, he would have to come back here and gather more. He preferred not to. His willpower was not that strong.

The light began to dim. It was time to go.

Wellington gathered up the long strands of fabric that once made an impressive overskirt, the underskirt, and the dress in his arms. He was about to leave when he paused on catching in the dim light the curves of Charlotte Lawrence, the sturdy corset still wrapped snug around her. A quick swipe of Sophia's knife later, and the corset rested spread over top the mass of fabric within his arms. The light of the illuminati was far from its original brilliance, but all Wellington needed to do was place himself before the macabre tableau, turn his back upon it, and walk straight forward. As it had before, the darkness seemed to swallow him. This time, his light seemed much dimmer, while the oubliette consumed sound and life. The gooseflesh along his arms tingled. Had the ladies moved from where he had left them?

He paused in the darkness for a moment. He had to keep calm.

"Wellington?"

In an instant he wished that was Eliza's voice, but then quickly changed that. He was glad his colleague was far away and safe.

The Archivist continued forward, and two forms sitting against the oubliette's curved wall slowly materialised out of the darkness.

"That illuminati does not have much time. Perhaps ten minutes," Sophia stated.

"Then we must make the most of each moment," he said, setting down the small collection of fabric before them.

"Monster," hissed Lena, jerking backwards.

"Perhaps," Wellington said, his eyes measuring the clothing bundled before them, "but as we have so little in our favour presently, we must make do with what we have."

Sophia ran her fingers through the strips of cotton and linen, keeping her eyes locked with Wellington's. "Your intentions?"

"I will show you the weave. While you do that, I will continue to cut. It may be tricky, especially in the dark; but it is a simple enough task so long as you keep a focus on what you are doing. When we are done, we should have enough of a rope to get one of us out of here."

The sharp sound of breath catching turned both Wellington and Sophia to the girl pressed hard against the stone wall. "One of us?"

"Yes, Lena. One." Wellington removed the corset, feeling its weight one more time before taking a seat on the oubliette's floor and positioning the dying illuminati next to him. "Between these strips, this cloth," Wellington placed a hand on the corset, "and our grappling hook, we must hope we have enough. Now, ladies, if you please?" he asked, motioning to the space before him.

Lena and Sophia looked to each other; and with a single nod from the Italian assassin they leaned toward him.

"In the few moments of light we have left, ladies," Wellington said, distributing the strips of cloth to them, "focus on the motion of your hands. We will, after all, be weaving in the dark."

"Weaving? In the dark?" The laugh from Lena was dry, completely free of mirth. "What a ladylike pursuit . . ."

Wellington looked at her, his eyes narrowing. The laughter stopped abruptly. "This is our only chance," he said. "Do as I do. Study your pattern. Know it intimately."

"And when we run low on our weaving, *Signore* Books?"

"Then, you let me know and I will supply more. If our supplies dwindle, we then utilise one—and only one—illuminati in gathering more fabric. We will need the last one for our escape. Now, let us begin."

Over. Under. Over. Tug. Over. Under. Over. Tug. Their pattern was a simple one, but as the shadows closed in around them, the challenge grew more and more clear. Satisfied that the ladies were comfortably in a routine, Wellington gathered up the underskirt and began slicing into it as he had done with its accompanying dress. He measured the width with his fingers. He would have to cut carefully, and slowly, hoping that the ladies and he had a good long time to achieve their task.

"Mr. . . . Books, is it?" came Lena's voice.

"Yes, Miss Munroe?"

"Would you mind if I sang a bit?" She sniffled, and then added, "My mother would do so when I was scared."

"*Signorina*?" Wellington asked.

"So long as the woman's voice is pleasant," the Italian snapped in reply.

Wellington took in a long, slow breath. "Go on then, Miss Munroe."

Her voice cracked now and again, but there was in fact a calming tone in her singing.

> *Sleep my child and peace attend thee,*
> *All through the night.*
> *Guardian angels God will send thee,*
> *All through the night.*
> *Soft the drowsy hours are creeping.*
> *Hill and vale in slumber sleeping,*
> *I my loving vigil keeping*
> *All through the night . . .*

As Lena Munroe sang softly in the darkness, the women toiled in their task. Wellington concentrated on slicing the fabric and holding the hope of their work before them.

CHAPTER TWENTY SIX

In Which the Troops Are Mustered

Driving the lococycle was much like wrestling a bull while perched between its shoulder blades. Eliza's dark hair streamed out behind her; her hands clenched tight on the steering horns, and her lips pressed together in concentration. She would have been having a throughly enjoyable time of it, were it not for the fact that her colleague was in mortal peril. Whoever the machine had originally belonged to, before Dottie made off with it, must have been quite the daredevil. Whipping through the streets of London, frightening horses, and causing hansom drivers and pedestrians to shake their fists at her was just a pleasant side dish. The main advantage was how she avoided the hurly burley traffic of the capital. Soon enough she reached her home.

Brakes were obviously the last thing the designer of this particular madcap creation had taken into account. Eliza had to rapidly work the levers to cut the supply of steam to the pistons, and then jerk the front of the lococycle to one side, least she smack into the wall opposite her property and decorate it in a most unseemly fashion. It was apparently the wrong thing to do. She was thrown to the right, and was forced to slam her boot down on the cobbles to slow her approach. The street gobbled up some of her shoe leather, but at last, panting, she brought the devil to a halt.

Racing up the stairs, ignoring the stares of her fellow apartment dwellers, she banged on the door. Her neighbours had seen many a strange occurrence in Miss Eliza D. Braun's domicile—the least of it being her running. Her excuses of owning a very large dog were starting to wear a little thin. Alice opened the door, and her mistress brushed past her.

"Bring me the *plures ornamentum*," she said pulling off her jacket. "No, wait—undo my buttons. I need trousers for what's to come." She would have jerked the dress off her, but it was a sturdy tweed.

Alice's fingers flew over the row of closures at Eliza's back. "And what exactly is to come, Miss?"

"Wellington's been taken." She swallowed hard on that admission. "I need to get to the Ministry and alert them."

"And then?"

Eliza was finally free of her feminine attire, and stepped out of it with alacrity. "Then we'll get him back."

The gears in Alice's legs spun, and her hand went to lift up her own skirt. "Then you'll be needing some assistance."

The maid had already made apparent that she had a soft spot for the Archivist, but that she would offer to step outside the apartment was unusual. Alice loved the house. It was something she was fiercely protective of, so much that Eliza wondered what her priorities were sometimes. Yet, here she was offering to take up arms for Wellington Thornhill Books. With a tilt of her head, Eliza considered. "I think the Ministry should provide more than enough in that department—besides, I need you to protect the apartments, just in case our enemies come calling again."

It was a sensible enough suggestion, and Alice gave a tight nod. "The *plures* then, Miss. And may I suggest a selection of knives and guns to go with it? No, high explosives, for Mr. Books' sake."

Eliza arched an eyebrow, but thought better of complaining. These two mad women were not the House of Usher, and this time she would not risk the Archivist's life.

While Alice hurried to the wardrobe to retrieve the powered arm, Eliza slipped into a pair of tweed pants, a worsted wool shirt, a shoulder holster, and a knife sheath, and swapped her short boots for a much taller pair. By the time her maid returned with her further accoutrements, she had slipped knives into the boots, the sheath at her waist, and slid her pistols into the holster. Then she held out her right arm.

Alice began to buckle the multi-tool on, taking care to make sure the straps that wrapped around the opposite side of her chest were firm, but not so tight as to restrict movement. The combination of pistons, gears and weaponry was heavy, but Eliza could bear it for a short time. It could be invaluable in the rescue of Wellington.

"Do you think he's still alive?" Alice's whisper conveyed more emotion than a shout would have.

The image of Wellington's lifeless body would not leave her, and every time it appeared, a knot of panic began to well up inside Eliza. She spun about and grabbed hold of her maid's hands. "Alice, I have made a terrible mistake— just terrible." Tears were welling in her eyes and she had the horrible feeling if she were not careful they would spill over. "What if he dies without me telling him . . ."

"Enough of that," Alice snapped. "He's not dead, and you're going to get him back. Then you can make everything right."

It was a bucket of cold water over Eliza's running thoughts. She'd gone into plenty of dire situations, but she now understood why this one was so terrifying to her. She straightened up. "Yes."

Alice held out her long winter coat. "Then hurry off. I have faith we'll be seeing Mr. Books back here for tea tomorrow."

Eliza abandoned protocol, grabbing her maid in a tight

embrace, and planting a kiss on her cheek. "Keep the pot warm then."

Pelting out of her apartments, she leapt much more gamely onto the lococycle. She always felt so much better when properly armed. It was only a short but exhilarating ride to Miggins Antiquities. This time she was better at releasing the pressure in the lococycle, and managed a far less alarming stop.

Springing off her transportation, Eliza sprinted into the building. It was, as usual, full of the worker bees scratching away on their ledgers. It was time for drastic action that they would most definitely not enjoy. Directly inside the front door stood a tall grandfather clock, ticking away the minutes until the regular workers could leave. Without hesitation, Eliza flipped open the case. Within was a large lever, painted bright red. She'd never had cause to touch it—but if now was not the time, then she didn't know when would be. Grabbing the lever firmly, she yanked it to the left with as much determination and assuredness as she possessed.

The reaction was immediate. The raised warehouse door dropped down like a guillotine, sealing the outside world away behind two inches of bound iron. Inside the klaxons began to sound and everything turned to figurative custard. The front shop workers leapt up from their desks and scuttled into the aisle between their desks. From there they raced towards the back of the warehouse where the safe room was. People only pulled the red lever when the Ministry was about to be attacked, and the general workers knew when to make themselves scarce.

Eliza tilted her head. Several noises all at once were coming from above: the whirling of the Gatling guns on the third floor as they slid into their firing positions, and the drumlike rattle of many feet. Everyone was dropping whatever they were doing, grabbing up their weapons and preparing to defend Miggins Antiquities. It was exactly what she wanted.

Yet she swallowed hard.

The entire population of the upstairs offices were now running down the stairs to the ground floor. Agents Hill, Campbell, the Director himself, and half a dozen others including Shillingworth. All of them, even the redoubtable secretary, were touting weaponry and looked ready for trouble.

Doctor Sound's eyes swept the area and then he strode over and cranked up the telescopic-viewer. When his examination of the scene outside revealed nothing, that same steely gaze turned on Eliza D. Braun.

She hadn't moved from her spot by the grandfather clock, even though her heart was thumping. Once she opened her mouth, all of their secret investigations down in the Archives would be revealed. Her future with the Ministry no longer mattered. She knew she needed backup. For Wellington. For Kate.

"Our Archivist has been kidnapped," she said loudly enough to ring down the length of the large building, "and we must get him back."

The Director's face tightened, so she knew he was thinking about the last time this had happened. The time when she had been given the orders to kill Wellington Books. It was ignoring that very command that had meant her exile to the Archivist's domain and started whole new adventures. Life had quite the sense of irony.

Doctor Sound tilted his head. "He's been kidnapped, you say? Did this happen last night while he was sleeping?"

Eliza knew where this line of questioning would lead, but she went on. "No. Sometime between yesterday and today."

"But Wellington would have been down in the Archives then, so now pray tell me how did that happen?"

Eliza glanced around: the other agents had their eyes fixed on her with breathless anticipation. Now was no time to back down. "No, sir, he wasn't—he was at home reviewing evidence."

The Director wasn't given a chance to reply to that as a grinning Bruce Campbell appeared at his shoulder. "Evidence? Eliza darling, sure sounds like you're working on a case." He stroked his chin, "But that can't be true since you don't do that anymore—not as a junior archivist."

She glared at him, ready to explode, but then heard the persistent voice of Wellington Thornhill Books in her head. *Not yet, Eliza. Not quite yet. Wait a little while.*

That damn well better not be his ghost haunting her. Ignoring Campbell, she fixed her gaze on the Director. Just him. "Mrs. Kate Sheppard asked me, as a personal favour, to look into the disappearance of the suffragists in the last few months. I convinced Wellington, against his better judgement, to assist me."

His expression was stern, but maybe she was imagining it, or was there a glimmer of respect in his eyes? "So instead of Wellington's cool head rubbing off on you, you have instead corrupted our Archivist?"

Bruce let out an almighty snort and muttered, "I could have told you that was coming."

Ignoring him, Eliza held her focus. "Time is of the essence for Wellington, Director. Disciplinary action against me can wait until after he is recovered—safe and sound."

Maulik Smith pressed the button on his throat, and his voice came out in the rasping croak that Blackwell's engineering skill had given him. "Considering what Books knows, considering what he has access to, we can't afford to be compromised. Director, I second Agent Braun's recommendation."

Agent Smith rarely spoke, so when he did it carried great weight. Eliza felt the tide turn her way, and her colleagues begin to come around to her way of thinking.

Bruce must have sensed it too, because he suddenly snapped, "Damn it, we can't afford to do that, since we're all up to our ears in active cases. As Assistant Director it is my duty to put the public first!"

Bruce's contradictory ethics incensed Eliza. They waxed and waned depending on what he wanted to get done. When he'd first arrived at the Ministry she'd thought he was merely a harmless moron. Now she was seeing he was more than that: he was a dangerous moron. He'd never once used the words "put the public first." She knew full well that in his mind there was only one person of any importance—Agent Bruce Campbell.

Still not yet, Eliza. Wellington seemed very close at this point.

Doctor Sound nodded. "You are absolutely right, Assistant Director, however Smith is also correct. Wellington Books is indeed a walking analytical engine that is a valuable asset to anyone who has him."

Brandon piped up from the rear of the room, "He's also a wonderful bridge partner."

The rest of the agents turned their heads, examining the Canadian curiously.

Doctor Sound cleared his throat. "Be that as it may." He fixed a look on Eliza. "We should do everything in our power to recover him. After all, allowing him to be eliminated would be a dreadful crime—wouldn't it, Braun?"

She tilted her head at his not-so-subtle dig at her past assignment. The Director could be as kindly as her grandfather, but then turn around and slice her with some well-chosen words. Before she could formulate an answer, she was cut off.

Bruce's face was beginning to redden. "Am I to understand then, Director, that you are putting the interests of one agent before citizens of the Empire?"

Doctor Sound's voice dropped very low, so that everyone in the room had to lean forward to catch it. "As Assistant Director you have every right to question my decisions."

Bruce was reaching some kind of full press, like a boiler ready to pop. "I do question it! I question your judgement in this situation most emphatically! You should be reported to the Queen immediately!"

No one moved—struck with shock and horror that Bruce had uttered such angry, disloyal words. The Australian went on regardless.

"After all, you are taking the word of a field agent who

was demoted due to insubordination. A person who has no evidence to prove what she is saying." He looked around, waving his hands, his voice now cracking with emotion. Eliza was not the only one who was revealing things here and now. "For all we know Books could have snapped and gone rogue. I mean, how much do we know about that bloke anyway, locked away in that dungeon all day? He's an odd bird that's never fitted in."

Eliza's hands were now white fists at her sides.

"Or even more likely he's already dead!" Campbell's face was beet-red with outrage. "For sure, he's a goner and that's the bloody end to it."

She swallowed hard. "If he was dead, then Chandi Culpepper would have displayed him like she did Ihita. No, he's alive, possibly with other women who have been taken as well."

"Bloody nonsense," Bruce snarled.

Now Eliza. Wellington whispered in the back of her head. *He's said quite enough.*

In the Archives she'd spent far too long hiding, far too long keeping her tongue in her head. This moment was going to feel very, very good.

"And the best bit of all, Campbell—the best bit is that if they are it's all your fault." She stepped forward and poked his finger at him. His lip curled back, but he stood his ground. "If you had done your job, then Ihita wouldn't have been murdered! If you hadn't thrown those files down in the Archives to rot instead of investigating as you were supposed to, we wouldn't have lost one of our own!"

"What is Braun talking about?" the Director asked mildly, as if he were questioning what time tea was.

Campbell went red to white in an instant.

"Not what, sir. Who." Eliza closed on her superior. (At least, her superior for the moment.) "Do you remember their names, Campbell? I do. Mildred. Glenda. Clara. Annette. Does that bring anything back to you?"

His eyes darted from side to side, but no one stepped in to assist him. No one dared to stop Eliza either.

So, she continued. "Tell me, Bruce, was Lena Munroe still at the forefront of your mind by the time you arrived home from York?"

"Campbell?" came Sound's voice.

"I don't care a jot where you believe a woman's proper place is in the world, until your inactions killed my friend, Ihita."

"Campbell," Doctor Sound said again, his voice somehow keeping Eliza at bay, "I suggest you explain yourself."

"Doctor Sound," Bruce finally responded, "this is not how it appears."

"Then refute the claim this instant, if you can with a clear conscience. Keep in mind: the Archives is only a flight of stairs underneath us." Sound cleared his throat and asked, "Did you really bury numerous missing person cases under your care?"

"Yes, Doctor Sound," Bruce began. "I did send the file to the Archives—but in my defence . . ."

"For abandoning your appointed duty," the Director growled, "there is no defence. An agent is dead and Lord knows how many other women as well. These are citizens of the Empire that could be alive now *if not for you*."

Bruce Campbell, a son of Australia and man of action, looked at his fellow agents assembled, and found himself utterly alone. For a flicker of an instant, Eliza felt sorry for her cousin of the Southern Hemisphere; but then she thought of Ihita, of the light in her eyes that would never be seen again because Bruce had his own personal bias.

There was something else in his confession before the Ministry, something Eliza couldn't pinpoint. Was that relief?

"You are correct, sir. Absolutely, without doubt. Therefore, in light of this, I hereby tender my resignation." He tried to look into the eyes of his agents, but his gaze returned to his feet. "I can only say that . . . I'm sorry."

"Apologise to Ihita," came a hard, tight reply from behind them.

No one needed to look towards the comment to know Agent Hill had dealt it.

His superior sighed, and his murmur was so soft that only Eliza really heard it: "I wish I hadn't seen this coming, but I had hoped . . ." When he straightened, his voice was louder. "I accept your resignation, Assistant Director Campbell." He gestured to her. "Braun, we will indeed follow your lead to rescue Agent Books."

This day suddenly seemed like it might be redeemed. "Thank you, sir." She slammed the address for the Culpepper country estate down on the nearest desk. "Unfortunately, Books wasn't wearing his Ministry tracking ring when he was taken, but I have from reliable sources that this is where we will find him."

Picking up the piece of paper, the Director nodded. "Essex it is then," he replied, before turning to the rest of the agents. "We will need every one of you on this—including," his lips lifted into a brief smile, "You Cassandra."

Miss Shillingworth's grin in return was terribly frightening. "Thank you, Director, I would be glad to assist."

"Then send a message to the Grey Ghost. Tell her we have need of her and the *Blithe Spirit* immediately. We will be underway within the hour."

"I'm happy to help also." Bruce tilted his chin up. "As you say, you could need everyone."

The Director sized him up for a moment, and then replied with all the chill of an Antarctic winter, "You've done more than enough in this organisation, Mr. Campbell. And what's more I think you've done more than enough for Lord Sussex."

Eliza blinked, as they all did. Doctor Sound was suggesting more than laziness and incompetence. He was suggesting treachery.

Doctor Sound stood aside as the rest of the agents filed back up the stairs and towards the armoury. All, that is, except Axelrod. The tall clankerton's eyes fixed on the *plures ornamentum*, and his gaze shot to Eliza's.

The circumstances of her having the power arm were not exactly within Ministry protocol, and Eliza blushed a little. Undoubtedly the inventor had got into some trouble over the loss of the experimental weapon. Yet his behaviour over their single dinner outing had deserved punishment.

When she raised one eyebrow in return, it was he who reddened. He definitely remembered the incident as well as she did. Quickly he turned away and followed the rest of the agents, without saying a word. The large iron door hissed upwards once again, and the rattle of the main guns could be heard as they returned to their hidden positions.

Eliza glanced out the door, doing the mental calculations of distance and what could be happening to Wellington right now. An hour could mean the difference between life and death for the Archivist.

Campbell was hanging around by the door. His expression was one of a kicked dog that still didn't want to leave home. Perhaps he was regretting his actions, perhaps he was merely regretting that he'd been caught—but either way, Eliza couldn't afford to care.

"Tell Sound I will meet him there," she snapped at her now former colleague. "I've got to get to Wellington now."

The man's eyes met hers and there was a kind of longing that she'd never seen in them before. Gone was the bluster of past years. It was uncertain if it would ever come back.

"All right, Eliza," he said, tucking his hands into his pockets. "I'll wait around and tell him. Be careful how you go there."

If women hadn't died, if he hadn't been so disloyal, she would have spared him a kind word. As it was, she had none to offer and no time to find any shred of sympathy. At the moment she had an Archivist and an old friend to rescue. After that she would have some rather stern words with a fellow suffragist.

Perhaps fatally stern.

CHAPTER TWENTY-SEVEN

Wherein Our Dashing Archivist
Finds Himself Walking with Madness

"**R**ight then, that should do it."

Wellington looked over the thin rope the three of them had woven together. Lena's lullabies had ceased a long while ago. They were all exhausted, and he'd had to return to the grizzly collection of corpses at least two more times for more fabric. For Lena's sanity and Sophia's loyalty, this had to work, and had to work the first time.

"The final illuminati, if you please, Sophia," he said, his voice a ragged rasp.

Her sigh echoed in their pit, followed by a rap hard against stone. The green light blossomed around them as Sophia shook the stick back and forth. Finally, she handed it to Wellington.

The Archivist peered up into the darkness above him, taking a few steps back as he again tried to catch in the shadows any hint of the lip of the pit.

"And you are sure about the sturdiness of this illuminati?" he asked, still peering upwards.

"Yes, most certain," Sophia answered.

"Well, let us hope Fortune favours us."

With a quick, silent prayer Wellington threw the stick upwards, and watched the illuminati fly. His throat tightened as it cleared its apex and descended.

Then it disappeared from view, and a few terrifying seconds later it clattered against a stone floor. Now the glow of the illuminati could just be discerned against the distant edge.

"A bit closer than I'd expected," Wellington said, slowly walking his way forward, hands reaching into the darkness.

What they reached first wasn't brick, firm as what he touched might have been.

"Why, *Signore* Books," cooed the Italian, "I do like what successful ventures bring out in you."

The Archivist snatched back his hands. Wellington was thankful they were back in darkness.

"Not quite yet," he said, his voice trembling a bit. Clearing his throat, Wellington bent down, now feeling his way across the oubliette floor. His hand finally came to rest on the steel strips he'd salvaged from the corset. He gave the four-pronged hook another check, and then began to coil the rope. "Once we are out, I will revel in my success but not before."

"I look forward to it," she whispered in reply.

Wellington took a few steps away from the wall and studied the now-visible curve above him. *Yes,* he insisted silently, *this will work.*

I would hope so, the old man spoke in his ear. *Otherwise, the deaths of these women fall upon you.*

Wellington felt a chill on hearing his father's whisper. *No.*

Oh yes, Wellington. His father's ghost was gloating. *And imagine, if you will, what havoc those hell-spawn will wreak, due to your failure.*

Quiet, Wellington spat silently.

How proud your mother would be.

Wellington felt the chill replaced by heat until Lena asked, "Mr. Books?" There was a pause, and then a more desperate, "Mr. Books, what's wrong?"

The Archivist looked back up to the curve, gave the hook a bit more slack, and said, "Nothing. Just judging distance."

"Please," she said, "judge faster."

"*Signore.*" Wellington felt a hand on his arm, and the assassin's breath warm on his neck. "Do you have much experience with grappling hooks?"

Wellington cleared his throat.

"So I thought." When her fingers touched his, Wellington recalled how taken he once had been with her. "Perhaps this calls for a lady's hand?"

"Need I remind you that when I last trusted you," Wellington said, his grip tightening on the rope, "I found myself in the hands of the enemy, bound for the frozen wastelands of Antarctica."

"Hush now, that was purely business. Right now, there are no clients, no ulterior motives. There is only me, a frightened girl, and a devilishly handsome archivist nurturing a grudge." She sighed and stroked his hand. "Trust me, Wellington, as I have trusted you."

This opportunity was their only one, and Sophia had far more experience at this sort of thing. It was a logical conclusion, and that made Wellington hate it all the more.

His fingers slipped free of the hook and rope as her own fingers tightened around them.

"Stand clear," she said as Wellington moved forward towards the wall.

The whipping sound filled his ears; and then with one final cut of the air, the silence returned. Wellington held his breath. A silly thing, but he didn't wish to chance anything disturbing the silence. This moment now rested on an assassin and a blind throw into the darkness.

The rope slapped against the wall of the pit. Moments crept by, and then came another sound. Fabric whispering against fabric, and then something moved against his pants leg. Their rope was now gathering by his leg. *Please, Lord . . .*

A valiant effort, my son, but I'm afraid—

Sophia let out a gasp, which turned into a laugh. A glorious, beautiful laugh. "The rope has caught!" she exclaimed, her voice echoing around them.

Wellington felt a smile on his face. *You where saying, Father?*

No reply from his ghost.

"I won't be but a moment, *Signore*," Sophia said, her voice trembling with something Wellington would have described as ecstasy.

He reached towards her, and then gave a soft sigh of relief. He had grabbed hold of an arm.

"Just a moment; but for Lena's sake and myself, exactly what are you planning?"

She placed a hand on his chest. Her touch caused him to flinch. "I have been working this plan through since we began to weave. I climb out, find you both a proper rope, and then we find our way free of this place. I am the most qualified to climb, the most apt at this sort of espionage, the best chance against any opposition."

Wellington rested his other hand over hers. "Indeed, but there is one tragic flaw in your strategy."

"And that is?"

His grip tightened on her hand. "The part where you are climbing out of the pit?"

She gasped. "Wellington, you think me so heartless as to abandon my compatriots?"

An advantage of the darkness was that she couldn't see his face, so there was no tell to let slip when he pulled her closer to him, and farther away from the rope. "I believe your opportunistic spirit is far more passionate than you believe we think it is."

He felt her muscles twitch, so the break she attempted on his hold was to no avail. The same went for her attempt to twist against his arm and turn his bind against him.

"How are you doing that?" she grunted, her third attempt quickly countered as Wellington spun her and pushed forward, not stopping until she slammed against the oubliette's wall. "For a librarian," she gasped, "you are quite apt in the martial arts."

"Archivist, if you please; and yes, I read. A lot." He leaned inward to whisper in her ear, "Do not play me for a fool. My trust is already at its limits."

"Oh, Wellington," Sophia purred, causing his skin to tingle, "I think we should get to know one another better. Such as the same experience I have in throwing our quaint creation. Tell me—how many structures have you scaled in recent years?"

"As I told you, I read a lot." He grabbed her shoulders, and shoved her back against the wall, pinning her there. Wellington could feel her cheek on the tip of his nose, and her smell was quite the welcome respite from the scent he had grown accustomed to. He quickly pulled back and guessed exactly where her face would be. "A brilliant plan you have there, Sophia, but it will be yours truly that will be climbing out."

He suddenly felt something strike his chest hard, then his feet kicked out from under him immediately followed by the feel of a flat-soled boot against his chest.

"Forgive my forwardness, *Signore* Books, but I think you are blinded by your English chivalry . . . or panic. Sometimes the two are most hard to distinguish." He was expecting to be left there, but was surprised at feeling himself lifted back to his feet by her. "I was planning to relieve myself of weapons for they make me close to the same weight as yourself. The lighter our climber, the less strain on our rope."

Wellington was truly loathing this woman's logic. "Perhaps, but if you think even in the darkness of this cell I will trust you—"

"You have no options!"

"There are always options," Wellington snapped.

And so there were, as the scuff of feet against stone proved to be true.

"*Mio Dio!*" Sophia swore as she felt for the rope while Wellington called, "*Lena!*"

A sole snarl was her reply. In that fleeting moment Lena Munroe made clear her desperation for freedom. Her grunts were growing harder, sharper, like borderline sobs; and if she were to fall midway through her climb, she could endanger all their lives. A body, even as frail as Lena's current condition, could snap a neck or incapacitate one of them.

Then Wellington heard a sound that brought him equal parts of hope and despair. Lena's open palm struck stone. The groan she gave cried now of determination. Her voice rang through the dankness above their heads, and then came a thick silence.

"Lena?" Wellington cried out. "Lena, please answer us!"

"Lovely." Sophia seethed. "Now our fate rests in the hands of a madwoman."

"As if placing our faith in you would be any more comforting?"

Sophia gave a dry laugh. "So, how comfortable are you now?"

Wellington looked up. The illuminati's glow was beginning to fade. "Not very. If she is caught . . ."

"Exactly."

Wellington gave the rope another tug. How far could he scale before one of the Culpeppers or even house servants were to discover them? He slid his back against the wall and ran his fingers through his hair. "Well, at least we did accomplish something."

"And what was that?"

Wellington let his breath out slowly. "The rope. It held."

He then felt Sophia take his arm and nuzzle closer to him. She was laughing softly, even sincerely.

"That it did, Archivist. That it did. Perhaps on our next attempt—"

"If we find such an opportunity," he interjected, "I will follow your lead on the escaping bit." Wellington gave her hand a gentle squeeze and added, "I may not like your logic, but it is most sound."

"I do love it so when men tell me that."

"I am sure you do." He unfolded his knees, seeing nothing around him. Wellington had not pictured his demise quite so bleak as this. Best to make the most of it. "I am sorry that our night ended as it did. It would have been a delight to have gotten to know you better."

She slipped free of his arm and then he felt something—no, he felt trained assassin and wanted mercenary Sophia del Morte—straddle him in the darkness.

Her hands took his hands and placed them gently on her breasts. "We have time now, don't we, Wellington?"

Was she serious?!

A sudden light blinded them both; and then their odd, awkward silence was disrupted by the flickering of flame. Only a few feet from Wellington and Sophia burned a torch.

"Mr. Books?" Lena called down to him. "Please move back. I don't wish to hit you with this ladder."

Wellington gave a little laugh of his own, but it stopped abruptly as he saw his hands had not moved from where Sophia had placed them.

She gave a sly wink. "Later," she mouthed before removing herself from his lap.

Wellington scrambled up to his feet and joined Sophia by the flame.

"Have a care, Miss Munroe!" he called up to her. "We cannot risk you being discovered."

As the ladder clattered down the stones, Lena replied, "Oddly enough I think we're the only people in here."

"And what gave you that idea?" Sophia grunted as she started her climb up.

"I checked the top of the staircase. No guards."

Wellington steadied the ladder as Sophia climbed. "There's no one else up there? Not even house staff?"

"Not a soul!"

Once he saw Sophia disappear, Wellington hoisted himself up the ladder. He was pleasantly surprised to reach the top of the pit without fail. Perhaps Sophia del Morte was not the same ne'er-do-well she had portrayed herself as in previous encounters. Wellington now stood in the dying glow of their last illuminati, now being held aloft like a torch in the grasp of the frayed Lena Munroe.

Sophia was saying nothing, merely considering the suffragist. Wellington looked back and forth between them, not entirely certain what he had missed or what he was currently missing.

"I assumed you two would have continued to prattle on like fishwives," Lena hissed, "but I wanted out! As I had served my time with the Womens' Explorers Auxiliary, I know a thing or two about climbing." Wellington and Sophia merely stood there, silent. "Oh, I may have been bordering on madness down there, but there is a fine line between insanity and stupidity. Considering your resourcefulness and this woman's"—Sophia lifted an eyebrow as Lena paused and then continued with—"unique skills, I was not going to assume you would simply stay down there if I didn't return. You would, no doubt, come up with a new plan of escape. What else would you do down there?"

Sophia turned her glare, softening quickly, towards Wellington. He felt a hotness grow in his cheeks.

"The way out?" Sophia asked.

"Follow me," Lena said, motioning behind her.

It was only a few steps and a single stone staircase later that returned the three of them back into a world of light and colour, simple and stark as that colour was. Where Wellington found himself was a palatial estate somewhere in the country as a quick glance from the windows told him. It was a crisp, brilliant day outside, but still the wind pushed through the treetops, making them sway with the grass outside.

And that was when Wellington noticed the décor of the house: there was none.

No side tables. No divans. Not even portraits or paintings of any kind. The house was empty. So much in fact that their footfalls echoed around them as their voices had in the oubliette.

"See what I mean, Mr. Books?" Lena asked him in a whisper, as they paused in a corridor.

They continued their run into another hallway, but this time, Wellington stopped.

"Ladies!"

Both Sophia and Lena skidded to a halt. They knew they were alone, but hearing his call so sharp and loud gave them both a fright.

"Wellington," Sophia asked, her tone far from the one she had given him in the oubliette. "Where are you going?"

"The conservatory."

Her head inclined to one side, allowing curls of raven black to spill across her face. "Is there a reason of utmost importance that you must pay that a visit?"

"Yes," Wellington said, motioning for them to follow. "It's the only room in the house that has furniture in it."

Sunlight reflected off the exotic plants and flowers; and unlike the other stark, barren rooms of the mansion, this parlour was immaculate, warm, and inviting.

The Culpeppers had taken great care with this room indeed, but it was not what any civilised Englishman would have called normal. The three escapees stood slack-jawed at the intricate patterns painted in garish colours through the conservatory. Many-limbed figures climbed their way up the walls and columns. They were black, brown, yellow and white, and all appeared to be wearing halos.

"How very curious." Their predicament suddenly faded to insignificance as Wellington continued into the centre of this manic art display. His fingers itched for a pen and paper as his neck craned back to take the detail in and attempt to make sense of it all. "Seems rather to resemble the Vimanam in the Dravidian style found in the south of India, but also . . ." He squinted at some of the figures and scenes depicted on the ceiling. No, his eyes were not playing tricks. " . . . but also the medieval decorations of Sulsted Church in Jutland."

When he finally reached the top of the rotunda, he felt a

strange, queer feeling overcome him. A part of him wanted to cry in outrage at the blasphemy he saw, but the analytical part of him was trying to decipher the bizarre imagery and the minds behind it: a pair of intertwined figures—one was a pitch-black, many-limbed woman, the other a bearded young man.

"That's Christ and Kali," Sophia pointed out before he could, indicating that she had some knowledge of the East, and then surprised him further when she stepped over to the space beneath the figures. "It even looks like they have constructed a kind of twisted Vedic altar here."

Wellington saw that indeed a hallowed-out shell carved with crosses and dancing figures contained ash and the remains of a fire. He shuddered to think what the Culpeppers had been sacrificing in it.

"Look at this." Lena had pushed aside some of the foliage, revealing two final figures. These though were of a far more realistic nature: a man, dressed in a classic gentlemen's khaki attire, with a broad, angry face, and a beautiful Indian woman dressed in the London fashions of perhaps twenty years ago.

"The parents," Wellington said, leaning forward to examine the photograph.

"I know Chandi spent many years in isolation. Her father went mad after the death of her mother."

Wellington straightened. Sophia del Morte certainly did know a lot about the Culpeppers. Observing his look, the assassin's expression tightened. "At least that was what I heard."

"An upbringing of two cultures, two religions—and knowing how Christianity is frowned upon in Indian cultures—might explain some of this. Add to this that they were born twins, the torment and isolation they must have felt . . ." The Archivist's voice faded away. "They seem to have created an elaborate religious theme of their own."

Sophia spat. "Religious zealots—my least favourite kind of person."

"Totally mad," Lena whispered, moving away from the drawings as if they frightened her. Instead she looked out the windows, and Wellington finally took note of the breath-taking panorama beyond. The whole house was built on the edge of a massive ravine, and as the sunlight hit the window all was revealed. The three of them approached the window, then looked down.

"Dear Lord!" Wellington gasped.

At the bottom of the ravine was an airship. The rock walls had kept its massive size hidden. Wellington squinted to see if there was any activity underneath the hulk of a hull. Though the gondola was completely hidden from view, he could make out small shadows going about in forced, stiff movements from airship to a nearby structure.

He felt a soft tap on his shoulder. "That platform out there," Sophia noted, motioning out to the ridge closest to the house, "would seem to be the access point."

"Indeed, but a concealed airship?" Wellington looked around the conservatory. The only furnished room in the house. "There has to be a method to this madness."

Just then, his eye fell on a small patch of glass in the window. Red. Not a discolouration or some odd trick of light. It was purposefully red. Wellington stepped back and noticed more shards of red glass, along with green and blue. These markers within the glass wall would have appeared nothing more than random dots; but the longer Wellington stared, the more the pattern took hold.

"So where is the key?" And then his eyes went up to the top of the conservatory window. "Oh, very clever, ladies."

With some excitement, Wellington grabbed a nearby hook and yanked the grand blind down. The translucent fabric now added the outline of the world map, as well as an expanded section of London streets that filled where the expanse of the English Channel would have been.

"This is a map of navigation, do you see?" Sophia motioned to the grid along the top and side, and within the larger grid there appeared to be a secondary one.

Wellington looked closer, adjusting his spectacles. "Quite right. This is a map providing accurate longitude and latitude. And these marks . . ."

His eyes happened to fall on the expanded map of London. He tilted his head to one side, narrowing his eyes on one marker a little outside of the city proper.

It was his home. The mark was red.

"Sophia," Wellington said as he stared at the marker on his address. "Where exactly were you snatched?"

"From the Culpepper townhouse. Thirty-four Craven Street, in Charing Cross to be precise."

Charing Cross, Wellington saw, possessed a red mark similar to his own.

He pointed to another between London and Edinburgh, and glanced back at Lena. "That one is you."

Lena covered her mouth in horror. There were well over twenty markers decorating England, Africa, and India.

Then there were the green marks. "Canterbury, Rome, Jerusalem, Mecca, Varanasi," he whispered as his gaze flicked once more to the figures hanging above them. They were scattered across the Empire. Another ten in England, five in Scotland, and twelve in Ireland. Ten in Canada. Seven in New Zealand. Four in Australia. Twenty in India . . .

"A religious war," Sophia hissed, "was not part of our arrangement."

"It will be the ultimate crusade," Wellington said, turning to the Italian, "and with their device the Culpeppers will be able to start it. Imagine them snatching whoever they want from the holiest places in the world—and where they could drop them . . . this cannot be allowed to happen."

Sophia gave a nod and led Wellington to the window she had been standing at.

"Then now is the only chance to stop them," she said, motioning to the airship outside the window.

"Mr. Books," implored Lena, "perhaps I should stay here and gather my wits about me. I would love to assist, but I have had nothing to eat, and I—"

"I understand completely," Wellington said, taking her hand and leading her out, "but we cannot leave you here."

"Why," she protested, much like a petulant, tired child might when being told it was time for bed, "this place is abandoned . . ."

"All for the conservatory. Why leave their plans behind unless—"

"Unless they intend to destroy this place," Sophia added, now looking to every corner of the building. "Explosives?"

"Possibly, or a barrage from the airship's armament shortly after liftoff."

Wellington opened the front door of the mansion and was delighted to see two horses tethered by the house. It stood to reason. If the Culpeppers were going to leave the three of them to rot, what were two horses on their conscience? He untethered one and set it loose. The other one he handed to Lena.

"Ride fast. Ride hard," Wellington told her as he lifted her onto the steed's back. "Do not stop until you reach the London suffragists, and have them contact Miss Braun immediately!"

With a nod, Lena heeled the horse and began her ride away from the mansion. Wellington turned back to Sophia and motioned back to the mansion. "Shall we pay a call on our hosts?"

Her grin was broad and terrifying. "Most assuredly. I think that is long overdue."

CHAPTER TWENTY-EIGHT

In Which Curious Allies Are Made and Enemies Must Make Do

The lococycle roared through the snow-sprinkled lanes and between the mounds of the hedgerows. Essex resembled a Christmas card this time of year, which would have been charming if Eliza had been able to enjoy it. She'd been forced to stop once already and fill the boiler with water from a stream, but she would still be ahead of the Ministry airship. Every moment could count towards Wellington's life.

She reached the Culpepper lands long after her cheeks grew slightly numb from the speed at which she cut through the winter chill. She looked around her at the property that appeared surprisingly well-tended, considering the farms and the smaller homes that had whipped by her were all woebegone buildings with little to remark on. Though coming from an impressive and aristocratic upbringing, the Culpeppers were not located in the most affluent part of the English countryside.

From a distance, the house at the end of the long drive appeared dark and quiet. The Culpepper country home showed a Georgian style with grand white pillars at its entrance and lines of windows overlooking a barren garden. Again, the grounds around the house were kept, but only at the minimum. There was no feeling of the tenant's style. Simple, straight lines. A general lack of any finesse. It was almost as if the house were tended to by automatons.

Eliza shielded her eyes from the sunlight and peered harder at the lone house. It appeared as if the front door was wide open, adding to that feel of abandon. No butler—not even the faultiest of McTighe's creations—would leave such a detail unattended.

"This can't be the right place," Eliza muttered to herself.

On those words leaving her lips, a lone rider crested the rise in the long causeway between the main road and the Culpepper manor. The animal thundering down the path was a skinny nag, its head held high, eyes wide; and on its back was an equally frail-looking Lena Munroe, clinging to the horse like a burr. Their eyes locked in surprise and amazement, and by a process of hauling on the beast's bridle, the suffragist was able to slow her escape.

"He's back there," she shouted, her voice cracking as she pointed behind her. "Wellington Books and an Italian woman—they're back there!" Then the horse tossed its head and galloped on, carrying Lena out of sight. The agent looked back where she had gestured and saw the broad shape of an airship rising above the hill.

"I stand corrected," Eliza muttered, revving the lococycle's engine. "This looks exactly like the place."

Her teeth ground together as the lococycle rumbled down the dip in the causeway adding to her speed. Somewhere in that house was her partner and an Italian? Another suffragist they hadn't encountered yet? She would know soon enough. She glanced up at the house, and that was when she could make out the growing curve of an airship hull taking to the sky. Her well-honed instincts told her that this was where she would find Kate. Once the causeway opened around her, she turned the handlebars and made for the ascending craft.

The sun was glinting off the airship, making it sparkle

prettily. Some kind of quarry must lie on the other side of the rise—quite a clever place to hide the bulk of an airship if you didn't want the neighbours to talk. Eliza had a few moments to think about such things as she strained the engine to its greatest limits, racing across the lawn.

Airship engines roaring hard now provided a steady thrum under the clatter of the machine between her thighs. Eliza bent low over the control bars, her heart racing and her palms becoming sweaty. Sizing up the blimp, she knew of only one way to get on board that leviathan at this crucial moment. The realisation both terrified and exhilarated her, and served as a sudden reminder why she needed this. Much like Kate, this was Eliza's calling and she would not be denied.

Pulling her feet under her, she shoved the lever down hard as the airship cleared the edge of the quarry, and drove the lococycle into the intervening space. The experience was a moment frozen in time. Eliza felt the wind battering her face, caught glimpses of the hundred-foot drop beneath her, and her breath jammed in her chest. She windmilled her arms, and one of her hands caught a trailing mooring line.

Her arm was nearly pulled from her shoulder. "Bloody hell," she groaned, as her full weight swung from the abused limb. Unfortunately, it was not the one with the *plures ornamentum*—but then that was usually her luck with these sorts of things. For a moment she was in a most precarious position, her whole body hanging off a single rope dangling in open space. She spared a glance down to give herself an incentive to do something. The monumental drop, the sharp rocks below, and the lococycle's boilers exploding on meeting its rather grand end in the quarry did the trick. She threw her free arm upwards and began the slow climb.

Suddenly, the mooring rope began to pull her in. The line was retracting into some internal housing within the vessel. When the winches finally came to a stop, she found herself inside the hull, somewhere near the back of the airship. She pulled herself upright and dusted herself off.

"Do you have to destroy everything you touch?" The accent was Italian, and the voice burned into Eliza's brain. Pushing aside her dark tangled hair, she looked up into the icy glare of Sophia del Morte. The assassin looked a little dishevelled—which was satisfying—but she also appeared as deadly and beautiful as the last time they had met.

It was such a surprise to find her here that Eliza was distracted from greeting the other standing just behind her. Wellington Books was looking less than dapper. His coif was rumpled, his glasses chipped, and his face smeared with dirt. He appeared hale and hearty, and for that Eliza could only be deeply grateful. Still, she knew her priorities— keeping an eye on Sophia.

"That was my lococycle," the assassin went on coolly, her hand slipping down her thigh, to probably what was a concealed weapon

Eliza flexed her fist in the *plures*. "I'm sorry, I didn't know." Her lips twisted. "If I had, I might have set fire to it on the way down."

She had not forgotten or forgiven the Italian for her slaying of Harrison Thorne. The man might have been mad and confined to Bedlam, but he had still been her partner in the Ministry. Sophia del Morte was a cowardly killer who had escaped justice for too long.

Both women drew their pistols in a heartbeat and pointed them at each other with unwavering aims.

Wellington cleared his throat, and gestured down the deck in the direction of the ship's bow. "Ladies, may I be so bold as to ask of you to come to some sort of truce considering our current circumstances?"

Sophia locked her gaze with Eliza's. "Those traitorous Culpeppers have a machine that both your employer and mine want destroyed."

"Update, Wellington?" Eliza growled to her partner, not believing a word that came out of the Italian trollop's mouth.

"Long version, or short?" he asked.

She looked at Sophia, and then back to Wellington. "Short."

"Mad twins. Teleportation device. Plans of a Holy Crusade." He paused, nodded, and then added, "And they have Mrs. Sheppard."

Eliza took a deep breath, filing all that information away. "Ducky."

"As for any resistance, you need not worry," Sophia began. "When Wellington and I snuck aboard, we noted the only crew apart from the twins themselves are automatons. The same ones she had tending to her manor and townhouse."

She then turned to face Sophia. The urge to smash that look right off the assassin's face was powerful, but this was not the first time Eliza had been forced to make uncomfortable bedfellows. "I think I can put aside history for that long with the understanding once we are off this airship we can settle our scores."

Sophia tilted her head, and smiled prettily. "I agree."

"Now that we have that settled for the time being," Wellington said, "perhaps we should move onto the bridge and find the device, and Mrs. Sheppard."

Mention of Kate made Eliza's rage at Sophia gain focus; she had more important things.

"Come on then," she said, flexing her arm in the *plures*, "Let's get this over with!"

CHAPTER TWENTY-NINE

In Which Confrontations Occur, Hearts Are Broken, and Eliza Takes Flight

This was hardly déjà vu for Wellington Thornhill Books. On the contrary, this was quickly becoming all in a day's work. Once again, he found himself on the heels of Eliza D. Braun, running deeper into the belly of chaos and calamity. This time, that belly was inside a leviathan soaring above the clouds. They reached what was apparently an observation deck and were stopped mid-stride by a brilliant flash. They watched as guns from underneath their gondola fired again on the now-abandoned Culpepper estate. The mansion struggled to stand, but a third and final volley brought the once-grand country home to its foundation.

"They are covering their tracks," Wellington said to them. "So no one will ever discover the truth."

"We will make sure people will know about this," Eliza growled, flexing her fingers in her massive sidearm. "Come on. We must be close."

They reached a heavy iron hatch that would have done any underground lair proud. Sophia grunted as she tugged vainly at it.

"Stand back," Eliza snapped and wrapped her metal-encased fingers around the wheel mechanism.

The gears and pistons along the *plures ornamentum* began to spin. Faster. Faster. Eliza planted her feet wider as her mouth twitched slightly and a low groan shuddered underneath Wellington's feet. Then came a hard, sharp crack that knocked both Wellington and Sophia back. The door flew open and slammed against the wall.

He didn't bother to call out to Eliza to wait for him. It was pointless. Wellington heard Eliza scream "Kate!" as he raced up the staircase, and his heart made a leap for his throat. He emerged onto the bridge of the airship, eyes wide and palms slightly sweaty.

At the captain's wheel stood an automaton, keeping the airship on a steady, straight course. Wellington recognised it as a model used for housework. Before them stretched a brilliant blue sky with only the odd cloud marring the expanse. It was a beauty that Wellington didn't have long to admire.

A pair of arms wrapped around him and knocked him sideways behind the stout oak and brass of the navigator's station. As he crashed into the floor, he heard the distinct crack of a gunshot.

Wellington peered around the corner of his cover. Two more household automatons had appeared, however these mechanised servants were brandishing pistols. The third, piloting the ship, now turned and joined its compatriots as their ocular devices scanned the bridge.

"The Culpeppers are not receiving guests at present," spoke the middle servant in Chandi's calm voice. Hearing it delivered thus made Wellington cold all over.

"Welly?" called Eliza from her hiding spot. "Are you all right?"

"A little winded at the current time," he moaned in reply, "but otherwise unharmed."

Sophia wiggled her hips against him and giggled lightly. "I can certainly vouch for that, *Signore*."

Wellington looked over his shoulder at the Italian, her smile dark and wicked. This woman was something rather incredible—more frightening than Eliza D. Braun. Still she had saved his life.

With a nod of gratitude, Wellington peeled himself free of the Italian's embrace and crawled to the corner of the podium. He attempted to peer past the wood in order to get a more accurate count of automatons, but another gunshot caused him to withdraw his head quickly.

"Miss Culpepper," Wellington called, "is there any possibility we can convince you to surrender?"

"That is most kind of you, Mr. Books, but I am afraid that is out of the question seeing as my house staff has the arsenal, and I have Mrs. Sheppard and the electroporter."

Good, Wellington thought. *It has a name. Now I need to know how to dismantle it.*

"Eliza," called Mrs. Sheppard, her voice level but stained with anger, "stay where you are! This bitch is as mad as a hatter! She's pushed back the movement twenty years at least!"

He screwed his eyes shut, pushing his spectacles up as he pinched his nose. *Don't antagonise the Mad Hatter. She has a small arsenal on command.*

"Kate, I'm not going to leave you," his colleague yelled back.

"You have to get out of here," the suffragist implored. "Tell the movement what has happened; stiffen their spines!"

"And therein lies a puzzle," Wellington called out. "It is most difficult to negotiate while the reasons of Miss Culpepper remain unspoken."

"Mr. Books, your being a learned man, a cultured man, I would assume this would not be hard for you to grasp." He heard their opponent move across the chamber. She was adjusting something. Dials, perhaps? That couldn't be good.

Then a low hum joined the rumble of the airship, and it grew louder with each passing second. No doubting it: Chandi was bringing the electroporter to life.

"The Queen does not believe in this movement!" Miss Culpepper's reply was high-pitched and rapid. Extremely disconcerting. "My country does not believe in this movement, and yet this cheek—this effrontery—is tolerated! Had it stayed in the isolated southern corners of the world, there would be no need for this sort of discipline, but this is a sickness that must be purged!"

Sophia looked at Wellington and shook her head. "A sickness?"

"Now it is here on the shores of England, and this woman is its eternal flame!" Wellington could hear something large being rolled into place as Chandi continued, "Well, I intend to put out this flame once and for all."

"Kate—" Eliza called again.

"Don't you dare!" Mrs. Sheppard barked. Wellington, had he not already been impressed with the suffragist, now understood how she could rally so many to her cause. "Go on, Chandi. Make me disappear. Do what you will, and the movement will make me a martyr. A banner that will always fly high and proud."

"Will I?" Chandi's laugh was cracked and terrifying. Then came the sound of a lever being pushed forward, immediately followed by a soft crackling of power. The machine was rapidly reaching its critical point. "I think Mrs. Sheppard's body impaled atop the clock tower might send an entirely different message. So will the deaths that follow."

"Most ambitious of you," Wellington shot his comment over the top of their cover. "We saw the map."

Sophia gave a flick of her wrist and a small, silver blade dropped into her waiting palm.

"No!" whispered Wellington, grabbing her arm. "We have no idea where the twin is. She could be in hiding. She could be elsewhere on the ship."

Chandi's diatribe rattled on. "You see how the sickness has spread, even in my own home country where women begin to gather. They watch. They plan. And they will rise. One day, they all will. This is not the mother's will. This is not the son's will. It was Eve who cast humanity out of Paradise. We must have order! We must—"

The airship rocked suddenly to one side, and in the corner of Wellington's eye he caught sight of another approaching craft. He recognised the banner of the *Blythe Spirit*. The cavalry had arrived.

Just a heartbeat after that realisation, there came a distant thud, followed by a heavy jolt that caused the airship to bounce. Wellington watched the captain's wheel compensate and the massive craft continued on.

He placed a palm against the bridge floor and shot a look at Sophia. "Chandi's twin is in Engineering."

The assassin arched an eyebrow. "How could you possibly know that?"

"We're picking up speed." The Archivist rolled to one side, switching places with Sophia in their cramped, shared space. "Even without a porthole down there, she must know we are under attack and be starting evasive manoeuvres." He pointed to the wheel as it spun towards the right. "I need to get to the controls."

"Wellington," Sophia whispered tersely, "should we not try to communicate with your comrades?"

"No time," Wellington said. "Finding such a device would take too long."

"But why are they trying to—"

"Kill us?" He gave a sharp laugh. "If you were piloting an airship with rescue in mind, and saw the stronghold where you knew your people were being held suddenly go up in flames, what would you think?"

"I could take her with one of these," Sophia said holding up the blade.

"Provided her rather hostile house staff didn't shoot you first. I have an idea of how to disable them, but I need cover."

Their eyes held one another for a long moment. It was a gamble. Once more his fate was in the hands of a skilled, ruthless assassin. Still, what were his options? As it was in the pit, they had only one chance; and Wellington knew that Eliza would not miss her own cue to rescue Kate Shep—

The feel of Sophia's strong, hungry kiss completely shattered any and all thoughts Wellington was piecing together. He only tasted her mouth, her tongue. She continued the sentiment in a most European fashion, delicious, soft moans escaping her.

With a final gasp, she stepped back and then glanced over to the controls. "You will have your moment. Do not look over your shoulder. That would be the hesitation her automatons will take full advantage of."

Who will? Wellington's mind was a complete blank. *My God, I think I'm sweating.*

"Do not worry." She held the throwing blade between them. "I won't miss."

"I know you won't," he replied dryly. He then rolled onto his stomach and fixed his eyes on Chandi at the electroporter controls. He could smell the building electricity in the air. He only had moments remaining.

Wellington tucked his leg underneath him, and whispered, "Now!"

He launched himself out from the hiding place and felt his shoulder connect with Chandi, knocking her free of the controls. His eyes immediately looked at the gauges, all indicating the device was at full power. Finding a control knob that appeared to control power output, Wellington turned the knob to its highest setting.

Behind him, Wellington heard the sound of mechanised feet advancing, followed immediately by the sound of a whip, the sharp *clang* of something striking metal, and the grinding of metal against metal. He swore he could have heard Chandi mutter "That is most inappropriate behaviour for this household, miss. I must ask you to leave." He then had to brace himself against the control panel as the ship listed sharply. Then it lurched upwards as it began to gain altitude. The Archivist heard two women exchange quick words followed by the sound of running. A scream of pain. He could not afford to pay them any mind. As Sophia said, he couldn't hesitate. He had to make sure this worked. The electroporter suddenly flashed, blinding him and no doubt those around them.

When he heard the automaton fall he dared to steal a glance. There was one mechanised servant still standing and its pistol was aimed directly at Wellington's temple. His timing was impeccable; the pulse had reached it first. Maxwell's paper, it seemed, has some really interesting applications.

A small explosion and the smell of electricity filled his nostrils, but instead of being blinded by another brilliant flash, he flew over to the captain's wheel and hit something hard. He fell against the floor, next to an unconscious Sophia del Morte.

A crackle of energy took his eyes away from the assassin. Slowly stepping forward towards him, wielding what appeared at first glance to be a swagger stick as found in the care of a sea or airship captain, was Chandi Culpepper. He still found her quite striking, even as her staff's tip sparked with dangerous, fatal energy. She made the Italian appear as demure as a country girl.

"Poor thing," she said, wielding her simple weapon awkwardly. Wellington could only glance at her other arm. She was bleeding. Sophia had obviously kept her promise to him. "I think that will leave a bit of a bruise."

"Miss Culpepper," Wellington grunted, feeling the airship shudder as another salvo struck the gondola. He scrambled back as the lethal tip slowly came down before him, sending sparks in all directions, some disappearing in the air while others bounced against the floor and faded away. "Miss Culpepper, please . . ."

"Mr. Books," she chided softly, shaking her head, "don't beg. It's hardly befitting from a gentleman." Chandi pulled back her weapon as if it were a spear. "Don't worry. I'll be certain to make the pain last."

Chandi didn't get the chance. Arising from beside her, Eliza backhanded Chandi with the *plures ornamentum*. Her body was abruptly lifted off the bridge floor when the gauntlet struck her hard in the chest. Her swagger stick clattered to the ground as she was tossed into the double archway of the electroporter. Wellington watched silently as Eliza glanced over the controls and reset the power dial. With a flip of a switch, lights flicked on and small generators within the metallic lace and webwork hummed to life.

"We trusted you." Kate now stood over Chandi, the one human eye visible to Wellington hard and cold. He could only imagine how the other with its eerie emerald radiance would look like from the Culpeppers' point of view. "You were embraced by the movement." Kate might be battered and bruised, yet she held herself erect as a queen. "You broke your the oath to the cause. For what? Some antiquated religious ideal?"

"Kate," Eliza said, slowly bringing the electroporter up. The machine's hum turned into a crackle. "Stand back."

His colleague's gauntlet must have hit her far harder than he initially thought. Chandi was having a rough go at catching her breath, let alone looking up. She did manage to do so, and her dusky skin went pale at seeing Eliza raise the final lever and stop at its halfway point.

"Her name was Ihita Pujari," Eliza spoke evenly, her voice icy cold. "She was a dear friend of mine."

Chandi's lips moved, but any sound she made was drowned out by the electroporter after Eliza completed the final circuit.

Bolts danced across the arches and crawled like angry, anxious insects up along the frame. The space around the array rippled and pulsed, causing the air to stir. The smell of electricity overwhelmed them and made Wellington's eyes water. Louder and louder the hum grew, and then the bridge disappeared in a great flash of white.

Blinking back tears, Wellington pulled himself to his feet, his eyes still looking at where Chandi Culpepper had once been. The air was settling as the generators within the device spun down.

He turned to congratulate Eliza; but instead her name rose to his lips as a warning shout.

It couldn't have been Chandi appearing behind his colleague; it did, however, look exactly like her. Eliza spun about and barely managed to evade the doppelgänger's knife Chandi's twin brandished; but even still, the blade dug deep into her shoulder. With a backhand motion, Eliza used the *plures ornamentum* to slap away her assailant. Then the agent slumped into Mrs. Sheppard's arms.

Wellington bolted for the two women, as Eliza's blood seeped onto her fellow New Zealander's dress. He tore off his lab frock and nicked the hem against one of the *plures ornamentum's* sharper edges. Once he had torn the fabric, he began binding Eliza's arm. As he continued wrapping the wound, his mind whispered, *Where is she?* The sister. She should have attacked again by now.

He looked up from his dressing to find Chandi's sister working the controls frantically. She turned dials, threw switches, and wept as she hammered her palm against button after button.

Wellington could just make out the frantic whispers in between her sobs. "Trajectory. Time. Distance. Reverse polarity. Designate point of origin as destination . . ." she rambled, her voice trailing off as she connected the circuits. The thrumming generators that were now decelerating gave a sharp clack of protest, and then began to rise in volume. "Yes, destination is point of origin . . ."

"She's . . ." Wellington began, but his voice caught in his throat. He swallowed, and finally looked over to Eliza. "She's trying to bring her back whilst in transit."

Eliza understood immediately. "Oh my God."

Light filled the bridge and clogged their ears with a thick, unnatural silence, the one similar to before . . .

Wellington yanked Mrs. Sheppard down between the two of them as the shock wave passed over. It destroyed glass panels around them and threw everything loose all over the place. The flash subsided, while sparks arced in the machine.

Someone, in amongst the dying generators and odd pops of overloaded instruments, was laughing. Wellington and the ladies looked up to see the two identical, exotic sisters, one still standing at the now useless electroporter controls and the other standing silent under the arcs.

"Chandi," the twin said, her breath catching in her throat as she cleared the control panel.

The sister in the machine appeared disoriented. No doubt, she would have been confused as she had been transported in a lying position and now she was standing upright. She opened her mouth, and her sister's name came out with a stream of blood and flesh. "Chandankika . . ."

Wellington swallowed back a bitter taste in his mouth on hearing the wail that came out of her. Chandi vomited up blood as her shoulders suddenly went slack. The knees failed next, collapsing in the opposite direction knees would normally bend. When Chandi hit the deck, Wellington, Eliza, and Kate flinched as one. It did not crumple as a complete body ought to.

Chandankika screamed, and it would be the last sound she would make. The twin's lament was cut short when a throwing blade embedded itself into her fine, smooth neck.

They turned to see Sophia massaging life into what had been, apparently, a throwing arm.

"Now I know I am sore," Sophia scoffed. "I was aiming for her skull."

"You can rest up," Eliza began, lifting up the *plures ornamentum* in the direction of the Italian, "at the Ministry headquarters. You have a few things to answer for, you bitch."

Sophia flicked her wrist and a blade appeared in her hand. "A sharp tongue you have there. Perhaps I should remove it?"

"I dare you to try."

"Ladies!" Wellington snapped. "Might we come up with a more amicable resolution to our differences once we are on God's green earth?"

The two ladies held their gaze, and to Wellington's surprise it was Sophia who relented as she lowered her blade. "Before Wellington knocked me out at the wheel, I managed to get us above your comrades for the time being. Perhaps that will avoid any of their artillery."

"Well done," Wellington said. "Now let's see if we can find that communica—"

A wet, thick cough cut him off and made them all turn. Sophia's aim, it seemed, had indeed been off. Chandi's double was dying, but not as fast as hoped. Draped over the electroporter's control panel, Chandankika was unlocking a small black box in the top corner. The housing popped up to reveal a large red button. Sophia threw her knife, sinking the steel into the woman's eye . . .

. . . after her hand slapped hard against the red button.

The crippled automatons flickered back to life, but remained stationary as Chandi's voice spoke softly, in unison, from all three, "Auto destruct sequence initiated. Please proceed to the nearest exit."

"We have to move." Eliza grunted, her stance not as sure or steady as Wellington was accustomed to. "Now."

"Quite thorough, those Culpepper girls," remarked Wellington.

"Then let us not waste time!" Sophia went to the electroporter, removed what appeared to be a transformer from the point where the arcs met, and headed for the closest hatch. "We must get to Engineering. That is where the escape hatches will be."

Wellington glanced at Eliza who was still a bit weak from the blood loss. She was not happy in following Sophia's lead.

"I can say without hesitation that I know exactly how you feel, Miss Braun," Wellington said. "Mrs. Sheppard, follow us."

"Gladly," she said.

Sophia, not hindered by a New Zealander draped across her shoulders, was making good speed along the dimly lit footpath between the bridge and the engine room. Occasionally, they would pass an automaton softly counting down. The fact it was Chandi's voice counting down Wellington found most unsettling.

Not as unsettling, though, as Sophia del Morte who was now closing the heavy iron door between them and Engineering.

"Sophia!" his voice boomed with echo, only to be drowned out by the door latching shut.

"Well, that tears it," Eliza grunted, pushing Wellington away. Her metallic hand wrapped around the hatch's wheel. "Welly, you get Kate to safety. This bitch is all mine once we get across this threshold."

Gears and cogs clicked and whined as Eliza put in whatever remaining strength she had in making the latch give. This time, however, the effort was much greater. Her groan matched the door's—until it became for her a primal scream. The *plures ornamentum* popped, puffed, and shrieked until finally the locking mechanism failed and the door swung open. With a cry of delight, Eliza led the charge into Engineering.

There were four automatons in sight, all of them standing still.

Over the rumbling of the engines, Chandi's voice announced through her house servants, "You now have fifteen minutes to reach minimum safe distance."

Wellington noted the Culpeppers' house servants were placed at strategic points. The automatons would ignite the boilers and make certain nothing of the airship would remain for salvage of any kind.

Yes, the Culpeppers had been very thorough indeed.

"There!" She pointed to a shaft of white light off to their left.

They only just caught sight of Sophia's boots clearing the landing before jumping into the vastness of aerospace. An envelope of silk opened into a parachute a moment before she slipped beneath the clouds.

"Bugger!" Eliza swore.

He felt his shoulders drop. Whatever was Sophia thinking?

When he went for the other parachutes, he soon found out.

Sophia's blade had made quick work of the remaining parachutes. The lifesaving haversacks, all save two, were brandishing gaping holes and deep tears. She had provided an escape—but not for all of them.

"Oh, she wants to make this personal, does she?" Eliza sneered.

"Go."

Eliza and Wellington turned to Kate. Had she just ordered them to leave her behind?

"Mrs. Sheppard," Wellington said, "have you forgotten we were here to rescue you?"

"I am well aware of that, Mr. Books, but you need to see the larger picture here." She dropped a hand on his colleague's shoulder. "Eliza, you have to carry on the fight for me, as you did back home. You can do this."

"Kate, no."

"Child, if today is my turn to die, I would rather do so as a martyr for the movement than as a freakish clockwork doll in need of oiling!" She laughed, in spite of herself. "I need to pass on the torch, and as God as my witness, I need to pass that torch to you. Douglas can make the proper arrangements, and back home you will carry on my legacy." She placed a hand on her cheek. "Don't let me die in vain. Promise me that?"

Her friend blinked, her eyes welling up with tears. "I promise you won't die in vain."

"Thank you."

With a grunt, the agent brought her free arm up, clocking Kate soundly in a vulnerable point between her brass jaw and fair New Zealand flesh. The leader of her home's suffrage movement fell to the deck, unconscious.

"You won't die, because you're not staying, Kate. Welly, dress her up." Eliza winced as she flexed her fingers back and forth. "Dammit, that hurt."

"That was your wounded arm," Wellington scolded her as he slipped the parachute on Kate. "So, of course it did!"

"Well I couldn't punch her with this bloody *plures ornamentum*, now could I?" Eliza said, moving the massive weapon back and forth. "I wanted to knock her out, not break her jaw." She paused, looking at her unconscious mentor. "Or dent it, as in this case."

"Does that thing have any sort of quick release, perhaps?" he asked, slipping goggles over Kate's closed eyes.

"Blackwell says she's working on it."

Always the bloody clankertons, Wellington thought bitterly.

With a final tug, the parachute was secure.

"Right then," she started, "your tu—"

"Hardly." Wellington raised a warning finger up to her, then tossing her a pair of aviator goggles. "I'm not leaving here without you."

He dragged Kate to the open port, grabbed ahold of the rip cord, and let her body fall into the void, her parachute opening mere moments later, clear of the Ministry's airship. The chute unfurled and Kate's descent slowed to a safe drift.

Wellington looked around them. If the parachutes were here, there had to be other gear, survival or otherwise, in this section of the ship.

"We really don't have time to debate the matter."

"Then I suppose," Wellington replied, his eyes still looking back and forth between cabinets and crates, "I will finally have the last word with you."

Where was it? It was standard on airships. The Culpepper sisters were industrious, but they certainly could not have built this airship. Therefore, standards would be in place.

"Wellington Thornhill Books, you bullheaded twit, look at me! I'm worse than a deadweight," she said, hefting her brass-encased arm.

"That is one thing I would never call you." His gaze fell on a long crate labeled "Emergency Rescue"—something very familiar from his military days. Opening it, he found a modified rifle loaded with a grappling hook and rope. Quite a bit of rope. "We will manage."

He glanced out the hatch. The *Blythe Spirit* was closing. He looked at the coil. He would have to make his angle of descent in freefall precise. There was no margin for error.

"Wellington, even if I could make that shot—which I could if I had an arm that wasn't wounded or heavily armoured—we don't have enough rope."

"We have enough rope if we get closer."

Eliza's eyes narrowed. "I can't make that shot."

"I know you can't." Wellington splayed his fingers around the rifle, and then took a step closer. "Do you trust me?"

She went to protest but stopped. He watched her eyes soften, a touch of blush rise in her cheeks. "I—"

Chandi's voice interrupted her. "You now have five minutes to reach minimum safe distance."

"I will take that as a yes," Wellington said, throwing the final parachute on her. He then grabbed a smaller coil of rope and secured Eliza to his back. "When we go, angle us towards the *Blythe Spirit*. When I shoulder the grappling hook, pull the cord."

Eliza nodded. She took in a deep breath while Wellington worked between them the accompanying belt where excess rope fed the rescue rifle. Both of them lowered their goggles even as the automatons announced that one minute remained. Underneath them was the *Blythe Spirit*. Exactly where Wellington wanted her. He looked over the rifle one more time, the feed line to confirm it would feed without fault, and finally the rope belt that bound Eliza to him.

"Twenty," came Chandi's voice again. "Ninteen . . . eighteen . . . seventeen . . . sixteen . . . fifteen . . ."

Wellington with his Braun-enhanced parachute leapt out in the open air, their bodies angling towards the *Blythe Spirit*. They were falling. Fast. He knew their collected weight was going to be too much for the parachute, but all he needed was a moment—a single, solitary moment—for the shot. The goggles pressed against his face, hard enough to make his eyes narrow; and in his vision he saw the *Spirit* draw closer. Closer. A few more feet . . .

Angle of descent . . .

Speed of descent . . .

Acceleration decay . . .

Now.

Wellington shouldered the weapon, and he felt Eliza tug between them. He waited a few more heartbeats, felt a sudden stop, and—compensating for the force of resistance—pulled the trigger.

The hook was away. Reaching. Reaching. The rope from the rifle continued to unwind and then the hook disappeared into the cabin. He was certain it had shattered a window.

Their parachute failed, and the world began to fall away once more. Something far above him thundered, and he caught a flash in the corner of his eye. Wellington's arm snaked around the rifle and pulled up in anticipation for the coil to catch. Now, they were swinging forward, flying underneath the *Blythe Spirit*'s cabin, and then arching upward. Like a pendulum, the archivist and his skilled assistant swung to and fro for a time.

It must have hurt, but Eliza's bloody arm reached around and pulled Wellington closer to her. All he heard was the wind in his ears, but Eliza was doing something against him. Crying with joy? Laughing? Hard to be certain.

Wellington Thornhill Books, Esquire was most certain of one thing though: once back in the Archives, he would have a lot of explaining to do.

CHAPTER THIRTY

In Which Friends Return Home
and Nearly All Is Forgiven

"I am quite sure this will be impossible to explain to the committee." Kate smiled as Eliza helped her down from the airship gangplank. She was trying to make light of it, but her friend could feel the tremble in her hand.

"All they need to know is that the disappearances will not happen again." Eliza looked back to the deck, where Doctor Sound was talking to Shillingworth. The Director's gaze flicked to her, and it was not exactly kindly. Consequences, she had a feeling, were about to fall on her once more. She'd expected as much.

Kate leaned in. "I wish our sisters could be told what you did."

"Now that would get me into trouble!" Eliza squeezed her hand. "I am happy they know I work in the government, but that's all we can really share. Besides"—she smiled wryly—"who would believe it?"

The suffragist looked up at the clouds. "I know, Miss Eliza D. Braun, that if I were told it rather than having seen it, I certainly would not." Then she touched the brass-covered half of her face. "We have a lot to thank you for—myself most especially."

"Mother!" Douglas was pushing dockworkers out of the way and causing quite a commotion as he raced towards them. Eliza's heart sank as he began to get near.

"I am glad of one other thing," Kate whispered to her. "I am ever so glad you didn't start your relationship with my son up again."

Such a pronouncement made Eliza straighten. Never in all their time together in New Zealand had Mrs. Sheppard ever mentioned any opinion on the matter. "Really?" she stammered, "I suppose I'm not your class, or not—"

"Oh, it's nothing like that," her friend replied, as she gave Douglas a reassuring wave. She let out a long sigh, one that spoke of maternal love and unending patience. "I adore my son as a mother should, but he can be a bit . . ." Her words disappeared as she considered the world-renowned adventurer. "Douglas is like one of his mountains—set, immovable in many ways, and just difficult to understand." She smiled and nodded in his direction. "You, my dear, would most likely kill him eventually."

Kate winked with her mechanical eye, and Eliza could not stop a snort of laughter escaping. "Very possibly," she choked out. "Yes, indeed, most probably."

"That does not mean," Kate began turning to her, "I still do not look upon you with a great amount of pride. Eliza, while the history books will not know of your contributions to the movement, I will. Never forget that."

Eliza swallowed back a growing lump in her throat. "That means a great deal to me."

They walked the rest of the way to meet him. Douglas abandoned all protocol and snatched Kate up in an embrace. "I'm so sorry, Mother. I was in town when I heard and I—"

"Now, now, please don't fuss. It was quite the adventure, but I am wholly safe and well." She turned and grinned at Eliza. "Though I do think I am feeling far too old for such high-jinks, and quite ready for a cup of tea before we set off for home."

In all the commotion Eliza had completely forgotten that the Sheppards were leaving by their own, much more sedate, airship this very evening. Before she could say anything Kate was hugging her, and planting a kiss on her cheek. "I shall send word to your family that you are safe and well—though I may leave out the bit about parachuting from a burning airship." She laid a hand on the agent's cheek. "It has been lovely to see you again, Eliza. I know now you have made yourself a good home here. When you return to Aotearoa, call on me. Until then, look after yourself and that delightful Mr. Books too." Then before she could be questioned further, she moved off so that Douglas and Eliza could say their farewells.

It was more than awkward, but it had to be done. "Good-bye, then." Douglas cleared his throat. "I hoped perhaps you might reconsider . . ."

"When have you ever known me to do that?" she replied as gently as she could, but when he stepped in to kiss her, she offered only her cheek. "Thank you for the past, Douglas. You really did help make some things clear to me." When he stepped back, Eliza could see he was struggling to maintain a veneer of control over genuine annoyance. Still, he had been her first love, and she didn't want this goodbye to end badly.

"Go find a girl more suited to you than I." She laid a hand on his arm. "You're a fine man—just not the man for me anymore." She pressed her lips lightly on his cheek, and then turned away, setting her sights elsewhere.

Wellington was coming down the gangplank to meet her. His wheaten hair shifted in the wind, quite naked to the elements. It was rather endearing. His gaze flickered over her shoulder. "So the Sheppards are going already?"

"Their airship for New Zealand leaves this evening," Eliza said, tucking her hand around his elbow, "so we got the timing perfectly right for a rescue."

"Aren't you sad you're not going with them?"

His voice was calm, but there was a strange note to it that made her smile. "Oh Welly, I have been quite won over by the charms of London. I'm not missing New Zealand as much as I once did."

A long exhalation followed from him, and it sounded as though he'd been holding it in. "That's wonderful, though, unfortunately, one part of London is far less charmed with us at the moment."

Both of their gazes drifted to the airship and the Director. Sound had finished his conversation with Shillingworth, and now had both hands locked on the railing, leaning out, and looking straight at them. His secretary inclined her head in a gesture that could almost have been a salute to her employer and strode down the gangplank. She completely ignored the Archivist and his apprentice as she made her way to the rank of hansoms. They could hardly guess what the Director had said to Shillingworth and certainly did not dare ask her as she passed them.

Eliza felt her mouth dry up, but still she managed to choke out, "So the jig is up then?"

"Quite."

"And he knows all about the cases we've worked from the Archives?"

"Naturally—he's not a stupid man. He wants us to meet him in his office." For a man about to lose his employment Wellington sounded remarkably chirpy.

Taking a chance, Eliza slid her hand down his arm and clasped her fingers on his. He didn't flinch, so she squeezed a little tighter. "I'm sorry," she murmured to him. "This was all my fault. It was my idea to chase these cases."

His hazel eyes met hers, and there was not one ounce of anger or accusation in them. "That is absolute rubbish, Eliza. I could at any stage have stopped you merely by going to the Director. I chose not to, and because of that, you and I have done a lot of good."

"I suppose," she replied in a small voice.

"Please keep sight of the fact that the Empire itself could have fallen under the weight of another religious crusade, Eliza. I would count that as most worthy."

"I hope the Director takes that into account." She said it as cheerfully as she could manage, but they both knew that Doctor Sound could not tolerate division in the ranks. Everyone—including the Archivist—had to be trusted to obey direct orders.

"So you see," Wellington said straightening to his full height, "I will not apologise for our actions."

They might be losing their jobs, and the scene that awaited them would be monumental in its scope, but they were at least united. "Then better to go out with a bang," Eliza squeezed his fingertips again, and only just managed to stop raising them to her lips. "That is the way I have always preferred to leave a party."

The Archivist looked down at her, while a small smile tugged at the corners of his lips. "Despite my protests, I have come to realise I would not have it any other way."

Together they walked down the street to find a hansom, and face whatever music the Director had ready for them.

CHAPTER THIRTY-ONE

Wherein Wellington Books Handles
a Situation with Aplomb

They arrived back at the Ministry before the Director—though not before Shillingworth. By some miracle of transportation, the secretary was sitting at her desk shuffling paperwork when Eliza and Wellington stepped out of the lift.

The Archivist observed that there was not one white-blonde hair out of place on her head, and it was impossible to imagine her toting firearms and hanging from the rigging of an airship only hours before. It could have been another woman.

She showed them into the office, saw them settled on chairs, and then turned to them with a smile. "Can I get a cup of tea for you while you wait?"

In all his time at the Ministry, Wellington had never seen Miss Shillingworth offer refreshment or a smile. It was a banner day apparently, yet when he exchanged a glance with Eliza she also appeared to be taking it as a bad sign.

"Thank you," his colleague replied, "I think that would be lovely."

They sat in silence while Shillingworth bustled out, to

reappear a short time later with a tray. On it was a fine porcelain teapot and cups in a lovely willow pattern, and also a tray of tiny biscuits. Then with another smile, the secretary returned to her desk, shutting the door noiselessly behind her.

Eliza poured, while Wellington nibbled on a biscuit. Somewhere just outside Ministry headquarters both of them had let go of each other's hands. It seemed the proper thing to do when entering one's place of employment, but the Archivist found that he missed her fingers wrapped around his.

Being in the oubliette had made a number of things clear to him—none of which he could discuss with Eliza at this very moment. If either or both of them were dismissed from the Ministry he could not foresee the consequences. Perhaps Eliza would end up working for another government organisation, and he could enquire at the British Library. The thought gave him great concern. It was not that the venerable library was not a wonderful place—it was just not the place for him. And Eliza . . .

Wellington glanced across at her. Though her hands were folded atop each other on her knees, he could detect real tension in her shoulders. The Ministry of Peculiar Occurrences was unique in Queen Victoria's government, and it was unlikely any other place would suit Miss Eliza D. Braun's skills as well.

For both of them then, this was quite the moment. Wellington was about to reach across and pat Eliza's hand again, when the door was flung open and the Director strode in. Like Shillingworth he appeared untouched by this afternoon's events, but he looked considerably less happy about that.

He took a seat behind his desk, and fixed them with a stare that should have been reserved for insects beneath glass. "Once again," he began, steepling his fingers before him, "I find you two in my office—a situation I was hoping never to have repeated."

Wellington swallowed, glanced across at Eliza, and then when she showed no signs of speaking, addressed his superior. "Director, I just want to express my colleague's and my own distress at being here as well. We never expected—"

"—To be caught?" Doctor Sound tilted his head. "That was a very foolish expectation then. I may be a shuffler of papers, as Agent Braun here once called me, but I am not without intelligence."

Wellington began mentally running through his contacts at the British Library.

"I gave you leeway after the Phoenix Society affair— even though your excuses were as transparent as glass— because you did the Empire a service, and I expected one incident would be enough for you both." He pulled a stack of brown folders over to sit in front of him. "Do you have anything mitigating to offer?"

Eliza brushed her skirt, and gave Wellington a warning stare before replying. "Yes, I do, Director. This was all my fault."

The Archivist went to protest at her throwing herself in front of the carriage like this, but she held up a hand. Wellington's good breeding forbade his interrupting a lady.

She turned back to the Director. "It was at my insistence that Wellington helped me investigate both the Phoenix Society and the missing suffragists. Both cases were dear to me. As Harrison Thorne and Mrs. Kate Sheppard were and are personal friends, I felt I needed to help them—especially since neither was being investigated properly by the Ministry."

Eliza sat tall in her chair, meeting the Director's eye, and Wellington had never been so proud of her. Ever since setting out on their first adventure she had expressed concerns that he would abandon her to the wrath of Doctor Sound. Yet now here she was, claiming all the responsibility.

It was not going to make a difference.

The Director's forehead furrowed. "You are once again, Braun, taking me for a fool. Our Archivist was aware of what you were doing, and could have easily reported your activities at any time."

392 PIP BALLANTINE & TEE MORRIS

"Yes indeed," Wellington replied, "I could have, but decided that the greater good was being served."

"You feel you are qualified to decide that?" The Director's glare flicked between the two of them, and sensibly, both remained silent.

"Yes, sir," they replied together.

Doctor Sound jerked back in his chair and peered at them in surprise. "And pray tell, what gives you this authority over me?"

"The number of cases that have gone unsolved by our agents. I have to look at them daily." Wellington leaned forward in his chair. "When do you see them, sir?"

The Director's mouth opened, then shut as he considered. Finally, he nodded. "*Touché*, Books. The truth of the matter is that both the Ministry and I are in a precarious position. We are under constant scrutiny by Her Majesty." He adjusted himself in his seat. "On one hand I cannot have you undermining my authority while our venerable Queen is keeping such a close eye on us."

"And we all know how she feels about the suffrage movement," Eliza muttered. "She called it a 'wicked folly' after all."

The Director cleared his throat and silenced her with one look. "However, I also cannot with a clear conscience dismiss the two of you for such heroic acts." He flipped open the folder. "My own investigations have revealed that you have solved six of our forgotten cases."

"Beg your pardon, sir," Wellington couldn't help interjecting, "it was actually seven."

Doctor Sound glanced down and made a notation in the folder. "Thank you, Books."

Eliza shot the Archivist an exasperated look.

"Fortunately, a solution to this little pickle has fallen into my lap. Tell me, have you ever been to the Americas?"

It was such an unexpected comment that Wellington barked out, "No, sir."

"Well then, with Eliza by your side it will be quite the

education, since our American counterparts have asked for assistance."

"I didn't know that the United States had an organisation like ours," Eliza said, tilting her head.

"They did not consult with you, Agent Braun? How shocking!" Wellington was not so foolish as to think this touch of humour from their superior meant they were out of the woods just yet. "As a matter of fact," Doctor Sound continued, "it is still somewhat in the formation stages, but they have a case that resembles one from your forgotten files section." He tapped his finger on a case file in front of him. "So both our Ministry and their organisation may benefit from this exchange of minds."

"We'll do our best," Wellington offered, trying to keep his voice level.

"I would expect no less. Airship passage has been booked. You leave at midnight. I will have the particulars of this peculiar occurrence waiting in your respective staterooms to study while you travel. Here is a brief summary," Sound continued, handing Wellington a single sheet of paper. "As it is close to five o'clock, you should have some time to gather a few case notes from the Archives before returning to your respective homes to pack." He looked between them both. Wellington knew he was smiling. Broadly. "I suggest you do not dilly-dally—lest I change my mind."

The Archivist was so giddy with relief that he really didn't care exactly which case it was, for it appeared that they were being temporarily exiled rather than dismissed. Eliza, too, looked as if she had been given a gallows reprieve. Both agents leapt to their feet immediately and made for the door.

"One last thing." The Director stopped them before they could get there. Wellington held his breath but dared not turn around.

"I also suggest you pack what things you need from down in the Archives. Miss Shillingworth will be overseeing them while you are away. I presume, as our Archivist, that meets with your approval?"

Wellington turned and gave a thoughtful nod. "I cannot think of anyone better, sir."

"You know, Welly," Eliza whispered as they made their escape, "I think we have bloody well earned a holiday."

Her bravado was thin, but still attached. Still for once, Wellington did not rise to the bait. Not today.

Wherein the Duke of Sussex Makes a House Call

Music played in the library of the Duke of Sussex. Peter Lawson was allowing himself the briefest of recollections to how things had been once, when he had been a younger man of wilder passions—passions that threatened his standing. That was another lifetime ago.

He had learned control since then. Control had brought him to one of the highest offices in the land. Her Majesty the Queen had given him the task of assessing the Ministry of Peculiar Occurrences. And that was what he finally felt he could do.

The transfer of rogue agents Eliza D. Braun and Wellington Thornhill Books to the Americas, while an admirable effort on Doctor Basil Sound's part to bring order to the fledgling agency, hardly restores his authoritative control over the agents he is responsible for. The insubordination of these agents, coupled with the unexplained and tragic death of Thita Pujari, only confirms my suspicions that the Ministry of Peculiar Occurrences is no longer the institute of logical deduction or reason it once was. Doctor Sound's inability to adequately discipline his agents as well as keep them safe from the opposition has displayed the Ministry of Peculiar Occurrences' scant regard of the voices of authority, including, I would dare say, the Crown itself.

He smiled, slowly nodding his head at that bold proclamation. True, he hardly had any proof to back up those words. At least, not yet. His colonial would provide him what he needed for such a claim. Still, he had compiled the assessment, ready to be presented right after Campbell brought him the secrets of this mythical "Restricted Area" deep within the Archives of the Ministry. This small piece of paper would cut out this cancer from the monarchy.

It would also appease the Maestro, and maybe Sussex would finally be free of the abhorrent presence once and for all.

His pen returned to the paper as incidental music from Shakespeare's *A Midsummer Night's Dream* continued on the gramophone.

What disturbs me most of all in the decay within the Ministry is Doctor Sound's delusions in believing he can employ the Ministry's resources for his own benefit. Underneath the offices of the Ministry of Peculiar Occurrences is an area Sound refers to as "Restricted Access," which is just that— restricted from all personnel save for Sound himself. At one time, it was unclear exactly what was kept in this dungeon within a dungeon; but in concluding my own investigation—

"Sir?"

Fenning's voice stopped his master's pen in its tracks. Sussex had made it very clear that he was not to be disturbed. Most nights, he did not mind the tending to from his London house staff, but tonight he needed total concentration.

"Fenning?" Sussex asked, lifting his eyes to the butler. "I do hope you have a very good reason to disturb me."

"A Mr. Bruce Campbell is at the door, sir." His voice quivered slightly as he spoke. "He was most insistent on seeing you immediately. He would not set an appointment, nor would he take no for an answer. I threatened to call the constable." Fenning paused and then added, "He welcomed it."

Sussex glanced at the assessment under his fingertips. Could he possibly earn his freedom that quickly?

"Show him in."

When Fenning reappeared, Bruce remained a few paces behind him, strangely hunched somehow.

"That will be all, Fenning." Sussex kept his eyes fixed on Campbell.

The butler glanced over the colonial with an air of contempt before leaving the study. Campbell stood there, gripping his bowler hat tightly as his eyes darted around the room.

Sussex turned a chair towards his visitor and started back to his own. "Please have a seat."

"I won't be staying long, sir, so I'd rather stand."

"Tosh," Sussex said, waving to the chair, "I believe we have a great deal to talk about."

"No, Your Grace, we do not."

The insistence in Campbell's voice made Sussex pause in taking his own chair. Finally, they were looking at each other, and the Duke did not care for what he found in the colonial's hard, cold gaze.

The Australian said softly, "I'm leaving London."

Sussex chuckled, shaking his head. "What? You've been reassigned? Well, I can certainly—"

"I have been dismissed."

A tight, gripping sensation—perhaps the cold grip of an armoured hand—began to slowly squeeze around Sussex's throat. "Campbell, whatever are you on about?"

"I'm not on about anything, Your Grace. Doctor Sound terminated my service with the Ministry."

Sweat. He felt sweat on the back of his neck. "Why?"

"Dereliction of duty. It came to light I was letting certain cases go unsolved on account of personal bias. That personal bias led to the death of Agent Ihita Pujari." Campbell smiled bleakly.

The Duke's head swam, as if he had drunk far too much brandy, or perhaps quaffed it too quickly. His heart pounded in his ears, but a single, deep breath later, he could feel himself back under control. "I will speak with Sound on this matter first thing in the morning."

"No," Campbell said, "you won't."

He wanted to sit down. "I beg your pardon."

"I'm going home." The Australian crossed the office to a shelf of small books—his collection of William Shakespeare—and read along the spines until he found the volume he was apparently looking for. "Now *Henry VI, Part 3*. That's a funny ol' play, Your Grace, if there ever was one."

Sussex blinked. What was Campbell on about?

"Loads of high falootin' muckity-mucks just blithering and blathering away. My wife wants the children cultured and all, so I humour her. But this play—" Campbell nodded, tapping at its spine, "This play has a speech."

Sussex felt himself torn between the sudden jovial notes of Mendelssohn playing on the gramophone and the colonial's sudden appreciation—apparently a begrudging one at that—of one of William Shakespeare's history plays. He had to focus on one thing. *Focus*, he told himself, *on one thing*.

Strangely enough, he chose the Australian.

"The Duke of Gloucester—gives this speech about 'a kingdom for Richard' and how he would make the world his. We colonials, you see, like a good ol' story of adversity, you know?

"But then that toff Gloucester kept on about what he was going to do to get that crown, so you might be surprised to know I was first in line to get tickets for the next play about that bloke, Richard. Cost of the crown. That bastard stepped over a lot of graves to get what he wanted. It caught up with him. Bloody killed him, it did."

Bruce tightened his grip on the rim of his hat and locked a dark gaze with Sussex. "I wanted my own little kingdom too, you know? Let a lot of loudmouths disappear, thinking one less voice asking for equality and all that would keep things as they should be . . ." His voice trailed off as he looked out of the study window. "I wonder now how many deaths were on account of that, Your Grace."

Sussex took in a long, slow breath, but Campbell went on before he could speak. "I don't doubt you could get my job back at the Ministry; but even if I were willing, no one trusts me there. Not anymore." The Australian turned back around to him and put his bowler back on his head. "I'm sorry, Your Grace, but I have failed you. I have failed the Ministry. So it's back to Australia with me. Maybe there, I can find some peace."

With a final nod, Campbell saw himself out—just as the "Wedding March" of Titania and Oberon commenced.

The trumpets seemed to herald the oncoming madness that now slipped around Sussex. Each breath hurt. *I have failed*, he heard Campbell say; but the colonial hadn't been the only one. The echoing sentiment, *I have failed*, began to sound less and less like the Australian, and ring more with a tone of refinement.

Yes, whispered the other voice in his head, *you have failed me, Peter.*

When Sussex opened his eyes, he half expected the Maestro to be there, lurking in the gloom, his presence made known only by the single, malevolent eye of deepest red piercing through the shadows.

No, he wanted to scream, but his throat was too tight to allow for voice. *I can't have failed. I am the Privy Counsellor to Her Majesty Queen Victoria. I cannot fail.*

Gaily the music played on, of the faeries gathering within the glade to celebrate the young lovers discovering one another, the reuniting of Faerie King and—

Sussex was a strong man. He knew that. He was now under the care of a progressive physician who believed in better health through purposeful exercise, and his own regimen of such activity produced amazing results.

However, Sussex also knew his own limits. He should not have been able to lift the gramophone, as he did. Nor should he have been able to lift it over his head, as he did. Nor should he have been able to hurl it across his study to smash against the bookcase, bringing down the complete works of Shakespeare and the other accompanying classics, as he did.

He landed on his knees, finally feeling the air rush into his body. He then vomited against the fine carpet; but even the putrid smell assailing his nostrils could not calm him from his fit.

His fit.

The temper.

He had to get a hold before—

"Peter!" cried a familiar voice.

It was Ivy.

He spit the remnants of bile from his mouth; and when he addressed his wife, his voice sounded hard and dry. "Have Fenning—" he wheezed. Then after a few coughs, he tried again. "Have Fenning bring the coach around. Take me to my—"

Sussex did not faint, but he did feel himself surrender to something. The cries were muffled. So far off. He could hear the word *physician* as the world underneath him moved.

No, it was *he* who was being moved. The world remained under his feet, but there was a person on either side of him, one short, another considerably taller; and through the strange haze of vision he could see the door.

A door that opened into darkness.

He should have been afraid as that was where his temper took him—into a darkness that would have consumed him completely had he not stood against it. This darkness, though, was far different. It felt painful, perhaps a bit . . . bumpy? And cold. A biting cold caressed his face as the darkness tossed him from side to side. The chill now made his way into his nostrils, down his throat, and into his stomach, or at least that was how it felt. He took another breath, and the fog surrounding him began to lift. How many times had he ridden in this carriage? Sussex had never noticed how firm the cushions in his coach were. Normally, he appreciated its solid, supportive feel, but at present it only made his body ache more. He needed something to drink. At the very least, to get the taste out of his mouth.

Another long, deep breath, and now London's night came into a sharp focus. No fog tonight. That was nice. Also helpful, as he needed to know where the line was between the Empire and his own personal hell. When the fits took him on foggy days, that tended to make such distinctions difficult. Sussex gripped the handle over his head and pulled himself upright. His faculties were far better than when he felt the fit overcome him in his study, but he couldn't order his driver to turn around and head home. He wouldn't. Not when he was this close.

The carriage turned a corner, and when Sussex's grip tightened, a ripple of agony worked through his arm and shoulder. He was exhausted, dizzy, but at least he could see the façade of his physician's home. "Finally," he sighed aloud as the horses slowed before the front door.

When the servant opened the carriage door, Sussex's hand grabbed for the man's arm as he pulled himself free of his seat. *You are the head of the Privy Council,* he chided himself silently. *You represent Her Majesty. Get yourself together, man!* He gave the lapels of his vest a slow tug, and fought to keep his steps strong and solid as he entered the doctor's home.

The young physician appeared in the hallway tightening a sash around an impressive smoking jacket. However, on seeing the Duke, his brow knotted with concern.

"Doctor . . ." Sussex managed.

The physician looked him over once and shook his head, "I need you to calm yourself, Your Grace, and come with me." As he escorted Sussex into the familiar library, the doctor called out over his shoulder, "Wadsworth, have Eucinda fetch me a bowl of water with rags. The water should be warm. Not hot, mind you. Warm."

"Very good, sir." The butler nodded as they lowered Sussex onto the plush settee.

A modest fire was burning gaily in the doctor's tiny hearth, and Sussex found the flame's dance oddly hypnotic. He was about to try and sit up when his young physician immediately propped his feet back onto the settee's one arm, keeping the Duke's feet elevated above the level of his head.

"Did your doctor tell you to sit up?" he chided. "I don't recall giving you those orders."

"The temper," he panted softly, again and again. His eyes screwed shut. "The temper came over me again . . ."

"Breathe, my friend. Breathe," the doctor replied, placing a hand gently on Sussex's chest. "Conjure the images. As I taught you."

Sussex nodded and attempted to settle into the pillow underneath his head. He recalled the Van Gogh-Brunel exhibition he had taken in two summers ago. With a flair for the dramatic which the engineer prided himself in indulging, Henry Marc Brunel had purchased several original Van Goghs, cut out specific shapes from the one-of-a-kinds, and created dioramas with mechanical movement. He had called it *automa-art*, while artists far and wide called it an effrontery to Van Gogh and his legacy. As for Sussex's own opinion, it was quite the contrary. He dared not share this with anyone. Not even Ivy. Such a common thing, this automa-art; but in secret, he found it charming. So, he committed this one work—*Starry Night with Rolling Clouds and Rising Moon*—to memory, with its clockwork melody of Beethoven's "Moonlight Sonata" softly tinkling in the background.

He would not let this temper of his bring all he had achieved to ruin.

"Peter," came the voice of his physician, his friend, "don't dwell. You must relax before we can talk about it. Find your solitude, and grant yourself the moment's peace."

Without protest, Sussex focused on the various shades of yellow rotating against one another, emulating star-shine, while Beethoven's sonata played.

"Excellent, Peter." His praise also lifted his spirits. "Now after I count to ten, I want you to slowly open your eyes, and then bring yourself up to a sitting position. You may be dizzy at first, but this will pass. Remember to breathe deeply. One . . . two . . . three . . . now begin to remove the sound from your solitude. Look upon it in silence."

The Moonlight Sonata diminished. Softer. Softer. He wasn't ready to leave this place.

He should have bought the piece. Society and artists alike be damned.

"Four . . . five . . . six . . . remove any colours you might see," the doctor said gently. "Don't worry. This place will be waiting for you whenever you wish to return."

Yellows faded into white while the blue grew darker and darker, until finally the night was black. So it went with the various hues, their colours seeming to melt like snow under sunlight. Soon it would be a flat, barren vista before him.

"Seven . . . eight . . . dim the lights, Peter. Just for a moment. And then, see the world again. Properly."

It was time to return. He knew that. The diorama slipped into darkness, inky black tendrils slipping around and between any open space. Soon, there would only be darkness.

"Nine . . . ten."

Sussex slowly opened his eyes. His friend's gaze was not judgemental or even condescending, but warm and assuring, much like the tiny, confident fire burning in the hearth.

"Welcome back, Peter," the doctor said, extending a snifter to him.

As Sussex pulled himself up, the room felt as if it listed sharply for a moment; but it was only for a moment. He paused, waited for the room to become level once more, and then resumed his ascent.

"Good to be back," Sussex sighed, taking the snifter. He had to get rid of this foul taste on his tongue.

"This must have been a bad one."

"I couldn't stop it." He took a drink and gave start. The amber liquid scorched its way down his throat, but oddly enough it did remove the chill. Still, hardly what he expected. "What kind of brandy is this?"

"It's unlike any brandy you'll find," the doctor said with a small chuckle. "It's scotch."

Sussex sneered. "Ah, yes, I forgot you were a scotch drinker."

"A taste for a more refined palette."

The Duke rolled his eyes at that. "Bugger off."

"Such language from the private secretary of Her Majesty." The young man clicked his tongue as he crossed over to the small collection of decanters. As he poured himself a drink, he continued with, "What will the higher minds of Her Majesty's Council think?"

"You're my physician," Sussex growled. "I'm allowed."

"Perhaps." The doctor pushed his hair back. Sussex marvelled at how young his friend appeared. It defied logic that he was a mere lad of twenty-two years and yet brilliant in his practice beyond such years. "So, as your physician, why don't you tell me about tonight?"

Sussex bowed his head. He was uncertain if it was the scotch or the fit that was making his head fuzzy. "I—" He took a deep breath. "I wanted to kill a man tonight."

"Was this a professional acquaintance, or personal?"

He looked up from his drink. How much could he tell? "Both."

The doctor scoffed and shook his head. "Peter, I'm sure you meet a good amount of peo—"

"No, I mean, I wanted to kill a man. I saw myself picking up the figurine. I could taste his blood on my lips. And when he left . . ." He should not have been able to do what he did, but that didn't change what had happened. By morning, Fenning would have made certain any and all evidence of the incident were gone. "I destroyed my gramophone."

"An interesting transference there."

The humour went without acknowledgement. "I threw it across the room."

"I see." Setting aside the drink cradled in his hands, Sussex's physician lowered himself to one knee and checked each eye carefully. "How have you been sleeping?"

"Not well."

The doctor's youthful face hardened, and Sussex swore he watched it age ten years in that instant. "I need to know, so do not play elusive with me—have you been feeling a build towards tonight?"

Sussex swallowed hard. There had been the night the Maestro left him the summons. Then the evening in that madman's company. "Yes," he admitted. "I think it has been. A slow build, but a build nonetheless."

"I was afraid of that," his doctor said with a sigh.

"What do you mean?"

"You may be developing a tolerance to your medication." The doctor stood up and turned back to the hearth, his own eyes staring into its flames. "I'm wondering if suppressing that temperament of yours is something akin to a dam, and once that dam begins to fail . . ."

"No, it *can't* fail," Sussex implored. "*I* can't fail. Not when I have come this far . . ."

"No," his friend said. "No you cannot, Peter. With everything we have accomplished together, I am not going to see you fall. Not now." He polished off the drink and then went to his desk. From a smaller selection of books held by two small bookends, he pulled out a volume and flipped through its pages. He stopped, nodded, and then proceeded a few more pages. "The good news is your dosage is still within safe limits. There's always a risk involved when changing a routine, of course, but I believe this is one worth taking."

"Are you certain?" Sussex asked. He took another breath and said, "I know your treatments have been incredible. I sleep quite peacefully, a welcome change to be sure; but . . ."

"Yes, Peter?"

"But usually I can remember dreams. Or at least I am aware of dreaming. Since taking your prescription—"

"I did warn you that this could be a side effect to the treatment."

Sussex nodded. "You did. You did." He took another deep drink of the scotch. His options were few. Actually, they were all of one. "Are you certain the risks are worth taking?"

His friend closed the book with a soft *snap*. "I'm a physician, Peter. I have your best interests at heart."

Sussex nodded. Yes, this would make things right. "Thank you, Henry. Thank you so much."

He was so very lucky to have a doctor he could trust implicitly. Not everyone was so fortunate.

CHAPTER THIRTY-TWO

Where Our Dashing Archivist Finally Gets in the Last Word with Our Colonial Pepperpot

Wellington gazed up the height of his analytical engine. It was more than just a tower of modern technology, but his own personal triumph. Even those arrogant *schlock-workers* in Research & Design could not fathom how he did it, nor could they replicate it. Not without his plans. Of course, Axelrod and Blackwell could have tried to dismantle it, deduced how he had solved the computation delay, managed the timing of the cogs, and kept in flawless order the various commands that did everything from play Mozart to file away artifacts from the field to make a fine pot of Assam. He wondered if it was coming down here and having to deal with him directly, that held those clankertons at bay.

He placed a hand on the outer pipes, feeling their slight warmth—again, another mystery he had solved in keeping the analytical engine at a precise temperature—and gave a long, hollow sigh. Should anything befall him over in the Americas, there would only be the redoubtable Miss Shillingworth to protect the engine.

Reaching down to the ring of keys, he slipped the smallest of them into a keyhole, releasing six latches with a single turn. The compact keyboard and tiny monitor slid free of the main housing, and with a slight groan he hefted the contraption onto his desk. While lacking a bit in the power of its mother engine, it would serve them well in the Americas. Perhaps as well as it had served him in interfacing with the ETS in order to track his reluctant partner on that fateful summer day.

He glanced back at where the keyboard and monitor had been hiding in plain view, and the gap did not appear as anything extraordinary. He grinned at his little touch of detail in that, and how his design was the reason this secondary keyboard had remained his little secret. Even with Eliza staring at him from the other side of the desk, Wellington didn't worry about tipping his hand about this portable analytical engine of his. She might have noticed that the keyboard and monitor collapsed neatly not only in its hiding place, but onto itself, reducing the array to a mere twenty pounds.

Eliza might have observed quite a few details about what he was packing for their journey across the Atlantic, if she hadn't been staring at him so intently.

"Eliza," Wellington sighed, "shouldn't you be arming yourself with the assistance of Axelrod and Blackwell? Or is this how you usually prepare for a mission abroad—by staring at your partner?"

"All. This. Time."

Ah, this conversation—the one he had been dreading since their free fall. Here it was.

Wellington placed the key in a different hole and gave it three quick turns. There was a hiss and several pearlescent puffs as four palm-sized objects resembling perfectly smooth bricks slid free of the engine. Inside the case on his desk, he lowered a protective panel over the secured interface, and slid two of the four bricks into indentations that fit them perfectly.

"That shot was a once-in-a-lifetime shot. Even at my best, I don't know if I could have made it." Her voice was calm—though tinted with simmering rage.

The Archivist scoffed as he pushed the remaining memory cases back into the Archives' engine. "As usual your attempt at humility is failing miserably."

"We were plummeting to the Earth, Wellington!" she snapped, slapping her hands against the desk.

Eliza rose from her chair and got in close to him. She was angry; and as such, she would never bother about his particular physical boundaries. Wellington took in the scent of her perfume. He kept his knees steady and hoped she didn't notice his jaw twitching slightly.

"Bruce, Maulik, Brandon—I'll even wager Harry—none of them could have made that shot. Yet you did." She had been holding on to this since their return to the Ministry, and there was no way she was letting him loose without an answer—that much was plain.

"Yes. Yes, Eliza. I did." He placed a protective cover over the brains of his portable engine and secured the carrying case. Hefting it off his own desk, he was quite pleased at the balance and lightness of its thirty-five pounds.

"You. An archivist with *basic* field training."

Wellington shuffled awkwardly past Eliza, crossing to the base of the Archives' entrance where an open satchel awaited. He placed the packed analytical device beside it and peered inside the second bag. Not much left to pack from the Archives, apart from what waited back at his house.

Then there was the matter of his work-in-progress, but that was something he could complete while in the air. Tonight he'd been able to call in a favour from Brandon Hill, who owed him a few shillings from their bridge games together. His colleague was more than eager to pack and deliver the items that Wellington requested from his workshop.

In fact, that eagerness made him a tad nervous.

"As you may recall," Wellington said, brushing his hands together, his eyes focusing on his desk, "from the odd conversation between independent investigations and cataloguing properly sanctioned cases of Ministry agents, I have prior experience with the military."

He attempted to open the main drawer in order to retrieve his new journal. The drawer stopped on hitting Eliza's rear. Still he gave it a slight tug, hoping the subtle gesture would politely nudge his partner out of the way.

Eliza's hips shot back, her rear end slamming the drawer shut.

"Since when does the Queen's Army train its soldiers to shoot like that?"

Go on, his father whispered to him. Wellington closed his eyes, pushing back the migraine threatening him. *Tell her. Let's see just how learned this colonial tart of yours is.*

"Very well then," Wellington sighed, sinking into his chair. He looked up at Eliza, a wave of exhaustion wrapping around him. "Eliza, my father was a right bastard. The worst of his kind."

You ungrateful shit, his father spat. His temple throbbed with a sudden jolt of pain, but Wellington merely swallowed back the bitterness in his mouth and continued.

"I—" He still couldn't prove anything about what really happened. At least, he had not found anything yet. "I lost my mother when I was very young. My father preferred occasional companionship versus something more permanent. I was raised, for a time, by my butler and nanny; and then my father decided after his 'mourning' to take a more vested interest in my upbringing. He trained me for survival. At least that is how he referred to it. While boys my age were trained in sport and etiquette, I was trained in physical endurance, sharpshooting, and the regimental lifestyle. Hardly befitting a boy at eight years of age, but such was life in the Books manor."

Eliza took her seat, staring at him as if he were a total stranger. Taking the opportunity, he opened the desk drawer, removed his new journal, and waved it lightly in his hand. "You never know when we might need this, yes?"

"Wellington," she said softly, but insistently.

He cleared his throat, and continued. "When I served in the African campaigns, I found out just what my father

had intended—he wanted me to be his gift to the Crown.
I was to be the example of a new breed of soldier. I would
take my childhood upbringing and train others in the same
manner, only my discipline would be of a different manner."
He laughed dryly. "Ingenious, if you think about it. My father's legacy would be a new generation of unstoppable kill-
ing machines and I would cement a place in proper society
with my own contributions. Not that I would be completely
comfortable in said proper society, as my skills in mixed
company are tenuous at best."

Eliza chuckled lightly at that. It was not meant as mali-
cious or insensitive. He could see that in her eyes. It was
lovely to make her laugh.

"After my service, I decided on a different path for
myself, a path my father did not approve of. So here I am,
in the Archives, applying the skills I had honed on my own.
Without my father's influence. I called upon many favours
owed to my father's name to bury my test scores and the odd
military record or two. Here, I was out of the way. I was out
of sight. And I preferred both to what my father intended."

Wellington stopped. Eliza remained silent. She wanted to
know more. He shook his head in disgust, snatching up his
journal and tucking it in his coat pocket. He then reached
over to Eliza's side of the desk, glanced at the case summary
provided by the Americans, and nodded.

"Right then," he said, turning back to the analytical
engine. His fingers quickly danced across the keys, and the
machine awakened, sending puffs of steam in several directions as its wheels spun faster. On the monitor, lines began
to slowly appear, forming what he recognised as a map of
the Archives.

"No mistakes?" He didn't look over at Eliza, even when
she clicked her tongue. "Really, Mr. Wellington Books, after
your speeches about trust and faith in your partner, and yet
you live by a different set of standards."

"I have to," Wellington said, tracing a path on the screen
from where he stood to a tiny *X* blinking somewhere in the

1857 shelves. "It was how I was raised, and the best way to protect you."

"Protect me?!"

Perhaps Wellington should have thought that statement through before uttering it.

"Eliza, we have a four-day journey ahead of us, and our airship leaves promptly in a matter of hours, and I for one would not care to miss our quickest passage out of London, lest we spend a week at sea." He gave his desk a final look, glanced at the map, and headed for 1857.

Eliza remained on his heels. "Please tell me: when did I represent myself as some sort of delicate flower in need of protection?" Wellington suddenly felt himself turned on his heels. Eliza had always been stronger than she looked. "Dammit, will you look at me when I talk to you? I have earned that much at least."

Wellington stared at her a moment before replying. "I beg to disagree. You have earned my respect in what we have accomplished together, but if you believe yourself entitled on account of my deception, I believe you are mistaken. Gravely, I will add."

Her eyes narrowed. "What are you on about?"

It was high time to reveal all. Both of them. "Eliza, I will ask this once and only once. Your answer will, in truth, guide me." He took a deep breath, and adjusted his spectacles, fixing her with a stare. "Were you sent to rescue me in Antarctica?"

When she blinked, he had his answer. Her response, perhaps if it was said in another place at another time, might have made him laugh in its absurdity. "I was sent to retrieve you from the House of Usher."

"We have only been partners for a year, but I do think you should not take me for a fool, nor should you mince words with me."

"God damn you, Wellington!"

"He already did, when my mother was taken from me." The hum of the generators seemed louder than ever. He broke the silence again. "Tell me truthfully—were you sent to rescue me?"

It was impossible to read Eliza's eyes in the dim lighting, but her posture told him all he needed to know. She was shaking.

"No," she finally ground out.

Wellington smiled. He didn't expect to, but he was sincerely relieved. "A spare pair of goggles, and those were your only considerations for someone kidnapped from the Ministry?"

"You suspected?"

"Of course." Wellington turned back to the terminal for the 1857 aisle and punched in the reference code he had earlier accessed on the engine's screen. "I'm sure I could have confirmed my suspicions by accessing confidential Ministry records, but that would indeed be a most slippery slope." A basket lowered from the darkness above, coming to a jerky stop beside them. "I would have rather got the answer from you instead."

Eliza's brow furrowed. "Why?"

"It would have meant more. Granted, I would have preferred to discuss this under different circumstances, not as we plan for an unscheduled journey to the Americas." He sighed, turning his attention to the evidence from the Ministry's previous case. "So, you see, we all had our secrets to keep, didn't we?"

He felt himself shoved away from the basket. Eliza was approaching some kind of boiling point.

"You have got some polished brass balls!"

"Whatever do you mean?"

"You chose to keep your abilities a secret from me when we were investigating these forgotten cases throughout the year when at any time—"

"I am not in the Archives because I was ordered. I *volunteered*, because I did not want to put anyone at risk. Not the Ministry. Certainly, not you."

"I can take care of myself," she said punching him hard

in the shoulder, "but it would have been jolly nice to have an ace up the sleeve like you!"

Wellington winced, rubbing the spot where she had hit him. Why did she always hit him there? "And then, once it became known in our clandestine circles of my abilities, how many would stop at nothing to recruit me into their ranks? How many would attempt to use you as a ways and means to do so?"

"That's very sweet of you, but please, there's no need to fret like a hen over her chicks. I am perfectly capable of protecting the Ministry and its secrets—even you."

He reached out and grabbed her, pinning her shoulders against one of the nearby shelves. "Dash it all, Eliza, this has nothing to do with protecting the Ministry! I could give a flying toss presently about any of them. The Ministry can fortify itself with a simple push of a red button, but you—" He drew closer to her, making sure he could see her eyes. "It's you. I don't want them to hurt you in order to get to me." He released her, slowly shaking his head. "I could not bear that. Not for a moment."

They stood before each other, the generator thrumming low in their ears. Perhaps he had finally got his message through. Maybe now she understood his intentions.

"Sorry, mate," she replied, "but you're still saying I can't look after myself!"

Was he *completely* invisible to her?

"Bugger it," Wellington swore.

He pulled her towards him and kissed her—rather hard and with great urgency. No, perhaps it was not the way a gentleman would have kissed a lady; but it was the way he wanted to kiss her in that moment. For all Wellington knew, this would be the one chance he would have to kiss her, so he would bloody make it count.

He felt her embrace tighten on him, her hands running along his back, her breathing deeper and wilder. Eliza's curves against his own surpassed any fleeting expectation he nurtured previously. Wellington prolonged his kiss by nibbling and nipping on her lips. They were soft, faintly tasting of strawberries. A delicious surprise, to be certain.

With a final touch, he pulled away. His heart was now pumping at full steam, so much so that he felt quite light-headed. He hoped that any physical reaction he outwardly displayed to such an erotic embrace (which, being human, he could not help) did not offend Miss Braun. Her brilliant blue eyes were now blinking quickly as she looked at him. Wellington hoped that, at best, she would simply slap him for offending her morality and making assumptions that were far beyond any intended or welcome by her.

Knowing too well her fondness for explosives, he preferred not to think of the worst reaction she could have to this.

"You stopped," she stated, her breath short and laboured.

"Um . . ." Not quite the reaction he expected. "Yes. Yes, I did, Eliza."

"Why did you do that? Did you want to stop?"

"Well . . ." Brash honesty. It was what he wanted. "No."

Her hand grabbed the back of his neck and pulled him close, so quickly, he gave a little yelp as he found himself nose-to-nose with his fellow Ministry agent.

"Then don't," she whispered just before bringing her lips back into his.

Wellington had never quite taken much notice of the smell of the Archives. Perhaps the smell of ageing wood and paper was something that he had grown accustomed to. Eliza's light touch of perfume—far too faint to have been freshly placed on her skin this morning—reached him. The two scents complimented each other quite well. In fact, the smells of old books and her skin, the feel of her hands running along his arm and back, and his own fingers feeling the softness of her cheek and curve of her bosom, and the faint taste of strawberries and tobacco—

Tobacco? Did Eliza smoke cigars?

He was in his own domain, deep within the shelves and stacks of the Archives, and yet, Wellington found himself